W9-AOZ-429

LEAVING BERLIN

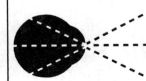

This Large Print Book carries the
Seal of Approval of N.A.V.H.

LEAVING BERLIN

JOSEPH KANON

THORNDIKE PRESS
A part of Gale, Cengage Learning

GALE
CENGAGE Learning®

Farmington Hills, Mich • San Francisco • New York • Waterville, Maine
Meriden, Conn • Mason, Ohio • Chicago

GALE
CENGAGE Learning®

Thorndike Press® Large Print Core.
The text of this Large Print edition is unabridged.
Other aspects of the book may vary from the original edition.
Set in 16 pt. Plantin.

LIBRARY OF CONGRESS CATALOGING-IN-PUBLICATION DATA

Kanon, Joseph.
  Leaving Berlin / by Joseph Kanon. — Large print edition.
    pages cm. — (Thorndike Press large print core)
  ISBN 978-1-4104-7507-7 (hardcover) — ISBN 1-4104-7507-7 (hardcover)
  1. Berlin (Germany)—Fiction. 2. Large type books. I. Title.
PS3561.A476L43 2015b
813'.54—dc23   2015000489

Published in 2015 by arrangement with Atria Books, a division of Simon & Schuster, Inc.

Printed in the United States of America
1 2 3 4 5 6 7 19 18 17 16 15

For
Martha, Gregg, and Tess

AUTHOR'S NOTE

As most readers will know, postwar Germany was divided by the Allies (the United States, Britain, France, and the Soviet Union) into four zones of military occupation. The capital, Berlin, was similarly divided into four occupied sectors. Located deep inside the Soviet zone, Berlin became an inevitable bone of contention as wartime cooperation deteriorated into the open hostility of the Cold War. Finally, in June 1948, the Soviets decided to force the other Allied powers out of Berlin by cutting off all land access to the Western sectors, a blockade to which the West responded with the Berlin Airlift (July 1948–May 1949), often considered the first battle of the Cold War. At its height the airlift provided Berlin with eight thousand tons of supplies a day.

The events of *Leaving Berlin* take place in January 1949 while the blockade was still a daily presence and occupied Germany had not yet formally split into two states. It was a time, like our own, fond of acronyms. A few key ones that are used here: SED (the Socialist Unity Party of Germany, which incorporated the old Communist Party and effectively replaced it), OMGUS (Office of Military Government, United States), SMA or SMAD (the Soviet Military Administration, governing its zone from the Berlin suburb of Karlshorst), BOB (the CIA's Berlin Operations Base), DEFA (the largest German film studio, successor to Weimar's Ufa, located in Babelsberg, just outside Berlin and hence in the Soviet zone). Earlier, the SA (Sturmabteilung) was the Nazi storm trooper unit.

Readers with even a glancing acquaintance with the eastern German Democratic Republic (GDR) will be familiar with the notorious Stasi (Ministry for State Security) and its armies of IMs (*Inoffizielle Mitarbeiter* — unofficial collaborators), but the Stasi was not founded until February 1950, and the term IM was used only after 1968. The first German secret police in the Soviet sector was the Interior Administration's Intelligence Information Department (K-5), who worked with the city police. On December 28, 1948, a new independent secret police division was established, the Main

Directorate for the Defense of the Economy and the Democratic Order. K-5 continued to exist, both organizations under the direct control of Erich Mielke, who later ran the Stasi (1957–1989). Informants were then called, as here, GIs (*Geheime Informatoren* — secret informers).

Although I have tried to be accurate about details of time and place, one deliberate chronological liberty has been taken: the SED party purge, and its attendant show trials, actually began a year later, in the summer of 1950. Finally, the real people in these pages — Bertolt Brecht, Alexander Dymshits, Anna Seghers, Helene Weigel, et al. — appear only as I imagine them to have been.

■ ■ ■ ■

1
LÜTZOWPLATZ

■ ■ ■ ■

They were still a few miles out when he heard the planes, a low steady droning, coming closer, the way the bombers must have sounded. Now loaded with food and sacks of coal. After Köpenick he could make out their lights in the sky, dropping toward the dark city, one plane after another, every thirty seconds they said, if that were possible, unloading then taking off again, the lights now a line of vanishing dots, like tracer bullets.

"How does anyone sleep?"

"You don't hear them after a while," Martin said. "You get used to it."

Maybe Martin had, new to Berlin. But what about the others, who remembered huddling in shelters every night, waiting to die, listening to the engine sounds — how near? — the whining thrust as the nose was pulled up, free of the weight of its bombs, now floating somewhere overhead.

"So many planes," Alex said, almost to himself. "How long can they keep it going?" *Die Luftbrücke*, Berlin's lifeline now, with little parachutes of candy for the children, for the photographers.

"Not much longer," Martin said, certain. "Think of the expense. And for what? They're trying to make two cities. Two mayors, two police. But there's only one city. Berlin is still where it is, in the Soviet zone. They can't move it. They should leave now. Let things get back to normal."

"Well, normal," Alex said. The planes were getting louder, almost overhead, Tempelhof only one district west. "And will the Russians leave too?"

"I think so, yes," Martin said, something he'd considered. "They stay for each other. The Americans don't leave because the Russians —" He stopped. "But of course they'll have to. It's not reasonable," he said, a French use of the word. "Why would the Russians stay? If Germany were neutral. Not a threat anymore."

"Neutral but Socialist?"

"How else now? After the Fascists. It's what everyone wants, I think, don't you?" He caught himself. "Forgive me. Of course you do. You've come back for this, a Socialist Germany. To make the future with us. It

14

was the dream of your book. I've told you, I think, I'm a great admirer —"

"Yes, thank you," Alex said, weary.

Martin had joined him when he changed cars at the Czech border, straw-colored hair slicked back, face scrubbed and eager, the bright-eyed conviction of a Hitler Youth. He was the first young man Alex had met since he arrived, all the others buried or missing, irretrievable. Then a few dragging steps and Alex saw why: a Goebbels clubfoot had kept him out of the war. With the leg and the slick hair he even looked a little like Goebbels, without the hollow cheeks, the predator eyes. Now he was brimming with high spirits, his initial formal reticence soon a flood of talk. How much *Der letzte Zaun* had meant to him. How pleasing it was that Alex had decided to make his home in the East, "voting with your feet." How difficult the first years had been, the cold, the starvation rations, and how much better it was now, you could see it every day. Brecht had come — had Alex known him in America? Thomas Mann? Martin was a great admirer of Brecht too. Perhaps he could dramatize Alex's *Der letzte Zaun,* an important antifascist work, something that might appeal to him.

"He'd have to talk to Jack Warner first,"

15

Alex said, smiling to himself. "He controls the rights."

"There was a film? I didn't realize. Of course we never saw American films."

"No, there was going to be, but he never made it."

The Last Fence, a Book-of-the-Month-Club Selection, the lucky break that supported his exile. Warners bought it for Cagney, then Raft, then George Brent, then the war came and they wanted battle pictures, not prison-camp escapes, so the project was shelved, another might-have-been on a shelf full of them. But the sale paid for the house in Santa Monica, not far from Brecht's, in fact.

"But you were able to read it?" Alex said. "There were copies in Germany?" Really asking, who are you? A representative from the Kulturbund, yes, the artists' association, but what else? Everyone here had a history now, had to be accounted for.

"In Switzerland you could get the Querido edition." The émigré press in Amsterdam, which explained the book, but not Martin. "Of course, there were still many copies of *Der Untergang* in Germany, even after it was banned."

Downfall, the book that had made his reputation, presumably the reason Germany wanted him back — Brecht and Anna Seghers and Arnold Zweig had all come home and now Alex Meier, Germany's exiles returning. To the East, even culture part of the new war. He thought of Brecht ignored in California, Seghers invisible in Mexico City, now celebrated again, pictures in the paper, speeches of welcome by Party officials.

There had been a lunch for him earlier at the first town over the border. They had left Prague at dawn to be in time for it, the streets still dark, slick with rain, the way they always seemed to be in Kafka. Then miles of stubby fields, farmhouses needing paint, ducks splashing in mud. At the border town — what was it called? — Martin had been there with welcoming flowers, the mayor and town council turned out in Sunday suits, worn and boxy, a formal lunch at the Rathaus. Photographs were taken for *Neues Deutschland,* Alex shaking hands with the mayor, the prodigal son come home. He was asked to say a few words. Sing for his supper. What he was here for, why they offered the resident visa in the first place, to make the future with us.

He had expected somehow to find all of Germany in ruins, the country you saw in

Life, digging out, but the landscape after lunch was really a continuation of the morning's drive, shabby farms and poor roads, their shoulders chewed up by years of tanks and heavy trucks. Not the Germany he'd known, the big house in Lützowplatz. Still, Germany. He felt his stomach tighten, the same familiar apprehension, waiting for the knock on the door. Now lunch with the mayor, the bad old days something in the past.

They avoided Dresden. "It would break your heart," Martin had said. "The swine. They bombed everything. For no reason." But what reason could there have been? Or for Warsaw, Rotterdam, any of them, maybe Martin too young to remember the cheering in the streets then. Alex said nothing, looking out at the gray winter fields. Where was everybody? But it was late in the year for farmwork and anyway the men were gone.

Martin insisted on sitting with him in the back, an implied higher status than the driver, which meant they talked all the way to Berlin.

"Excuse me, you don't mind? It's such an opportunity for me. I've always wondered. The family in *Downfall?* These were actual people you knew? It's like *Buddenbrooks?*"

18

"Actual people? No," Alex said.

Were they still alive? Irene and Elsbeth and Erich, old Fritz, the people of his life, swallowed up in the war, maybe just names now on a refugee list, untraceable, their only existence in Alex's pages, something Fritz would have hated.

"It's not us, these people," he'd yelled at Alex. "My father never gambled, not like that."

"It's not you," Alex had said calmly.

"Everybody says it's us. They say it at the club. You should hear Stolberg. 'Only a Jew would write such things.' "

"Well, a Jew did," Alex said.

"Half a Jew," Fritz snapped, then more quietly, "Anyway, your father's a good man. Stolberg's just like the rest of them." He looked up. "So it's not us?"

"It's any Junker family. You know how writers use things — a look, a mannerism, you use everything you know."

"Oh, and so now we're Junkers. And I suppose we lost the war too. *Pickelhauben.*"

"Read the book," Alex had said, knowing Fritz never would.

"What does it mean, anyway? *Downfall.* What happens to them? The father gambles? So what?"

"They lose their money," Alex said.

19

Old Fritz turned, embarrassed now. "Well, that's easy enough to do. In the inflation everybody lost something."

Alex waited, the air settling around them. "It's not you," he said again.

And Fritz believed him.

"But the camp in *The Last Fence,*" Martin was saying. "That's Sachsenhausen, yes? They said at the office you'd been in Sachsenhausen."

"Oranienburg, in the first camp there. They built Sachsenhausen later. They put us in an old brewery. Right in the center of town. People could see through the windows. So everyone knew."

"But it was as you describe? You were tortured?" Martin said, unable to resist.

"No. Everyone was beaten. But the worst things — I was lucky." Hands tied behind their backs then hung from poles until the shoulder joints separated, torn from the sockets, screams they couldn't help, pain so terrible they finally passed out. "I wasn't there long enough. Somebody got me out. You could still do that then. '33. If you knew the right people." The one thing old Fritz had left, connections.

"But in the book —"

"It's meant to be any camp."

"It's nice, though, don't you agree, to

20

know what the author has in his mind, what he sees?"

"Well, Sachsenhausen then," Alex said, tired of it. "The layout was described to me, so I knew what it was like. Then you invent."

" '33," Martin said, backing off. "When they rounded up the Communists. You were in the Party even then?"

"No, not then," Alex said. "I just got caught in the net. If you were sympathetic. If you had Communist friends. They scooped up all the fish and you were caught. You didn't need to have a card."

"And now the Americans are doing it, putting Communists in jail. They said that's why you left." A question. "They're trying to destroy the Party. Just like the Nazis." The only way it made sense to the Kultur-bund.

"They're not sending people to Sachsen-hausen," Alex said evenly. "It's not illegal to be a Communist."

"But I thought —"

"They want you to tell them who the others are. Give them names. And if you don't — then that's illegal. So they catch you that way."

"And then to jail," Martin said, following the logic.

"Sometimes," Alex said vaguely.

Or deportation, the Dutch passport of convenience that had once saved his life now something to use against him. "Might I remind you, you are a guest in this country?" The congressman with the thick athlete's neck, who probably thought exile a greater threat than prison. And let Alex slip away.

"So you came home to Germany," Martin said, making a story.

"Yes, home," Alex said, looking out the window again.

"So, that's good," Martin said, the story's end.

There were city buildings now, the jagged graveyard streets of the newsreels, Friedrichshain probably, given the direction they were coming from. He tried to picture the map in his head — Grosse Frankfurter Strasse? — looking for some familiar landmark, but all he could see were faceless bombed-out buildings heaped with rubble. He thought of the women handing down pails of debris, hammering mortar off reusable bricks — and four years later the rubble was still here, mountains of it. How much had there been? Standing walls were pockmarked by shelling, marooned in empty spaces where buildings had collapsed, leaving gaps for the wind to rush through. The streets, at least, had been cleared but were still lined on either side with piles of bricks and smashed porcelain and twisted metal. Even the smell of bombing, the burned wood and the sour lime of broken cement, was still in the air. But maybe, like the airlift planes, you didn't notice after a while.

"You still have family in Germany?" Martin was asking.

"No. No one," Alex said. "They waited too long." He turned to Martin, as if it needed to be explained. "My father had the Iron Cross. He thought it would protect him."

But did he? Or was it simply a cover for a fatalism so knowing and desperate that it couldn't be admitted? It was almost as if he had exhausted himself getting Alex out. How much had it cost? Enough to wipe out Fritz's debts? More?

"You owe him your gratitude," was all his father would say.

"You should come too," Alex had said.

His father shook his head. "There's no need. Not for me. I'm not the one they send to prison for having such friends. The Engel boy, he was always trouble. Who does he think he is, Liebknecht? Times like these, you stay quiet." He took Alex's shoulder. "You'll be back. This is Germany, you know, not some Slavic — So it passes and you'll come back. Nothing is forever. Not the Nazis. Now don't worry your mother."

But it turned out the Nazis were forever, long enough anyway to turn his parents into ash, seeping into the soil somewhere in Poland.

"There's Alexanderplatz up ahead," Martin said.

The welcome lunch and bad roads had made the trip longer than they'd expected, and it was late now, their car lights stronger than the occasional streetlamp shining a pale cone on the rubble. On the side streets there were no lights at all. Alex leaned forward, peering, oddly excited now that they were really here. Berlin. He could make out the scaffolding of a building site and then, beyond a cleared, formless space, the dark hulk of the palace, singed with soot, the dome just a steel frame, but still standing, the last Hohenzollern. Across from it the cathedral was a blackened shell. Alex had expected the city center, the inevitable showcase, to be visibly recovering, but it was the same as Friedrichshain, more rubble, endless, the old Schinkel buildings gutted and sagging. Unter den Linden was dark, the lindens themselves scorched clumps. There was scarcely any traffic, just a few military cars driving slowly, as if they were patrolling the empty street. At Friedrichstrasse, no one was waiting to cross. A sign in Cyrillic pointed to the station. The city was as quiet as a village on some remote steppe. Berlin.

All the way in Martin had talked about the Adlon, where Alex was to stay until a flat could be arranged. It was for Martin a place of mythic glamour, of Weimar first nights, Lubitsch in a fur collar coat. "Brecht and Weigel are there too, you know." Which seemed to confirm not only the hotel's status, but Alex's own. But now that they were almost there, with no lights visible up ahead, no awning or doormen whistling down taxis, he began to apologize.

"Of course it's only the annex. You know the main building was burned. But very comfortable I'm told. And the dining room is almost like before." He checked his watch. "It's late, but I'm sure for you they would —"

"No, that's all right. I just want to go to bed. It's been —"

"Of course," Martin said, but with such heavy disappointment that Alex realized he'd been hoping to join him for dinner, a meal off the ration book. Instead, he handed Alex an envelope. "Here are all the papers

25

you'll need. Identity card. Kulturbund membership — the food is excellent there, by the way. You understand, for members only."

"No starving artists?"

A joke, but Martin looked at him blankly.

"No one starves here. Now tomorrow we have the reception for you. At the Kulturbund. Four o'clock. It's not far, around the corner, so I will come for you at three thirty."

"That's all right. I can find —"

"It's my pleasure," Martin said. "Come." Nodding to the driver to bring the suitcase.

The functioning part of the Adlon was in the back, at the end of a pathway through the gutted front. The staff greeted him with a stage formality, bowing, their uniforms and cutaways part of the surreal theatrical effect. Through a door he could see the starched linen on the dining tables. No one seemed to notice the charred timbers, the boarded windows.

"Alex?" A throaty woman's voice. "My God, to see you here."

He turned. "Ruth. I thought you'd gone to New York." Not just gone to New York, been hospitalized there, the breakdown he'd heard about in whispers.

"Yes, but now here. Brecht needs me here,

26

so I came."

Martin lifted his head at this.

"I'm sorry," Alex said, introducing them. "Ruth Berlau, Martin —"

"Schramm. Martin Schramm." He dipped his head.

"Ruth is Brecht's assistant," Alex said, smiling. "Right hand. Collaborator." Mistress. He remembered the teary afternoons at Salka's house on Mabery Road, worn down by a backstairs life.

"His secretary," Ruth said to Martin, correcting Alex but flattered.

"I'm a great admirer of Herr Brecht's work," Martin said, almost clicking his heels, a courtier.

"So is he," Ruth said, deadpan, so that Alex wasn't sure he could laugh.

She seemed smaller, more fragile, as if the hospital had drawn some force out of her.

"You're staying here?" he said.

"Yes, just down the hall. From Bert."

Not mentioning Helene Weigel, his wife, down the hall with him, the geography of infidelity. He imagined the women passing in the lobby, eyeing each other, years of it now.

"Of course a smaller room. Not like the great artist's." An ironic smile, used to servants' quarters. "They're going to give

27

him a theater, you know. Isn't it wonderful? All his plays, whatever he decides. We're doing *Mother Courage* first. At the Deutsches Theater. He was hoping for the Schiff, but not yet, maybe later. But the Deutsches is good, the acoustics —"

"Who's playing Courage?"

"Helene," she said simply. Now finally Brecht's star as well as his wife. Alex thought of the wasted years of exile, keeping house for him, ignoring the mistress, an actress without her language. "You'll have to come to the theater. She'll be pleased to see you again. You know Schulberg is here?" Wanting to gossip, California in common. She jerked her head. "In the army. Over in the West. Which is lucky for us. Food packages from the PX — he's very generous." Alex felt Martin shift position, uncomfortable. "Not for Bert, of course. They give him anything he wants. But for the cast, always hungry. So Helene gets food for them. Imagine what they would say if they knew they were flying in food for Weigel?" She looked up at him, as if the thought had jogged her memory. "So tell me, what happened with the committee? Did you testify?"

"No."

"But there was a subpoena?" Asking something else.

Alex nodded.

"So," she said, taking in the lobby, his presence explained. "Then you can't go back." Something else remembered, glancing behind him. "Marjorie's not with you?"

Alex shook his head. "She's getting a divorce." He raised his hand. "We should have done it years ago."

"But what happens to Peter? The way you are with him —"

"He'll come visit," Alex said, stopping her.

"But he stays with her," she said, not letting go.

"Well, with the way things are —"

"You like a fugitive, you mean. That's what they want — hound us all like fugitives. Only Bert was too clever for them. Did you see? No one understood anything he said. Dummkopfs. And what? They *thanked* him for his testimony. Only he could do that. Outfox them."

"But he left anyway." His bridges burning too. "So now we're both here," Alex said, looking at her.

"We're so happy to have our writers back," Martin said before she could answer. "A wonderful thing, yes? To be in your own country. Your own language. Think what that means for a writer."

Ruth looked up at this, then retreated, like

a timid animal poking its head through the bushes then skittering away, frightened by the scent in the air.

"Yes, and here I am talking and you want to go to your room." She put her hand on Alex's arm. "So come see us." But who exactly? Brecht and Ruth or all three? A hopeless tangle. She smiled shyly. "He's happy here, you know. The theater. A German audience. That's everything for him." Her eyes shining a little now, an acolyte's pleasure. The same look, oddly, he'd seen in Martin's, both in thrall to some idea that seemed worth a sacrifice.

"I will," he said, then noticed the overnight bag at her feet. "But you're going away?"

"No, no, just to Leipzig. They want to put on *Galileo*. Bert doesn't think they're serious, but someone has to go. One day, two maybe. It's all right, they keep my room for me here. You can't make such arrangements by letter. You have to go." So someone would.

The room, on the third floor, still had blackout curtains hanging heavily to the floor, and the bellboy, barely in his teens, made an elaborate show of drawing them, then demonstrating the light switches, the candle and matches, in case of power cuts.

He nodded to the luggage rack with its single suitcase.

"Are you expecting more bags?"

"Not tonight. In a few days." The rest of his life, sitting somewhere on a railway siding, waiting for the new flat to be ready. But why wasn't it? It occurred to him, now that he'd seen the city, that flats must be prizes awarded by the Party. It wasn't ready because someone was still in it, packing, being shuffled off somewhere else, the way Jews had been told to leave.

"Is there anything else I can get for you?" A bottle from the cellar, a girl, a bellboy's usual late night services, but offered now without innuendo, vice out of style in the workers' state, the boy himself too young to know the old code. Maybe one of the boys defending the city with panzerfausts during the last days. Now waiting for a tip.

"Oh," Alex said, picking up one of the envelopes from Martin, his walking-around money. He handed a note to the boy.

"Excuse me, perhaps you have Western currency?" Then, almost stammering, "I mean, you are coming from there."

"Sorry. I came through Prague. No West marks. Just these."

The boy looked at him. "Not marks. Do you have a dollar?"

Alex stopped, surprised. The contact line, sooner than he expected. Not even a day to settle in. The boy was still staring at him. Speaking code after all, a new vice, not too young for this. Or was Alex imagining it all?

He took out his wallet and handed the boy the folded dollar bill, watching as the boy looked at it, then handed it back.

"You are from Berlin? From before?"

Alex nodded.

"Naturally you would be interested to see your old home? A matter of curiosity. It's often the first thing people want to do. Who've been away."

"Lützowplatz," Alex said, waiting.

Now the boy nodded. "In the West," he said, already another city in his mind. "You can walk there. Through the park. In the morning." Instructions. "Early. Before eight, if you would be up."

"There's no trouble crossing?"

The boy looked puzzled for a second. "Trouble? To walk in the Tiergarten?"

"At the sector crossing."

The boy almost smiled. "It's a street only. Sometimes they stop a car. To inspect for the black market. But not someone who walks in the park." He paused. "Early," he said again. "So, now good night." He held out his hand. "Excuse me. The East marks?

Since you don't have West? *Vielen Dank,*"
he said, palming the note and backing
toward the door, a practiced move, part of
the Adlon touch. But did he have any idea
what he'd done? Just delivering a message,
pocketing a tip, no questions asked. Or
something more, already part of it?

Alex took off his coat and lay on the bed,
too tired to get undressed, staring at the
dim chandelier overhead. They'd told him
the most likely places for bugs were tele-
phones and lighting fixtures. Had the chandelier been listening? He thought over
everything the boy had said, how it would
sound. But what could be more innocent
than a walk in the park?

In the silence he could hear the planes
again, muffled, as if he were listening from
below in one of the hotel shelters. Some of
the guests would have been in furs, not
wanting to lose them if their rooms disappeared by the time the all clear sounded.
Could you actually hear fire, flames licking
at walls just overhead? Then the shelter
became the cell in Oranienburg, not the
barracks, the interrogation cell, airless, the
old nightmare, and he willed his eyes open,
short of breath, and went over to the windows.

Why have blackout curtains now, live in

the dark? In California you could keep the windows open, never be shut in. He pushed the heavy drapes apart, then felt the first draft of cold air seeping through. Still, better than living in a tomb. Anything was better than that.

The view faced the back, the hills of rubble that had been Wilhelmstrasse off to the left, an empty stretch of wasteland ahead, barely visible by moonlight. The new view from the Adlon. Maybe that's why the curtains. Inside, cocooned, you could still imagine the ministries lined up in their grave permanence, not the ghost town that was actually there, a faint ashy gray in the pale light.

What Lützowplatz would be like too. The world of his childhood already belonged to memory, to old photographs. Bicycles by the Landwehrkanal, afternoons in the park, Aunt Lotte's fussy visits — you didn't expect any of these to survive. Things changed. Cars in the photographs looked faintly comical. But now the city itself was gone, streets no longer there, wiped not just from memory but from any time, the standing ruins like bones left behind, carrion.

And he'd come to feed on it too, a prize catch, already caught, the bargain he'd had to make. Do whatever they wanted. And what would that be? Not just a walk in the park. He lay there, the room getting colder, seeing Ruth's cautious eyes. Did you testify? In exile you learned to get by, principle an extravagance you could no longer afford. A lesson he thought he knew, all those years of it, and then thrown away in one heedless refusal. Would it have mattered, giving them names they already had? What if he'd done the practical thing, cooperated with the committee? But no bargain had been offered, not then. And he'd seen the faces before, the jowls and smirks, when they'd been Nazis, the same bullying voices, and he couldn't do it. An act of contempt, cause for deportation, and then a different bargain, the one the committee would not know about.

"It's perfect," Don Campbell had said when they met in Frankurt. "Telling the committee to go fuck themselves? Not even Brecht did that. Talk about lefty credentials. The Russians would never think — Perfect."

"Perfect," Alex had said, a monotone.

"And they want you. They think they're pulling a fast one, getting you."

"But I'm pulling the fast one," Alex said, his voice still flat.

Don looked up. "That's right. A fast one on them. And a fast one on the committee.

Work with us, we'll get you back in. New papers from State." He nodded. "A guarantee. Uncle Sam takes care of his own." He paused. "And you see your kid."

The closing argument, why it was perfect, Alex's cuffs.

"How long do I do this?"

"They'll give you privileges," Don said, not answering. "They do that with writers. Like they're movie stars. Extra *payoks.*"

"What?"

"Food packages. Off ration. You'll need them too." He lowered his voice. "Wait till you see it. The Socialist paradise."

"I am a Socialist," Alex said, a wry turn to his mouth. Fifteen years ago, before life had tied him up in knots. "I believe in a just society."

Don looked at him, disconcerted, then brought things back. "That's why you're perfect."

He drifted into a half sleep, eyes closed but his mind still awake, sorting through the long day, the mayor's welcoming speech, posing for *Neues Deutschland,* and now there was tomorrow's reception to get through, and all the days after that. His picture would be in the papers. Irene would know he was here, if she was still alive. But why would she be? Any of them? You still have family in Germany, Martin had asked. His parents' deaths at least had been confirmed.

"We had to check, if you had any people left," Don had said. "The Russians use that sometimes. If the family's in their zone."

"Use them how?"

"Pressure. Bait. Make sure you cooperate."

"Imagine," Alex said.

Don looked up at him. "But it's not an issue here. We have the records. They're both gone, your mother, your —"

"I could have told you that."

"We like to make sure."

"I had an aunt. Lotte. She married into a Gentile family, so —"

"I wouldn't hold out a lot of hope." He took out a pen. "What's the married name? I can put a query through the OMGUS files."

"Von Bernuth."

Don raised an eyebrow. "Really? Von?"

"Really. They got it from Friedrich Wilhelm himself. After the Battle of Fehrbellin." Then, seeing Don's blank stare, "It's an old name."

"Nice. Rich relatives."

Alex smiled. "Not anymore. They went

through all the money. Lotte's too, probably."

"Where was this? Berlin?"

Alex nodded. "And Pomerania. They had property there."

Don shook his head. "Commies broke up all the big estates. If she's still alive, she's probably somewhere in the West. A lot of them left after."

"That would make her easier to trace then."

"Easy. Try to find records in that —"

"But if you do turn anything up — on any of them." He caught Don's expression. "I knew the family."

"But they're not related. Just the aunt."

"That's right, just the aunt."

Not related. Everything else.

But nothing came back on Lotte. Old Fritz had died and Erich's army records listed him as taken POW in Russia, which probably meant the same thing. But Irene and Elsbeth had vanished. The final downfall, even the name itself gone now.

It was Elsbeth who had kept the family genealogy, in a large leather book that sat on a sideboard in the country house.

"The christening records go back to the thirteenth century," she had said, a caretaker's pride.

"Ouf," Irene said, "and what were they doing? Getting drunk and planting beets. What else is it good for?" This with a wave of her hand to the flat fields stretching toward the Baltic. "It's still beets. Beets and beets. Farmers."

"What's wrong with farmers? You should be proud," old Fritz said.

"Anyway, the Poles do all the work. Nobody in this family ever did anything."

Lazily picking up her lemonade and leaning back against the lawn chair, as if offering herself as living proof. One of those summer afternoons, the air too still to carry the smell of the sea, just the baking fields. Irene in shorts, her long leg propped up, making a triangle.

"Well, now is your chance to do something then," old Fritz said, already sipping beer. "Instead of hanging around with riffraff. Drug addicts. Pansies. Out every night."

Irene sniffed, an old complaint, not worth answering. "But still living at home."

"Of course living at home. A girl not yet married."

"So what should I do? Drive a tractor maybe."

Alex smiled, imagining her up on the high seat, her hair a braided crown, like the model worker in a Russian poster. Women with wrenches, rolling up their sleeves. Not languidly painting her toenails, as she had been doing earlier, each stroke a kind of invitation, looking up and meeting his eyes, even the nail polish now part of the secret between them.

That had been the summer of sex, hanging thick in the air like pollen. The first time, every guy feels like a conqueror, a producer in California had once told him, but that hadn't been how it had felt. A buoyant giddiness he was afraid would show on his face, a heat rising off his skin, like sunburn, flushed with it. The furtive pleasure of being let in on a secret no one else seemed to know. People just kept doing what they'd been doing before. As if nothing had changed.

No one suspected. Not Erich, not old Fritz, not even Elsbeth, usually aware of the slightest change in Irene's moods. The risk of being caught became part of the sex. Her room at night, trying not to make a sound, gasps in his ear. On the stairs, a maid's footsteps overhead. An outbuilding on the farm, smelling of must, the hay scratchy. Behind the dunes, naked to the sharp air, with Erich only a few yards away, at the water's edge, the wind in his ears so that he couldn't hear Irene panting, her release.

Every part of her body open to him, his mouth all over her, and still he couldn't get enough. Not that summer, when they were drunk with sex.

"Do? You can marry Karl Stolberg. That would be doing something. The Stolbergs have a hundred thousand acres. At least a hundred thousand."

"Oh, then why not a von Armin? They have even more. Twice that."

"There's no von Armin the right age," Fritz said, not rising to the tease.

"Then I'll wait," Irene said.

Fritz snorted. "You think a girl has forever to decide this?"

"Anyway, who needs more land? Why don't you auction me off? Get some cash. Good Pomeranian stock. Untouched." She looked over at Alex, a sly smile. "How much for a bridal night?"

"Irene, how can you talk like this?" Elsbeth said, her mouth narrowing. "To father."

But it was Elsbeth, prim and conventional, who was offended, not Fritz, who enjoyed jousting with Irene, a daughter cut from the same rough cloth.

"Let's hope he doesn't ask for proof," Fritz said. "Untouched."

"Papa," Elsbeth said.

"Well, it'd be worth the wait. For a von

Armin," Irene said, enjoying herself. "But then — I don't know — maybe not. The von Bernuths only marry for love. Isn't that right? Just like you and Mama."

"That was different."

"Yes? How many acres did she bring?"

"Don't make fun of your mother."

A woman Alex remembered always in the same full skirt, piled hair held by a tortoise comb, a Wilhelmine figure who spent her days running the house — the long, rich meals, the polishing and dusting — as if nothing had changed outside the heavy front doors, the kaiser still in place, the angry noises in the street better ignored, a time before politics.

"I can also run a trace through CROW-CASS," Campbell had said.

"What's that?"

"Registry of war criminals. Convicted. Suspected."

"No. They weren't like that."

"If you say so. Nobody was, not now. Just ask them."

Alex shook his head. "You didn't know them. They were in their own world. Fritz — I don't think he ever had an idea in his head. Just shooting birds and chasing the maids."

"Shooting birds?"

"Game birds. And deer. Hunting. It's a big thing in that part of the world. Was, anyway."

The house parties, long cold days in the fields, beaters up ahead, then a rush of birds up through the trees, yellow birch against the dark green firs. Lined up for pictures with the day's kill laid out in front, bonfires, bottles of *Sekt,* dinners that went on all evening. Sometimes an invitation farther east, the thick forests of East Prussia, wild boar.

"I thought you said they were broke."

"It doesn't cost anything to be a guest — they were one of the old families. Anyway, they had enough for that." He looked at Don. "He didn't care about Hitler, any of that. They never talked about politics."

Until it was all they talked about, the unavoidable poisoned air everyone breathed, even the dinner table under siege.

"I won't have it in this house," Fritz said. "All this talk. Bolsheviks."

"Bolsheviks," Erich said, dismissive, his father's bluster by now a familiar joke. "It's not Russia here."

"So what, then? Hooligans? Maybe you prefer hooligans. Otto Wolff and the rest of your gang. Socialists. What does it even mean, 'Socialists'? Kurt Engel. A Jew —"

Catching himself, aware of Alex down the table. "Fighting in the streets. We had enough of that after the war. Spartakists. That woman Luxemburg. Of course dead. How else would she end up?"

"We're not fighting in the streets," Erich said, an exaggerated patience. "The Nazis are fighting."

"And cracking skulls. Yours, if you're not careful, and then what? Politics." Almost spitting it out. "I don't want trouble. Not in this house." What he wanted was his wife, with the tortoise comb, the boiled beef with horseradish sauce, and *Kaiserschmarren* for dessert, life the way it had been. He looked at Erich. "You have responsibilities."

"So go stick my head in the sand. How much room is left down there, where you stick yours?"

"Bolsheviks. And how do you think that's going to end? No property rights, that's how."

"Don't worry," Irene said, "by that time we won't have any property left, so what's the difference?"

"Quatsch," Fritz said, genuinely angry.

"Well, how much is left? This house, yes, Berlin. But the country? I know you've been selling it off. You think nobody knows, but everybody talks. How much is left?"

"Enough to feed you. Where do you think the money goes? You think your dresses are free? Food?" His hand sweeping over the long table with the silver carving dishes.

"So it's for us. Not the card games. Those women you —"

"Irene," Elsbeth said.

"Oh, what's the difference? Mother's dead. Everybody knows."

"Alex, you talk to them," Fritz said, shifting, suddenly embarrassed. "How can someone at this table be with the Bolsheviks? Does that make sense? They kill people like us."

"But what is the choice?" Alex said quietly. "The Nazis? They'll kill everybody before they're through."

"Hindenburg will never accept that man. Von Papen —"

"Has no one behind him."

"I tell you. He will never accept him."

"Oh, you know this?" Erich said. "Your friends at the club?"

"He has to form a government," Alex said.

"Not with Communists. Socialists."

Alex looked at him. "Then you've made your choice."

"I don't choose any of them," Fritz said, exasperated. "They're all —" He turned to Erich. "You'll see. All the same. Keep out of it. Keep your head down." Alex's father's advice too, burrowing in.

He opened his eyes. A sound, stopping. Not the airplanes, still humming in the distance. Closer, in the hall. Footsteps. He listened, holding his breath. Where had they stopped? Just outside? The way he used to listen after Oranienburg, an ear to the door even when he was asleep. The middle of the night. No, there was a faint light outside the window. Not yet morning but not night anymore. Then the steps started again, soft, not wanting to be heard. He got up and went over to the door, listening.

But why would they be checking on him at this hour? Suspecting what? We just want information, Don had said. Some ears to the ground. There's no danger to you. If you're careful. Hedging. Careful of what? People listening at doors. The hall was still. Alex turned the knob, easing the door open a crack. A dim night-light, empty corridor. But someone had been here. Then he saw the shoes at the next door, just polished, the Adlon overnight service, even in the ruins. He leaned against the doorjamb, feeling foolish. But it might have been somebody.

And now he was up, restless, the room closing in again. If he lay down they'd come

46

back, not dreams exactly, bits of his life that still hovered in the air here. He should change, have a bath, but he didn't want to run water now, risk pipes clanging, let everyone know he was up. What he wanted, just for a while, was to be invisible, someone nobody could see. Another ghost.

He pulled on his overcoat and started down the hall, as quiet as the shoe boy, keeping to the carpet runner. The lobby was deserted except for the night porter, half asleep, whose surprised look Alex had to answer before he'd unlock the door.

"Couldn't sleep. I thought I'd take a walk."

"A walk," the porter said. "It's not safe, nights. It's the DPs. I know, they've had a rough time, still —"

Alex looked out at the deserted street. "It'll be light soon."

"The kids are worse. Children, you think, and then they're all over you. They picked me clean. Me."

Alex nodded, glancing down at the door lock.

"Friedrichstrasse should be all right. Police by the station, so the gangs stay away. You don't want to go into the park, not at this hour." Hand still on the door, waiting. A concern for Alex's safety or something to put in a report later? The night porter at the Adlon would see things, be a useful source. Alex looked at him. Well, where? And suddenly he knew.

"I want to see if something's still there."

Outside he glanced across the square to the Brandenburg Gate, covered in scaffolding, the Quadriga gone, and turned right toward Wilhelmstrasse. Streets he would know even in the dark. He could walk straight down to Hitler's Chancellery, have a gloating moment. You didn't win, not in the end. But who did? Now that it was all just rubble.

Instead he made his way east, Französische Strasse to the Gendarmenmarkt, both churches in ruins, the concert hall smashed, only a path cleared through the wreckage. Given this, how could the house have escaped? But faster now, because maybe it had. Odd buildings had been spared, as if the flames had just skipped over them. The post office on Französische Strasse had made it through. Why not a town house tucked away on a side street, the pompous architecture at least solid, built to last. But as he reached Hausvogteiplatz, his heart sank. Every building on the square seemed to have taken a hit, the small park at the center now a huge gaping hole. Where the

U-Bahn station had been. He walked toward the edge, ignoring the warning signs, visible in the half-light. Why hadn't they at least covered over the open wound? People could fall in. The least of their worries. Out of the square, really a triangle, and then Kleine Jägerstrasse, just a dog's leg off Niederwallstrasse, not even a full block long, a few old buildings and the von Bernuth house. Still there.

He went farther into the little street. Not all of it. The roof was gone and most of the inside gutted, but the big old front doors were intact, and through a blasted section of the façade he could see the great staircase, hanging from its support wall, no longer going anywhere, the second floor open air. The sconces along the staircase wall, once gas, were still in place, even singed pieces of wallpaper, the same familiar pattern, now exposed to the street, all privacy gone, a woman whose clothes had been ripped away.

Alex stared for a few minutes, then stepped back to the pile of rubble across the street and sat down, taking out a cigarette. The von Bernuth house. All the thick carpeting and carved mahogany gone, presumably ash now. Had they rescued the silver or any of the Caspar David Friedrichs in their old-master frames? Or had all that been removed before the raids started?

The house had always been in the wrong part of town. Even in Fritz's grandfather's time the big town houses were being built near the Tiergarten, Vossstrasse, and then even farther west. But old Friedrich, whose lucky bet on a railway stock made the house possible, didn't know Berlin well — he liked the feel of Hausvogteiplatz, the bargain price for the lot. When the clothing factories began to move in, the new office buildings, it was too late. The von Bernuths had a mansion in the middle of a commercial neighborhood. More amusement than stigma attached to this — it was considered a joke on old Friedrich, another family story.

Alex had heard them all. How the elder Friedrich invested in railroad after failing railroad, hoping for the pay dirt of another Anhalter-Bayerische line. How Fritz's father accidentally shot a tenant, then gave him one of the farms when he recovered. How a note to a mistress was put in the wrong envelope. The sunny, overdressed years before the first war. He knew the stories because Irene and Elsbeth told them to him. It was part of their charm that the von Bernuths saw their family history as a comedy, a series of hapless misadventures. And then when the real stories ran out, he made up more, a book of them.

"You've made us more interesting than we are," Irene had said.

"Not you."

At night there were only a few lights in Kleine Jägerstrasse, so the house had seemed that much brighter, light pouring out the windows, the door lamps like beacons, waiting for guests. There were always people, the girls' friends staying over, parties when they were older. Elsbeth was the pretty one, creamy and delicate as a Dresden doll, but it was Irene people came for, her jokes and careless sensuality, the swollen lower lip, the tangle of blond hair, forever falling out of place. And after the parties, the house cleaned and aired, there were the Sunday lunches, the long table and stiff napkins, one rich course after another, swimming in gravy, the platters almost too heavy for the maids. Saddle of venison and red cabbage and spaetzle, or pork stuffed with prunes, soups thickened with cream, breast of veal, potatoes Anna, a full afternoon of food. His aunt Lotte, who'd married Fritz's brother Hermann, had warned him. "There's always another course, so just take a little or you'll never get through it." Lotte had giggled. "They have to lie down afterward. They can't move." Desserts. Stewed fruit and elaborate cakes, a Spanische Windtorte. A Sunday lunch of the last century, before the money had begun to run out.

He finished the cigarette and stood up, wiping the dust off his coat. In Hausvogteiplatz a few people were on their way to work, the sky finally morning. He could see details now, not just shadowy clumps. The brass knocker on the door was gone, valuable scrap, the interiors long since ransacked. He pushed at the door.

"What do you want there?" An old man with a worker's cap.

"Nothing." He hesitated. "I knew the family. The owners."

The man shook his head. "What owners? It belongs to the bank," he said, indicating the big office building on Kurstrasse, new to Alex. "The Reichsbank." An unexpected pride in his voice, not just any bank.

"Well, a family used to live here."

The man nodded. "I saw you sitting here. So you're looking for them? It's a long time now. Since anybody was here. The bank was going to knock it down. To put up a new building. That was the idea. But then the war started and that was the end of that."

"So it just sat here?"

"They used it for storage. Files, things like that. But then it was hit and everything went up. People thought maybe there were safes here. You know, for the gold. But we never moved it."

"We?"

"I was night watchman. At the bank. I saw it, you know. The gold. In bars. But it was never moved here. I thought that's what you wanted, to see if there was anything to take. But there's nothing. Here, look." He pushed the door open. "Nothing."

Not even broken pieces of furniture, scavenged for firewood, just bricks and chunks of plaster. He looked across what had been the hall to the suspended piece of staircase. The built-in closet underneath it, dumping ground for umbrellas and trunks and boots, had been cut away, surgically removed by blast. The newel post had been ripped away too. Where they used to stand the Christmas tree, the first thing you saw when you came in, draped with strings of electric candles.

"Careful of the glass," the old man said.

Alex took a step, then stopped. What was the point? "That's all right," he said. "I just wanted to see if the house was still here."

The man closed the door behind them, a watchman's instinct.

"A thousand years Adolf said. Now look."
He turned to Alex. "How is it you didn't
know? About the house. You were in the
army?"

"No. I was away." Evading.

"Away," the man said, leaping somewhere
else. "Not so many come back from that.
You hear the stories —" Wanting to hear
Alex's, what the camps were like, and now
it was too late to correct him, too many lay-
ers of embarrassment. When Alex said nothing the man sighed and looked away. "Well,
it was no picnic here either," he said, his
hand taking in the street. "Night after night.
A thousand years. What a liar. And now
we've got the Russians. That's what he gave
us instead. The Russians. A thousand years
of them." A quick glance at Alex, to see how
he was responding to this. "I never thought
I'd see that. Russians in Berlin. Any of it."
He hesitated, not sure how to ask. "You're a
Jew?"

"Half," Alex said.

"Half. That didn't matter to them, did it?"

"No."

"Swine. And now they blame us. The
Germans did it. Who? Me? No, those liars.
They say the Jews brought it on themselves,
but I don't agree. It was them. They took
everything too far." A pause, awkward, the

easiness gone. He touched his hat. "Well, so."

Alex watched him go, his shoes loud on the pavement. Kleine Jägerstrasse had always been an echo chamber, sounds bouncing between the buildings. That night they had heard shouts first, running footsteps, then heavy boots, stopping just outside, not sure where to go next, a tension you could almost feel through the door. Erich had outrun them only by seconds, just long enough to slip through the side door before the maid bolted it, eyes wide with fear. Kurt Engel was bleeding from a gash in his scalp, Erich holding him up, his own face bloody from a smashed nose. Fritz and the girls had rushed in from the sitting room, little involuntary cries, the whole house beginning to flutter. Then more shouts in the street.

Alex peeked through the curtains. "SA," he said. "Did they see you come in?"

"Who cares what they saw?" Fritz said. "Call the police."

"The police won't do anything," Erich said.

"What's that? Blood?" Fritz said. "Are you hurt? Ilse, get some water —"

The maid began to run then stopped short

as the brass knocker began pounding on the door.

"Open up! Scum!"

Alex could hear the sharp intake of breath in the room, the beginning of panic. Elsbeth was swallowing, her eyes darting nervously.

"Call the police," Fritz said.

"Papa," Erich said. "They'll kill us."

"In my house?" Fritz said.

"Open!" Another pounding, even the heavy door shaking with it.

"Over here," Irene said, opening the closet door under the stairs. "Quick."

Erich put his arm around Kurt's waist and half dragged him behind the Christmas tree.

"Turn on the tree lights," Irene said to the maid.

"Open!"

"You have to answer them," Alex said to Fritz, watching Irene shut the closet door and move two wrapped presents up against it, part of the display spread under the tree.

"Who is that?" Fritz shouted. "What do you want?"

"Open up!"

Alex nodded at Fritz, who looked around, a directive to stay still, then went over and opened the door.

"What is the meaning of this? What do you want? You should be ashamed of yourself. Are you drunk?"

The leader, a burly man in his twenties, rushed through, then stopped, not expecting the lights, girls in dresses.

"They came in here. There's nowhere else —"

"Who? What are you talking about?"

"Jewish scum. Communists."

"Here? Don't be ridiculous."

"We'll see for ourselves," he said, moving into the hall.

Fritz stood in front of him, a stage gesture. "How dare you? Make trouble in this house? At this time of year?" he said, taking in the tree. "Do you think you're in some beer hall? One more step and I'll get the police and then you'll see where you are."

"Get out of the way," the man said, pushing Fritz's shoulder, his nerve back, the men now behind him.

"Stop that," Alex said, reaching for the man's hand.

The man swerved, shoving Alex instead. "Oh yes?" Another shove, toward the tree. "What about you? Were you at the meeting too? Maybe another Jew. You look —" Peering at him, nose wrinkled, so that for one stopped second Alex wondered if there really was some telltale Semitic scent.

"That's my son," Fritz said. "Take your

hands off him." The voice icy, the authority of generations. Alex looked at him. No hesitation.

The SA man stepped back. "If you're hiding them —" He signaled for his men to fan out.

"What makes you think you can do this? What right?"

"What right?" the SA man repeated, jeering.

"Effie, call the police," Fritz said to another maid.

"Call them," the SA man said. "They're looking too. Let them do the dirty work for once."

"Dirty work," Fritz said. "That's all you know. You and your —"

"Here's the water," Ilse said, carrying in a pitcher, the old request.

"Water?" the SA man said.

Fritz looked at the rest of them, suddenly at a loss.

"Thank you, Ilse," Alex said, moving over to take the pitcher. "For the tree," he said to the SA man. "They dry out and then there's a danger of fire." He knelt down and poured some water into the support stand. "It doesn't take much," he said, hoping it wouldn't overflow, the basin already full. He glanced over toward the closet. Don't even look, draw anyone's attention. But then he saw the blood seeping out from under the door. Just a thin tickle but there, blood always jarring, something the eye went to, like a snake.

He stood up and went to the other side of the tree, away from the closet. Sounds overhead now, doors being slammed.

"So that's what it is now?" Fritz said, no longer looking at the SA man. "You do whatever you want. In my house. My *house.*" The only way he understood it.

The SA man ignored him, busy shouting to the men upstairs, then turned, his voice heavy with contempt. "A man who would hide Jews. Vermin."

"Nobody's hiding anybody. You're making a fool of yourself. Ah, now we'll see." The knocker rapped again. He went to the door. "Police. Now we'll see. Come. Thank you. This gangster and his men broke in. You hear them? They're all over the house."

But the policeman seemed more embarrassed than alarmed. "Well, Hans," he said to the SA man. "What's this?"

"Communists. Two. Maybe more. They're here — he's hiding them. There's nowhere else in the street."

"Hans, this is the von Bernuth house." He turned to Fritz. "I'm sorry for this."

"I told him. No one's here. And he comes right in —"

"Call your men," the policeman said quietly. "You have no business here."

A reluctant shout upstairs, Hans surly but not prepared to defy the police.

"Oh." Almost a gasp, involuntary. Ilse had spotted the blood. Still behind a wrapped present, out of the SA's line of sight.

Alex went over to her quickly, taking her elbow. "It's okay," he said, maneuvering her toward the sitting room. "Nerves," he said to the policeman. "She's easily upset."

"But —"

"I know. But it's all over. The police are here."

The SA men were clomping down the stairs.

"Now look. Frightening the maids," Fritz said. "I hope they *keep* you locked up."

"Get her out of here," Alex said, handing Ilse to Irene, almost a whisper, then went back to stand by the closet, in front of the blood.

"Is that everyone?" the policeman said, watching them file out, awkward and sheepish. "So. I'm sorry for your trouble. A misunderstanding. Now good night."

"But aren't you going to arrest him?" Fritz said.

"Arrest him?"

"A man breaks into your house —"

"Breaks in here?" He pointed to the door. "I don't see any signs of that. You opened the door to him, yes?"

"Do you think he was a guest? I'd have this rabble in my house?"

"It was maybe too much enthusiasm," the policeman said, "looking for Communists. Better, I think, to forget this evening. In the Christmas spirit." He glanced again at the tree, then the present underneath. A few inches.

"Yes," Irene said, coming back. "Just go. Leave us, please."

Fritz said nothing for a minute, looking at the policeman, then turned away. "Rabble."

Outside Hans was back at the steps, one last threat. "We'll watch. And when we get them, it won't go so easy for you. You'll see."

The policeman pushed him away from the door. "Shut up. Idiot. He's von Bernuth."

Alex closed the door, bolting it, then waved to the maid. "The drapes. Every window."

The room itself seemed to exhale, everyone stuck in place for a moment, listening for sounds outside.

Alex went over to Fritz. "Thank you. For saying that."

Fritz looked at him, a quick nod, then, confused by the intimacy, moved away. "Such things. In Germany."

"Oh God," Irene said, suddenly frantic, moving the presents and opening the closet door. "Help me."

"Are they gone?" Erich said, nose still bleeding. He slid out, pulling Kurt with him. "Now do you see?" he said to Fritz.

Fritz said nothing, his body slack.

"Here, let me," Irene said, moving into Erich's place, cradling Kurt's head in her lap. "Where's the water?" Dabbing at his head with her handkerchief to stanch the blood around the cut.

"Careful. You'll get blood on your dress," Elsbeth said.

"Oh, my dress," Irene said, dismissive.

Alex helped Erich to his feet. "Are you all right? Is your nose broken?"

"I don't think so. How do you know? I mean, how does it — ?"

"Never mind that," Irene said "This is going to need stitches. Ilse, call the doctor."

"Now?" Erich said. "You heard them. They're watching the house."

"Get Lessing. Tell him to bring flowers. A Christmas call," she said, but offhand, distracted, her eyes on Kurt.

It was then that Alex finally took it in, her

hand soothing the side of his face, her body draped over his. He felt a prickling on his skin, peeking through a crack at something he wasn't meant to see. The way her hand moved, soft, familiar. He stood still, hearing the blood in his ears. How long? All the while? Erich's friend. Always around. But when? Not the summer, the air thick with sex, no one but the two of them. That couldn't have been a lie. But then when? She looked up suddenly, feeling his stare, caught, and he knew again. How long? Did they do the same things? At least she didn't look away, pretend he hadn't seen, didn't know. It would be in his face. She held his look. I'm sorry. I'm not sorry. I didn't mean to hurt you. It's not about you. Don't look at me like that. It's different. I couldn't help it. You have no right —

"I'll get Lessing," he said, breaking into her look, all the words, and then he turned to the door and it was over.

Outside he had stood for a minute, expecting to see a waiting SA uniform come out of the shadows, but no one was there. The street had been as empty and quiet as it was now, and he wondered for a second if both of them, the memory and this gray morning, were part of the same Berlin dream. The people he'd just seen were dead, lost to the past. And in the half-light the grim street now seemed something he'd imagined too. When he woke up, the hot Pacific sun would be burning off the morning fog and he'd be getting Peter ready for school, hurrying him for the bus, nursing a coffee.

He turned back to Hausvogteiplatz. Except he was awake, here, and it had already started. "Just settle in and we'll be in touch," Campbell had said. Some vague timetable, a week or two, not the moment he got here, the first meeting already set. "You can walk there. Through the park. Early." Why so soon? He looked up. No fog to burn off. As light as Berlin was going to get.

Just as the bellboy had said, he had no trouble at the sector boundary. A barrier had been set up for car inspections, but even those seemed random and listless. Pedestrians just walked across the street. The Tiergarten had been broken up into garden allotments and was still bare of the tall trees of his childhood, but at least the debris he'd seen in photographs — a downed plane, burned-out trucks — had been cleared away. Now what? There were two ways to Lützowplatz, zig-zagging down past the embassy quarter or straight out to the

Grosser Stern and then down. Did it matter? No one had said how the meeting would happen, maybe not until he was out of the park, so he just kept to the road. A few people in dingy overcoats had already begun to gather near the charred Reichstag to swap watches and heirlooms and PX tins, the new Wertheim's. No birds, an eerie quiet.

He was almost at the Victory Column when the car pulled up.

"Meier? Get in."

An American voice. For a second Alex hesitated, not reaching for the door handle, as if there were still a choice.

"Get in." Boyish, no hat, short military hair.

In the car, he offered his hand. "Willy Hauck. Nice to have you here." Pronouncing Willy with a *v*.

"You're German?"

"Not since I was a kid. Detroit. My father took a job there and never came back. I didn't think I'd ever be back either, but here we are. *Berliner Luft.*" The German accented now with a lifetime of flat lake vowels, the voice crackling and on the run, like Lee Tracy's.

"You didn't want to come?"

He shrugged. "Things are happening here.

65

So they move you up faster. They recruited me out of the army. G-2. They like it better if you went to Yale, but what the hell, I had the language, so off you go — beautiful Berlin." He gestured toward the window. "That's how most of us got here. If you can speak Kraut. Campbell's got Polish too. His old man."

"Campbell?"

"It used to be something else. Lots of *z*'s and who the hell knows. So. We haven't got a lot of time. You want to be at Lützowplatz same time it would take to walk there." They were driving out the other side of the circle, toward Charlottenburg. "Anybody behind you?"

"I don't think so. Why the big hurry? I didn't expect you to —"

"Something came up. So, let's do exits first."

Alex looked at him, a question.

"In case something goes wrong and you have to exit."

"Oh."

"Try to remember this, you can't write it down, okay? BOB's at twenty-one Föhrenweg, out in Dahlem."

"BOB?"

"Berlin Operations Base. That's your *last* resort. We have to assume it's watched, so

66

you turn up there you're blown and all we can do is get you out of the country."

"Twenty-one Föhrenweg," Alex said.

"You know who used to live across the street? Max Schmeling." Oddly proud of this, as if it meant something. "But like I say, that's the fire exit. Otherwise, use the regular meetings if you need to get in touch."

"Which are?"

"Depends where they set you up. Writers, people like that, they've been mostly putting in Prenzlauer Berg. Not a lot of bomb damage, so the buildings are in fairly good shape. So we're assuming there. Close to Volkspark Friedrichshain, where you'll like to walk."

"And bump into somebody?"

"Near the fountains with the fairy tale characters. Know it?"

Alex shook his head. "Never been there."

Hauck grinned. "A real West Ender, huh? Berlin stops at the Romanisches."

"We never had any reason to go there, that's all."

"And now it's home."

"I go every day?"

"When you can. We'll set up a time. It would make more sense with a dog, but with the rationing — But you still like to get out, get some exercise, clear the cob-webs."

"I do, actually."

"See? So you establish a routine. If they put you further out, we'll have to change the place. Weissensee, you walk the lake. But that's bigger houses. They keep those for the elite."

"Not the help."

"I didn't mean it that way. The Party elite. Officials. Don't worry, they like writers. You're at the Adlon, right?"

"In the lap of luxury."

Willy looked at him from the side. "They'll want you to do things. Public appearances. They had Anna Seghers at a factory. Cutting a ribbon. Major Dymshits loves writers."

"Who?"

"I thought they briefed you. Chief Cultural Officer. Or whatever the title is. Anyway, he calls the shots for the Soviets. He's a big fan of yours. He's the one told them to make the offer. To bring you over. He loves German writers."

Alex gazed out the window, blocks of ruins, as bad as in the East.

"What am I supposed to find out about him? Whether he reads Thomas Mann?"

Willy turned. "What are you asking?"

68

"I don't know. Cultural Officer. Why? How is that useful?"

"Let me explain something to you. We got a couple of wars going on here right now. Not just the airlift. Dymshits runs the propaganda one and he's doing all right. The Soviets think they've got the moral high ground. Don't ask me how. They come in here and rape everything in sight and they're supposed to be the heroes. The first victims. The ones the Nazis hated before they hated anybody else. But they won. Not us, them. We're just passing out candy bars in France. And now we're the ones getting into bed with old Nazis. On the radio anyway. And anywhere else they can twist a knife in. Old Nazis — is that the future you want? Or the Soviet model? A fresh Socialist start. Of course the Soviets used the Nazis too — who the fuck else was there? — but somehow that never comes out, just ours."

"That's what you want me to do? Find out if they've got Nazis in the Kulturbund?"

"Sure. If they do," Willy said, looking away.

"What else?"

"What did Campbell tell you?"

"Whatever I could pick up. I still don't see the point, but never mind. I'm here."

Willy headed the car back toward the Tiergarten, then slowed to a stop, idling by the curb.

"Look, Campbell told me about it. Those fucks on the committee. Reds under every bed. If they knew what the Soviets were really up to — So we got you by the short and curlies. Sometimes that's the way it happens. But, like you say, you're here. You're going to meet a lot of people. I want to know who might be — open to a little business."

"This business."

Willy nodded. "Maybe the future doesn't look as bright as it used to. Maybe somebody's beginning to wonder, maybe he needs a little money. I want to know. That's the point."

"All right," Alex said quietly.

"Next, don't get yourself killed."

Alex looked at him. "I thought I was just collecting a little gossip."

"The Russians don't see it that way. It's Dodge City here. You want to watch your back. Everywhere. The sectors don't mean anything. They think it's all theirs. People disappear — broad daylight, they just grab them — and we complain and they say they don't know what we're talking about. People get killed too. It's a dangerous place for amateurs. I didn't ask for this, you know? Civilian, first time out. But Campbell said you'd be okay. Said you were motivated." Holding onto the word.

"That's one way of putting it. If you're a shit like Campbell."

Willy leaned back, surprised, then smiled. "Yeah. Well. It's a shitty business."

Alex looked over. "What else? You didn't get me out my first morning to tell me to keep my ears open. Something came up, you said."

Willy stared back for a second. "Good. You listen. That's something you can't —"

"What came up?"

"Pay dirt. For you. You've been promoted."

"To what?"

"You're a protected source now. Not just an information source."

"Protected."

"It means nobody at BOB knows about you."

"Except you."

"Except me. So there's less risk if there's a leak. BOB knows I've got a protected source in the East, but not who."

"Why?"

"Remember you asked us to run a trace on some friends of yours?"

71

"And nothing came up."

"That's because they got married. New names. Then one of them popped up in a CROWCASS file, with a cross-ref to the maiden name. Elsbeth von Bernuth. Now Frau Mutter. Frau Doctor Mutter."

"Why was she in a CROWCASS file?"

"He was. Doctor in the Wehrmacht. That automatically gets you a file."

"What's he supposed to have done?"

"Nothing. For the Wehrmacht. Just patch up the troops, what you'd expect. Before the Wehrmacht's a little different. He was knocking off people in mental homes. The euthanasia program, to keep the Aryan bloodlines pure. No more cripples or idiots. Just the ones in brown shirts."

"He was tried for this?"

"No. If we put every Nazi doctor on trial — Eugenics was a big deal here. Lots of doctors signed on. Not nice, bumping people off, but all legal. Anyway, that was before. CROWCASS was only interested in war crimes and there they came up empty."

"She's alive?"

Willy nodded. "Both. In the British sector. Practicing."

"And you want me to contact her?"

"That's up to you. Campbell said you were kissing cousins."

"My aunt married her uncle," Alex said, distracted. How had he done it? Injections? A pill before bedtime? Gas? Purifying the race. Had Elsbeth known? Or just waited at home, pretending not to. In exile you imagine people as you left them, not what they become. What had it been like here, day to day?

Willy was watching him.

"Why is this pay dirt?"

"This one isn't. But then I got the bright idea maybe the other one married too."

Alex looked up. "Irene?"

"Now Frau —"

"Engel," Alex said flatly.

"No, Gerhardt. Frau Engelbert Gerhardt. Enka to his friends. Funny thing is, he was supposed to be a little light in the loafers. Makeup artist, for chrissake."

"What?"

"Out at Ufa. Pictures."

"So why —?"

"Keep him out of trouble probably. They were putting them in camps. So, a happily married man. Goebbels didn't care as long as things looked okay. And he could screw the actresses." He raised his head. "Who's Engel?"

"An old boyfriend," he said, seeing her cradling his head.

Willy was peering at him. "What's wrong?"

"Nothing. She's alive?"

"And kicking. So we thought you'd like to see her."

Alex looked at him.

"Be friends again. Closer than ever."

A small jump in his stomach, wary. "Why?"

"It would be the most natural thing in the world. You were practically family." Willy took out a cigarette.

"Practically," Alex said, waiting.

"She'd want you to meet her new friends too, don't you think?"

"Just tell me."

Willy leaned forward, lighting the cigarette. "Gerhardt didn't make it. Bombing raid. Which left her a widow. Technically, anyway."

"And?"

"So now there's a new friend. Not that anybody would blame her for that. Not easy, a woman on her own in Berlin." He paused, taking a drag on the cigarette. "But a break for us."

"Why?"

"Alexander Markovsky. Not so bad. A wife back in Moscow, but that doesn't count for much. They all do, don't they? Anyway, very fond of your cousin. How she feels about him I don't know. You tell me. Let's hope she's crazy about him. We wouldn't want her to walk out on him, now that you're in the picture." A faint smile. "That's why I wanted to see you first, give you a heads-up. Forget Dymshits. You've got a real job."

Alex followed the trail of Willy's smoke, not breathing, then looked back.

"You want me to spy on her," he said, forcing the word out. "Nobody said anything about this. I'm not —" His voice trailed off, as if it were walking away.

Willy took a breath. "That's not the way this works. You don't get to pick."

"She's — a friend."

"We're not interested in her. We're interested in him," Willy said, explaining to a child. "He works for Maltsev. Major General Maltsev. State Security. That's about as inside Karlshorst as we're likely to get. We've never had a chance like this, somebody close to Maltsev. You want a ticket back, this is it."

A tightening around his chest, short of air.

"When did Campbell know about this?"

"I don't know," Willy said, surprised at the question. "You'd have to ask him."

"But he's not here."

Willy looked at him. "Does it matter?"

Alex turned, facing out. "And what do you think he tells her?" He paused. "In bed."

"Maybe nothing. Maybe something. And it's what he's going to tell you. Without even knowing it. Just because you're around. Anyway, it's a little late for second thoughts, isn't it?" He glanced at his watch. "I'd better get you to Lützowplatz. It's been awhile. Even for a slow walker."

"I never said I'd do something like this."

"Who are you worried about? Markovsky? He's a thug, just like the rest of them. Your friend? Ask yourself what she's doing with him. There aren't any good guys in this one."

"I thought we were the good guys."

"We are. You don't want to forget that." He tossed the cigarette out the window and put the car in gear. "Look, you have a problem, you'd better tell me now. You can go right back to the Adlon. Hang out with your new friends. If you want to live here. But I thought the deal was you wanted to get back to the States. Show us what a good citizen you are."

"By doing this."

"Well, this is what we have." Willy turned back into the park. "So what's the problem? Is there something I should know?"

Alex shook his head. "It's just — someone you know."

"How long since you've seen her? Irene."

"Fifteen years."

"A lot happens in fifteen years. Especially here. You think you know her? Maybe not so much anymore." He slowed the car. "Not someone sleeping with Markovsky."

Alex stared straight ahead. When he woke up, he'd be getting Peter ready for school.

"Here's the bridge. You should get out here. If anybody's watching, they'll be expecting you to walk over."

"Why would they be watching?"

"It's what they do." He looked over at Alex. "You all right? You look — You know, we all get cold feet in the beginning. You'll be okay. A chance like this." A verbal pat on the shoulder, part of the team.

Alex sat for another minute. The kitchen would be bright with sun, even that early.

"What do I do? I mean, how do I contact her?"

"She'll be at your party. You're a big deal. Everyone wants to meet you."

"With the boyfriend?"

"Unless he's out at Karlshorst."

"Doing whatever he does."

"At the moment, running interference between Moscow and the SED, the German Party. They have this idea that Moscow should stop robbing the zone blind with reparations. And send back the POWs."

"And he's going to talk to me about all this?"

Willy looked at him. "You'd be surprised what people will say. Once they trust you." He nodded to the window. "You'd better go. See if your house is still there. Which side of the square was it?"

Alex stared out the window. You think you know her? Maybe not so much anymore. It was easy to cross a line in Berlin, as easy as going from one sector to another. Finish your cereal, he'd be saying to Peter.

"The east side," he said finally.

"We're not expecting gold right away. It's all valuable. Just keeping track. Where he goes when he's away. When he's coming back."

Alex opened the car door and turned. "The kind of thing you'd tell your mistress."

Willy met his look. "We'll be in touch."

On the bridge, the one he'd crossed a thousand times coming home from the park, there was a stalled army truck with a Union Jack on its door, soldiers busy with wrenches. The British sector, where Elsbeth's husband was practicing medicine again. First do no harm. He glanced down

at the thick oily water of the Landwehrkanal. There had been bodies here after the
war, floating for months. A lot happens in
fifteen years. At the end of the bridge there
was a car parked across the street, maybe
waiting to see him come into the square.
What they did in Berlin. It didn't matter if
they were really watching, as long as you
thought they might be. Oranienburg with
the peek hole in the door.

Willy's car came up from behind and
passed him. Don't look. You've walked here
to see the house, the predictable motions of
homecoming. But when he reached the
square nothing was there, no sturdy door or
hanging staircase, just an empty space
where the house had been. For a second he
felt light-headed, lost, as if he had ended up
in the wrong street. He had expected at least
some fragment of their lives, maybe the
frame of the big window where his mother
had kept the piano, the ground-floor corner
where his father's study had been. Then the
evenings would come back, his mother's
music, her long conservatory fingers, hair
pulled back in a tight bun so that not even
a wisp would fall in her eyes, his father
wreathed in cigarette smoke, head back,
listening, the music rising and falling. How
he would always remember them, in a room

filled with music. But that had all been erased, not even a headstone of rubble left. A vacant lot. And a parked car waiting for someone. He crossed the street, looking preoccupied, as if he hadn't noticed it. Up ahead he could still see Willy's car, driving slowly, probably keeping a rearview eye on him until he turned back. Two cars watching.

He looked away from the parked car and started down Schillstrasse. The rubble had been cleared here, a standing wall without the usual heaps of brick in front. Behind him the sound of a motor, gears switching. Not the parked car, still motionless where it sat. Maybe the British truck. Then, suddenly, there was a screech of tires, a burst of speed, and another car shot into his line of vision then turned in toward the wall, cutting him off, brakes slamming, a man jumping out the back, grabbing his upper arm, the force of it shoving him against the wall. He felt a sharp pain in his shoulder, a pinpoint of focus, everything else a blur, too fast.

"Get in." A low growl, yanking him now toward the open car door and all he could think was, broad daylight, you do this in broad daylight. But only one. Shouldn't there be two to pin him, two to make the

snatch? The other was waiting behind the wheel. Easy pickings, a writer. If they knew who he was. Not just a man Willy had dropped off. A little drive through the park. Which made him the enemy now, just talking to Willy, and he realized suddenly, as the man was pushing his head down to force him into the car, that this would mean Oranienburg. Or a new Oranienburg. With no one to bribe him out this time. People disappear. Maybe for good, the car a kind of coffin. But only one of them.

Alex pushed back hard, swiveling, flinging the man against the car, and pulled his arm free.

"Scheisse!" Lunging for Alex again, pushing him against the standing wall.

Another screech of tires, Willy's car backing down the street toward them, a fishtail swerving. No other cars to dodge, coming fast.

The man had grabbed Alex again, a stronger grip this time, still sure of himself, one man. Not even thinking, jerking to some electrical charge running through him, Alex smashed his knee into the man's groin. A surprised gasp, then a grunt, the man bending over, still trying to hold onto Alex's sleeve. But this was the split second, the one chance, and Alex yanked himself free, starting to run. He heard a car door open, the driver spilling out in alarm. Two of them.

"Halt! Scheisse!"

And then a swirl of sounds, the kicked man howling and pulling himself up to lunge again, the driver's footsteps running back to block Alex that way, the scream of brakes as Willy's car stopped, another door slamming and then a loud crack, jarring, that made all the other sounds go away. For a second everything stopped, the shot still echoing in the air. Then Alex heard the driver inhale, a rasp, and fall to the street, a thump as his body hit. The first man turned, pulling a gun out of his pocket and fired at Willy, who ducked. A moan from the other side of the car, the driver clutching his stomach. Willy jumped up and fired again, hitting the first man, then crouching back down. But not fast enough, the man's return bullet catching him in the chest, his eyes widening in disbelief. The shot was deafening, loud enough to rip the air, to bring British soldiers running across the bridge, but the square was still empty, as if the sounds hadn't reached them yet, hadn't left the inside of Alex's head, where they drowned out his own ragged breathing. I could die. I could die here.

Willy slumped against his car and fired

again, this one higher, hitting the first man in the throat. He teetered for an instant, blood gushing, then fell across the hood of the car and slid to the ground, leaving a streak of blood down the side, his overcoat matted with it. His body went still, legs twisted at some unnatural angle. In the sudden quiet Alex heard the car engine, still idling, waiting for him to be bundled in the back, taken somewhere for questioning. Watch your back. He gulped some air, sidestepping the body, and started running toward Willy.

"Are you all right?" Still panting.

Willy was on the ground, his head propped against the car's tire. He winced, an answer. "It fucking hurts," he said, his breathing labored now. "I always wondered."

Alex looked into the square again. Still nobody, the parked car empty, not the one he should have been worried about.

"I never saw them," Willy said flatly. "That's how good they are."

They heard a groan from the other car, the driver trying to move. Willy looked at Alex, his eyes darting with alarm.

"Take the gun. No witnesses."

"Are you crazy — ?"

Willy grabbed his wrist, clutching it. "No witnesses. He's seen you." He looked at

Alex's face, then squinted from the pain and opened his eyes again, an act of will. "Nobody knows. You're still protected." He squeezed his wrist again. "Take the gun. Quick, before —"

"I can't," Alex said, almost a whisper. "I never —"

"They'll kill you. That's what this is. Do it. In the head. Don't think, just do it. Then run like hell."

"What about you?"

Willy twisted his mouth, then looked again at Alex. "Do it, for chrissake. Take the gun."

Alex looked at it, still clutched in Willy's hand, and started prying his fingers off. There was the sound of a motor in the distance. How far? He took the gun and walked over to the other car. A faint moaning, the driver opening his eyes at the sound of footsteps. A startled look, what prey must feel like at the end. The driver tried to raise his hand, his gun weaving. Do it. Don't think. Alex fired. A roar of sound, then a splat as the driver's head ripped open, the insides oozing, then stopping. No witnesses. Alex stared at the man for a second, feeling his stomach heave. But there was nothing to bring up, just the taste of bile, too early for food.

The motor again. He glanced toward the

bridge. The British truck. Don't think. Run. He raced over to Willy. Eyes closed. Alex felt his neck for a pulse but there was nothing, the skin already cool or was that his imagination? The morning was cold. You could see your breath, coming now in quick puffs. The sound of the truck again. Oddly, the other car engine was still running and for one crazy second Alex fought the impulse to turn it off. Disappear. Now. No one here but the dead. No witnesses.

He darted behind Willy's car and then followed the standing wall until there was a break and he could slip behind. Not as neat as the square here, piles of rubble. But what did it matter? Run. In a few seconds they'd be here. He listened to the sound of his shoes crunching on the dust and mortar and he realized he had never run so fast, that he was somehow trying to outrun the sound of his own running, make it disappear. An old woman was stopped at the next corner and turned, terrified, and he saw what she must be seeing, a man running too fast, still waving a gun in his hand, his shoes slipping on loose bricks as if he were splashing through puddles, and he knew he should stop, slow down, but he couldn't. He kept running, away from the British soldiers who must now be swarming over the cars in Lützowplatz. Running from the old woman, who must have seen his face. Running away from all of it, all the lines he never thought he would cross, sprinting over them.

It was only when he reached the Budapester Strasse bridge, where there were a few cars, that he put the gun in his coat pocket and slowed to a walk. He felt the sweat on his face. Sweating in the early morning cold. Slow down. Breathe. No witnesses. On the bridge, after a quick glance around, he tossed the gun over, a plop in the water, and then started to walk again, forcing himself not to run, draw attention. A man's startled eyes as you aimed a gun. His head opening. That's what this is.

By the time he reached the Adlon, he was breathing normally again, a guest just back from a long walk. A new doorman, the day shift, said good morning, and for an anxious moment Alex wondered if anything showed in his face. How do you look after you've killed a man? But the doorman simply waved him through. No one knew. Upstairs, he lay on the bed and kept replaying Lützowplatz in his mind. Willy's grimace. They move you up faster here. His panic, running, and now this strange troubled relief afterward. Nothing in his face. Getting away with something. And now what? A protected source, one contact. But someone knew enough to follow Willy. They knew he was here, even if they didn't know who he was. Three bodies in the square, two guns, an impossible arithmetic. They'd be looking. Whoever they were.

When he finally did close his eyes it was not so much sleep as sheer animal exhaustion, the body shutting down for repair, a void, like the space where his house had been. Irene with a Russian. Frau Gerhardt. Someone he didn't know, even if he'd known every part of her. It would be easier that way, someone he didn't know. You want a ticket back, this is it. When he heard the knocking on the door he was at the von Bernuth house, the SA pounding, Kurt bleeding, Irene meeting his eyes. But it was only Martin coming to collect him. His eyes were still scratchy, tired. No hot water, an astringent splash of cold. They'd be waiting at the Kulturbund, maybe one of them open for a little business. Not understanding what it would mean until he was in it, over his head.

■ ■ ■ ■

2
KULTURBUND

■ ■ ■ ■

The reception had been called for four, the early hour, Martin explained, because of the difficulties getting home in the dark. "The West refuses to sell us coal, so naturally there are shortages." "And we refuse to sell them food." "Because they refuse to sell us coal." The kind of airless, circular argument Alex remembered from meetings in Brentwood, before he stopped going.

Even at this hour, though, the sky was already dusky, filled with clouds promising snow. They picked their way along a path cleared through the rubble toward the light of the club windows. The Kulturbund was on Jägerstrasse, just off Friedrichstrasse, and suddenly familiar.

"Well," Alex said. "The old Club von Berlin." Where Fritz had often spent the afternoons, napping after a brandy.

"I don't know," Martin said, slightly stiff. "Now the Kulturbund." The only thing it had ever been to him.

"The Nazis changed the name. Herren-club, I think, but it was the same people. Landowners. Old money. Funny it should be here, the Kulturbund."

"Funny?"

"Culture was the last thing on their minds." Nodding over papers in the library. Playing cards in one of the private rooms. Buying each other drinks in the bar, maybe even where Fritz had arranged the favor for him, Oranienburg for a price.

"Then it's good, yes? Better."

"The waiters had tailcoats, I remember," Alex said.

"Yes," Martin said, uncomfortable.

"Still?" Alex said, amused. "So. Socialist tailcoats."

Martin looked away, not sure how to answer.

Inside they could hear tinkling glasses and voices floating down the marble staircase.

"I thought we'd be early," Alex said, giving up his coat.

"Everyone is anxious to meet you," Martin said, leading the way. "Goethe." He pointed to the portrait on the landing.

At the top they were met by a huddle of men, all wearing lapel pins with the SED handshake.

"Such an honor. Your trip was comfortable?"

One polite question after another until they blended into one, the usual official welcome. Alex nodded and smiled, automatic responses. No one knew.

There were two dining rooms, one with walnut paneling and the other, where the party was, with a burgundy satin brocade, the long members' table now pushed against the wall for a buffet spread. He smiled to himself. Anxious to meet him, but already filling plates, the eager freeloading of any faculty lounge. Someone handed him a glass of sweet champagne. The room looked neglected, the brass railings dull and the carpet tired, but it was otherwise much as he remembered, plush furniture and heavy drapes, like a room in the von Bernuth house. Was she already here?

"So, my friend. Ruth told me she saw you." Brecht, grasping his arm as he shook his hand, the stub of a cigar smoldering in his mouth.

"Yes, she's here?"

"Still in Leipzig. She likes to make these little trips. I said, send a letter. But, well, Ruth. So, you're here. All the little birds returning to the nest. And Feuchtwanger was sorry to see you go, yes? Always sorry, but he stays. How is it there now?"

"Still warm and sunny."

Brecht shrugged. "So, sun. But now everyone's here. Speaking German again." He waved his hand to the room, and, as if in response, the sound rose, lapping at them, the comfortable babble of one's own language. "There's a spirit, you can feel it."

"I hear they're giving you a theater." Making conversation, sleepwalking. Had the British soldiers seen anything?

Another shrug. "People come up to you in the street. They know who you are. In California, who do they know? So it's flattering. But the work we can do now. Not *Quatsch* for some studio. Wait till you seen Helene. Magnificent. You're at the Adlon too, Ruth said? It's comfortable. Better than a house, while this is going on." A finger to the ceiling, the unseen stream of planes. "They won't sell us coal, so it's a problem." Martin's explanation, what everybody knew.

Alex looked over Brecht's shoulder. The room was filling up, men in old suits and women without makeup in wool skirts and thin shapeless cardigans.

"You know who's also here? Zweig. Soon everybody. Except Saint Thomas maybe. The bourgeois comforts, very important to him. A Biedermeier soul, Herr Mann. Bied-

94

ermeier prose too," he said, a small twinkle, having fun. "A stuffed sofa, with tassels. In his case maybe Switzerland would be better."

"Why should he go anywhere?"

"He can't stay there. It's starting again. He thinks the Nobel will protect him? Not if they — well, you know this. Who better? I congratulate you, by the way. I didn't know — forgive me — you had such strong —" He paused, peering at Alex. "A dark horse. All the time — I didn't know you were even in the Party."

"I'm not. Other people were. But that was their business. Most of them left anyway. After '39."

Brecht looked around, hesitant. "Well, that time. It's not so well understood here. How people felt. To them, you know, it was a kind of disloyalty. Not to follow the Party."

"And be nice to Hitler. But of course Stalin knew what he was doing all along."

A flicker of caution, then a small smile, unable to resist. "He usually did," Brecht said, a boy being naughty. He looked at Alex. "They'll ask you to join now. Just tell them you're not a joiner. No organizations. A writer works alone."

"Is that what you said?"

"It's enough discipline with Helene," he

95

said, waving the cigar, then lowered his voice. "Then you're not obliged — to do what they say. A little independence. They have to work with you. Push-pull. And they will. It's a new start here." He cocked his head west. "Over there, business as usual. It doesn't change. Nazis. The Americans don't care, as long as they're not Communists. Like the committee. But here there's a chance." Believing it, like Martin. "But first, bread. They're reissuing your books?"

Alex nodded. "All of them. Even *Notes in Exile.* Pieces."

"Make sure they pay. They can afford it. They get a subsidy. It's a priority with the Russians, culture. Coal not so much," he said, another wry shrug. "You've met Dymshits?"

"Not yet."

"A lover of German literature — Goethe, by heart. There he is. Sasha," he said, approaching a slight man with dark hair and glasses, eyes slightly watery. "Meet our guest of honor. Major Dymshits."

"I'm so pleased," he said, taking Alex's hand. Another face from the faculty lounge, bookish, an eager smile. "Welcome."

"I gather you're responsible for bringing me here."

"Your talent brings you here," he said with

a quiet flourish, his German precise but accented.

Alex nodded, a court gesture. "My thanks in any case. And for this reception. So much —"

"My advice is have some ham now. It always goes first." A polite joke, the smile in place again. "Artists are always hungry, it seems. There is so much I want to ask you. The scene in *The Last Fence* when the shirt catches on the barbed wire — Perhaps a lunch one day, if you would like that?"

"Of course," Alex said. That easy. Just as Willy had hoped. When that was all they'd wanted.

People were still coming in, more men than women, none with her blond hair. She wouldn't stay in a corner, she'd come up to him. Almost family. How would she look? Fifteen years.

"This is your publisher," Dymshits was saying. "Aaron Stein. Aaron will be taking care of you at Aufbau."

"An honor," Stein said, bowing, a younger version of Dymshits, the same glasses and gentle Semitic face. "We're so pleased. I hope you will come to the offices, meet everyone. We're just down the street. *Notes in Exile* —"

"Of course it's a favorite with him," Dymshits said. "Both of you exiles. Aaron was in Mexico City with Janka and Anna Seghers."

"Mexico. What was that like?"

"All right," Aaron said tentatively. "Of course, foreign. Walter had a little Spanish, from his time in Spain, you know, but most of us — so we had each other. Los Angeles was better, I think. Anyway we used to think so. Everyone wanted to go to America."

"Even those of us who were already there," Brecht said, a growl in his voice. "Where was it, this America we'd heard about? In Burbank? Culver City? No, not possible. So maybe nowhere. No such place."

"Like *Mahagonny*," Dymshits said.

Brecht ignored this, taking a drink instead.

"Here's Colonel Tulpanov," Dymshits said, standing straighter. "He very rarely comes, so you see how popular you are."

"His boss," Brecht said.

Dymshits shot him a glance, pretending not to be annoyed.

Tulpanov, in military uniform and short-cropped hair, had none of Dymshits's easy manner. There was an awkward exchange, welcome and thank you, then a blank pause, waiting for Dymshits to fill it with small talk.

"You know where they are?" Brecht said, a nod to Tulpanov. "The Information Administration? Goebbels's old offices."

"The building doesn't matter," Dymshits said quickly, before Tulpanov could decide whether to take offense. "It's what we do inside. Anyway, there were not so many buildings left standing. In those days you took what you could get. You know, we had a theater open that first month. Then more." This directly to Brecht. "Newspapers. Film licenses. So Berlin would have a life again. Ah, Bernhard, come and meet our guest."

After that it was a succession of handshakes, a blur of introductions. Brecht had drifted away to provoke someone else, and Tulpanov held court by the drinks table, obviously just waiting to leave. Dymshits gave a formal toast, welcoming Alex home to build the new Germany. "As we know," he said, "politics follows culture," and people nodded as if it made sense to them. Alex looked at their bright, attentive faces, Brecht's cynicism as out of place here as it had been in California, and for the first time felt the hope that warmed the room. Shabby suits and no stockings, but they had survived, waited in hiding or miraculously escaped, for this new chance, the idea the Nazis hadn't managed to kill.

Nothing was being asked of him. He acknowledged the toast with a few words of appreciation, thanking everybody for the welcome, but no one expected a speech. It was enough that he was here. Dymshits wanted lunch, some literary conversation. Aaron Stein hoped that he would help Aufbau by giving an opinion now and then on an English book. Martin wanted him to make the Kulturbund a kind of second home. But all he really had to do was collect his stipend and work as he pleased. In America there had never been enough. Without Marjorie's paycheck, how would they have managed? And now here in the Soviet zone, of all places, he was comfortable, even prized. Everyone seemed oddly grateful that he had come. There were polite questions about America, whether he thought they would accept a neutral Germany or try to rearm their zone, asked hesitantly, fearing the answer, and it occurred to him, an unexpected irony, that despite the blockade it was they who felt besieged, that his welcome was that of a soldier who'd managed to get through the lines and rejoin his unit.

"I hope you won't mind." Someone speaking English. "I just wanted to tell you I think it was great what you did, standing up to them. It's about *time.*" A woman holding a plate heaped with salami and potato salad, the voice New York quick. "I'm Roberta

Kleinbard," she said, motioning with the plate as a substitute for a handshake. "God, it's such a relief to speak English. You don't mind, do you? Herb says I'll never learn German if I keep falling back on it. But it's hard. You read the papers and that's all right and then somebody wants to really talk and half of it just sails over your head."

"You're living here?"

She nodded. "We figured it was just a matter of time back home. You know, like you with the committee. Herb was in the Party. Nobody's going to hire him once that comes out."

"What does he do?"

"Architect. And what's an architect supposed to do if he can't do that? Work at Schrafft's?" She waved her hand in dismissal. "They won't be satisfied till they hunt us all down. It's not illegal, but tell that to the boss. The *client.* Anyway, he was from here originally and God knows they could use architects." She cocked her head to the invisible ruins outside. "So I thought, it's better than sitting around waiting for some sub*poena.* I didn't want to give them the satisfaction."

"And how has it been? For you, I mean."

"Well, it's not New York, let's face it. Try and get a decent lipstick. They're going

through a rough time. You know, just keeping *warm.* But Herb's working. He's not sitting in some jail for taking the Fifth. He
likes it. And the plans they're working on —
like starting over. But this time you build it
the way you want it to look. You're not going to do that in New York. So it's good for
him." She looked around. "I know he's dying to meet you. He wanted — did you
know Neutra? Out in California? Neutra's
like a god to him."

"No, never met him."

"But you were in Los Angeles, right? I just
thought, you know, Germans, they'd naturally know each other."

"Neutra's been there a long time. He
probably thinks of himself as American.
Anyway, he was Austrian. Vienna, I think."

"And not German, there's a difference,
and everybody here would know that, right?
And there's me with my foot in my mouth
again." She rolled her eyes.

Alex smiled. "Only the Austrians care. So
you're mostly right. Anyway, never met him.
What about you? What do you do while your
husband's building Berlin?"

"Well, they're not building it yet, so I'm
still helping him with the drawings. That's
how we met. I was a draftsman. And there's
Richie to look after."

"Your son?" he said, a sudden drop in his stomach, unexpected.

"Mm. But he's in school now, so he's gone most of the day." She looked away, following her thought. "You do get homesick sometimes. And some of the ideas they have. About the States. All we do is beat up people on picket lines and lynch Negroes. Not that things are so wonderful but —"

"They really say that?"

"Well, the Russians. But you see things in Richie's books now, so you wonder what they're getting in the schools. The evils of capitalism, all right, fine, plenty of those to go around, I agree, but lynching — are we talking about the same place?" She looked back. "But it's better than having his father in jail. And things'll improve."

"They might even have lipstick soon," he said lightly.

She flushed, as if she'd been caught at something. "I can't believe I said that. Lipstick when —"

"No, it's nice to see a woman looking her best. Even Socialist ones," he said, harmless party talk, then saw that she had taken it as a pass, her eyes moving to the room.

"Is your wife here?"

"No, she's — in the States. We're separated."

"I'm sorry," she said, meaning it. "Because of this — you coming here?"

"Because of a lot of things."

"They never talk about that, the strain it puts on people. Do you testify? Do you cooperate? What it does to the families. Always wondering. Are they watching? Friends of ours, they'd see a car parked outside — so, FBI? How do you know? It's the strain."

He looked at her, at a loss, not what he had meant, but now Martin joined them, slightly shiny from the wine.

"There you are. I have to steal him for a few minutes. You don't mind? Anna's here," he said, lowering his voice.

He led Alex across the room, his bad leg skipping over the floor, to a woman talking to a small circle of men. Anna Seghers was shorter than Alex had expected but otherwise the same woman he'd seen in jacket photos for years. Her hair was white now, pulled back around her head, a halo effect that made her seem radiant. Martin, clearly dazzled, presented Alex as if she were granting him an audience, a *gnädige Frau.* Alex dipped his head as he took her hand.

"Oh, I'm not as grand as that," she said easily. "Or as old. How nice to meet you finally. Not just in your books. Welcome home."

"And you not just in yours."

"Tell me, did you have anything to do with the film they made of *The Seventh Cross*? They said every German in Hollywood had a hand in the script."

"Not this one," Alex said, holding his hands up. "All clean."

Seghers laughed. "Good. Now we can be friends. But I suppose I shouldn't complain. It was very nice to have the money. Even in Mexico money doesn't go very far. So, a godsend. And how are you getting on here?"

"I've just arrived. Literally. Last night."

"The first few days, it's difficult," she said, her voice warm, confiding. "When you see Berlin now. The trick is to see what it's going to be. Germany without Fascism. Sometimes I thought I would never see that. I hoped, but — And now it's here. So never mind the mess, you can always clear bricks away. Fascists were a little harder, no?"

"You sure they're all gone?"

"Well, it's like weeds, always there. So you get new soil, not so good for them. Change the economic system and they don't grow so well."

"Maybe they become something else."

She looked at him, interested. "Maybe. Let's talk about this. Not here. You have to meet a hundred people. Say nice things. The *same* nice things. I know how it is. But maybe you'll come see me? Come for tea and we can talk all afternoon. About what the Fascists become. Martin, you'll tell him where?" Meeting everyone, just as Willy said. A true believer, used for ribbon cutting.

Martin nodded, impressed, the invitation clearly an honor.

"*Ach,* there's Brecht," she said, noticing him across the room. "Poking, poking with the finger. More mischief. He thinks he's eighteen years old still. Well, maybe that's the answer, he is. You knew him in America?"

"Yes."

"Not a happy time for him. He says. Imagine what it was for Helene. But of course he doesn't. Imagine it. And now making everyone dance. First this, then that. Now he wants a car and a driver. When everything is so difficult for people, scarcely enough to go around, he wants a car and a driver. Like a —" She searched for the word.

"Great dramatist."

Now it was Seghers who smiled. "I look forward to our tea. Come this week. You're free?"

Alex opened his hands.

"We have a few things scheduled," Martin

said, playing secretary.

"The Kulturbund," Seghers said, an indulgent glance to Martin. "They hate to see us actually *write*. Fill the days, fill the days."

"It's lunch with Dymshits."

"Well, then you must go. Our masters." She put a hand on Alex's arm. "It won't always be like this. An occupied country. Now they can do what they like — take away factories, anything. Well, so it's the spoils. It's difficult for the German Party, people think we're lackeys, but what else can we do? Wait. And one day, it's a German government. And at least when they leave, they leave a workers' state. A German idea. Marx always had Germany in mind. I often wonder, how would it have been if it had happened here, not Russia. Well, we'll see." She stopped, cutting herself off. Did Campbell, anyone, really want to hear all this? Just static in the air. "Go have your lunch with Dymshits. He's a cultivated man. Brecht says he reminds him of Irving Thalberg."

Alex raised an eyebrow. "Brecht never knew Thalberg. He was dead before Brecht got there. Years before."

Seghers snorted. "Typical Bert. So your wife is here? I'd like to meet —"

Alex shook his head. "In America. She's

American."

"Ah," Seghers said, looking at him, shuffling through stories, reluctant to ask. "Maybe later. When things are easier here."

"Yes, maybe later." A harmless lie, closing things off.

He felt someone hovering at his side and turned. A young man with wire-rimmed glasses and dark, neatly combed hair.

"So you don't recognize me."

Alex stared, trying to imagine the face fifteen years ago. Serious, sharp-edged now, not a hint of the youthful fuzziness he must have had in old school pictures. "I'm sorry."

"No? Well, who remembers the younger brother? There's a clue."

Another look.

"Never mind. I don't blame you. I was ten years old. So things have changed." He held out his hand. "Markus Engel."

"Kurt's brother?" His head in her lap.

"Ah, now the bell goes off. The little brother. Maybe you didn't even notice back then. But of course I knew you. All of Kurt's friends." He turned his head. "Comrade Seghers. We haven't met but I recognized you from your photographs."

"If only I still looked like that," she said pleasantly. "Well, I'll leave you to talk old times." She took Alex's hand. "So glad you're with us. I'll have Martin arrange the tea."

Markus watched her go. "A good Communist. There should be more like her."

Alex looked at him, surprised. "Aren't there?"

"I mean the exiles. So many years in the West, it changes people sometimes. But not her." He half smiled at Alex. "Or you it seems. You came back." He paused. "You didn't bring your wife, I think? She's staying in America?"

The third person to ask, but this time a hint of interrogation, something for the file. Alex looked up, alert. Not unkempt and eager like Kurt, controlled, a policeman's calm eyes, watching.

"Yes," Alex said.

"Let's hope, not too long. It's not good for families to be apart." Innocuous but somehow pointed, fishing for a reaction. The leverage of family left behind, what Campbell had wanted to know too.

"I'm afraid for good. We're separated."

"Oh," Markus said, not sure where to take this. "And still you come. So a matter of conviction. Admirable. But you know it's a serious issue, this exposure to the West. Not for you," he said hastily. "Not the writers. But the Russian soldiers, POWs — it confuses them. Comrade Stalin immediately saw the problem. How it's necessary to re-educate them if they've been in the West."

Alex looked at him, disconcerted. Re-educate. Kurt's little brother.

"It's a long time you're away," Markus said.

"So I'm hopelessly tainted."

A delayed reaction, taking this in. "I see, a joke. I'm saying only that you weren't here. You're meeting lots of old friends tonight? Ones you can recognize?" he said, smiling.

"You're the first."

"And your old house? Lützowplatz, I remember, yes? It's still standing?"

Alex looked at him, unable to speak. What did he know?

"Often people do that," Markus said. "Go to see if it's still there. An understandable curiosity."

"Yes, you wonder. So I went this morning." Something easily checked. Play it out.

"An early riser."

"Not too early," Alex said vaguely. "I slept in a little. A long drive yesterday. But what a memory you have. Lützowplatz."

"Well, I was reminded of it. There was an incident there this morning."

"Oh?"

"You didn't see anything yourself?"

"No. What kind of incident?" Keeping his voice steady.

Markus stared at him, then waved his hand. "Traffic accident. Carelessness."

"Was anyone hurt?"

"I think so, yes. Imagine surviving the war and then a stupid accident. A man was seen running away. Maybe the cause, it's hard to say." Then, at Alex's expression, "I thought you might have seen —"

"No. Nothing. Not the house either. It was gone. The whole thing."

Markus held his eyes for a moment, then decided to move on. "It's difficult, coming back. I was with the first group in '45. The streets — I didn't know where I was. I thought, what city is this? But then, little by little —"

Alex took a breath, half listening, his mind darting. Of course Markus could get times from the Adlon doorman. But they wouldn't be precise enough to put him there, already on his way back when the traffic accident happened. Why call it that? Why bring it up at all? And then back off. He saw him suddenly as a young boy, maybe even the boy he'd actually been, poking a toad with a stick, toying with it. Toying with him now. Don't react. Nobody knew. Nobody in this noisy room suspected anything.

111

"The first group?" he said, picking up the thread. "From the army?"

"No, I was in exile, like you. But east."

"East."

"Moscow. At the Hotel Lux." A name he assumed Alex would recognize.

"A hotel? All during —"

Markus smiled a little. "Not the Adlon. They kept all the Germans there, the German Communists. The SED leadership now, all Hotel Lux graduates. They say it was our Heidelberg. Well, if they could see it. Not so nice as the real Heidelberg."

"But when — ? I don't know where to start. What happened to everybody? Kurt?"

"He was killed in Spain. It was after that we left for Russia. My mother and me."

"I'm sorry."

Markus shrugged. "A long time ago. At least a hero's death. One of the first, in the International Brigade."

"I didn't know."

"She never told you? Irene? You were so close to them, the family. Always at the house."

Alex shook his head. "We weren't in touch. After I left."

"No, she wouldn't have time to write. That kind of woman."

"What kind?"

"The kind she is. She would already have another man by then. Kurt just dead and —" His voice unexpectedly bitter, a grudge he'd nursed for years. "Not that the others in that family were any better. Nazis."

"The von Bernuths? They weren't Nazis. They hid Kurt. From the SA. I was there."

"Oh, the famous night under the stairs? That was for Erich."

"I went for the doctor," Alex said slowly, making a point. "For your brother. He needed stitches, not Erich."

"Yes, and then what?"

"What do you mean?"

"Erich. He follows Kurt like a puppy. So, meetings. Leaflets. Illegal then. But what is it for him, politics? A fast car. Maybe a woman he shouldn't be seeing. It's exciting and then he comes to his senses and leaves her. And where does he go? Into the Wehrmacht."

"That doesn't make him a Nazi."

"Not drafted. The father arranged a commission. From his Nazi friends. You're surprised? Nobody forced him. The sister, Elsbeth, she even goes to rallies with her Nazi husband. We have photographs of this. An official party member."

"Doctors had to join, didn't they?" Alex said absently, his mind still back on *we*. We who? Who would have photographs?

"They live over in the West now," Markus said. "It's easier for them there." He looked at Alex. "You're like Kurt a little bit. He was always taken in by them too. But in the end —" His voice tailed off.

"And Irene?" Alex said. "You think she was a Nazi? She was in love with him."

"Whatever that means to her."

Alex ignored this. "They never married?"

Markus shook his head. "He said it was a risk for her. If he was arrested. And then he went to Spain. And that was the end of it."

"But you expected her to — what? Wear black for the rest of her life? A young girl?"

"Maybe wait a little."

"But she didn't," Alex said, curious, leading.

"A woman like that? Kurt thought she was — well, I don't know what. Not somebody who works for Goebbels. Who marries — a sham marriage, to hide her affairs."

"Worked for Goebbels how?"

"Everyone at Ufa worked for him, everyone in *Kino.* And what were they making? Propaganda. Our great National Socialist heroes. So how would Kurt have felt about that? A wonderful way to honor his memory — make films for the Nazis."

"But what did she do?"

"Production assistant," he said easily, familiar with her file. "Later, bigger jobs. So maybe she slept with someone. Then after, when there's no more Goebbels, she goes to the Americans. The old Ufa crowd, back again, but now for the Americans."

"Erich Pommer."

"Yes, exactly, Pommer. But it's not so easy getting a license to work. Even from old friends. Not after so many Horst Wessel films. So she changes sides again. Now DEFA. Soviet zone. Back to Babelsberg."

"Then why hire her, if she's so — what? Unreliable? It's a Soviet studio."

Markus hesitated, not expecting this, suddenly cautious, then raised his eyebrow, suggestive.

Alex looked away, just meeting his eyes a kind of complicity. "Why are you telling me all this?"

"What happened to everybody, you asked. So there's an answer. People you knew — maybe they're not the same."

"None of us are," Alex said, looking at him.

"No," Markus said, meeting the look. "You, for instance, are now an honored guest of the Soviet Military Administration." He waved his hand to the room. "A public figure. How you live, who you see.

These things are noticed. You want to be with people of the future, not the past."

"Are you telling me not to see them? The family?"

"I'm telling you who they are. It's not like the old days. People like you — guests of the state — set an example."

"Is this official or just some personal advice?"

"Official?"

"Hotel Lux graduate. Don't you work for the Party?"

"Don't you?" Markus said. "A very generous stipend." He paused. "No. I'm not speaking officially."

"Good. Then since it's just between the two of us —" He looked up. "And even if it isn't. Being a guest works two ways. You don't have to keep me and I don't have to stay. I travel on a Dutch passport. If the Party doesn't like the example I'm setting, I'll start packing. But Fritz von Bernuth saved my life. So if I want to see his family, I'll see them."

Markus's face twitched. "Your famous temper," he said finally, forcing a small arch smile. "Sometimes confused with political principle."

Alex dug his nails into his palm. Don't rise to it. Every answer reported.

"Not by me," he said.

Another pause, as if Markus's fingers were on a chess piece. Defuse it.

"I'm a little touchy about Fritz, that's all. He was a good friend to my father."

Markus nodded, accepting this.

"Now both dead," Alex said. "And yours? I should have asked earlier. Your mother?"

A flash in Markus's eyes that Alex couldn't interpret, almost panic.

"I'm sorry," Alex said quickly. "She's dead?"

Another flash and then the eyes cleared, Markus in control again. "She's in Russia."

"Oh. She's staying there?"

"For now," Markus said, a twist to his mouth. "Like your wife."

Alex sidestepped this. "It must have been difficult for you. During the war. To be a German in Moscow."

"By that time I could speak Russian, so not so difficult," he said, suddenly thoughtful. "But of course people were suspicious. The Wehrmacht did terrible things, and some people thought, well, maybe it's something in the blood. Not the Party, of course. To them we were Communists only. Even then they were planning for after the war. A new Germany. So we were well treated." He paused. "We were the future."

Said plainly, without his usual edge, maybe what he really believed.

"You're sure of that?" A voice next to them, waiting for an opening, stepping closer now. "Markus." A formal hello, with a bow, the awkward body of a tall man.

"Well, Ernst," Markus said, surprised. "In the east? What are you doing here?" Trying to keep his voice genial, but displeased. "You have joined the Kulturbund now?"

"A guest only."

"Yes? Whose?"

"I'll let you find that out," the man said, as if he were proposing a game. He turned to Alex, dipping his head and handing him a business card. "Ernst Ferber, RIAS."

Alex looked at the card. *Rundfunk im amerikanischen Sektor.* Then, underneath, Radio in the American Sector.

"The initials work in both languages," he said.

"Yes, it's convenient."

"Propaganda is the same word in both too," Markus said.

"As you say," Ernst said.

"You want to interview him? RIAS? A man who left America?"

"No, I wanted to be sure he's really here. The news can be so unreliable these days. And of course to pay my respects." This to

Alex, with another dip of his head. "*The Last Fence.* An important book for us. You must know that."

"Thank you."

"He is not giving interviews to RIAS," Markus said.

"Not now, no. I don't expect that. Perhaps later. Meanwhile, you can listen to the music. Everybody does. Even in Karlshorst, I hear. The Russians listen to us."

"Nonsense. What do you mean, perhaps later?"

"Well, he's here now. Under your protection," he said to Markus. "Let's see for how long. A man who writes *The Last Fence.*"

"I've come to stay," Alex said quickly, before Markus could answer for him.

"I know why you're here," Ferber said, looking at him, and for a second Alex stopped breathing, not sure if something else was being said. RIAS a natural cover. "A strange time in America. Some excesses, maybe." He turned to Markus. "You know how that can be." Then, back to Alex, "But as I say, you may change your mind, and that would be an interesting story for us. Meanwhile you are welcome to visit any-time." He nodded to the card. "Come have coffee, see the station. If you can travel. He's allowed?"

"Everyone's allowed to travel in Berlin," Markus said, annoyed. "Look at you. In the Russian sector. Who stops you?"

"Good," Ferber said to Alex, aware he was needling Markus by ignoring him. "Then I hope you will come. I knew your father a little. At the university. It would be a pleasure to talk. Maybe you could explain it, why you — Well, we'll save it for the coffee." He shook hands, a good-bye. "Markus, I'll do a favor for you. No need to turn the Kulturbund upside down. No one brought me. I just came. Not very gracious, I know, an uninvited guest, but I drank very little, so it's not too bad. So now maybe you'll tell me something. The men in Lützowplatz this morning. You've made an identification yet? Not the American, the Germans. All Karlshorst will say is 'Not yet identified.' Of course, records are not so complete since —"

"The accident, you mean?" Alex said, assuming a puzzled expression, waiting for Markus's response.

"An accident with guns?" Ferber said, raising an eyebrow. "Well, a Berlin accident. So, 'Not yet'?"

"Not yet." Markus paused. "Lützowplatz. The British sector. Why ask Karlshorst?

What makes you think they're from the East?"

Ferber looked at him. "Just a guess. Well, thank you for your hospitality."

"What did he mean, with guns?" Alex said when he left.

"I don't know," Markus said, shrugging this off. "Some joke of his. He's a great one for making jokes. Coming here like that. Be careful of him."

"Him too?"

"I say these things only to help you. You're new to Berlin — not the old one, this one. If you broadcast for him, it would be a provocation."

"Don't worry, I'm not going on the radio. Anywhere. Just the men's room. Would you excuse me for a moment?" Anxious to be out of it. How much longer? He looked around.

"Let me show you," Martin said, suddenly there, or perhaps there all along.

"I can find —"

"Please," Martin said, beginning to escort him, a bobbing motion, dragging his bad foot.

"You really don't have to —"

They were already out of the room, just under the portrait of Goethe.

"Herr Meier, a word?" Martin said, his

121

voice lower, almost conspiratorial. "Herr Engel, he's an old friend?"

"Not really. I knew his brother. He was a child —"

"You know he's state security?"

"Markus?" Alex said, pretending to be surprised. And then, curious, "A German?"

"They have a special department for Germans. Now under the police. But when the Russians leave —"

"Thanks for letting me know. I don't think I said anything —"

"It's not a question of that. You're free to say what you like," he said simply. "It's not Gestapo here anymore."

"Then why the red flag?"

Martin licked his lips, hesitating. "The Kulturbund. It's a very free atmosphere, as you see. Sometimes the police misinterpret." He looked up. "You don't want to say anything that might —"

"No, I don't want to do that." He looked around the old club. "Do the walls have ears too?"

"What?" Martin said, confused by the idiom.

"Nothing. Has there been some trouble with Markus?"

"No, no," Martin said quickly. "It's just something — to know."

Alex looked at him. Part of the air he breathed.

And then suddenly, over Martin's shoulder, he saw the lipstick, a tiny splash of red across the room, and she was there. He stopped listening. Martin was talking, his mouth moving, the whole room now just some indistinct hum. Lipstick, a plain white blouse, bright against the crowd of drab cardigans. And now she was turning her head, facing him, her eyes skimming over shoulders, finding his. What had he thought it would be like? Blood rushing through him, a purely physical reaction. He had wondered whether he would recognize her, whether the years had worn her away. But blood rushed through him, stopping up his ears, and they were looking at each other and what he felt was the secrecy of that summer, when it had been just the two of them, all these people oblivious, not even audible. Talking with her eyes, the way she had done that night at the house. My God. I never thought I would see you again. Do I look the same? I was afraid. What you would think. So many years. But we're here, aren't we? Both. Look at you. I remember everything. From that time. Do you? A sudden welling in the eyes. Don't say anything. Not yet. Just keep looking. One more minute.

Nobody sees us.

Then someone touched her arm, drawing her away from his gaze and she turned her head back, now only a side glimpse to Alex, something she'd done in Pomerania, the secret between them, while Elsbeth primped and Fritz drank and nobody knew. So close they could speak in glimpses. And now it was all here again, the hot afternoons with the smell of the fields, hiding in the dunes, the taste of her. He kept staring until she looked around again, then away, as if she knew what he was seeing, her head thrown back, his face between her legs.

A man's back, in gray uniform, cut her off. The Russian? Not alone after all. The look maybe the only private conversation they'd have all night.

"Herr Meier —" Martin's voice came back.

"Sorry. I've just seen somebody," he said, turning to go.

"You don't want the toilet? It's there." Holding out his arm.

"Oh, the toilet. Yes." How long had he been dreaming, not listening? Her hair was longer, not bobbed, but still the color of straw.

In the men's room he had to wait in line, the others smoking and grumbling, already unsteady from vodka. When he washed his hands, he looked up in the mirror. A conversation in a glance. What if it hadn't happened at all, the words in his head just what he wanted her to say? He splashed a little cold water under his eyes. Remember why you're here. Go and meet the Russian.

"You see who's here? That little shit Engel." Two men behind him, wiping their hands, thinking they were whispering, not alcohol loud.

"Ulbricht's ears. Everything goes straight to him. They're worse than the Russians."

"Careful," the first said, an elbow and a nod toward a closed stall.

Alex kept looking at the mirror, the face he had now, not the one she'd known. Different people. The words in his head.

A boy handed him a towel. "Herr Meier."

Alex turned. The bellhop from the Adlon.

"Hello. You're working here too?"

"Something extra. When they have parties."

The other men who had been washing left, now just someone peeing in a stall. The boy started brushing the back of Alex's jacket.

"You're enjoying Berlin?"

"Yes, of course." Saying nothing.

"There is so much to see," he said without

irony, a tourist brochure, so that for a second Alex thought he was making a joke. "You have been to Volkspark Friedrichshain perhaps?"

Alex looked up into the mirror.

"They are building a mountain there."

"A mountain?" Alex said, confused.

"Yes, with the rubble. Over the flak tower. Some day soon, just trees and grass. It's interesting to see."

Alex kept looking at the mirror. The man flushed the toilet.

"Go tomorrow," the boy said under the sound, no ambiguity now, looking at each other in the mirror. "The Fairy Tale Fountain." He gave a final whisk with the brush as the other man came to the sink and turned.

"Here," Alex said, reaching into his pocket for a tip.

"No, it's not allowed," the boy said.

"One good thing about Socialism, eh?" the man said, soaping his hands.

The boy had turned away, busying himself with the towels. Not much older than Peter.

"So. Another admirer who wants to meet you." Brecht, now wreathed in cigar smoke. "Matthias Fritsch," he said, presenting a bald man. "How can a man have so many readers when his books are banned? So maybe he hasn't read them really."

"Every one, I assure you," Fritsch said, taking Alex's hand. "A pleasure."

"Thank you," Alex said, distracted, still rattled by the message in the men's room. Tomorrow.

"Contraband literature," Brecht said. "The only kind that's worth reading. It's an idea. You could do something with that."

"You could," Fritsch said.

Alex noticed Markus, still there. "Markus Engel," he said, introducing him. "A friend from the old days."

Markus bowed, visibly pleased, but the others barely took him in, not someone in their world.

"Matthias is at DEFA," Brecht said. "Very important. Close to Janka. So maybe useful to you. You see how I arrange things? And for just a small commission."

"How small?" Fritsch said, an old familiarity. "He says it's a business for whores, and now who plays the pimp?"

"I said capitalism makes us whores. The film business, just more so."

Alex was only half following this. Capitalism as a brothel was a Brecht conceit he'd heard before, and it struck him that what Brecht had really been in exile from all these years was not Berlin, but the twenties, with their tart, almost thrilling nihilism. Now that the worst had actually happened, just outside, his cynicism sounded like posturing, dated.

"But perhaps we can tempt you," Fritsch said to Alex.

Alex held up his hands. "Books only."

"Come see us anyway," Fritsch said. "Babelsberg. So much damage, all the soundstages, but now a few are working again. I'll give you a tour."

"Wonderful films," Brecht said. "Boy meets tractor."

"He never changes," Fritsch said, indulgent. "Some good work too. Serious."

"Boy loses tractor," Brecht said, impish.

"I'd like that," Alex said, polite.

And then she was coming toward them, here, not a memory. How did they greet each other? A social kiss? A hug? Everyone watching. Even Markus, still hovering at the edge of the circle.

But Irene knew. She took his hands and swept them up in hers, holding them, a gesture as welcoming as a hug without its intimacy.

"My old friend," she said, voice husky. The same voice. "So many years."

"So you know our Irene," Fritsch said.

"Yes," Alex said, feeling her hands, touching.

She was smiling, not the stare of a few minutes ago, something for the room, reaching for her old lightness.

"Do I look so different?"

Alex shook his head, playing with her. "No, the same."

But she wasn't the same. Up close he could see the years, the sparkling eyes duller now, worn. Her face was thinner and yet somehow fuller, the skin slack under her chin, a little puffy.

"You see, Sasha?" she said to the Russian next to her. "It must be true. He knows me longer than anybody."

"I believe it," he said genially, then offered his hand. "Alexander Markovsky. Welcome to Berlin."

"Two Alexanders. All my men Alexanders. So confusing. So, Sasha, Alex," she said, pointing in turn.

Markus shifted on his feet.

"Markus, you're here too? How nice." She held out her hand. "Alex, you remember Kurt's brother?"

"We've just been talking."

"Oh, about old times?" she said airily, but wanting to know.

"What happened to everyone," Alex said.

"It's such a long time."

"Not always a pleasant story," Markus said.

"Who said history would be pleasant?" Brecht said, drawing on the cigar stub, still going.

"But a homecoming is pleasant," Markovsky said, steering back to Alex.

"Yes, and now famous," Irene said. "My old friend." The voice husky again as she repeated the phrase.

"An honor for the Kulturbund," Martin said.

"But if you're an old friend," Fritsch said to Irene, "get him to come work for us."

"*Ouf,* use my influence. What influence?" Then, looking up at Alex, "He doesn't listen to me now. It's too long ago." Two conversations, one for the room.

"He will. Everyone does what Irene says," Fritsch said, party chat.

"It's better. In the end," Markovsky said, the same easy tone.

Alex looked at him. Fleshy, but not fat, blunt hands. A wife in Moscow. Trying to be pleasant, not an occupier, the horrors of '45 someone else's bad behavior. Holding Irene's arm in his, her protector. What had it been like, at the mercy of the Russians? *Frau, komme.* Sometimes several in one

130

night, gangs of them.

"It's not true," Irene said. "No one does what I say."

"I will," Brecht said, dipping his head.

"Good. Then get me a ticket for *Courage,* yes? Opening night. Already people say it's impossible."

"Ah, for that you have to ask Helene," Brecht said.

"You see?" Irene said. "No one."

"You work together?" Alex said to Fritsch.

"Yes. Well, not so much anymore. But during the war —"

"*Kolberg.* We worked together on *Kolberg.* My God."

Alex waited.

"Goebbels's last big production," Markus said, intending a barb, but instead prompting a survivor's nostalgia.

"How crazy was that time," Fritsch said. "The Allies are advancing and we're staging battles. Uniforms. Cannons. Heinrich George in the lead — his salary alone. And the bombing is going on round the clock then."

"And no film stock," Irene said.

"No. And what does she do? She tells the director to keep shooting anyway. So week after week we shot scenes but there's nothing in the camera."

"Why?" Markovsky said.

"The crew," Irene said. "They would have been drafted. To defend Berlin. But as long as we're shooting, they're in an essential industry. Essential. *Kolberg.* Well, so at least it was good for that."

"You saved their lives," Fritsch said.

"Well, not me."

"It was a propaganda film?" Markus said.

"They were all propaganda films," Fritsch said. "It was wartime. Even Zarah Leander films — propaganda. The wife waiting at home? How many did? And *Kolberg*? A German victory. Just around the corner. Except when it opened — January, that last January of the war — there were no theaters left, almost none. All bombed. So all that expense —"

"You found the stock then to finish?" Markus said.

"It was already finished. We just kept filming to save the crew. She might have been shot," Fritsch said. "So it was a great thing, what she did."

"Oh —" Irene said, waving this off.

"Your husband was in the crew, yes?" Markus said. "Makeup, someone told me."

"That's right," she said, looking at him.

"Maybe that explains the lipstick," he said. "So difficult to get now. But maybe you had a good supply. From the old days. Your husband."

"No," she said, touching her lip. "This? A present."

"Yes, a present," Markovsky repeated, aware finally of Markus's tone.

Markus took a step backward, as if someone were about to raise a hand to him, his body wound tight.

"Of course," he said. "Lipstick wouldn't last so long, would it?" Not sure how to walk away from it.

Brecht, who'd been quiet, said, "Thank God for the black market. Where would our women be without it?"

"Bert," Irene said quickly, darting her eyes toward Markovsky, "don't be silly. Sasha doesn't go on the black market. It's from Russia."

But Markovsky missed most of this, focused now on Markus. "I'm sorry, you are — ?"

"Markus Engel." A military response, erect, without the salute.

"Ah, K-5. Under Mielke, yes?"

"Yes, that's right," Markus said, both pleased and wary that Markovsky knew who he was.

"What happened this morning?" Meant to

be an aside, but loud enough for Alex to hear.

"We're investigating," Markus said, voice low, reluctant, waiting to be dressed down.

"Such carelessness," Markovsky said, in charge. "Whose idea was that? And now the British. Making protests. All day, on the phone. Directly to Maltsev. You can imagine how pleased he is. So who answers for that? Formal protests."

"About what?" Alex said, unable to resist.

"Oh," Markovsky said, turning, checking himself. "The usual foolishness. Our allies refuse to accept the reality of the situation here, so they like to make difficulties. Isn't that right, Engel?" The tone dismissive, a question to a servant.

"Yes, Major. Exactly."

Alex watched, fascinated, as Markus looked away, embarrassed, then back to Irene, who had seen this, then finally to Markovsky again, dismayed at his own impotence.

"But usually it's not the British," Markovsky said, making the conversation general. "In the end, realists. Not like our American friends. You were a long time there."

"And an even longer time here. Before," Alex said smoothly. "It's good to be back."

"It's good to have you," Markovsky said,

playing host.

Markus glanced at Alex, annoyed, as if Markovsky had slipped his arm through Alex's, one more protected, off-limits.

"I must say good night," Markus said, formal.

"I never see you," Irene said, giving her hand, the only one who seemed to notice his leaving. "So busy you are always."

"What did you think of America?" Markovsky said to Alex.

"They took me in. When the Nazis — You don't forget that."

"And then threw you out again," Brecht said.

Alex smiled. "And then threw me out."

"Well, so it's good for us," Markovsky said, making an effect. "And now back with old friends. You were sweethearts maybe?" Half teasing.

"No, never sweethearts," Irene said, looking at Alex. "Something else." Then, quickly, "Anyway Elsbeth was the pretty one. So there was no chance for me." She looked again at Alex.

"Elsbeth," Markovsky said.

"My sister."

"Two of them," Markovsky said, shaking his head, an affectionate joke.

"And Alex, you know, was so serious. A

writer, even then. You had to watch what you said. You know we're in a book? My father said it was another family, but it was us."

"And what were you like? In the book," Markovsky said, familiar.

"Like I am. Well, like I was. A long time ago now."

"People don't change."

"No? Maybe. But the world does." She looked at Alex. "You remember the old house."

"I went to see it. This morning."

She nodded. "It's sad, to think of it like that. But you know he sold it to the Nazis, so —"

"To the Reichsbank. A man told me."

"Yes, the bank. So at least no one else ever lived there. Just us."

"Junkers," Brecht said. "Are we supposed to be sentimental?"

"No, polite," Markovsky said, turning to him.

"Oh, Bert, he's never polite," Irene said easily. "Are you, darling? It's part of his art."

Brecht took this and held on, a social lifesaver. "I still can't get you a ticket," he said, almost winking. "But what about a drink instead?"

"A drink also," Irene volleyed back, put-

136

ting her finger on his chest.

Brecht bowed, a waiter's gesture, and left with Fritsch.

"It's just the way he talks," Irene said to Markovsky. "And you know, he's right. There's no reason to be sentimental. I never liked the house anyway."

"But your family's house —" Markovsky said, and Alex realized that it was part of her appeal for him, someone who'd known that life.

"*Ouf.* It was like here," she said, waving her hand. "A museum. But the country house I always liked. And now that's gone too."

"Fritz sold it?" Alex said.

"No. All the big farms were broken up. After the war. They just took it."

"Land reform," Markovsky said, explaining, suddenly uncomfortable. "A more equitable distribution."

"Oh, I'm not blaming you. I'm sure it's right — give the land to the people who farm it. My father would have sold it anyway, so what's the difference? It would still be gone. Don't worry, I forgive you," she said, teasing.

"She forgives me. I'm the politburo," Markovsky said, but smiling, charmed.

Alex looked at them, a life together he

knew nothing about.

"Major Markovsky, the telephone." The bellboy from the Adlon, his eyes fixed on Markovsky, not even a glance to Alex. "They said urgent."

"Urgent. At this hour?" Markovsky said, checking his watch. "Excuse me a moment. There was some trouble this morning, so maybe it's that."

"The phone is here," the boy said, leading him away, still ignoring Alex.

"So," Irene said, her voice suddenly her own again, not at a party. "My God, what do I say to you? Why are you here? You leave America and everyone else wants to go there."

"I had to leave."

"And the whole world to choose, you come here? Who comes to Berlin?"

"People," he said, indicating the room. "Brecht."

"Oh, Bert. He thinks it's like before. Well, maybe for him. When he was first here, we took a walk up Friedrichstrasse, where the theaters used to be. Gone. I thought, now you'll see what it's like. And you know what he says? You see those people looking at us? They know it's me. So that's how it is for him." She paused. "Not for us."

"Tell me how you are," he said, looking at her.

"How I am," she said, flustered. "I'm — I still have the flat. Marienstrasse, by the Charité. The upper floors were hit, but not mine. So. Sasha brings food."

"And lipstick."

She looked up at him. "He's all right, you know. Don't judge."

"I wasn't."

"No? Well, so maybe it's me, I judge myself. You think it was so easy to survive here? The bombs every night. The shelters. Nothing to eat. My God, to have a bath. People on the street in dark glasses, wrapped in blankets — for the smoke, you know — I thought it's some Ufa film, people from space. Except, no, it's everybody, we're living like this. And then after, it's worse —" She stopped. "After a while that's all you think about. Getting through it. The reckoning? That comes later." She looked up. "So I go with him. Markus didn't tell you? He likes to do that, I think. He blames me for Kurt. Why, I don't know. Maybe I took a gun and went to Spain and shot him and that's how it happened. And you? Do you still blame me for Kurt?"

"It was a long time ago."

"Yes," she said and then for a minute

neither of them said anything.

"What about the others? Markus said Elsbeth was a Nazi. Elsbeth?"

"Well, but that husband of hers. A madman. I think he still believes, a little anyway. So of course she does what he says. And now, since the children were —"

"What?"

"He didn't tell you this? Both killed. A direct hit. She was away from the house and when she came back — the nanny, both boys, in the cellar, where they were supposed to go, but a direct hit. I think she went a little crazy then. You know, 'If I had been there, they wouldn't,' things like that. And now they only have each other, she and Gustav, so whatever he says —"

"Do you see her?"

"Sometimes. When he's out. Then I don't have to listen to him. You ought to go. She'd be pleased."

"And Markus said Erich was — I'm sorry."

"But at least not dead. I'd know if he were dead. I'd feel it." Putting a hand to her chest. "He'll come back."

"Irene —"

"No, it's true. You can feel these things. People you know. You don't believe it? That you can sense — ?"

"No."

"I knew something would happen to Enka."

"Your husband."

"I suppose you know all about that too? From Markus? Another black mark against me."

"He was killed?"

She nodded. "His own fault. But I could feel it, that something would happen. We were in a big shelter in Gesundbrunnen. Why there, I can't remember. Probably on a tram. They were always diverting the trams, you never knew where you'd end up. And then of course in a raid they'd have to stop. So, there. An old U-Bahn station. Small rooms, where they used to store equipment. Just phosphorus paint for light, a real cave. I knew Enka would hate it. And they had a candle, you know, to tell you when the oxygen was running out. So many people. They'd paint the number on the wall — how many could fit — but it was a joke. Sardines. Hot. And what could you do? Stop breathing to save the air? They put the candle up high, so you'd know when the oxygen was almost gone — the carbon dioxide fills the room from below, that was the idea anyway, but Enka just watched it burning and I knew he would panic. He was a coward about such things. Not everything, but a thing like that —" She stopped, aware that she was becoming lost in the story. "So he did. Panic. Sweating, trying to breathe, you know what that's like. No one could stop him. At the door, he just pushed them aside. And you know it was a danger to everybody if the door was left open — blast — so they let him go. Of course he was wrong about the candle, there was still air in the room. Another half hour, maybe more. And I just sat there and I knew. I could feel when it happened."

"A bomb?"

"Shrapnel. Like a knife in the air." She made a cutting motion with her hand. "So he bled out. Before the all clear. You don't think you can feel these things? I do." She paused. "Anyway, and if it's not true? Then Erich's dead? Is that better?"

"No."

"Oh, let's not talk about these things," she said, putting her hand on his sleeve. "Tell me something from before. A story. You were always good at that. Let's talk about those times. The way things were before."

And for a second he saw her then, eyes shining and eager, joking about Fritz, certain that life was on her side. Maybe the way he would always see her, having missed everything else.

"Irene," he said, at a loss.

"I'm sorry, I have to leave." Markovsky, suddenly there. What had he overheard? But what was there to overhear? "An emergency."

"What's wrong?" Irene said.

"Some trouble. A labor action. Down in Aue," he said, in a hurry, distracted. "They should have called me earlier. They always leave things too late, and then it's a mess. I have to go now. My apologies," he said to Alex.

"Tonight? In the dark? It can't wait?"

"No. I'll send a car to take you home."

"No, no, don't. It's not far. Alex can take me home. He's an old Berliner, he knows the way."

"A labor action?" Alex said. In a workers' state, the contradiction its own bad joke.

"Well, it's always something, you know," Markovsky said, brushing it off, no details. "One trouble or another. Maybe not so serious in the end. We'll see."

"But it's so far," Irene said. "At night. Can't you go in the —"

"No," Markovsky said, cutting her off. "I'm sorry. Oh, there's Franz. My apologies again. Anyway, now you can talk about old times, eh?"

"That's just what we were doing," Alex said.

"Good, good," Markovsky said, preoccupied. "The car is ready?" Then a quick kiss to Irene's hand, public behavior. "I'll call you tomorrow." And then he was gone, rushing to put out a fire.

"Where's Aue?"

"Near the Czech border. He goes there sometimes. I don't know why. He doesn't tell me things. Work things. Well, maybe I don't ask either."

But you have to, Alex thought. How else can I do this? He looked away.

"So shall we do that? Go somewhere and talk about old times?"

"I can't leave. I'm the guest of honor," he said, palms out.

"My famous friend," she said softly, raising her hand to the side of his head, then brushing her fingers over his hair. "Gray. So soon."

"Just a little." Feeling her fingers.

"Like your father. Very distinguished. So what has your life been? Safe in America. You have a wife?"

"I did. We're separated."

"So. What was she like?"

"She was like you."

Irene let her hand fall.

"The same hair. She looked like you. A little. But she wasn't."

"Don't."

"What difference does it make now? It was probably true. My fault, not hers."

"And what do I say? To something like that." She looked at him for a moment, unsettled. "Anyway, you don't mean it."

"No?"

"No. Just something to make me feel — I don't know what. I can tell. I always know what you're thinking. Remember? We wouldn't have to talk. I'd know." She glanced up. "I know you better than anybody."

He met her eyes, another minute, not saying anything, then she turned away.

"So go talk to them. I'll rescue Matthias from Brecht. It won't be much longer. Nothing goes late anymore. During the war people wanted to get home before the first sirens, so everything was early. You get in the habit. Imagine, in Berlin, where we used to — Yes, I know, don't look back. I don't. It's just seeing you, I think. You won't leave without me?" The old voice, ironic, flirtatious.

"I think it might have been true, though."

She stopped. "That you married me?" She looked down. "Well. But then look what

145

happened. So maybe I wasn't the best choice."

The party went on for another hour, wine and vodka being poured even after the food had run out. Alex had to thank the Kulturbund officers, which prompted another toast. In the smoky room, warmed now by body heat and alcohol, it seemed everyone wanted to see him again — Fritsch at Babelsberg, gentle Aaron Stein at Aufbau, Brecht back at the Adlon bar. Willy would have been pleased. Except Willy was dead. Alex put the drink down, his head already slightly fuzzy, and looked around the room, sweating again. How long before they knew? Some slip, an unexpected witness. Nobody got away with murder. In broad daylight. Irene, over with Fritsch, glanced toward him, her private half smile. I always know what you're thinking, she'd said, and for a moment Alex wanted to laugh, some perverse release. How about bodies crumpling over, Willy grabbing his sleeve, just do it, running through the streets, Markus checking times with the doorman? He lit a cigarette, steadying his hands. No one knew. All he had to do was be who they thought he was.

The lights dimmed twice, like the end of a

theater intermission, and people finally began to leave. Glasses were tossed back, coats retrieved, the noise louder than before, shouting good-byes, and then they were all out in the street, where it had begun to snow, covering the ruined buildings in white lace, drifting down through the open roofs. There were a few official cars, leaving skid marks behind, but most of the guests were walking, their footprints crisscrossing the snow in all directions, like bird tracks.

"I love it like this," Irene said, lifting her face. "Everything clean. Well, until tomorrow. And listen." They both held their heads still. Somebody laughing farther down Jägerstrasse, the end of a good-bye, then nothing but the steady hum of the planes heading to Tempelhof, even their drone muffled tonight. "So quiet." She was tying a scarf over her head, a few flakes landing on her face. "You'll ruin your shoes," she said. "Should we get a car from Sasha? I can call."

"No."

"Oh, you don't approve."

"I didn't say that."

"No." She put her arm in his. "So, you know Marienstrasse?"

"Behind Schiffbauerdamm."

"Yes, but it's blocked that way. I'll show you."

They walked up Friedrichstrasse, lighted only by the snow. At Unter den Linden it was even darker, a long empty stretch without traffic. The city felt like a house shut up for the season, the furniture covered in white sheets.

"You remember Kranzler's used to be here," she said. Then, "Nobody approves. So it's not just you. Maybe I should find an Ami. Would that be better?"

"I didn't say anything."

"You think I don't hear you? What you think?"

"I wasn't here. I don't blame —"

"Sasha was later. It wasn't for that, to protect me. Nothing could protect you then. Not the women."

He turned to her, waiting.

"You want to know what happened? I was like all the others. Afraid to move. I was in Babelsberg then. I thought it would be safer. And Enka's friends disguised me — you know, the makeup department. They made me look like someone dying from syphilis." She forced a small laugh. "If that's what they look like."

"Did it work?"

"No."

Alex said nothing, the only sound their soft footfalls in the snow.

"They didn't care. Mongols. Maybe they don't have it there. Maybe they didn't give a damn." She paused. "You know, when it happens you think, well, now I know the worst. And I survived it. And then it happens again and that's the worst. So you think, what if it doesn't stop? Every night. They're drunk, they come looking. If you hide, it's worse. They get angry, sometimes they shoot. They shot my friend Marthe. She was screaming and it upset them."

"Irene —"

"Yes, I know." She shrugged. "It was a bad time. Nothing's the same after. Even when it happens to everybody, you think it only happens to you." She looked over at him. "Damaged goods."

"Are you all right? I mean —"

"Yes. I only meant inside. You want to know everything? I got pregnant, of course. Imagine, a Mongol baby. You see how I can say these things? Before, I never would have told you. I don't know why — ashamed maybe. And now —"

"Did you have it?"

"Are you crazy? A child of rape. Every time you look at it. And no food. Anything. No, I had it taken care of. They had clinics for that then, there were so many, but it wasn't safe. Soviet army doctors, sometimes just some orderly, they didn't care what happened to you. So I went to Gustav, Elsbeth's husband. The Nazi. He didn't want to do it. Imagine, all the people he killed and he didn't want to kill this one. But he was in hiding then, waiting for the Amis. He wanted to give himself up to them, not the Russians. So I said I'd tell the Russians where he was and he did it. No anesthesia, nothing for the pain, but no Russian baby either. So that's how the war was for me. Another story, just like the rest. You wanted to know."

"Yes."

"And how does it end? Well, how? All those people back there," she said, tossing her head toward the Kulturbund. "What do they think it's going to be like? A paradise." She snorted. "They're worse than the Russians. They believe in the Party. The Russians know better." She turned to him suddenly. "You don't believe in it either. Not like that. I know you. Why are you here?"

"I had nowhere else to go," he said.

"So we're a fine pair. They make parties for you and give you *payoks* and I'm — both of us kept by the Russians. How things turn out."

Up ahead he saw the lights of the elevated station, soldiers guarding the stairs. Still an occupied city.

"Why are you?" he said. "With a Russian. After what happened."

"Sleeping with him, you mean. You can say it, we don't have secrets from each other."

"No," he said, looking away.

"Well, why not? He didn't rape me. And the Russians — they're here. I live in the Russian sector. How can I move? Even to get a room in Berlin, it's impossible now." A sly look toward him. "Unless of course you're a guest of the Party. But then you're still in the East. So, a Russian."

"Do you care for him?"

"Oh, care for him. What does it mean? He helps me. It's useful to have a Russian friend. You saw how even Markus doesn't make trouble for me."

"And when they leave?"

"When is that? Maybe never. I used to think the Nazis would be forever too. It felt like it. You never see the end of things when you're in them."

"No."

They were on the bridge now, collars up against the wind off the water.

"How pretty it is, in the snow," she said, stopping at the rail, looking down at the narrow Spree.

In fact it was the same raw landscape they'd just walked through, piles of bricks and scaffolding and empty lots, but the few lights were flashing now on the water, a lantern effect, soft through the scrim of snow, and you could see the city you wanted to see.

"Remember all the cafés?" She pointed to the terrace along Schiffbauerdamm. "At night. And the boats." Seeing it through her own lens, sun umbrellas and waiters with trays, not the cold black water and rusting girders. "Oh, it's so good to see you," she said, reaching up to brush some snow off his coat, her hand on his chest. "I never thought — And now you're here. Just the same."

"No, not the —" The rest swallowed by an S-Bahn train squealing into the overhead station.

"Well, the same to me. I know, everything's different. But it feels the same. Nobody knew me like you did. The way it was with us. Just a look."

"What about Kurt?"

"Well, Kurt. Now you're going to be angry again. So that's the same anyway. Jealous," she said, turning, putting her arm in his again to walk. "It's getting cold here. You want to talk about Kurt? After all this time?

It was something different, that's all."

"Different how?"

"It was like being in love with a pilot. Or a — I don't know, skier, something like that. The way a little girl is in love. With her own idea, not the person."

"And what was your idea?"

"Oh, the revolutionary, the fighter. Someone to save the world, while everyone else sits around and watches it go to hell. Maybe someone I wanted to be myself. When all I could do was argue with my father, stupid things like that. But he was really going to fight. So, very romantic. And then a week later, he's dead, so what was the point? We were — how old? Now you can see what foolishness it was, but then —"

"Then you were in love with him."

"Shall I tell you something? I never knew what he was thinking."

Alex stopped, looking at her.

"Never. So it was different. You know, it's different with different people. Enka — we never made love but I loved him. So what was that? Kurt. Well, Kurt. I'm not sorry — except that it made you so angry. Why did it? All right, I know. You thought I loved him *instead.* It was never instead. But it ruined everything between us. I used to think about that sometimes. What if it had never happened? But you would have gone anyway. The way things were after Oranien-burg. I kept wanting to tell you, it wasn't instead. It was — just something else."

Alex said nothing. They had turned off Friedrichstrasse.

"You don't believe me?"

"It doesn't work that way for me, that's all."

"And do you know what? If it were Kurt here, not you, I could never say these things. He never knew me. Not like you did."

Alex looked away. "Well, he was busy sav-ing the world."

"Don't." She stopped, looking around at the street. "Anyway, nobody saved it." She turned to him. "He thought he was, though. So you should leave him that."

"Why does Markus blame you?" he said, starting to walk again, away from Kurt.

"He blames everybody. So angry and he used to be so nice, remember? Well, you can imagine what it was like there for him. People being taken away. No mother —"

"He said his mother is still there."

"Well, buried. She must be by now. They sent her to one of the camps. Siberia, wherever they send them. And they don't come back."

"Sent her why?"

"Why. A spy, probably. Isn't that what they used to say about all of them? She was German, that was really the reason. They purged the Germans."

"Not all of them."

"No, so imagine what the survivors are like. Well, we know. Lapdogs. Please don't arrest me. A wonderful incentive for loyalty. You ask them now, they say it was right that people were taken away. Their colleagues. Anyway, poor Markus. A child. They tell him his mother is an enemy of the people. And after a while you believe them. What choice? Everyone else does. And you want to be like everyone else. It must be true. So that's how they make a Markus. Show us you're not her. A model Communist. Sasha says that first group who came back, the German Communists —" She tapped the side of her head. "Nothing here but the Party. You had to watch yourself. Maybe they'd report *you.*"

"Then Moscow will have nothing to worry about. When they pull out."

"No, just us. They protect themselves — the rest of us don't matter. Even Sasha is surprised sometimes, how they go along with everything. As long as it doesn't touch them."

"Like what?" Alex said, trying to sound

155

indifferent.

"I don't know. Labor quotas, things like that. People don't like to work in the mines. Sasha says it's difficult, there are never enough."

"So they force them? Work gangs?"

"No, they pay them. It's not Siberia. The labor exchanges assign all the workers anyway. That's how it works — go where you're needed. But no one likes the mines. So the SED has a hard time filling the quotas."

"But they do?"

"Not always, so it's a headache for Sasha."

"He's in charge?"

"You're so interested in this?"

"No, I'm interested in him. He's — somebody you're with."

"You don't have to worry about him. It's not Kurt. Or you. Something useful, that's all."

"Useful."

"Well, to have a friend at Karlshorst. He works with Maltsev."

"Who's Maltsev? What does he do?" Any information, Willy had said.

"What they all do. Give orders. Anyway, important. You know how I know? Markus. I could see it in his face, the first time he saw me with Sasha. This way," she said, leading him, "it's a shortcut." The street branched off to a wide connecting footpath. "It's better at the Luisenstrasse end. They cleared all the streets near the hospital first." There were lights finally, people at home. "You see how lucky we were here. Not too bad, only some top floors. Fires. It was like that. Not too bad in one place and then one street away, everything gone. I'm just down there, near the end."

They passed under the sound of a radio, loud enough to be heard through the closed window. Waltz music, which Alex heard somewhere in the back of his mind, the rest preoccupied with SED quotas. Sasha says it's difficult. Would any of this be useful? What else? And then suddenly the music stopped and the lights blinked out, the street pitched into darkness.

"A power cut," Irene said, a weary resignation. "Careful where you walk. It's all the time now. But they say it's worse in the West."

"How long have you been with —" Alex started, not wanting to let Markovsky go, then stopped, blinded, as a bright light swung into the street behind them. Two lights. Headlights, the same shape as the car in Lützowplatz. He swung his head away and grabbed Irene's elbow. But where was there to go? A long street, straight, impossible to outrun a car, no heaps of rubble to duck behind, the footpath back at the corner. No Willy to help this time. In the Russian sector, no questions asked. Run. Where?

Without thinking he pushed Irene into the building entrance, pressing her into the doorway corner. Get out of the light. A couple huddled in a doorway. The car began to race toward them, close to the curb, headlamps blazing, tracking. Alex pressed more tightly, away from the street. Make them come for you, get out of the car, not just run you down. He raised one arm, a shield, ready to swing it around in defense, waiting for the crunch of tires stopping in the snow. The car swept past. He took a breath, then realized he'd been panting, running over the rubble again. He looked over his shoulder. Almost at Luisenstrasse now, not even aware of him.

"Alex —"

He dropped his arm. "Sorry." Still catching his breath.

She put her hand up to his face. "What is it? You're shaking."

"I thought I knew the car. Saw it before."

"Saw it before?" Hand still on his cheek. "When?"

Well, when?

"Before. Following us."

"Following us? Why? You think Sasha — ? No. He doesn't —" She stopped, looking up at him. "My God, how this feels." The hand now behind his neck, drawing him down, kissing him, kissing each other, tasting her, his breathing still ragged from fear, now something else, blood rushing to his face, pushing up against her in the corner. "Alex," she said, kissing him again.

He pulled away.

"Come upstairs," she said, a whisper, her breath warm on his cheek.

"No."

"It's dark. No one will see." A small giggle. "Really no one. If we can find the stairs."

"Irene —"

"I knew it would feel the same. When I saw you." She touched his temple. "All gray. But I knew it would be the same."

"It's not."

"I don't care." She put her head next to his. "I just want to feel like before." The words warm in his ear. "It's not so much. When we were nicer. Just that."

"Irene —"

"Why? You don't want to? What a liar you are," she said, reaching down, feeling him.

"Cars following us. So maybe that was an excuse too." Playing, oblivious to the look on his face. Another kiss, his mouth opening willingly. "Nobody ever wanted me like you. Nobody. Remember on the beach? My God. And now you don't want to anymore?" She shook her head, still close to his, her hand gripping him below. "What a liar."

He looked over her shoulder at the threshold, another line to cross. Don't. This betrayal worse than the other, or maybe just part of the same one now. What they wanted. More.

"I know you," she said. "Don't I?"

Already betrayed, so that when he nodded, his head filled with her, nobody ever wanted me like you, the nod seemed like a small lie.

"Be careful in the hall. Don't make too much noise." She was whispering, her breath faster, the same reckless eagerness as before, the way he remembered. "Frau Schmidt. I think she listens at the door. She used to be the block warden. Now she can't stop." She put her fingers to her lips, turning to the door, opening it slowly. A small foyer, the stairs opposite. "Can you see? Should I light a match?" Still whispering, conspiratorial. She turned, holding him again. "Maybe it's better. You can't see me. How I look. We'll be the same," she said, kissing him again. "This way. It's better by the stairs." The one visible part of the room, under a skylight.

Her foot bumped into something — a pail, a child's toy, something that clattered.

"Ouf." She giggled again. "Now she's setting traps. Wait." She reached into her purse and took out a match, lighting it, and waving it over the floor. "Okay." She took his hand, leading him to the stairs. "Just hold the rail. Here. It's the first step."

A faint noise, furtive, from out of the dark, beside the stairs. "Irene."

She froze.

"Over here."

Someone moved away from the wall, approaching them. "Thank God. I've been waiting."

Almost there, the thin pale face ghostlike in the dim light.

"Erich," she said. "Erich?"

"I didn't know if you were still living here." Both whispering.

"Erich." Almost a sob now, falling on him. "My God. How you look. So skinny. My God."

They held each other for a minute, Erich shaking, a nervous relief, exhausted.

"*Shh.* It's okay," Irene was saying, patting him. "Everything's okay. Erich."

"I have to hide. Can you hide me?"

"Hide?"

"We escaped —" He raised his head, noticing Alex for the first time. An odd, startled look, seeing the dead. "Alex?" His eyes darting, confused. What had he heard, waiting by the stairs? Irene giggling, intimate.

"Yes."

"It's you?" An inexplicable presence.

"What do you mean, escaped?" Irene said, now studying his face. "You're all right?" She looked down. "Like a skeleton." Her voice broke, a whimper at the back of it. "My God, what have they done to you?"

Alex looked at him, the boy they'd hidden under the stairs. His hair, once the color of Irene's, was now indeterminate, cropped short, prison style, easy for delousing. Dirty, streaked with grime, his skin drawn tight over the bones, so that his eyes seemed to bulge out, too big for his face. Holding onto the newel, some support.

"Come," Irene said. "Alex, help me with him. Just hold onto the rail."

A flickering light appeared, a candle coming out of a door.

"Who is it? What's going on?"

"It's only me, Frau Schmidt. Another power cut — it's hard to see."

Erich swerved away, his back to the candle.

"Frau Gerhardt," Frau Schmidt said, holding the candle higher. "Two visitors?"

"Can I borrow the candle?" Irene said, breezy. "For the stairs? So kind. I'll replace it tomorrow. Thank you." She took the candle before Frau Schmidt could object.

"It's late," Frau Schmidt said. "For parties."

"It's not a party," Irene said. "It's my —" Then stopped, catching herself. "Well, it's to make sure I got home safely."

"And now you are home."

"Yes," Irene said, not biting. "Thank you again." Moving up the stairs, the others shuffling behind.

At the door, she asked Alex to hold the candle while she fumbled for the key, Erich leaning against the wall, holding himself, drained. "In the old days, she'd make a report," Irene said. "The old witch. Quick, inside. Erich, can you walk? What's wrong?"

"Nothing. Just tired." He sank onto the couch, looking dazed. "Alex," he said. "What are you doing here?"

"Never mind," Irene said, fussing with his jacket. "We'll explain later. You're freezing.

You don't have a coat?"

"A coat," Erich said with a laugh, some joke only he knew.

"Here, put this around you." Irene draped an afghan around his shoulders, then began stroking his face. "What's happened to you? Are you hungry?"

"Something to drink maybe."

"Alex, it's over there," she said, nodding to a side table. "My God, so cold." Rubbing Erich's hands.

"Well, the truck. No heat."

"What truck?"

"Rudi had a cousin with a truck. That's how we got away. But no heat in the back. Thank you," he said, taking the glass from Alex, then looking up. "I don't understand. You're in Berlin? I thought you were —"

"I came back. Drink. It'll warm you up."

Erich tossed it back, then shuddered.

"Are you hurt?" Irene said. "Escaped from where?"

"The camp. Where they shipped us, the POWs. Back to Germany, but not home. Slave labor." He looked over. "People die in the camp. They get sick. I can't go back there." His voice wavering, involuntary tears.

"*Shh.* You're here."

He looked again at Alex. "You're with

164

Irene?" The confusion nagging at him.

"I just brought her home. From a party."

"A party." Something unimaginable.

"Did they feed you? You look —"

Erich shook his head. "They don't die of that."

Alex and Irene looked at each other. The illogic of hunger.

"There's plenty here," Irene said. "Sasha sent —" She stopped and went over to the kitchen counter. "Some cheese maybe?"

"Do they know?" Alex said. "About the break?"

Erich nodded. "It's only because of the truck we got away. Rudi's cousin. Usually they catch you. In one of the villages. The police track you down. German police. Our own people. Sometimes you can get to a bigger town, it's easier to blend in, but you still have to get through the roadblocks. That's the Russians. The whole area, all the towns, are blocked off. So they always get you." Talking partly to himself.

"Well, not here. You're safe now," Irene said. She cocked her head to the door. "Except for Frau Schmidt." Trying to make a joke, but Erich looked up, alert again.

"They'll come here. I can't stay here."

"Don't be silly. Where would you go? I'll get Sasha to help —"

"Who's Sasha?"

"A friend."

"A Russian friend?"

"Yes," she said, turning her head, embarrassed.

"He'd turn me in. They have to. It's a rule with them."

"They know you're in Berlin?" Alex said.

"I don't know. Rudi's cousin left us in Lichtenberg. If they trace the truck, they'll know we got that far. So maybe yes. Then it's the first place they'll look. Here."

"I'm Frau Gerhardt, not von Bernuth, so how would they know?"

"They'll know," Erich said, irrational now. "They know these things. And then they'll take you for helping me. Make you work. In the slime. No boots. That's how they get sick."

"What slime? Erich —"

But he was standing up. "No. They'll come. Both of us. I have to hide."

"All right," Irene said, humoring him. "But first something to eat. There's some soup. Let me warm it up for you. If they come, Frau Schmidt will sound the alarm. She's good for that at least. What's that on your legs?"

"Sores," he said, looking down at two lesions. "From the slime."

"What slime? You keep saying —"

"I can't go back there. I'll die."

Irene took his hand. "You're safe. Do you understand? Now let me get the soup."

"They have to get us, you know, so the others won't find out. Then everyone would —"

"It's a POW camp?" Alex said.

"POWs, criminals, anyone they can find. They don't care what happens to us. If we die. People think we're dead already."

"No," Irene said from the stove. "I never thought that."

"It's worse than in Russia. They don't want anyone to think he can get past the patrols."

"How did you?"

"Rudi's cousin drives the truck for the TEWA plant. In Neustadt. The same run, every week. So the Russians know him. They don't look in the back."

"So they don't actually know how you got out."

"They will. Someone always talks. Then they have to track you down."

"Look," Irene said. "Across the street. Lights. The power must be back."

She turned the switch, then stared, appalled at Erich in the light.

"What about upstairs?" Erich said. "Is

there an attic?"

"It's open from the bombs. You'd freeze."

"Then I'll find something."

"*Ouf,* be sensible. It's safe here. Where would you go?"

"They'll come," he said stubbornly. "They'll find me here." Pacing now, determined.

"Come with me then," Alex said. "They'll never look for you at the Adlon."

"The Adlon?" Erich said, another confusion.

"You can't get a room without papers," Irene said. "If he stays with you they'll report —"

"Not with me. There's a room he can use. Someone who's out of town," he said vaguely. "They'll never look there. He'll be safe, at least for a day or two. Until we figure out what to do."

She lowered her head, thinking, then looked up at him. "You'd do this? It's a risk to you."

"So was the SA. Remember, under the stairs?"

"Yes," she said, still looking at him. "How could I forget that night?"

"This'll be easier. I just have to talk him in. You can't go like that, though. Let's get you cleaned up. Look like you're actually staying there."

"At the Adlon?" Erich said, slightly dazed.

"I'll light the geyser," Irene said, busy. "It never gets really hot, the water, but it's a bath. Just don't run it too fast. A trickle, then it's warm. I still have some clothes from Enka." She went over and opened a closet door, assessing. "The coat will be big but you have to have a coat. Who walks into the Adlon without a coat? Shall I come with you? We'll have a drink, everything normal, then you say good-bye —"

"No. We don't want to draw attention. You kept his clothes?"

"Most I sold. On the black market. That first year, how else could you live? But I never sold the coat. It's a Schulte, hand tailored. Enka liked things like that." She watched Erich go into the bathroom, then turned back to Alex. "So much for old times," she said softly, a faint shrug of the shoulders. "Anyway, it was nice, that you wanted to." She put her hand on his arm. "How things turn out," she said, then folded her arms across her chest, holding herself, as if she were going to spill out. "What are we going to do? Look at him."

"We'll hide him until he's better."

"And then what?"

"Then we'll do something else. First, let's

get some food in him. Did you keep any shirts? He can't wear this."

She kept holding herself, swaying a little. "If they find him, they'll — shoot him. That's what they do."

"What's the difference, he's dying where he is." Then, hearing his tone, "They won't find him. We'll think of something."

"You will, you mean. The Adlon. Imagine. Why do you do this? It's trouble for you."

"You think I'd walk away from Erich? Any of you?"

She stared at him, not saying anything.

"Maybe it's for Fritz," he said, avoiding her eyes.

She smiled to herself. "How sentimental you are. He did it for the money. Your father paid him."

"But he did it."

"And now you. But nobody pays you." She glanced toward the bathroom, fidgeting, suddenly nervous. "He shouldn't use so much. Frau Schmidt will be up. She thinks she owns the water too. The *Gauleiter.*" She turned back to him. "So it's for Fritz. Not me. But maybe for me a little."

Waiting for him to agree, something from the lost part of the evening. He looked at her for a minute, listening to the water running. A trickle to get the most out of the geyser.

"I'm not the same person," he said quietly.

She tipped her head back, not expecting this.

"I have a family."

She nodded, still surprised. "The wife who wasn't me."

"A son."

"Yes?"

"Everything is for him now. What I do. Sometimes things I don't want to do. It's not about me anymore. I can't explain —" He paused. "It's not the same."

"Just now. In the street. It wasn't the same?" She looked away. "Why are you telling me this? You want to be faithful to a woman you divorced?"

For a second he almost smiled. An Irene response, tart, fast.

"You know before, it was the same for me. So let me think that. Not that everything's different." She rapped on the bathroom door. "It's enough water, Erich. There's soup ready." She started setting out a bowl, willed activity, still fidgeting. "So this son. What is he like? A wunderkind?"

"No. Just a boy. A beautiful smile, when he smiles. Serious. He thinks about things."

She held the soup spoon in midair. "Like

his father. And have you thought about this?" She nodded toward the bathroom. "What it means? It's prison, helping a POW escape. I'll keep him here. You don't have to do this."

"Yes, I do."

"Because of some old debt? It's foolishness. Paying back Fritz?"

"I don't know why. Does it matter? He needs help."

"Is that what happened in America? Why you left. Something you had to do. Why? Because you had to. And now look."

"That's right. I had to." Ending it. "Where are the clothes? I'll pick some out."

"Who is the friend at the Adlon, the one who's away?"

"A friend."

"Oh, without a name."

"She doesn't know she's helping. Neither do you."

"But how can I go then? See him?"

"You don't. Not yet. He's not really there. There's nobody in the room."

"Then what do I do?"

"For one thing, don't tell Sasha."

"But he could help."

"You mean that much to him? That he'd do this for you? Maybe you believe it."

"You don't know him."

"He couldn't. He's not just some Ivan — five wristwatches and a German girlfriend. He's a big shot at Karlshorst. Who do you think is after Erich?"

"Oh, Sasha. Chasing soldiers," she said, dismissive.

"He works for Maltsev," Alex said, thinking out loud. "Security. So he might hear. Any escapes, there'd be reports. You could keep an ear open — you could do that."

"How do you mean?"

"If he says anything. What they're thinking. Do they know he's in Berlin? They might still think they're hiding in the woods by the camp. Do they know about the truck? He'd hear things."

"And if he never says?"

"Ask him how his day was. Talk to him."

Irene looked at him. "Spy on him, you mean."

Alex took a breath. "Yes, spy on him." That easy, the line not even visible.

They left by the Luisenstrasse end of the street, under the elevated tracks, with the charred wreck of the Reichstag looming up on the right. No cars, nobody following. The snow had stopped, patches already disappearing in the streets, leaving a wet sheen. Erich was dressed for the cold, his lower face wrapped in a scarf, a hat covering the

173

rest, safely indistinguishable. But eventually they'd be in the lobby. Work out the logistics. Not the bar, where Brecht might be holding court, with some spillover group from the Kulturbund.

They were lucky. The bellhop was there, immediately at his side, eyes wide, scenting trouble.

"Frau Berlau's room," Alex said, a low voice, almost a mumble. "What number?"

"One forty-three." No hesitation, already part of it.

"Get the key. Meet us there."

The boy slid away. Not much older than Peter.

On the first floor, no one in the hall, they only had to wait a minute before he reappeared and opened the door.

"The maid won't come in," he said. "But she's back Friday. Frau Berlau."

Alex nodded, leading Erich inside. "Let me give you something." He reached into his pocket, but the boy waved it aside.

"Don't forget the park tomorrow. The Fairy Tale Fountain," he said, pulling the door closed, this just part of the same drama, in on it.

It was the room of a nun, tidy and austere, a single bed and neatly stacked piles of books, Brecht's plays, copybooks with production notes and reminders.

Erich began taking off his coat. "Someone's already in the room?"

"Ruth Berlau. Can you remember that? A friend of yours. She said you could use it. If anyone asks. Don't go out. No noise. No one's here, understand? It won't be for long."

"And then what. What's going to happen?" He started shaking, a nervous tremor, crying without tears.

Alex took him by the shoulders. "We'll get you out. But right now, you need some rest." He glanced at the bed. "Better sleep on top. Then nobody'll know. They usually keep a duvet in here," he said, opening the armoire.

"Out," Erich said, brooding. "The house in Pomerania maybe. The Poles would hide me."

Alex shook his head. "It's gone. Here, this should be warm enough. Off with the shoes."

"So where? They have to send you back if they find you. It's an agreement. If I go there," he said, cocking his head to the West. "They have to send me back. So where do I go?"

"We'll get you out, don't worry. But first sleep, okay? In you go." Talking to a child.

"I can't stay in Berlin."

"No. We'll get you to the West." Suddenly sure, now that he'd said it. "I have friends there. We'll fix it, all right? Do you need anything else? Don't open the door to anybody. Just me. Three knocks like that, okay?" He knocked lightly on the night table. "Three."

"Like in a story," Erich said and for a second he did seem like a child, tucked in, drowsy, trusting.

"Good night, my friend," Alex said. His responsibility now. The last thing he needed. He looked down again. Not a child. An old man's face, gaunt, a death mask.

Get out of it. Go down to the bar and find Brecht or some other alibi. But his mind was racing, planning. He felt in his pocket and pulled out a business card. Ferber. Happy to give him a tour. He'd need something to get them to keep Erich. Some chip. He owed Fritz this much at least. His stomach tightened, a dread he could feel rushing through him, like blood. Knowing he'd pay somehow. Don't. And then the odd relief of having no choice, suddenly calm, the way it had felt standing up to the committee.

■ ■ ■ ■

3
RYKESTRASSE

■ ■ ■ ■

The man was standing next to the statue of Gretel, his back to Alex, collar pulled up against the cold. A worker's cloth cap and peacoat, slightly bent over, no longer young. Earlier there had been a woman with a dog but no one since, so it must be him. But how to do this? No password or coded signal, just turn up in the park. The fountain basins, drained for the winter, were covered with snow, the Grimm figures and the Baroque colonnade beyond like pieces of confectionary, but he couldn't look at them forever. It must be him. Or just an old man out for a walk.

"Herr Meier?" the man said, barely turning.

"Yes."

"You got the message. Good. Dieter," he said, introducing himself. "We can talk here, there's no one. You have a cigarette maybe?" A Berlin accent, brisk.

179

"What's up?" Alex said, offering it.

"You, Herr Meier, what else?" He leaned in to light the cigarette. "You haven't tried to contact anyone, I hope?"

"No."

"Good. And if anyone tries to contact you, don't respond."

"Just you."

"That's right. Campbell's orders. At BOB they think Willy was running you himself. Whoever 'you' are."

"And the Russians?"

"If they knew, you wouldn't be here. The two who saw you in Lützowplatz? No longer with us, alas. A rare distinction, Herr Meier. Unknown to the Russians, unknown to the Americans. How many in Berlin can say that?"

"If I'm so unknown why did they try to kill me?"

He shook his head. "Not kill you. Kidnap you. Maybe turn you. Trade you. Any possibility. But the point was to find out who you were. So they follow Willy and what happens? They still don't know."

"You're sure?"

Dieter nodded. "A source there."

"What about them? Do they have a source with us?"

Dieter sighed. "Well, they must. How

180

would they know to follow Willy exactly then? So there's a leak. He was right, it turns out."

"Who?"

"Campbell. He wanted someone outside BOB. An independent contractor."

"That's you?"

Another nod. "So you talk only to me. Until he comes. That's his message to you."

"And what if it's you, the leak?"

"Well, it might be. You decide. Do you enjoy such puzzles? Maybe you like to think the worst. Me, I like to hope for the best." He turned to the statue, looking at it. "The witch wanted to bake her in the oven. What kind of men do you think they were, the Grimms, to tell children such stories? How the world really is. So," he said, shifting gears. "It's clear? You don't contact anyone. Just me — if you can trust me. Come here for a walk. I'll find you. If there's something wrong, Peter will —"

"Peter?"

"The boy at the hotel."

"His name's Peter?" Alex said, unexpectedly thrown by this. "How old is he anyway? I mean, a child, how did he get —"

"My nephew's son. So it's safe. He doesn't know. He thinks I'm working in the black market. So he's training for that. It's exciting for him. It's what he wants. That's the choice now in Berlin. Be a criminal or a spy. So, a criminal. I don't blame him. The money's better."

"They why don't you do it?"

The man looked at him, then rubbed out the cigarette. "You want to know why I do this? If you can trust me? So. I work for the Americans because they're not the Russians. That's the politics of it, nothing else. I used to think things. A better world. Anyway, better than the Nazis. Then the Russians came. They raped my daughter. They made me watch. Then they beat her — she was fighting them. And she died. So that's my politics now. Stop the Russians. You think it's wrong to use Peter? He doesn't do much — messages, little errands. Those last weeks of the war I saw boys younger than him hanging from trees — traitors because they ran away from the Volkssturm. And then the Russians came. There are no children in Berlin." He motioned toward the statues. "So maybe they were right, the Grimms. Come, walk with me."

They headed behind the colonnade into the park.

"Have they asked you to do things?"

"Like what?"

"The radio, for instance. A talk. Why you

chose the East. How it's the right path for Germany, a united Socialist Germany. Maybe a literary interview. Whatever they suggest, do it. The more valuable you are to them, the safer you are. Don't worry," he said, suddenly wry. "No one will hear. No one listens to their radio." He paused. "You're in the Party?"

"No."

"Join. Make them feel sure about you."

"Brecht didn't."

"Well, he's Brecht."

Alex looked at him, amused. "That's what he thinks too."

"He's a friend? Do a radio with him. The Kulturbund party, it was a success? Comrade Markovsky was there, I hear."

"Yes."

"So you met? And how was that?"

"Pleasant. But short. He had to leave. Some crisis."

"In Karlshorst?" Dieter said, interested. "Maybe something with our friends in Lützowplatz."

"No, out of town. Someplace called Aue."

Dieter turned. "Aue? Are you sure? He said Aue?"

"That's what it sounded like. A long drive at night, apparently. There was talk about that."

"What kind of crisis?" His voice more urgent. "Did he say? It's important."

"Some labor problem. Maybe some kind of strike, that's what it sounded like anyway."

"No, not a strike," Dieter said, thinking. "That's not possible there. Did he say anything else?"

"No. Oh, how they always leave it too late. They should have called him earlier. That was it. He didn't seem particularly upset. More annoyed at having to leave the party."

"But he drives to Aue. A labor problem. In Aue."

"That's important?"

"In Aue, yes."

"Why?"

"It's in the Forbidden Zone."

Alex looked at him, the phrase out of a magazine story.

"Aue is where they send you first, the distribution point. They call it the Gate of Tears."

"Forbidden Zone?" The sound of it still implausible.

"The Russians sealed off the whole area. It's controlled by Moscow, all the operations there, so it's difficult getting information out. For the Germans too. The SED has no say, they just take orders. So something like this — it's a break. Anything you could hear —"

"What am I listening for?"

"Yes, of course," Dieter said quickly, distracted. "You don't know. The Erzgebirge, they patrol the whole range. Fences sometimes, three meters."

"Why?"

Dieter looked at him, surprised, something he assumed Alex already knew. "The uranium mines. You remember Oberschlema, famous for radium baths? In the old days it was good for the health. Well, they thought. Over on the Czech side, more spas, it's the same region. Now the mines. The whole operation is called Wismut. If you ever hear him talk about that —"

"And no one knows?"

"No, people know. And they don't know. We're good at that. Ask anyone now, did they know about the Jews and no, they didn't know a thing. Except who's living here then? Who else would know? And at first, of course, when the Russians are using criminals, Nazis, it's easy not to know. But they start drafting ordinary Germans and then the rumors start."

"Who's using criminals?" Alex said, not following.

"The mines. At first people went for the

185

wages. Jobs that pay, that wasn't so easy last year. And the papers made it sound good. *Neues Deutschland.* So not a secret. But then word got out about the conditions and no one would go. So Ulbricht sends ex-Nazis, political prisoners. He empties the jails and still not enough, so they start drafting forced labor. Twenty-five, thirty thousand last year. And they ask for seventy-five thousand more. These are rough figures," he said with a side look to Alex. "Myself, I think it's even more. And Ulbricht will find them. His own people — well, if you still think someone like that is German. The Russian bear just gobbles them up — feed me more. And Ulbricht does. People who have never done work like that. For them like a death sentence. Unless they can get to the West — anything to avoid the mines. We're losing many that way. Last night, did you meet your publisher from Aufbau?"

"Aaron Stein?" Alex said, remembering the watery eyes.

"Yes. A decent man. You know he resigned from the central committee last year, the secretariat, to protest this. He said the SED should say no. Of course, how could they do that? A great embarrassment to Ulbricht, a respected man like Stein. We thought maybe a chance for us, someone we might recruit, but no, still a believer. So what happens? He resigns and Ulbricht sends more workers anyway. Thousands. And they don't come back now, they keep them working, so it's hard to know how it is there. How much are they shipping out? Why do they keep asking for more people? So you see, when you tell us he's going to Aue — this is better than we hoped, to know that."

"It's not a lot."

"Yes, but why? What happened? So now we listen. Even rumors. We have ears outside the zone. In the processing plants. We go to Farben in Bitterfeld and ask, what do you hear? The TEWA plant at Neustadt."

"Neustadt?" Alex said, raising his head. But how many Neustadts were there in Germany? A hundred?

"Yes, near Greiz, but outside the zone, so we can talk to people there."

"Do they use POWs? The mines?"

"Yes, of course. They were among the first. They're already prisoners, so they can't pick up and leave if they don't like the work. Why?"

Alex looked up. "No reason," he said, wary. But Dieter was still looking at him. "I just thought, useful, if we could find some to talk to."

"Well, yes, anyone, but here you are with

such a source —"

"I met him for two minutes. Do you really think he's going to talk to me about any of this?"

"But he already has. Every lead is useful. And of course there's the woman. An old friend of yours, yes? Campbell said."

"Did he? When?"

"She sleeps with him. A man will say anything in bed."

"Mining conditions in Aue? Is that what you would talk about?"

Dieter smiled. "My friend, at my age you don't talk. You have to save your breath." They had been walking gradually uphill and he stopped for effect, catching his wind. "It's not so difficult for a woman. All she has to do is listen."

"What makes you think this one will?"

"Well, I leave that to you." They were rounding a small hill. "It's kind to walk with an old man, but you should go now. Or someone might wonder. But first, let me show you something interesting. This way."

"But don't you want to know who else I met? I thought that's what —"

"Another day. Nothing's more important than this. Aue," he said, repeating it to himself. "You understand, we've been trying to get good information for a long time.

What grade ore are they shipping? How? In what form?" He stopped. "Excuse me, it's a lot all at once maybe. I'll make a list, what to listen for. Right now, anything. You know, the propaganda value alone —"

"What, that the Russians have labor camps? Everybody must know —"

"But who's in them? Who's supplying them? The Russians are capable of anything — yes, old news. But Ulbricht, the German Communists, feeding the beast? With Germans? Their own citizens. Who would trust a government like that? My friend, keep your ears open. Keep your ears open."

"All right. When do I see you again?"

"Just come to the park. I'll know. Otherwise, next week, same time, if you can. Look." He pointed toward what appeared to be a construction site. Narrow-gauge rails had been laid across the park, sloping uphill, the open tram cars loaded with rubble sent up from Friedrichshain. "You see they're making a mountain. On the flak tower. What's left of it. They dynamited it, but you know they were built to — anyway, now it's covered. So, higher and higher. And then some grass, trees, and in a few years it's gone, buried. The war? No sign. All the sins covered up. That's what we do. The Russians cover theirs with memorials. Have you been down to Treptow? The memorial they're building there? Stalin's words, now in granite. A statue higher than this hill. A Soviet soldier rescuing a child. From Fascism. A broken swastika. Maybe someday somebody believes it. You have one more cigarette?" He coughed as he lit it. "Peasants. They didn't know how to flush a toilet. You know what happens when you give a peasant a gun? You make a monster. That's what the statue should be."

"But they did break the swastika," Alex said.

"Yes," Dieter said, glancing at him. "You're a Jew, yes? Meier? So, all right. We had monsters too. Maybe worse. But they didn't rape my Liesl." He flicked away the end of the cigarette. "Barbarians. Now they want to do it to Germany. No. Not them. That's my politics now."

Martin was waiting for him at the hotel.

"We have your housing assignment," he said, pleased with himself. "In Prenzlauer Berg. A very nice area. So. You can pack now?"

"Now?" Erich, still in Ruth's room.

"Yes. I have a car for us. You will be anxious to see it."

"What's the address? I want to write it

down." He took out a notebook.

"But I will take you," Martin said, puzzled.

"For the desk here," Alex said, improvising. "To forward mail."

"You are expecting mail here?"

"From America. It's the only address they have. Until I send the new one."

"Rykestrasse forty-eight. Near the Wasserturm. A very nice street."

Alex jotted down the address, two copies. "For me," he explained, "if I forget it. I won't be long. A few minutes."

And then, before Martin could say anything more, he was on the stairs. Three knocks. Erich opened the door, still looking sleepy, but not as drawn as last night. Alex slid in.

"They're moving me. To a flat." He handed him the address. "You know where it is?"

Erich looked at the paper and nodded. "Your flat? But it's trouble for you."

"It's more trouble if Ruth gets back early. Put the duvet away. No one was here. And make sure there's nobody around at my place when you come. Three knocks, just like here, okay? Better wait an hour. At least. I don't know when I can shake Martin."

"Who?"

"Nobody. My keeper. Okay, let's go. Neat

as a pin, right?"

"What about the key?" He cocked his head toward the night table.

Ruth's key. Impossible to explain at the desk. A fuss if it went missing.

"Give it to me. I'll put it back." How? Surprisingly heavy in his palm. Adlon luxury. At the door he turned. "Erich? The work camp. It was mines? Near Aue?"

"Yes. How did you — ?"

"The people who got sick — what happened?"

"They got tired. Well, everybody was tired. But more tired. Sick in the lungs, from the dust. And no boots. You had to work in the slime up to here, no rubber boots, so it was easy to get sick."

"Did they tell you what you were mining?"

"No, but we knew. Pitchblende. Uranium. Everybody knew. The doctors would check. If someone got sick from that. Radiation. But with them, everyone was healthy. Unless you couldn't work at all." He looked up. "Why do you ask this?"

"No reason," Alex said, thinking of the lesions on Erich's legs. "We'll talk later. I want to hear — how it was."

"They said it was our patriotic duty. As Socialists. The Americans didn't want anyone else to have it, uranium. And we had so little. We needed more. So, that cough? It's nothing important. Go back to work. It was like that."

Alex put his hand on the doorknob. "How many of you escaped?"

"Five. We were afraid, if we told too many someone would betray us. You know, for special privileges."

Alex stood there for a minute, at a loss. No end to it. "Give me an hour," he said finally. "And keep this locked from inside."

His packing, the shaving kit and the extra suit, only took a few minutes. Down the hall, Ruth's key in one hand, his key in his pocket so they wouldn't get mixed up. No bellhops in sight. Where was Peter? Who'd know what to do. And then, near the bottom of the stairs, he saw the long overcoat and stopped. Markus Engel, talking to the doorman. Martin leaped off the lobby couch, reaching for Alex's suitcase.

"Let me help. You need only to sign the paper," he said, pointing to the desk. "It's all been arranged." Anxious, clearly wanting to leave.

Alex took out his key and handed it to the desk clerk. Hurry, before he sees you. But Markus was already coming over to them. Alex clutched Ruth's key in his palm. What if he wanted to shake hands?

"Ah, you're leaving?"

"Markus."

"And I was hoping we could have coffee. Continue our conversation. Well, another time."

"Yes. But soon?" Alex said, friendly, keeping the fiction going. "I'd stay now except they've got a car waiting for me."

"An honor for an honored guest," Markus said, managing a smile. "So, a flat already. It's very efficient, the Kulturbund." This to Martin.

"No, it was the housing authority," Martin said. "But lucky, certainly."

"Yes, lucky. Perhaps a word from Major Dymshits."

"I don't know," Martin said, uncomfortable.

"Was there anything in particular you wanted to talk about?" Alex said, feeling the key in his hand, squeezing it.

"No, no, just to talk. Maybe a good thing, your having to go. I should be getting to work, not drinking coffee." But not moving, a speech that seemed endless, each word like a rope tying them to the floor. And still the key. Alex turned to the desk.

"Is Peter here this morning? The boy?"

The desk clerk nodded and whispered something to another bellhop, presumably a go-find-him request.

"I wanted to say good-bye," Alex explained.

"We should hurry," Martin said. "The car —"

"There is one thing I wanted to ask you," Markus said. "I just remembered. You will find this odd, maybe."

Alex waited.

"Do you carry a gun?"

"A gun?" Alex said, surprised. "No. Why? Do you think I need one?"

"Need? No. But many people keep a gun here. Berlin can be a dangerous city. I was curious if you had brought one from America. And someone took it maybe. We had an incident with American bullets. So to find the gun —"

"Markus, there must be thousands of American guns in Berlin. Thousands."

"Army guns, yes. But not this one. A gun a civilian might have. Or so the bullets suggest. There are not so many of those in Berlin. So we have to check."

"So you ask me?"

"To eliminate you," Markus said calmly. "Someone just arrived from America. Someone who was in Lützowplatz —"

"What does Lützowplatz have to do with it?"

"That's where the incident took place."

"The traffic accident you mentioned."

"Well, perhaps it was more than that."

"With bullets? Yes. Well, I didn't see anybody shoot anybody either. Just my house — or what's left of it."

"It was a simple query."

Alex looked at him, saying nothing, then spied Peter across the room. "There he is. Excuse me a moment." He went over quickly, before Peter could reach them and took his hand, a tip movement, a bill slipped into a maître d's palm. Peter's eyes widened at the feel of the key, then looked up, a kind of approving glance for the smooth hand-over. He put his hand in his pocket, then saw Markus.

"You know he's K-5?"

"Yes. Don't worry. He's just poking around. If he asks you —"

"I know what to say. He talks to Oskar." Indicating the doorman.

"Thanks for this. I'll tell Dieter."

Peter bowed, backing way, Adlon training.

"You know it's not necessary to tip here," Markus said when he came back.

"I know, I keep forgetting. Old habits."

"Bourgeois habits."

"Well, he's just a kid."

"He did a special service for you maybe?"

196

"No. It's just, a kid —"

"Not the best lesson, perhaps. I know, you mean to be generous, but what does such an exchange do? Reinforce an artificial distance between the classes."

"It was only a mark," Alex said easily. "An East mark." Something Peter was likely to have.

"Well, I am perhaps too didactic. I've been told this. But you know, it's true all the same."

"We should go," Martin said. "The car —"

Markus glanced at Alex's suitcase. "A light traveler."

"Just until the rest of my things arrive. Well, until our coffee then."

"You can leave messages at the Kulturbund," Martin said to Markus. "In fact, there is good coffee there. You would be most welcome."

This seemed to amuse Markus, who smiled. "I will find you, don't worry," he said to Alex. "You don't mind my saying? A very nice coat." He ran his eyes over it, appraising. "It's English?"

"No, just Bullocks Wilshire." And then, at Markus's blank expression, "A store. In California."

"When people say 'English coat' what do

they usually mean? I'm so ignorant of such things."

"Tweed, I guess," Alex said, wondering what he was asking. "Anyway, not Bullocks."

"Of course, if it's not German, they might say any foreign coat was English. American. English. How many would know the difference? It's a difficulty with witnesses. Sometimes they don't know what they're seeing." His eyes cool again, steady, not letting it go at all. The old woman? One of the English soldiers? Or nobody? Just his way of pulling a string to see if anything twitched.

The flat was in a nineteenth-century block of pale stucco and ornamental balconies, facing the street, not one of the gloomy back courtyards. Rykestrasse seemed to have escaped any serious bombing, the buildings shabby but intact. A few doors down there was a synagogue that had been converted to stables and at the end a small park with the red brick water tower that Alex could see from his window if he leaned out and craned his head.

"The SA took it over," Martin said, pointing out the tower to him. "They tortured people in the basement." He pulled his head back inside. "So, it seems comfortable to you? I realize, not so big, but the light is good. And even —" He paused for effect. "A telephone."

"It's wonderful," Alex said, looking at the phone, clearly a great rarity. "I'm very grateful. You've gone to so much trouble."

"No, no, we are so pleased you're here." Meaning it.

A separate bedroom, a worn sofa in the living room for Erich, small galley kitchen and a table by the window facing the street where he could write. A pressed glass pitcher with flowers. Lace curtains, recently ironed. Home.

"I have brought food packages but there are also shops in Schönhauser Allee." As if everything were there for the asking, shelves filled.

Alex glanced at his watch. Erich would have left by now. "Thank you for everything. I don't want to keep you."

"No, no, it's my job." He took out a notebook, a secretary. "Perhaps now is a good time to look at your schedule?"

"My schedule?"

"A radio interview. We were hoping —"

"Can't it wait?"

"But everyone is so anxious to hear what you have to say. A talk at the Kulturbund naturally would be later. So you have time to prepare. But the radio —"

"What kind of interview?"

"A conversation. Like talking over coffee. How it feels to be back. Conditions in America — why you left. Your hopes for the Socialist future. And your work, of course." His voice implacable, something Alex would have to do sooner or later.

"All right. Let me know when. Anything else?"

Martin looked up, hesitant. "We're preparing a *Festschrift.* A special book for Comrade Stalin's birthday. It was hoped that you might contribute."

"Contribute?"

"A short piece, whatever length you like. Some members are writing poems, but you —"

"Write a piece," Alex said. "Praising Stalin."

Martin turned his head, embarrassed. "His leadership during the war perhaps. A heroic period." He waited for a moment, as if he were testing his words first. "Shall I say that you are thinking what to say?"

"Who else are you asking to do this?"

"Our prominent members. You of course —"

"Brecht? Brecht is writing something?" An impossible idea.

"A request has been made."

Alex raised an eyebrow, saying nothing.

Martin licked his lips, nervous. "It's an awkward situation. We want to show a certain solidarity. You understand."

The more valuable you are, the safer you are. Alex nodded. "When do you need it?"

"The end of March. So the printer will have time. Sometimes, you know, there are delays, with the shortages."

"Not for this, surely."

"No, not for this." Embarrassed again. "The Kulturbund appreciates —"

"Anything else?" Alex said, cutting him off.

"For now, no. May we expect you for lunch today? I can keep a place at the members' table."

"No, not today."

"But Comrade Stein will be disappointed. He wanted to take you afterward to Aufbau. To meet the staff. I think they are expecting you."

"Oh. I didn't realize. It's just — I'd like to get some work done. It's been awhile since I had a place to work." He waved his hand toward the table.

"Then coffee perhaps. I know they have prepared something. Say four o'clock? I can have a car —"

"That's all right. I can get there." Imagining a car idling, Martin on the stairs, Erich hiding.

"Of course," Martin said, smiling. "An old Berliner. So. Four o'clock then. I'll let Comrade Stein know." He looked over at the table. "What are you working on, may I ask?" Eyes eager, interested.

"A story about a marriage. How we deceive ourselves. When we want to believe in something."

"A political metaphor?"

Alex smiled. "I hadn't thought —"

"As in *The Last Fence*," Martin said, earnest.

"If you like. But really it's about the marriage. A bourgeois subject, our friend Markus would say."

"Well, Markus," Martin said, putting his notebook away. "I think it's because he knew you before that he's so curious. Everything. Even your coat."

Alex shrugged this off. "Cops are like that."

"It was the same in America?"

"Well, they never asked about my coat. Just my politics."

Martin looked at him, not quite sure how to take this. "I'll tell Comrade Stein to expect you at four."

And then, another embarrassed nod and

he was finally gone, the room suddenly quiet, not even a clock ticking. Alex looked around. How long would he be here? Long enough to tell the world Stalin was a hero? Even longer? He went over to the window, watching Martin go down the street. No parked cars, nobody lurking in doorways, flowers on the table.

Erich got there an hour later, worn out from the walk. He was shivering, even in the heavy coat, so Alex made tea, spiking it with some schnapps he'd found in Martin's food package.

"You need to see a doctor."

Erich shook his head. "No papers and then they report you and you're finished."

"Does Irene have a phone?"

"Now? I don't know. Before, yes."

"Do you remember the number?" Had they kept the same numbers? But she answered.

"Irene? Alex," he said, holding the receiver close, aware of his own voice. A phone was a privilege. Why had they given him one? To listen? "I have a flat. I thought I'd give you the address."

"You're not at the Adlon?" she said quickly, worried.

"No, they found me a flat. Very nice. Big enough for two."

"For two?" she said, trying to read his tone.

"If I had a guest. Some day. Bigger than the Adlon. Even a phone. Do you have a pencil? I'll give you the number."

"Is everything all right?"

"Yes. Everything. Very lucky to find a flat so soon, don't you think? To have my own place. Do you have an address for Elsbeth?"

"Elsbeth?"

"Yes, I want to visit her. Say hello. She's married to a doctor, you said, yes? So useful, having one in the family."

"Yes, useful," she said slowly, putting this together.

"She'd be so angry if she knew I was here and didn't come to see her."

"Shall I come too?" she said, playing along now.

"No, no. You're busy. Why don't you come this evening? See the flat and then we'll get something to eat."

"I don't know when Sasha —"

"Well, just call if you can't. Nice having a phone, isn't it? Here's the number."

They left separately and sat apart on the tram down to Alexanderplatz and then on the S-Bahn to Savignyplatz. Dr. Mutter was only a few blocks down on Schlüterstrasse, but Erich seemed winded by the walk.

The door was opened by a nurse who seemed to be doing double-duty as a maid.

"You have an appointment?"

"We're here to see Frau Mutter. Tell her Alex Meier."

"Meier?" she said, a slight twitch, perhaps reacting to the name. Only Aryan patients still. "Wait here."

A vestibule with a coatrack, drafty, separated from the hall by another door. Elsbeth came almost at once.

"Alex? It's you?" she said, forehead wrinkled in disbelief, her hand to her throat, a film gesture. She had become her mother, hair wrapped around her head in a braided crown, her face an old woman's, pinched. Then she noticed Erich, a sharp intake of breath, now clutching her throat, and her face seemed to dissolve. "Erich?" she said, a whisper. "Erich — ?"

He reached over to her, hugging her, both now crying.

"I thought you were dead," she said, touching him, making sure he was real. "Dead. Back from the dead. Unless maybe it's me who's dead. They say that's when you see them, when you're dead yourself."

"Elsbeth," Erich said, disconcerted by this, something she was saying to herself.

"And you," she said to Alex. "Back too. I

205

thought I would never see you again. But how is it possible?" she said, turning to Erich. "The POWs don't come back. They keep them there."

"They've started to release them," Alex said. "Three weeks ago. It's taken him that long to get to Berlin. He needs to see a doctor. Is your husband here?"

"Gustav? Seeing patients." She motioned her head inside the house. "It's his day at home. From the hospital. Are you ill?" she said to Erich. "What?"

"He's been in a prison camp," Alex said. "Somebody needs to look at him."

"So you brought him to Gustav? I don't understand," she said to Alex. "Why are you with him? How did you know where — ?"

"He went to see Irene."

"Oh, Irene," she said, a slight stiffening. "And she sends him here? She won't even talk to Gustav."

"Elsbeth," Alex said, a willed patience. "Can we come in? He's very weak. You can see for yourself."

"Weak. Yes, yes, come in. I'm sorry." She took Erich's arm. "You're all right? Did they make you walk? Is it possible, all the way from Russia?"

Erich touched her hair, a faint smile, familiar. "A truck."

"And you go to Irene?"

"I didn't know where you were living. She told me."

She stared at him again. "Back from the dead. Maybe everyone comes back. Wouldn't that be — ?" She turned, leading them in.

The flat was filled with furniture, almost a prewar feel after the austere rooms he'd seen in the East, some leftover Christmas greens still on the mantel. But there were none of the porcelain knickknacks that must have been here before, the clutter of silver frames on the piano, all sold, he assumed, to the men in long coats in the Tiergarten for PX food tins during the first hard winters. Elsbeth, thinner than before, was buttoned up in a nondescript sweater, her old creamy complexion drained away.

"Would you like some tea?" she said, an almost surreal politeness.

"Elsbeth, is your husband — ?" Leading her back.

"Yes, I'll tell him. I hate to interrupt when he has patients. Oh, but what am I saying? It's you, isn't it? Come back. But Erich," she said, a new thought, "did you want to live here? It's only a flat, as you see, and Gustav —"

"He's staying with friends of Irene's," Alex

interrupted. "He doesn't need a bed. Just a doctor."

"Yes. Let me get Gustav. Oh, look at you, so thin. You came back. You know father's dead?"

Erich nodded. Something that had happened years ago.

"And the boys. Both. I was doing volunteer work at the hospital. So many people — the raids. So I wasn't here. I saw them later, when they dug them out. Both. You can't imagine how they looked. At first I didn't recognize them, just the size, so small, so it had to be them. If I had been here — well, Gustav says, don't think that, but he didn't see them. All smashed. Like dolls." She stopped, catching herself. "I'll get him."

Erich looked at Alex, not saying anything. Back from the dead.

"Well, Erich," Dr. Mutter said, coming in and clapping him on the shoulder, a public family welcome. "Thank God. We thought — you know, so many stories." Tall, with thinning blond hair, a long Nordic face. He turned to Alex, waiting.

"This is Alex Meier," Elsbeth said. "A friend of the family. A long time ago. Before you knew me."

"And now here again," Mutter said, nodding, pointedly not offering his hand. "With Erich."

"He's sick," Alex said plainly. "He needs you to examine him. See what's wrong."

"Why didn't he go to the hospital? We're not supposed to —"

"He lost his papers," Alex said, looking at him.

"Lost or never had? Elsbeth said he was released but I haven't heard they're doing that. If he's here illegally, you know it's against the law to —"

Alex stared at him, his head swimming. The kind of unforgiving precise face that might have been at his parents' selection. Able to work, over here. The others, there.

"Really, Gustav —" Elsbeth began.

"And if I lose my license?" he said to her. "What happens to us then? I don't understand why you come here. Or you," he said to Alex. "Meier, it's Jewish, yes? Many Jews have tried to make trouble for me. Maybe you want to report me."

"I couldn't do that," Alex said smoothly. "I've never been here. Neither has Erich. And you never treated him or gave him medicine. None of that happened, all right?"

Mutter said nothing.

"He's sick. I want to know with what. What to do."

"You want to know."

"Alex was close to us," Elsbeth said, explaining. "Like cousins."

"A Jewish cousin. And you come back to Germany? Why? To gloat over us?"

"Just tell me what's wrong with him. It shouldn't take long."

"For God's sake, Gustav, he's my brother," Elsbeth said.

"And what does he say if they catch him? He implicates us."

"They're not going to catch him," Alex said.

"I have never broken the law."

"That must be a comfort."

"Alex," Elsbeth said, alert to his tone. "You don't know how difficult it's been for Gustav. Such accusations. Lies."

"All of them?" Alex said, looking at Mutter.

Mutter said nothing, then turned to Erich. "Come."

Alex started to follow.

"No. You stay here."

"Do you mind if I sit on your furniture?"

"Alex," Elsbeth said, disapproving. "You mustn't talk that way."

Mutter left, taking Erich to a back room.

"Sit. I'll have Greta bring some tea," Elsbeth said.

"No, don't bother."

"It's been a difficult time for Gustav," she said, her voice apologetic. "You know, these things he did, all legal — he was *asked* to do them — and then after they try to make him a criminal. Gustav a criminal, imagine. Of course he was exonerated, but the experience, so unpleasant."

"What things did he do?"

"Medical things. All legal," she said again, clinging to it. "But of course difficult to explain after."

"Yes."

"We were in the American sector then. For the denazification hearing. And you know the lawyers, the translators were all Jews. Who else knows German there? People from here. Jews who left. That's why he said that to you. He thinks they came back for revenge. To make trouble for him. So when you come here —"

"With your brother."

"Yes, well, he sees only the other thing. He's suspicious. After all that happened." She paused. "He's a good man. A wonderful father. You should know that. And you know, some of them did make trouble. Jews are like that." She caught herself. "Not you —"

"Just all the others."

"I didn't say all. Excuse me, but you don't know what it's been like here. Oh, let's not talk about these things. I'm so surprised to see you. And Erich. From the dead. I never thought — Where are you living? Are your parents — ?"

He shook his head. "Dead. Both."

She sighed. "That whole generation. Gone now. I think of my father all the time."

Alex stared at her, at a loss. As if the deaths were remotely comparable, a quiet passing, not murder.

"You know he's in the Französischer Friedhof now? At first he was buried on the farm, of course, as he wanted, but when the Communists gave it away in the land reform, well, they call it reform, not theft, which is what it was. Anyway, Irene had him moved. She knew someone who could arrange that. So now he's in Berlin. But I don't like to go to the Russian sector, so I don't visit the grave the way I should. Funny, isn't it, his ending up in Berlin. He never really liked it here."

"But don't you go to the Russian sector to see Irene?"

"I don't like to," she said, suddenly prim. "Russians. Those first few weeks, after the war. You've heard the stories? I'm afraid, even now. Just to see them. So she comes here. Ah, Greta, thank you." A tray with teapot and cups was put before them. "And honey cake, yes?" She put a slice on a plate and handed it to him. "Such a treat, since the blockade, even a little sugar. POM they send, dried potatoes, not even like real food. Of course, Irene, it's different for her," she said, switching back, confiding. "You know she goes with them, the Russians. At first I thought for her work — they own the studios now. But Gustav says no, someone high up. A protector. What kind of protection? People who steal your land. Of course, Kurt Engel was a Communist too, but that's different."

"How?"

"He was German." She stopped for a minute, some vague, disturbing thought, then looked at him. "It's like a miracle to see you again. But to come back — after everything. How was it in America? You didn't like it? Everyone dreams of going there now."

"They offered me a position here."

"A position?"

"A publisher. A stipend. And — Berlin."

"Oh, father always said there was never a Berliner like you. How you liked it." She looked up. "But you know that's all gone. How do you bring that back? Bring the people back? So many in the raids. Night after night —" Her voice trailed off.

"I'm sorry about the boys."

"Rolf would have been twelve now. Tall, I think, like Gustav. The same stubbornness too." She smiled to herself, then looked up. "He says I shouldn't think about them. That it will make me sick, living in the past. Where else can I live? That's where they are. Not here. How can I leave them?" Her eyes had begun to shine, moist and pleading. "I don't care if it makes me sick." She lowered her voice. "I don't care if I die. Maybe I'll see them again then. It's possible, no? We don't know —"

"What's possible?" Gustav said, coming in.

Elsbeth looked up, startled, somehow caught out. A scene they'd had before.

"To visit her father's grave," Alex said. "Now that he's in Berlin. The Französischer Friedhof, yes?" he said to Elsbeth, who nodded quickly, grateful.

"Such morbid thoughts," Gustav said, looking at her, really asking something else.

"No, I was fond of Fritz. I'd like to pay my respects."

Gustav had nothing to say to this, just another stern look at Elsbeth, and Alex saw, in one awful second, that all the bullying, the righteous will that used to exorcise itself in rallies now had nowhere to go and had become domestic, Elsbeth's grief a sign of weakness, something to be overcome.

Erich sat down next to Elsbeth. "Cake. My God, I haven't seen cake —"

"So?" Elsbeth said, fussing over Erich, touching him. "And what does Gustav say? You're all right?"

"I'm not dying yet," Erich said, a forced casualness. "So it's better than I expected. Can I have some —"

"Come with me," Gustav said to Alex.

They went into Gustav's consulting office, a desk and a console dispensary, health posters on the walls, food groups and the circulatory system.

"He's not dying yet. But he will be. Unless he can get treatment."

"For what?"

"A guess only? I need to see X-rays to be sure. We don't have such equipment here." He looked around the spare office. "I can listen with this," he said, touching a stethoscope, "but I can't take X-rays, so I can't say for sure. Maybe simple pneumonia — which is never simple, of course. Or cancer. It's possible. But more likely, tuberculosis. A feeling only, but tuberculosis takes its time, and he hasn't been well for months."

He paused, hesitant. "He is also maybe a little erratic in his mind, I think. Maybe just the fever, maybe — It was common with soldiers. Especially on the eastern front. But that — that's something you heal yourself. A question of time. The lungs are the problem now. So."

"But it's not radiation poisoning."

"Radiation poisoning?" Gustav said, surprised. "Why would you think such a thing? Where would he be exposed to radiation? Do you think the Soviets are exploding bombs? That would be news."

"What about the lesions on his legs?"

"Rat bites," he said, matter of fact. "He said they were forced to work in wet conditions. It's easy to infect a puncture in the skin."

"The wet conditions were pitchblende waste. Uranium. They'd be radioactive."

Gustav looked up. "You're sure about this? Where? You should go to the authorities with such information."

"Yes, but first let's get him well. If it is radiation —"

Gustav shook his head. "It doesn't work that way. Everything depends on the exposure — how much, how far away you are. A bomb, of course, death. But other exposures, a matter of weeks, no more. A big exposure, you vomit the first week, less than that the second week, and so on, but almost never more than four. He's been sick longer than that. So poisoning, no." He stopped. "Of course, a continued exposure, even a low dose, can lead to cancer. Maybe the case here, I can't say."

"What would that mean?"

"Lung cancer? There is no cure for lung cancer."

"It's the lungs?"

Gustav nodded. "That's why I think tuberculosis. He hasn't been coughing blood. Yet. Otherwise, the signs are there. But I need —"

"An X-ray, I know. So where can we get one?"

"A hospital. But without papers? An escaped prisoner? We are obliged to hand such a person over."

Alex started to say something, then stopped, pressing the edge of the desk to stay calm. The only doctor they could see.

"And if it is TB? What do we do?"

"Do? Well, in the old days, a sanitarium. Lots of eggs and mountain air. Like Thomas Mann." A nod to Alex, as if this were a writer's joke. "Now streptomycin. If you could get it. It's effective. They've only been making it since '44 but the results with tuberculosis are good."

"Can you get some? At the hospital?"

"In Berlin? My friend, even penicillin is difficult. We keep asking for more. Streptomycin?"

"So where — ?"

"The Americans would have it. Their hospital, down in Dahlem. But that's only for the military. If you really want to do this, start this treatment, you have to get him to the West."

"The West?"

"Herr Meier, the Russians think *aspirin* is a miracle drug. There is nothing over there. The American hospital won't treat civilians. You have to take him west. The hospitals there —"

"Now? Through the blockade."

"Yes, thanks to your new friends." He raised his eyebrows. "Erich told me, you're a guest of the Soviets. And what will they think, your hosts, of you helping a fugitive?"

Alex looked at him. "Who would tell them? And implicate himself?"

Mutter said nothing, turning this over.

"And meanwhile he's sick. He's family."

"Not yours."

"No, yours."

"Let me say again. I can't help him and neither will the Soviets. You need to get him west." He looked over, almost pleased. "An interesting dilemma for you."

"There must be something you could give him. He's shivering. Even I can hear it when he talks, all the congestion, maybe it's pleurisy, pneumonia, I don't know. You're the doctor." He stopped. "He won't have to wait for TB to get him if he doesn't get through this."

"You understand, it's illegal, what you're asking."

"You're a doctor."

"Now you sound like the Americans. A doctor should answer to a higher authority. What authority, an oath? The conscience? Then everything breaks down."

"Everything has," Alex said quietly.

Mutter looked up. "All great humanitarians, the Americans. When it's someone else on trial. What would they have done, do you think?"

"I didn't come here to put anyone on trial. I just want medicine for Erich. He's sick. You're a doctor."

Mutter turned away, hesitating, then went over to the dispensary bureau. "Wait a minute," he said, rummaging through the drawer. He came back with a tube and a handful of vials and small bottles. "For the legs," he said, handing Alex the tube of salve. "Once a day only. These twice, once before food, yes? It's not much, but it should help. Believe it or not, rest and liquids are even more important. The old remedies. Of course, this does nothing for whatever's really wrong. Working in mines — the dust, think of the damage. The conditions were harsh?"

Alex nodded.

"Well, I don't put anything past the Russians."

"No."

He glanced up, catching Alex's expression. "Or the Germans? Is that what you were going to say? You don't come to judge, but you do. Such terrible people. So now we're all guilty. Do you include yourself?"

"You don't have to explain anything to me."

"No? Why, because you already know? Someone not even here? How can I tell you what it was like? What we had to do? I wouldn't know where to start."

"Start with my parents. They were — what? Racial impurities? Now they're nothing. Smoke. Start with them."

"And you blame me for that?"

"Who do you blame? I'd like to know. Or do you think it happened all by itself?"

For a minute neither said anything, then

Alex held up one of the bottles.

"Thank you for this. I won't say where we got it."

Mutter half turned, waving his hand in dismissal, no longer meeting Alex's eyes. "He needs antibiotics," he said quietly. "Streptomycin. Get him to the West."

Alex fed him soup and more tea and put him to bed, under the covers.

"But it's your —"

"I'll take the couch. We can switch when you're better." He held Erich's head up, spooning him medicine. "Gustav said this would bring the fever down."

When Erich lay back his face became Fritz's, the same tall forehead and high cheeks, so that for a second Alex felt he was nursing the old man, some odd transference. Not blustering for once, eyes half closed, a child's trust. Alex lifted the edge of the sheet and started spreading the salve on Erich's leg. "Gustav said these were rat bites. Yes?"

"In the barracks. At night. They waited for you to go to sleep." He reached over to Alex's arm. "I won't go back there."

"No."

"But if they come?"

"They won't. Go to sleep. I'm just outside."

But what if they did? Alex walked through the apartment. A good view of the street from the windows. An armoire, big enough to hide in, if this were a French farce. The back door out the kitchen led to service stairs, a utility closet on the next landing, not locked, something Erich could reach in seconds. Alex looked up — presumably the stairs went all the way to the roof. But why would anyone come, unless they'd been told, in which case they'd search everywhere and there'd be no real escape. The only way to be safe was to be non-existent, unseen, unheard. Alex scoured the apartment for listening bugs — lightbulb sockets, behind the watercolor of a Wilhelmine street scene, the telephone mouthpiece. Nothing. A trusted guest of the Soviet Military Administration.

Erich was asleep when Alex left for the reception at Aufbau Verlag. A table with coffee and cakes had been set out in the boardroom, the staff crowded around it, curious and deferential. The art director showed him mock-ups of the jackets for his books. There was a polite joke about the author's photo, now a good ten years old. Aaron Stein, after a public toast, introduced him to smaller groups, department by department, then led him into his office.

"I know, I should give them up," he said, offering Alex a cigarette. "Helga says they'll kill me. Well, something will." A cultured, almost elegant voice that reminded Alex of his mother. Someone who'd been to school, who could play the piano.

"The new editions look wonderful. Thank you."

"It's we who should thank you. Our writers are so important to us now. To know there is another Germany, of culture, not just Nazis. If that's our only history, we'll die of shame. We are more than that."

Alex nodded another thank-you, waiting, watching Aaron fidget with his cigarette, working up to something.

"Alex — you don't mind I call you Alex? I wanted to have a word. Something — delicate."

Alex raised his eyebrows.

"Martin tells me — you know he's a great admirer of your work? He tells me you had — a reservation, perhaps. About the *Festschrift*. For Stalin."

"No, I said I'd do it."

"Yes," Aaron said, uncomfortable. "We appreciate that." He paused. "I don't want you to feel that you are being asked to do something against your will."

"No, I said I would. A Kulturbund project."

"Well, that's just it. I wanted you to know, so there's no misunderstanding, the project did not originate with us. The SED asked. Of course, it was an appropriate idea, we were only too glad to help." He looked up. "You know, it needn't be long. The fact that so many contribute is really the point. For him to know he has our support."

"I understand."

"The Kulturbund — sometimes we find ourselves in an awkward position. To make German culture live again. And also to please the occupation authorities. A question of balance. Anyway, we are so pleased to have you with us."

Alex nodded again.

"So," Aaron said, evidently finished, then looked down at his cigarette, rolling it against the rim of the ashtray. "You know, there are fashions even in politics. Today, something is popular, tomorrow not. Things change. Sometimes even the logic of things. But the logic of the Socialist system, that doesn't change. Nobody ever said it would be easy to make a new society. Think who must be against it. So, sometimes a disappointment, sometimes a compromise. But how else to get there? And think what's at the end. A just society must be worth a few sacrifices, no?"

Alex felt the hairs on the back of his neck. A phrase he'd used himself.

"And you cannot have a just society without a just economic system. That's the logic that never changes for me. The rest —" He waved his hand.

"Can I ask you something then? I heard that you resigned from the secretariat last year."

"And you want to know why, if I'm such a good Communist?" Aaron said, a wry smile forming around the cigarette. "Well, it's a question. Should I say I'm too busy here with my work? That I wanted more time with my family? No, you ask, I'll tell you. A change of fashion maybe, like I said before. I come from the Comintern days when there was an international ideal. All Communists, the same belief. But now the SED answers only to the Russians, to their issues. I understand. Germany lost the war. You have to expect a certain amount of — what? — hardship. Looting, all the terrible things of war. But three, four years later, they're still dismantling factories. Our soldiers are still prisoners. Four years later. This isn't good for Communism, only for

Russia. If it really is good for them, who knows? But it's not good for Germany. Why did I resign? I want the SED to be Socialist *and* German." He stopped. "Well, I'm giving you a speech. You didn't ask for that. Anyway, you think they were sorry to see me go? An old Cominterno who went to the West? Another fashion. If you went to the West you're suspect. Cosmopolitan. Although that's only another word for Jew. Whenever you hear that, you know what's coming —" He stopped again. "A good time, maybe, to mind your own business. Until the fashion changes."

"That's what people thought before."

Aaron looked away. "Yes, I know. The head in the sand." He shifted in his chair. "But this will pass. It's not possible, you know, anti-Semitism in a Socialist state. A contradiction. It's against the logic." He took off his glasses, wiping them with a handkerchief, his face suddenly boyish, pale. "So there's an answer. About the secretariat. Maybe I wasn't practical enough for political work. My wife thinks that." He smiled. "It's true. But it's just as well. There is so much to do here. Can I stop them taking a factory? No. And in the end, what's more important? Today's problem, which goes away, or to bring German literature back to

Germany?"

"But what about the forced labor? I heard that's why you —"

"No, no, no," Aaron said, cutting him off, head up now, glasses back on, alarmed. "Nothing like that. Such nonsense. Berlin, you know, is a great place for rumors. People will say anything. But come," he said, standing up. "I'll walk with you. You're taking a tram? From Hackescher Markt?"

Alex looked up, surprised. Everything abrupt now, rushed. Coats, a word with his secretary, and then they were on the street, walking up to Unter den Linden.

"What is it?" Alex said, stopping.

"Nothing. I —" He stifled a cough. "Please, walk. It's better. Forgive me. You learn to be careful."

"About what?"

"Forgive me," he said again. "You know, you're with us now and I'm so pleased. But not everything is perfect. This matter of the forced labor — it's a great sensitivity."

"So we have to go out here to talk?"

"Yes, maybe a foolishness. But people listen. Herschel — a journalist, a friend — wrote about this and he was arrested. A Kulturbund member. A book coming from us. We can't have that kind of trouble. What I said to you before — it's old news. What

Comrade Stein is always saying. But this — they don't like talk about this. I've been warned."

"But it's not a secret."

Aaron shook his head. "No, that's the hypocrisy. I said not everything is perfect. People know about this. Thousands sent to the mines. How can you keep that a secret? But the Russians pretend it is. They don't want to talk about it. Well, of course, it makes them unpopular. But it also makes the SED unpopular. To go along with this policy, forcing their own people —" He shook his head. "So short-sighted. So I resigned. You ask the reason, that was it. I think the SED should protect Germans from this. I won't lie to you. But I can't talk about it there," he said, cocking his head back toward the office. "I don't want to make trouble. You're disturbed — I can see in your face — but the final logic is still correct. You were right to come. Don't ever doubt that." His voice earnest, a hand on Alex's arm. "You know, with everything else, the Russians try to work with us. Look at the subsidies to Aufbau. A priority for paper. The schools. The theaters. But this — on this one thing, an iron fist. So all the rest of it, all the good efforts — who gives them credit for that when people are being worked like this? Like slaves. So they don't want them to know. The Siberia mentality — people disappear. No one knows where. No one talks. So here too. They don't want any talk. Then it doesn't exist. Just the good news in *Neues Deutschland.* Forgive me," he said, slowing, his voice calmer. "There is good news, you know. Real progress. We mustn't forget that. This is — a problem. And you know, problems can be solved. The underlying logic is still right."

"But the West — you'd think they'd have a field day with this. The propaganda. If they really want to hit the Soviets."

"It's hard to get information. Not so many leave now. And of course the ones who do speak are discredited. So it's rumors." He looked up. "Conversations like this."

"Which we're not having."

"No," Aaron said, a faint smile. "Literary conversation only."

"I didn't mean to pry — about the committee. Thank you for being so frank."

"Frank. Indiscreet, Helga would say." He looked up at the sky. "You know, it's not always like this here. It's just a sensitivity, the mines. When you think — how desperate they must be to risk all this good will, for pitchblende."

"Maybe they don't care."

"No, I don't think it's that," Aaron said, thoughtful. "I hope not. How can we do this without them?"

"Do what?"

"Make a new life for Germany. The Russians are here. What other choice is there? When I was in Mexico I used to think how it would be, when the Nazis were finally gone. When it was our chance. And now it is." He looked over at Alex. "So you work with what you have. Well, I'm talking too much. I should get back to the office. You can find your way?"

"Were you ever tempted to stay? In Mexico?"

"In Mexico? My God, no. I couldn't wait to get back to —" He stopped, laughing at himself. "Civilization." He looked around at the ruins. "Well, it doesn't seem so now, does it? But you know, we are a civilized people." He paused. "Don't worry, you've done the right thing. We'll clean all this up. You'll help. And then we'll see what we can be."

It was already dark, Unter den Linden like a long open field swept every once in a while by the headlights of military transports, high off the ground, and the fainter beams of a few cars. In the quiet he could hear the airlift planes overhead. How to get Erich out? Train, car — the usual exits were closed. Getting to the frontier now would mean traveling across the Soviet zone, a desperate risk for a POW on the run. He could walk to a Western sector in Berlin, but that was no guarantee — the Soviets picked up people wherever they felt like it, snatched them right off the streets. He thought of Lützowplatz, the squeal of tires. And who would hide him? Gustav, with one hand already on the phone, doing the right thing? Willy might have done Alex the favor of getting him into the American hospital, but Willy was dead. Any approach now to BOB would put both of them at risk. And Erich would still be in Berlin. He looked up. The only way out was by plane, and for that he'd need more than a favor.

It took him a few seconds to realize the sidewalk was being lit up by a car behind him. Not speeding, not passing, trailing at his pace. Instinctively he glanced away from the road. The buildings were set back from the sidewalk here, not flush as they'd been at Lützowplatz. Any grab would involve leaping the curb, pinning him in with the car. A showy maneuver, drawing attention. If that mattered. The bridge soon, the blackened city palace beyond, the light still steady behind him. His throat felt dry, the saliva drained away. Then the light moved up, alongside.

"Alex."

Impossible to pretend he hadn't heard, impossible to run. He turned to the car, the rolled-down window. Markus.

"Come, I'll give you a lift."

"I don't want to take you out of your way," Alex said, leaning toward the window.

"Not at all. A pleasure. Get in." Not quite an order, the voice genial.

The car was warm, a heater blasting from under the dashboard.

"A cold night for a walk," Markus said. "I thought it was you. The other man, that was Stein?"

"Yes, there was a reception at Aufbau. To meet the staff. A nice occasion."

"And then he came out to walk with you."

"Just for some air. He had to get something, I think. I don't know what."

"Cigarettes, perhaps. A great smoker."

"Yes." Not saying anything more, waiting.

"A serious conversation. What were you talking about? Do you mind if I ask?"

"My books. They're bringing out new editions. They showed me the jackets earlier."

"You found them attractive?"

"Yes, very."

"So you're pleased with Aufbau? Good. He's very respected, I think, Stein. For his literary opinions. What else did you talk about?"

Pressing. Or testing? What if the walls did have ears?

"Books, mostly. A *Festschrift* they're putting together. For Stalin's birthday."

"Ah yes? That will please him, I think. A loyal gesture. You're contributing?"

"Yes, I was pleased to be asked. Being new here."

"So, a change of heart since '39? No more objections to the non-aggression pact? All is forgiven?"

"Anyone can make a mistake. He made it right in the end. That's all that matters now."

"This is not — do you mind my saying? — the version of history you should offer in the *Festschrift.*"

Alex looked over. As close as Markus could come to making a joke. He was smiling, pleased with himself.

"No. Anyway, it's a long time ago now." A new thought. "How do you know I objected to the pact? You were, what, fourteen, fifteen?"

"It's in your file."

"I have a file?"

"Everybody has a file. Some, more than one."

"Really. And what's in mine?"

"Good things. Don't worry."

"Just curious. Why would anybody be interested?"

"You were invited to be a guest of the SMA. Naturally such invitations are only extended to persons who are — reliable."

"Well, then I must have passed."

"Oh yes. Your statement to the Fascist committee was really admirable." Said warmly, without his usual innuendo. "And you have made a good impression here."

"Oh," Alex said, not expecting this.

"Yes, it's very pleasing. Not just to me personally — you know, to see an old friend so well received. But it makes it easier."

"Makes what easier?"

"People are comfortable with you. They'll talk to you."

For a minute, Alex said nothing, letting this sink in.

"Which people?" he said finally.

"For instance, Comrade Stein. He is sometimes outspoken, sometimes not. What does he say to you? It would be interesting to me. To know that."

"For his file?"

Markus shrugged, something irrelevant.

Alex sat looking out, then turned in his seat. "Are you asking me to be an informer?" Hearing himself, struck finally by the sheer implausibility of the moment, a laugh somewhere in the pit of his stomach, trying to rise then curling in on itself, one knot tightening into another.

"Informer," Markus said, dismissing the word. "I am asking you to help me in my work. To keep Germany safe."

"Germany."

"Yes, I know, we are not yet a state. But we will be. The West is already making theirs. A new currency. Soon, a country. Armed. Against us. So how do we defend ourselves? How do we protect the revolution?"

"By snitching on Aaron Stein?"

Markus looked over. "More jokes. It was a worry to me at first, all this joking. Then I saw that it was useful. It puts people at ease with you. No, not 'snitching.' If Comrade Stein is working for the Party what does he have to fear if we know what he says?"

"And if he's not?"

"Then it's important for us to know. To help him correct his mistakes. As you say, we all make mistakes. He will be grateful for this, I think."

"Markus, I'm not —" The words sticking

somewhere in the back of his mouth. "No one asked me to do anything like this. When they invited me."

"No, I'm asking you. When I saw you, at the Kulturbund, I thought, yes, someone in an excellent position to hear. And with a debt. A state that took you in, that treats you as —"

"Are you saying I have to do this if I want to stay here?"

"It's not a question of bookkeeping, this for that. But think how pleased the Party will be, knowing how you help them." He paused. "And, you know, very useful for me. To use this old association, the trust we have for each other. It's just a matter of time before someone else suggests this. I'm not the only one to see your position, how convenient it can be. And eventually the Party agrees and you will do it anyway and then someone else gets the credit. But to do this work now, at my suggestion, it would be a great personal favor to me. I know, it's only the younger brother, but we have a history. A friendship."

"I'm not —"

"Think about this. Think of all the advantages. Before you decide. There are many who do this."

"Who tell you what Aaron Stein says to them?"

"Stein, others. An informal arrangement. No desk at K-5," he said lightly, another joke. "A talk, from time to time. Of course, confidential. Comrade Stein will never know. No one will." He looked over again. "It will be our secret."

Alex felt his stomach clench, some rush of acid.

"This is what I ran away from. The FBI watching —"

"Is it? I don't think so. I think you were running away from prison. For your admirable Socialist principles. Now you have — the opposite. A good life. It's a small price, to help those who helped you. Especially when they need this help. To protect themselves." He took out a business card. "Think a little. How easy this will be. And how useful. Call here. We'll meet for coffee. Another advantage. A friend from the old days, what could be more natural? A friendly visit, coffee. What could be more natural?"

"You're so sure I'd be good at this?"

"You don't have to be good. Just tell me what you hear. I'll do the rest."

They had left Alexanderplatz and were heading up Greifswalder Strasse. "Turn up here," Alex said.

"I know where you live," Markus said, smug.

But not who's living there with me.

"Do you have someone telling you what *I* say?"

"Alex, so suspicious," Markus said.

"You know, something I don't understand. You ask me to do this and all the time I've been feeling — all the questions —"

"I wanted to be sure of you."

"And now you are."

"They say in the service you should never be sure of anybody." He turned, a small smile. "Yes, I'm sure. At first, just a worry only. Another service rule — there are no coincidences. So you go to Lützowplatz. A coincidence? The service rule says no. But life — it's a different thing. We have someone now for questioning."

"You found him?" Alex said, his stomach tightening again.

"I think so. Someone in the service, so maybe the first rule is right. I've been suspicious of him for some time. So now we'll see."

Answering questions. Or just screaming in pain. Claiming to be innocent. Feeding on each other.

"I can get out at the corner here," Alex said, suddenly aware of the street. What if

Erich was up, a light on? One small detail, a light, and everything would unravel.

"It's no trouble," Markus said, turning into Rykestrasse.

Had he told Erich to keep the light off? He couldn't remember. The utility closet on the stairs, the escape route, the knock signals, but maybe not the light. One slip. The world he lived in now.

The car stopped in front of the building. Alex looked up, counting floors. No light. He breathed out, then realized Markus was talking.

"How things turn out," he was saying, the end of a thought. "When I was young, you were — all of you, all of Kurt's friends — like gods to me. I wanted to be with you, do what you were doing. And now look. Here we are, working together. It's such a pleasure for me. Well, so think." A farewell touch of his fingers to his temple. "You can call me. You have a telephone, I think?"

Alex nodded.

"You see, only the best for you. One more thing? When you were talking to Comrade Stein, it was about books only? Nothing else?"

A trap if Markus already knew, listening through walls.

"No, I asked him why he had resigned

from the secretariat last year."

"Ah," Markus said, pleased, another test passed. "And what did he say?"

"Nationalist feelings. He thinks the SED should be more protective — of German interests."

"Yes, I have heard this."

"But that's all," Alex said, looking at him. "He's a loyal Communist."

"That is your assessment?"

"Yes. Completely loyal. I'm sure of it."

"The first rule of the service?" Markus said. "Don't be sure of anybody." Teasing, almost waggish. "Well, perhaps you're right. We'll see. Good night. It's such a pleasure for me, all this. Who could have predicted it?"

Alex watched the car pull away. We'll see. Inside he stopped at the foot of the stairs, suddenly unable to move, as if his knees had given out, and leaned against the wall. Now what? Maybe he could get out before he had to do anything. But what if he never got out? Writing odes to Stalin and looking and listening, betraying everybody. What both sides wanted. Because of course in the end he'd have to do it. Think about it, Markus had said. But who said no to such a request? From a grateful Party. A refusal would make him suspect, someone to watch, the last thing he could afford. Make yourself valuable to them.

His breath was coming faster, running in place. What if Campbell never got him back, kept him dangling here, waiting to drop into Markus's net? One slip. Who got out of Berlin now anyway, all blockaded up, his Dutch passport something the Soviets could flick aside, like a gnat. Their property now, with his privileged telephone. Making reports for Markus's files. Another line crossed, maybe all of them just lines after that first one, a raised gun in his hand. No witnesses. Except there had been. Had Markus dug the old lady up? Someone to tighten the noose around his hapless colleague's neck. Markus, who now believed in coincidences. And being sure of someone.

He turned his head toward the stairs. Voices. Only one flight up, his flat, unless they were loud enough to carry down another floor. He started up, instinctively on tiptoe. Had Erich let someone in? But there was no light under the door. Voices again, rising, then falling. No, not voices, one voice, talking into a void. At the door, he listened. Nothing, then the voice again. Erich's. A few words, a falling off, then a sound of distress, almost a whimper, no words, as if someone had twisted his arm, caused some sudden pain. Alex put his hand on the doorknob, beginning to turn it quietly, surprise whoever it was, but it stuck, still locked. No one then, just Erich, but loud enough to be heard by some curious neighbor, loud enough to give himself away.

Alex unlocked the door and switched on the light. Another sound, muffled, talking to himself in the dark. Alex went into the bedroom and sat, trying to wake him gently. A startled cry, eyes still closed, afraid, wherever he was.

"*Shh.* Erich. It's all right." Hand clammy, some night sweat on his forehead. "It's a dream."

Eyes open now, staring at Alex but not seeing him, then filling with tears.

"I didn't know. What they would do to me."

"*Shh.* It's all right." Quietly, almost a whisper.

"But I couldn't. At first I couldn't."

"Couldn't what?"

"Shoot. Not after the women. Nobody ran. Why didn't they run? That would have been — like a hunt. Not like this. Lined up, then in the pit. Then another group. And no one runs."

"In the pit? In the mines?" Alex said, trying to make sense of it.

"No," Erich said, his eyes focusing now, grabbing Alex's sleeve. "Not in the mines. Before. We made them dig the pit and then we shot them. It's a dirty business, Schultz said. But we had to do it. They gave us vodka before, for our nerves. You know, when you see them fall in like that, over and over, it does things to you. So we tried to help each other —"

"Who did?" Alex said, sitting up, motionless.

"Us. The soldiers. They said somebody had to do it, so we did it. And then I didn't have the stomach for it, but I thought what will they do to me? Some punishment. So I had to keep going."

"Shooting," Alex said.

Erich nodded. "Until it's done. The whole village."

"And then what?"

"Then we covered the pit. Not us, other soldiers. The shooters were excused from that. And you know what Schultz said? A good day's work. They don't give medals for this, but —" He looked up at Alex. "He said we should be proud."

Alex froze, hearing the thuds of the bodies falling in. He moved his hand away. What had happened to everybody?

"Now I dream about it sometimes," Erich

243

said. "The way they looked at us. Before we shot them."

Alex looked over, dismayed. The man he was risking everything to help. Fritz's son.

Erich turned his head on the pillow, somewhere else again, back in his waking dream.

"The children stayed with the mothers. It was easier. Sometimes hiding the face in the skirt, so those we didn't have to see. And once, after they fell in, we saw one of them crawling — we had missed him some- how — so Schultz went over to the edge and did it himself. Two shots, to make sure." His voice had begun to drift. "And you know that night we had more vodka and what do you think comes? A letter. From Elsbeth. How she knew I must be suffering in the cold, it was always cold in Russia, but everyone in Germany was so grateful, how brave we were. And I thought, how can I tell her? What we were doing. Dirty busi- ness, he said. But it was worse than that, wasn't it? I couldn't tell her. Anybody. Schultz said we couldn't tell." He turned back, facing Alex. "Anybody. You won't report it? That I told you this?"

"No."

"We couldn't tell the Russians. In the camp. They would have killed us. Revenge.

It was bad enough, just being there. So we didn't tell. But you, it's different. An American." He stopped, his face wrinkling in confusion. "I thought you were there."

"I was."

"They don't know about such things there. You think you can't do it. Then someone tells you to do it and you do it."

Alex looked away, hearing Willy's voice, his own panicked breathing.

"To help each other. If one stops, what does that say to the others? So you do it. And then it's everybody shooting, not just you, you know?"

Alex looked at him, saying nothing. How old was he now? Twentysomething. Line after line, everybody shooting so nobody was shooting. He turned away.

"Try to get some sleep."

"A few minutes. Sometimes when I sleep —" He clutched Alex's sleeve more tightly. "So what should I have done? Somebody had to do it. They said so."

Alex stood up. "Go to sleep. I'll be here."

"Yes, from America," Erich said, still a puzzle piece to him, but he did finally close his eyes, his shallow breathing slowing, getting easier. Alex stood for a few minutes, watching him drift off, Fritz again, a boy's smoothness spreading over his features.

He was still asleep when Irene got there.

"What did Gustav say?" she said, wiping his brow, barely touching it, not wanting to wake him.

"He needs medicine he can't get here. He needs to get to the West."

"The West? How? The border's —"

"I know."

"Maybe Sasha will help."

"He can't. You know that."

"But it's only one man. A boy. And you know Sasha's —" She stopped, an awkward pause. "He's very fond of me."

"He's not going to help you."

"But if he dies here — It's that serious? He might die?"

Alex nodded.

"Then what choice? He stays here, he dies. He goes back to Russia, another death sentence. What choice?"

"None. We have to get him out. You realize, he can't come back. It's a one-way trip."

She put her hand back on Erich's forehead, her face soft, then looked at Alex. "People come back."

"Not always. Not this time."

"What do you mean? Tell me."

He started back to the other room, waiting for her to follow, then closed the door quietly.

"The only way out is by plane. That would mean military authorization. American. And somebody to take care of him on the other end. So they'd have to want to do this for him. Even break a few rules."

"And why would they do that? For a German." She looked up. "You mean they'd do it for you. Some favor. You know someone like that? Who would do this for you?"

"For me?" He shook his head. "I'm practically a fugitive. In contempt of Congress."

"What does that mean?"

"Nobody in the American zone is going to do anything for me." Hearing himself, the smoothness of it, not even a hesitation. "Unless I have something to trade, enough to pay Erich's fare."

"What are you thinking?" she said, looking at him closely. "You have some idea?"

"I met a man at the party from the radio. Their radio — RIAS. If Erich did an interview with them, I think Ferber would have enough clout to get him out."

"An interview about what?"

"He hasn't been in a POW camp. A slave labor detachment. Down in the Erzgebirge."

"Where Sasha goes," she said quietly. "Do you think he knew? That Erich was there?"

Alex shook his head. "Erich was just a number. Not even a name. How would he have known? He wasn't supervising work parties. Not Maltsev's assistant. They're not names to him." He paused. "Just slaves."

"If I thought that," Irene said, not picking up on this. "That he knew all along — And now? Does he know now? The men who escaped —"

"They're probably just numbers too." He looked over. "It would be something to find out."

"When I spy on him," she said, a wry shrug, then looked up. "And Erich would talk about that on the radio? The mines? That's the idea?"

"A firsthand report about what it's really like there. From a former war hero."

"War hero."

"If he's alive, he's a hero."

She looked at him. "It's propaganda."

He nodded. "But in this case, also the truth. He almost died there. He might die here, if we don't get him out. I think they'd want the interview — eyewitness, not rumors."

"And get Erich on a plane?"

"That would be the deal. But you understand what it would mean. Right now, he's a POW on the run. If he does this, he becomes an enemy of the state."

For a minute she said nothing, then breathed out, a kind of sigh.

"An enemy of the state. What state?"

"Sasha's state," Alex said.

She raised her eyes, holding his for a second. "But he would have his life."

"Yes."

"The Americans want to put you in prison, but you arrange propaganda for them," she said, a question.

"They're Germans in the mines."

"And if they find out here you arranged this? You'd be an enemy of the state too."

"Probably."

"Then you'd go to prison here."

"Do you have another idea? We can't just walk away from this."

"From Erich? No. He's all that's left now, from that life." She lifted her head. "And you'd do this? Hiding him, it's one thing, but —"

"It's a lot easier to do it if you don't think about it. What it could mean."

She was quiet for a second, then looked away. "Yes. That's often how it is, isn't it?" She moved toward the bedroom. "Is it good to sleep so long, do you think?"

They woke him to give him the scheduled medicine, but even after more tea all he wanted to do was sleep.

"Alex has an idea. To get you to the West. Would you like that?" Irene said.

"You'll come too."

"*Ouf,* how could I do that? DEFA doesn't move for me. But I'll come visit. They have medicine there. Things you need."

"I can't stay here," Erich said, not really a reply, some conversation he was having in his head. "The ones they catch, they put them in the worst mines. That's what happens. They put you back, but worse."

"Nobody's going to catch you," Alex said. "You warm enough?" He closed the bedroom curtains. "If you need light, stay in here. They took the blackout curtains down in the other room, so any light shows. Remember what I said about the stairs if there's any trouble?"

Erich nodded. "Where are you going?"

Alex turned to Irene. "Where are we going?"

"The Möwe. Sasha said he'd meet me there. You don't know it," she said to Erich. "It's just a place people go to. Sleep now and I'll be back tomorrow."

He nodded, closing his eyes. "You know what Elsbeth said? Her flat is too small."

"It's not her. It's him."

"My own sister. Blood."

"Never mind, it's better here. Alex is like family."

Erich smiled, eyes still closed. "Ha! What would papa say? An American in the family. A spy."

The hairs on Alex's arms moved suddenly, as if some electric pulse were running along his skin. "Yes? Why a spy?"

"All Americans are spies. That's what they told us. Don't talk to them. If you see one in the village, report it. They're all spies. Imagine how stupid — to think we could recognize them. How? Wearing uniforms? In Aue?" His voice drifted off.

"Yes, stupid," Alex said, turning off the bedside lamp. "I'll be back. Remember, no lights in the other room."

"So careful. So maybe Erich's right," Irene said, teasing, then looked at her watch. "Anyway, there should be a power cut soon. They like to turn it off during dinner, so you can't see how bad the food is." A Berlin joke, tart, a shrug of the shoulders.

On the stairs the lights did go out, a quick flicker, then darkness, so that after they felt their way to the courtyard entrance they almost collided with a woman trying to get a flashlight to work.

"Oh, Mister Meier," she said. "You're in the building too? I didn't realize." Then, backing up, "Roberta Kleinbard. We met at the Kulturbund."

"Yes, I remember. From New York. The architect."

"Well, Herb's the architect. But I help with the drawings."

"You remember Frau Gerhardt?" Alex said, not sure if they had met. Both nodded.

"We're across the courtyard," Roberta said. "Did you just move in?"

"Yes, just."

"So they're putting all the Americans in one place, I guess. Tom Lawson's in the back courtyard. He was the first. Here we go," she said as the flashlight finally went on. "Follow me."

They trailed the light, single file, out the entrance to the street.

"Thank God I bought extra batteries. Hard to get now," Roberta was saying, but Alex barely heard her, his mind still back in the courtyard. All the Americans. Is that how Roberta saw him? What Erich thought too. He felt he had just seen himself in a mirror, rubbing bathroom steam away, seen finally what all the others saw, Markus and Martin and Erich making spy jokes. Not a

German anymore, someone who hadn't been here, couldn't know what it was now to be German. Exile was irreversible, where he lived.

"You can still buy them in the British sector," Roberta said. "But who knows for how long? They're going to end the dual currency any day now, that's what people say, and then what? Who has West marks unless you work over there?"

"Can we drop you somewhere?" Irene said, pointing to the waiting car, sent by Sasha from Karlshorst.

"Oh," Roberta said, taking it in, impressed, then glancing at Alex. "If you're going by the Kulturbund. But I can —"

"No, no, it's on the way. Please."

They got in, Irene giving the driver instructions. Roberta, who had assumed the car was Alex's, now looked puzzled, a little wary.

"Another party?" Alex said.

"No, just dinner. With Henselmann. You know he's in charge of the Friedrichshain project. New buildings all the way to Frankfurter Tor. Herb's designing two."

"Frankfurter Tor," Irene said. "That's miles."

"A showcase street," Roberta said, nodding. "Herb said they're going to call it

Stalinallee."

"What, Grosse Frankfurter Strasse?" Alex said, remembering his drive into the city, the endless blocks of piled rubble. "But it's always been —"

"Well, I know. But really, what difference does it make? And it's the kind of gesture that might get the funding started. You know, once you start a construction project, it's hard to stop it. But getting started — And Herb's designs are ready to go. He was at the Bauhaus, you know. Years ago. So this is like a dream for him. Come for a drink sometime and see. So convenient, being just across the courtyard. Do you face the street?"

"Yes."

"They must think a lot of you," Roberta said.

"No, it's probably what was available, that's all."

Roberta looked at him, about to correct this, then decided to say nothing. Instead she turned to Irene.

"Can I ask what you do?"

"I'm at DEFA."

"Oh, an actress," Roberta said, excited, looking around, as if the answer explained the car.

"No, I work on the production staff."

"Still. Just to be there. I was always crazy about movies, from a kid on. Of course, here it's harder. But my German's getting better. My son laughs at me now. It's so easy for them at that age."

"You've been here a long time?"

"No, just long enough to get homesick once in a while. For friends, you know. My sister was coming to visit, but with this going on," she said, jerking her head up to the airlift, "it's impossible. But soon. I mean how long can they keep it up? Their coal allowance is lower than ours now, and that won't get anyone through a really cold one." She had been looking toward the front seat, still trying to work out the car. "Your driver. He's a soldier? It's an official car?"

"A friend lends it to me. It's so hard to get around at night. Almost as bad as during the blackout." Which still didn't explain why he lent it.

"Yes, thank you for the lift," Roberta said, looking at her, but reluctant to push it further. "The lap of luxury. Herb'll be jealous. Here we are. Just at the corner. I must say, I don't know what we'd do without the Kulturbund. Meals off ration." She caught herself. "And of course the people — everyone is so interesting. There's a real seriousness about the arts here. Not like —"

Alex, on the street now, offered his hand to help her out.

"Thank you again," she said to Irene. "And your friend." She got out, her hand still on Alex's. "Thanks. Alex — can I call you Alex? — I wanted to ask you —" She lowered her head, her voice almost conspiratorial. "I mean we don't know each other really, but to tell you the truth, I don't know who else to ask."

Alex looked at her, waiting.

"I just wondered if it was us, people who'd come from the States. For some reason."

"What?"

"Have they asked you for your Party documents? They said they were calling them in for review and I was just wondering why. You know, whether it was everybody or just Herb —"

"Party documents?"

"Membership books, you know."

"But I'm not a member. Not yet."

"Really? I thought — well, never mind. It's probably just some office thing. They love all that official paper, all the stamps. I just wondered is all." Her voice trying to be light, but anxious, her eyes troubled. She raised her head. "You're going to join, aren't you?"

"Yes," he said, remembering Dieter.

"I mean, it makes everything so much easier here. And of course it's — the Party. It's why we're here, isn't it? Anyway, come for a drink and see Herb's drawings. It's really wonderful, what Berlin is going to look like."

■ ■ ■ ■

4
MARIENSTRASSE

■ ■ ■ ■

"Don't worry, I'm worth the wait," Irene said, offering her cheek to be kissed. "I brought Alex. You don't mind. He wanted to see the Möwe. Look, there's Brecht."

Across the room, Brecht took out his cigar stub and half waved it.

"The more the merrier," Sasha said. "You remember Ivan?" The other Russian stood and bowed his head, military polite. "A real Ivan," Sasha said to Alex. "Not *an* Ivan. His name. Sit, sit. He came with me to celebrate."

"Oh yes?" Irene said, sitting down. "What are you celebrating?" She glanced at the vodka bottle, half gone.

"Tell her," Ivan said. "He's so modest. She'll be proud of you."

"I'm already proud," Irene said. "So now?"

"A big promotion," Ivan said. "Moscow!"

He raised his glass, a toast they'd made before.

"Moscow?" Irene said, paling a little.

"In the director's office." Ivan slapped Sasha on the back. "Now what do you think of him?"

"When?" Irene said to Sasha. "You never said."

"I didn't know."

"It's all the good work," Ivan said, clinking glasses with him. "Come, have a drink," he said to Alex. He raised his hand to get the waiter. "You need a glass."

"Just beer for me," Alex said to the waiter. "Irene?"

She shook her head. "When?" she asked again.

"I don't know. Soon. Any day. Whenever the new man arrives. It's a question of arranging transport."

"You'll be sorry to go," she said, looking at him.

"Sorry? To go to Moscow?" he said, answering something else, as if he'd already left her. "After Berlin?" He laughed, then stopped, finally aware of her look. "Of course I will miss you."

"Maybe not so much."

"Every day," he said grandly, raising a glass to her.

"You won't be lonely," Ivan said to Irene. "I can see to that."

"No, I won't be lonely," Irene said to Sasha. "It's a surprise, that's all. Moscow. It's a big job?" Her voice tight, eyes troubled, sorting through all the implications.

Sasha nodded.

"So. Your wife will be pleased."

Sasha poured another glass for Ivan, avoiding this.

"And here I thought you and Alex would get to know each other," she said. "Become friends."

"We are friends," Sasha said, smiling. "One night. It's like that in wartime."

"To Moscow," Alex said, raising his beer glass to Sasha.

He drank, feeling the beer work its way down to his stomach, clenching again, his one chance of buying his way home about to disappear. They wouldn't care anymore what people said at the Kulturbund, now that they'd almost had Markovsky, the promise of indiscretions on Irene's pillow. Maltsev's assistant, the best keyhole at Karlshorst, leaving town.

"Don't worry," Sasha said, leaning toward Irene. "You'll be all right at DEFA. The *payoks,* I can arrange to keep you on that list.

Is there anything you need?" When she shook her head, "We always knew this would happen, no? Someday."

"But maybe not so soon."

"You're sorry to see me go?" he said, a little surprised, teasing.

"Of course."

"Well, a woman like you. You'll have no trouble finding someone else." Said lightly, intended to flatter, but Irene turned red, as if she'd been slapped, a public embarrassment.

"At your service," Ivan said, moving his arm to his chest in a bow.

"Anyway, I'm not going tonight," Sasha said, a wink in his voice, touching Irene's hand.

"No," she said, looking down, away from Alex.

"That's right," Ivan said, louder. "Tonight we celebrate."

"Yes," Irene said. "I'll have a drink now." She picked up a glass. "To Moscow."

"Moscow," Ivan echoed.

"You see?" Sasha said. "Not so sorry after all. How long before you forget me? A week?"

"No. I have a good memory," she said, then smiled, a party mood. "Maybe a month."

"Me, never," Sasha said, suddenly sentimental, drunk now. "I'll never forget Berlin. It was a good time here."

"For you maybe," Irene said. "Not so much for us."

"You think it was bad here?" Ivan said. "You should see what the Fascists did in Russia."

"Well, that's in the past now," Irene said easily.

Alex glanced at her, thinking of Erich. Things she would never know.

She raised her glass again. "To Moscow."

"To Berlin," Sasha said, clinking his glass to hers. "Someday I'd like to come back, see what it's like then."

"Like Moscow," Irene said, fingering her glass.

"No. Something new. I don't know what, but new. All of this gone." He waved his arm, as if clearing the rubble outside. "You know what I saw today? They leveled the Chancellery. The whole building. And I asked one of the men, what happens to the stone? Marble some of it, nice. And he said the best goes to the Soviet memorial in Treptow and the rest to a U-Bahn station. Like what happened in Rome — you take the good stone and build something else, a new city right on top of the old one. It's interesting to think about Berlin that way, no? One city on top of the other."

"And what happens to the people in the old one?" Irene said.

"I thought you were in Aue," Alex said, breaking in. "There was some trouble, you said."

"Trouble, no. An overreaction. Some workers left the job. This happens all the time. And you know they are always found. No need to sound the alarms. *Bah.* And there I am, on those roads at night because some fool panicked."

"They just walked away?"

"A truck, apparently."

"And they can't do that?"

"At the end of their contract, yes," Sasha said, slurring a little. "A man has to live up to his contract. Anyway, these were POWs. For them it's not a question of choice."

For a moment no one said anything, as if Sasha had committed some impropriety, broken a delicate vase.

"POWs," Irene said finally. "Germans, you mean. Do you know who they are? The runaways." The word somehow making it a lesser violation.

Sasha shrugged. "Somebody must. They have lists. So they find them. But meanwhile it makes trouble for everybody — the morale, you know? And what can one do? The work has to be done. For the uranium."

"Sasha," Ivan said, putting his finger to his lips.

"I read about that," Alex said quickly. "The mines in the Erzgebirge."

"Yes, that's right. The Erzgebirge. It's not a secret," Sasha said, looking at Ivan.

"Well, half a secret," Alex said. "The area's cordoned off. That's what they say anyway."

Sasha nodded, a little bleary. "We had to do it. The Americans were offering people jobs, more money. They send agents to the villages, to recruit the best workers. It's a distraction, something like this. When there are quotas to fill."

"And who fills them?" Ivan said. "Every time? Who gets Moscow?"

"It's high grade?" Alex said as they drank again. "Good enough to make a bomb?" Trying it.

"Of course we'll make a bomb," Sasha said, answering a different question. "They think we won't catch up, but we will. What should we do? Let them destroy us? No. There's nothing more important than this," he said, leaning forward, confiding. "That's why I was promoted. I gave them what they wanted. Every quota. High grade? So we have to make it higher. But we'll do it. Some worker doesn't like it — what, the work is too hard? Some Fascist who tried to destroy us? We should be soft with him?"

Irene looked up, watching him.

"People complain? So complain. Nothing is more important than this. Our future. Our safety —" He stopped, aware that his voice was getting louder. "Nothing," he said quietly. "What's a few workers when this is at stake?"

"But we're a society of workers," Alex said, just to see how he would respond.

For a second, a delayed reaction, Sasha just blinked, then slammed his hand on the table. "Fine. Then let them work. Not shirk. For that, no excuse."

"You have to admit," Ivan said drunkenly, "a worker should work."

Sasha started to laugh. "But they don't. You have to make them. Sometimes a carrot, sometimes a stick."

"A stick," Ivan said, nodding.

"I'll be right back," Irene said, standing up abruptly. "The ladies'."

"She's upset," Ivan said, watching her make her way through the crowded tables. "She's upset you're leaving." A playful punch to Sasha's arm. "Don't you see that? Such an oaf not to see that. Talking about workers. Talk about *her*. That's what they like."

"I know what they like," Sasha said.

"To women," Ivan said, clinking his glass against Alex's. "You're married?"

"Divorced."

"Yes? You were seeing other women?" The only logical explanation.

"I came home — here. She stayed in America."

"That's right, Irene said you went over there. And now back. Maybe you want to offer my workers jobs too? Did they send you here to do that?"

Ivan thought this was funny. "That's it, take Sasha's workers. Now that he's going to Moscow."

"Don't worry, they're safe. I wouldn't know who to ask. I've never been in a mine."

"They don't want the miners," Ivan said. "They're nothing. *Muzhiks.* They want the scientists."

"Well, I don't know anything about that either." He turned his hands up, empty.

"You think Sasha knows? Numbers for the quotas, that's all. What more do you have to know? Remember at Leuna?" he said to Sasha. "The heavy water? Sasha doesn't know, he thinks it means it's heavier to carry. You should have seen the look on their faces. The big boss, and he doesn't know what it means. So they try to explain and who knows what they're talking about? Remember? Protons, neutrons — Greek."

"Oh, and you knew. A scientific expert. You understand everything."

"No, it was Greek to me too," Ivan said good-naturedly. "Deuterium," he said slowly, a careful pronunciation. "So what does it mean? Who knows? It goes right over your head."

"Make sure it stays there," Sasha said, a stern look. "Then it doesn't go to the tongue."

Ivan gave him a look, surprised at the reprimand, then backed away, raising a finger to his forehead in a mock salute. "Well. So you don't need to know anything," he said to Alex. "Be a dummkopf like me."

"I was in Leuna once," Alex said to Sasha. Keep it going. "Long time ago. But that's not in the Erzgebirge, is it?"

"No, outside the area. A plant there."

"Heavy water," Ivan said. "And he thinks it's heavy to carry." Still a joke to him.

"What's so funny?" Irene said, back at the table.

"Too much vodka, that's what," Sasha said, then leaned his head into her neck, nuzzling her.

"That's more like it," Ivan said.

"What were you talking about?" Irene said, trying to move away without being obvious, a pained expression, embarrassed.

"Nothing," Sasha said, his face now at the back of her neck. "Workers. Nothing important."

"What happens if you catch them?"

"We put them back to work. Never mind. What happens if I catch you?"

"Sasha."

"So you'll miss me? You don't show it."

"You're not gone yet."

He pulled away, smiling. "You see, that's what I like," he said to Ivan. "That spirit. An answer for everything."

"Everybody has an answer for that," Irene said.

"So you were her first sweetheart?" Sasha said to Alex, a question out of nowhere.

"We were children," Irene said. "Don't be __"

"It was the same then? An answer for everything?"

"Yes," Alex said, trying a smile, keeping it friendly. "Everything."

"You know she's from a very good family," Sasha said to Ivan, then looked at her. "So what were you like then? I wish I knew that."

"Oh, now that you're leaving."

"Maybe I'll come back."

"Yes? Should I wait? How long?"

"You don't have to wait now," he said, leaning forward again. "I'm still here." His face near hers.

Alex stood up. "The beer goes right through you, doesn't it? Excuse me."

Not able to look anymore, suddenly claustrophobic, the air heavy with smoke. He squeezed through the narrow spaces between the tables. Try to remember. Leuna. A grade that needed to be enriched. But didn't they all? Was that relevant? Don't write anything down, just remember it. Say a word three times and it's yours for life. He pushed through the men's room door. No one. He peed, then leaned back against the washbasin, going through it all again. Someone arriving from Moscow, not a promotion up the ranks. Nuzzling Irene. I know what they like.

"Ah, it's you," Brecht said, coming in. "What are you doing, going over your lines?"

"Taking a break."

"From the Russians?" Brecht said, smiling, then turned to the urinal to pee, a wisp of cigar smoke circling his head. "I saw you. A lively party. Good jokes?"

Alex didn't answer. Brecht finished, flushing the urinal, but not bothering to wash his hands.

"So, my friend, I hear you're going to write something for Comrade Stalin."

"Good news travels fast."

Brecht looked up. "As you say. They thought it would encourage me. To follow your good example. A poem, just a poem. They think that's easier, only a few lines, not so many words."

"Will you do it?"

Brecht sighed and leaned against the wall. "It's my last country here. Denmark, Finland, Russia, those idiots in Hollywood — I look at my passport and I feel tired just looking. We can work here. And Berlin —" He broke off, drawing on the cigar.

"So you will."

"I don't know. I'm not such a model citizen." He nodded toward Alex. "Anyway, it's interesting, to make them wait. Some old theater advice." He held up a finger. "Leave something for the second act." He started for the door. "So Irene is still with him? When you think how that family — Well," he said, a twisted smile. "She makes a contribution her way, eh? To the *Festschrift*."

The room seemed even noisier now, several more drinks in.

"There he is," Ivan said. "So now you can decide for us. All those years in America. I said, he'll know."

"Maybe," Sasha said, speaking into his chest, stifling a burp.

"Know what?" Alex said, looking at Irene, sitting awkwardly, one of Sasha's arms around her.

" 'GI,' what does it mean?"

"A soldier."

"Yes, but what does it mean? The initials?"

"Government Issue," Alex said. "They used to stamp it on army equipment. Then it started to mean anything in the army. The men."

"Ha! You see, he knew."

"So what?" said Sasha, moody.

"So it's a good joke. In English, a soldier. And in German? *Geheimer Informator,* a secret informer. So that's the difference."

"What's the difference?" Sasha said.

Ivan jerked his head back, not sure how to answer, his eyes unfocused.

"GIs. Both sides. But ours —" He stopped, losing the thread.

"Do excellent work," Sasha said. "Without them —" He picked up the glass. "When you have so many enemies, you need —" He tossed back the drink. "How else to keep

274

the Party safe? You know that," he said to Alex.

"Can I ask you something now?" Alex said, directing this to Ivan but wanting Sasha to hear. "You're at the Ministry with Sasha? What does it mean when the Party calls in membership books? For review. I hadn't heard of this before."

Sasha raised his head, suddenly alert. "This has happened to you?"

"No, no. Someone I met. I didn't understand why. It's a security measure?"

Sasha shrugged. "A routine check, are your papers in order, dues, maybe it's that. And maybe more serious. Without documents you can't travel. It gives the Party time to investigate, decide what to do." He looked down at his glass. "I have seen this before. It starts this way. And then —"

Alex looked at him, expectant.

"And then the Party cleanses itself," Sasha said, answering his look. "And always after, it's stronger. No weak elements. You say they've started asking for this?"

"I don't know. Just the one. But wouldn't this come from your — ?"

"No. The Party itself. We're instruments only. It's always like this in the beginning — the element of surprise. An innocent review.

275

But maybe not so innocent, not what it seems."

Ivan nodded, familiar with this. "Sometimes the reward that isn't a reward. They used to do that in the Comintern days. Call you back to Moscow for a medal, and then —"

"Don't be an ass," Sasha said, angry.

"Oh, not you, Sasha. An example only. How the mechanism works."

"Mechanism," Sasha said, sarcastic. "You're drunk."

"Well, all right," Ivan said, backing off, making a zipper motion across his mouth.

"Ass," Sasha said again, then looked over at Alex. "So maybe it's nothing. But stay away from your friend. Until you know." His eyes moved down to his glass again, an unguarded moment, suddenly anxious, then shot another angry glance at Ivan. "They don't have to promote you to call you back."

"No, of course not, I didn't —" Stopping before he stumbled.

"I picked Saratov myself."

"Who?" Alex said.

"My replacement here. A colleague." Then, to Ivan, "My choice. Do you think they ask you to choose if they — ?"

"Sasha —"

"Ach," Sasha said, waving him quiet.

"Let's have another drink," Ivan said, making peace.

But Sasha had turned to Irene.

"It's true, I will miss you," he said, his voice maudlin now. "At first you think, ah, Moscow, you don't think — We had some good times, yes?" He leaned forward to her neck again.

"Sasha. Not here."

"Why not here?" he said, looking around the room. "You think anybody will mind? In a place like this? With a Russian? Those days are over."

"I didn't mean that."

"No? What then?"

"We're not alone here." Opening her hand to take in the table.

"Ivan? You think he can see anything? After the vodka? Ivan, can you see?"

Ivan wiped the air in front of his eyes, a blind gesture.

"Alex? You think he minds? You think he's jealous? You were children, you said."

"Yes, and now you're the child. It's getting late. We should go," she said, then turned her head, a commotion at the door.

Helene Weigel, making her entrance, hair covered in a kerchief tied in the back, her face gaunt, tired from rehearsal, but pleased at the attention, actually touching people as she passed, regal.

"Alex, how nice. Bert told me you were here," she said, offering her cheek to be kissed.

Introductions were made, but neither Sasha nor Ivan seemed to know who she was, so the conversation became intimate again, Weigel and Alex standing, Irene trying to placate Sasha at the table.

"How is it going?"

"Exhausting. I get *up* tired. But it's going to be good, I think. Well, you know the play."

"Bert says you're wonderful."

She waved her hand. "He doesn't say it to me. Well, Bert. You know what's interesting? Everyone's coming. Today, the French cultural officer — can he have four tickets? And where do I get them? The Americans, the British, they're all coming. Even with this." She raised her eyes toward the ceiling. "The planes, all this trouble, and everyone still comes to see Brecht. So Marjorie," she said, shifting gears. "You've heard from her? The divorce, it's official?"

"I haven't had the final papers yet. Any day, I guess."

"Well, I'm sorry. But maybe you're not? And sometimes it's for the best. You'll see. Peter will come visit, and I'll make my chocolate cake."

"He'd like that."

Helene nodded. "It's better than Salka's. But don't say that to her." As if they had just come for the weekend and were expected back to Sunday dinner on Mabery Road. "Anyway," she said, glancing around, "the life here. I don't think it's for her."

"No."

"Well, for anybody right now. But soon. And they're all coming for Brecht. They won't sit with each other in the Kommandatura, but they come to the Deutsches Theater. So maybe they should meet then, eh? They're all there anyway, just bring the agenda."

"After the curtain calls."

Weigel smiled. "Of course after. Look, there's Bert. Now he's going to give me his *notes* — everything I did wrong."

"Do you listen?"

"Well, you know, he's a genius. So I listen." She looked up. "Sometimes."

"Everybody knows you," Sasha said when Alex sat down again. He raised his glass. "Our famous author."

"Well, at the Möwe," Alex said, the mood pleasant again.

"We should go," Irene said.

But Sasha was sitting back, comfortable, at peace. Ivan, half stupefied, was quiet.

"The new man — he's a protégé of yours?" Something more for Campbell.

"No, no. Older. We met only at the Ministry."

"But you recommended him?"

"I agreed he was the best," Sasha said smoothly. When? "A good head on his shoulders. You need that here."

"Like you," Ivan said.

"You know, everyone lies. Were you a Nazi? Oh, no. And then you read the file." He paused. "Denazification. How is such a thing possible anyway? Who else was here?"

"Not everybody was like that," Irene said.

"Not you," he said, touching her hair, "I know. But the rest — So you need something here." He tapped the side of his head. "To pick out the lies."

"A lie detector," Alex said. "But no wires."

"That's right," Sasha said, amused. "A lie detector. Up here." He tapped his head again. "And then something here." He held out a clenched fist. "A little steel."

"And he has that?" Alex said.

"Stalingrad," Ivan said. "Political officer. They were all bastards. Tough. No trouble in the mines with him."

"There is no trouble in the mines," Sasha said.

"No, of course not. I just meant —"

280

"You think that's all it takes? Tough? Anyone can be tough. You have to know how to run things. Eighty, ninety villages in the district. Workers? Thousands. You think it's easy, to keep all that going? Make the quotas? Things happen. You can't always predict — It's not just a question of being tough. Let's see how he does, Saratov. I want to see that."

"But you'll be gone," Irene said.

"Yes," Sasha said, his face clouding, as if that hadn't occurred to him.

"In Moscow!" Ivan said. "Think how wonderful. Maybe two secretaries — why not? One for the typing and one for —"

"Don't talk foolishness," Sasha said, cutting him off, then turned to Alex. "Who is the friend? The one under review?"

"Not a friend," Alex said, wary. "Just someone I met. I don't even know his name. He wanted to know if they had called in my membership book. I think because he had been in America, so maybe —"

"Yes, they're suspicious of that. Maybe it's that." His expression still thoughtful. "But it's often the way. A few, a handful, then so many all at once."

"So many what?"

But Sasha was distracted by another commotion at the door. Not Weigel's entrance

281

this time, two Russian soldiers scanning the room, people turning their heads, avoiding eye contact.

"Rostov. Now what?"

Sasha got up and went over to the door, a hasty conference, then made his way back to the table.

"Excuse me. I must go," he said curtly, his voice completely sober.

"Again?" Irene said. "Another drive?"

"No." Not saying anything more, on duty.

"Shall I wait for you?"

He looked at her, thinking. "No, don't wait. It's an interrogation. Sometimes it goes fast, sometimes not, so I don't know. Anyway, it's enough tonight. Look at Ivan. Put him in the car, yes? I'll go with Rostov. Don't let him sleep on the table."

"Who's asleep?"

Markovsky bent over, a public kiss, but Irene moved her head, an involuntary shying away.

"So, I'm already gone?" Markovsky said.

"People are —" she said vaguely, taking in the room.

He took her chin in his hand and tilted her face up, kissing her.

"I paid for that much, no?" he said.

"That much, yes," she said, turning away.

He took her face in his hand again, turning it back. "The rest tomorrow."

Her eyes flashed, looking for a comeback, but he had already begun to move away, and she took a drink instead, looking down at the table.

"I'm sure it's a promotion," Ivan said, half to himself. "I didn't mean —"

"Come, let's get you home," Irene said. "Can you stand?"

"Can I stand? Of course I can stand." He pushed himself up, holding the table, weaving a little. "I'll take you home."

"I'm around the corner. You take the car. Come on. Alex, help him."

"You don't want me to take you home?" he said, leering. "No, not some Ivan." He turned to Alex. "She wants to wait for Saratov, the next one. Only the boss, not —"

"Go to hell," Irene said, dropping his arm and turning.

"Come on," Alex said, holding him up. "The car's outside."

"German cunt," Ivan said after her, loud enough for the next table to hear.

She turned, staring at him, a silence.

Ivan shook himself free of Alex's hand. "I don't need any help," he said, taking a step, then rocking a little, finally sitting down again.

Irene looked down at him. "And what will

you do when he's gone?" she said. "You think Saratov wants you?"

"Cunt."

"Have another drink," she said, leaving.

Outside she told the Karlshorst driver to take care of Ivan and started down Luisenstrasse alone, heels clicking on the pavement, then stopped at the corner, head bent. Alex, following behind, put his hands on her shoulders.

"He's drunk," he said to her back.

Irene nodded. "But he can say it. If Sasha were — But now he can say it. So he's right. I should see what Saratov is like. Maybe a new possibility for me, eh? Another wife in Moscow."

He turned her around. "Don't."

"What do you think of your old friend now? A man talks to her like that. And what can she say?" She grimaced. "Look how we all turned out. Elsbeth with that crazy. He still thinks they were right. Me. Well, so there's Erich — he's the same. One von Bernuth left. One."

Alex looked at her, unable to speak. A pit with a crawling child, vodka to steady the nerves.

"Don't talk like that," he said finally.

"No? How? It's what I am. Someone he puts his hands on. In front of everybody.

His property."

"He had too much to drink, that's all," he said, reaching up to her hair, smoothing it back.

"I'm used to it. But tonight —" She broke off, turning her head. "In front of everybody. In front of you."

His hand stopped, as if he'd heard a sound, unexpected.

"Looking at me. Seeing that. I felt — ashamed. Imagine feeling that now, after everything. To still feel that. Even a — what Ivan said."

"Who cares what he says?" His hand on the back of her neck now.

"Maybe Sasha's worse. I'll miss you — so one last time before I go. As if it's a love affair he has with me. Ha. Maybe I'll say no. Just to see his face." She lowered her head. "But then it's trouble, so —"

"He's leaving. All that's over."

She looked up. "Yes. Then all my troubles will be over. Until the next one. So there's an opportunity for you. You can catch me between," she said, trying to smile, then dropping her head forward, almost to his chest. "Alex," she said, just his name. "You don't think I'm like that?"

"*Shh.* How could I think that?" he said, kissing her, not thinking, falling into it. "I

285

know you."

"You used to say that," she said, her breath on his neck. "Just like that. The same way."

"Yes," he said, kissing her.

"Tell me something more. Even if you don't mean it." Both of them kissing now, his head beginning to sway, like Ivan at the table, drunk with her. "I don't care if you lie to me. I just want to hear you. Like before."

"Irene," he said into her ear.

"Look at us," she said. "In the street." She leaned up, kissing him. "It's like before."

"No," he said, still in the kiss.

"Then let it be something different. I don't care. I just want to feel — like myself. Be Irene again. The one you used to like. Come," she said, taking his hand. "Now. We're so close. Around the corner. But no noise," she said, almost giggling, finger to her lips. "Frau Schmidt. Oh, but she's gone. I forgot. Her sister in Halle. There's no one to hear." She stopped. "Alex. Say something. Say you love me. You used to say that. Even if you don't —"

His head still swimming, the taste of her now in his mouth, their faces wet. "I've never loved anyone else." The words making him feel bare, as if he had just taken off his clothes.

She looked at him, suddenly still. "Is that true?"

"Yes."

"Then it's still true." She reached up, brushing the hair back from his forehead. "We'll be the same. I'll be nice again."

"Don't be nice," he said, kissing her neck, wanting her. "Be the way we used to be."

They went up the stairs in the dark, afraid the timer switch would wake someone, feeling their way up the railing, then huddling at the door while she found the key, short of breath from the stairs, everything now just smell and touch, invisible. Inside she locked the door, then fell back on it as he kissed her, urgent, that familiar moment when he knew there was no stopping, turning back. She reached for the light switch, but he blocked her hand.

"Someone might see," he whispered, his hands on her behind now, holding her, excited, the way he remembered, furtive, something stolen in the dark, muffled gasps people couldn't hear below.

"I don't care," she said, more breath in his ear, helping him with her clothes, both in a rush now, hurrying. She moved him toward the bed, clothes dropping, then sat, unbuckling his belt, tugging at his pants, his rigid prick springing out. Kissing it, a lick, a courtesan giving pleasure, too quick almost, unbearable, so that he backed away, then fell on her, pushing her down on the bed, his mouth on hers, opening it, tasting the inside of her.

"Don't wait. Don't wait." Grasping him below and guiding him until he felt her, already slick, ready, and, excited by the wet, he pushed in and stopped, just feeling the warmth around him. She moved against him until all of him was in, as far as he could go, and he thought he would come then, before they'd even started, and pulled back, but then couldn't stay, pushing forward again, giving in to it, faster, a rhythm that seemed beyond their control, his ears filled with the sound of creaking springs and his own blood. There had been times when they'd lingered, working up and down each other's bodies, stretching out the afternoon, but now they were back in the dunes, tearing at each other while Erich walked down on the beach. Deep inside, what seemed like the end of her, then out, a mindless thrusting, hearing her panting, the sound like some hand pushing him, an almost violent rocking, feeling the pleasure beginning to work its way up through his body, racing through him, about to spill over. Too soon.

But she was there before him, the panting now coming in gulps, little cries, and then an actual cry, loud in his head, squeezing him below in spasms, as if she were literally pulling the sperm out of him, the moist walls clutching him until it was finally there, splashing out, draining him, so that when he finally stopped, resting on her, he felt empty and full at the same time.

She reached up, cradling his face.

"I'm sorry. I was too —"

But she was shaking her head, still stroking him. "Alex," she said.

He rolled off, lying next to her, and she turned, facing him, her hand on the side of his head. "Nobody ever wanted me the way you did."

He said nothing, just breathing, slower now.

"You don't know that until you're with someone else." She paused. "But then it's too late."

He lay still, wanting a cigarette but too lazy to get it. Another minute, quiet.

"What are you thinking?"

He smiled to himself. What women asked when you weren't thinking about anything.

"I wish it were that summer," he said, talking to the ceiling. "And I could put you in my pocket and take you away. Before anything happened. To any of us."

"In your pocket," she said. She looked down, tugging the skin on her hip. "If I could fit now. Not like then."

"Yes, you are," he said, turning.

"Liar."

"You told me to lie," he said, a smile.

"Well, for a joke. I knew you wouldn't. You couldn't. Not to me. I'd know."

"Would you?" he said, no longer drowsy, suddenly uncomfortable. He got up and found his jacket, taking out the cigarettes.

"Of course. We know each other."

She took the cigarette he offered.

"We used to," he said, all the flushed well-being draining away. Her face soft, unaware. What he told himself he wasn't going to do. Not this line.

"No, we do," she said, sure. "Oh, white lies maybe. Things you don't like to tell me."

"Like what?"

"The wife who looks like me. She doesn't really, does she?"

"No," Alex said, the easier answer.

"No. I thought so. You see, I'd always know."

He looked away, no longer able to play, then put out his cigarette and sat on the bed.

"Irene, listen to me. There's something —"

"No, don't tell me anything. Let's not tell each other anything. Do you think I want to know?" She stopped. "Do you think I want to tell you about me?"

"You don't know —"

She put her finger to his lips.

"You don't have to explain anything. Your wife, any of it. Everything that happened to us — it happened somewhere else. Not here," she said, touching the bed. She looked over at him. "Nobody ever wanted me so much."

He looked back, the same falling sensation.

"It's not about that."

"What, then?"

Everything he couldn't say.

"We can't, that's all. I'm sorry, I should have —"

"No, it was me," she said. "I wanted it." She raised her eyes. "We both did, didn't we?"

He said nothing, at a loss.

"You remember that summer. We thought we had — all the time we wanted. And we didn't. Only a little." She moved toward him on the bed. "And then in the war, you know what I learned? I could die any day." She opened her fingers, something invisible flying out of them. "Any day. So that's the time we have. One day." She sat up, her face close. "One day," she said, kissing him.

Feeling her next to him, his skin alive again, warm.

"So tell me everything later." The words curling up like ropes, wrapping around him, then folding over each other in knots.

This time it was slower, almost gentle, hands all over, touching what they hadn't before, so that every part of them felt aroused, blood rushing to the skin, and then a release that went on and on, their bodies pulsing with it, lingering even after they fell back, away from each other, and began to drift.

After a few minutes her breathing changed, the slow, even sound of sleep, her hand still resting on his chest, and he covered her shoulder with the duvet, suddenly aware of the cold seeping through the cracks around the window. No one burned coal at night, burrowing instead under blankets in cold rooms. He lay there without moving, wide awake, watching the faint light from outside on the ceiling, dread moving over him like a cold draft. Everything Campbell had hoped, in her bed, listening. But for how much longer, the golden source back in Moscow, Irene no longer useful. Tell me everything later. But he couldn't tell her anything, not even that he would leave too. One day. Unless he never got out. And then what? Afternoons in her bed, still lying. Coffee with Markus. His real life bleeding out, Peter a memory, no longer in his life, the best part of him. Irene moved onto her side, her back warm against him. No one ever wanted me the way you did. He couldn't do this. Give Campbell something else.

He heard the footsteps one flight down, clumping, not worried about being heard. The click of the timer switch, a slit of hallway light under the door. Now on the landing, just outside. He waited for the knock, suddenly apprehensive, then heard the scratch of a key in the lock. Someone with a key. He jumped out of bed, grabbing his pants off the floor, just zipping up when the door swung open. Markovsky, outlined by the hall light behind him. Alex picked up a shirt. Now what? A series of Feydeau doors slamming? People darting in and out? But there was nowhere to go, the bedroom straight off the living room, the old hinterhof style, and now the overhead light was on, catching them like a flashbulb. Irene sat up, holding the duvet to cover herself.

"Sasha," she said faintly.

Markovsky looked from one to the other. "It didn't take you long, I see. Get up."

"It's not what you think," she said, but he waved this away, not even interested.

"Get up."

"What's wrong?" she said, reaching for her robe.

He watched while she put it on and belted it. "What's wrong. I knew what you were. But not a liar. Where is he?"

"What are you talking about? Coming here like this —" Trying to go on the offensive, parrying.

"Do you think I'm such a fool? Asking questions and all the time —" He turned to Alex. "And you? Did you know too?"

"What?"

"We captured one. With this type it usually takes a few hours. The interrogation. But no, this one right away. The truck. Lichtenberg. Names. Who else? Ah, von Bernuth? And they just take everything down and I'm standing there and what do I think? How you lied to me. To my face."

"What are you talking about?" Irene said. "What von Bernuth?"

"Erich. Your brother, no? One of the little birds that flew out of the cage. But now we put him back. Where is he?"

"Erich? Erich's in Russia. Dead, maybe, I

294

don't know. What birds? What are you talking about?" she said again, avoiding Alex's eye, playing it out.

"No, not in Russia. In the Erzgebirge. But now not there either. So where? Here? Where I pay the rent?"

"The Erzgebirge," Irene said, a gasp. "The mines?" She looked up. "You knew he was there? In that terrible place?"

"You think I know the people there? To me they're mules, that's all. Something to haul the stuff out." Almost spitting it out.

"So you come to me?"

"He got to Berlin, we know that. Where else would he go? The big sister, ready to hide —"

"Sasha, I swear —"

"Where else?" he said, louder.

"Look for yourself," she said, spreading her hand to take in the flat.

His gaze followed it, landing for a second on Alex, now buttoning his shirt. "And what do I find? Already at it. Old friends. What a slut. And to think I came here to protect you."

"Protect me?"

"They hear von Bernuth, they don't know it's Gerhardt now. Not yet, anyway. But I know. So I think, get him out of there before they see she's involved. No one has to know.

Do you know what it means, helping such a person?"

"But he's not here. I never saw him. I didn't even know he was — I thought he was in Russia."

She turned and picked up a cigarette, a pause between rounds. "Protect me," she said, lighting it, her hand shaking a little. "Protect yourself, you mean. Your girlfriend, right under your nose. It doesn't look so good for you, does it? Protect me."

"Where is he?" He looked at Alex. "With you maybe? This is how she pays?" He nodded toward the bed. "To have you hide him? Once a day? How many times?"

"Bastard," Irene said. "And what does that make you?"

He crossed over to her, grabbing her arm. "Where is he?"

"Take your hands off me. I don't know. Anyway, how do you know it's Erich? Because somebody says so? Maybe he's lying."

"He was in no condition to lie," Markovsky said flatly.

For a minute, no one said anything.

"So it's true? He's in Berlin?" Irene said.

"You know he is."

"And if I did know, I would tell you? Sasha, he's my brother," she said, her voice softer, tacking. "How can you send him to such a place? My brother."

"I didn't send him there."

"But you'd send him back."

"No one leaves. Until we say."

"Oh, we. Who? You and God? It's one man, that's all."

"If he can do it, so can others. It's not possible, to allow it."

"So he's a slave?"

"He was a German soldier. And he pays for that."

"For how long? The war's over and we're still paying. The new lords and masters," she said, cocking her head toward him. "First the rapes. Animals. And now what? Drunks like Ivan. Pawing me at the table. Like peasants."

Markovsky colored, then looked down, not rising to this. "That's what they think, you know," he said to Alex. "They lose the war. Everything. And they still know best. The great German *Volk*. All gentlemen. Not like us."

"At least they could flush a toilet," Irene said, her voice suddenly haughty, von Bernuth. "The Russians — a mystery to them. Where were they from? I don't know. The back of beyond somewhere. You never got the chance to ask. Before they raped you. That they knew. Experts."

"What are you doing?" Markovsky said. "Talking to me like this. Me."

"Why? Are you going to send me to the mines too? More slaves for the masters? Erich's not enough? Or maybe you want to rape me first."

"I never had to rape you," he said, his voice a kind of growl. "A few cigarettes, some ham — that's all it took for you to open your legs. Not rape."

"No? That's what it felt like. Every time."

The hand came up so quickly that Alex heard the slap before he saw it, a blurred movement, her cheek twisting away from it, a little cry.

He reached for Markovsky, all instinct. "Don't —"

"Mind your own business." He turned back to Irene. "That's what it felt like? And what did it feel like with him?"

"Get out," she said, touching her cheek, still red.

"Tell me where he is."

"I don't know."

"Then get dressed. You can tell someone else."

"Who?"

"A man at Hohenschönhausen. Very persuasive. Another Russian peasant."

"Sasha, I —"

"Get dressed," he said, grabbing her upper arm.

"Leave her alone," Alex said, pushing him away.

Markovsky looked down where Alex's hands had been. "Well. The hero of the Kulturbund. You think it's another story? The damsel in distress? So. Assault a Russian officer? Sleep with his — well, what do we call her? No need. Let me tell you now how it ends."

"Leave her alone."

"We take you into custody," Markovsky continued as if he hadn't heard, "while we search your place. No one there? Then maybe you're released. No embarrassment for the Kulturbund. And then your whore tells us where he is. And she will. That's the ending. Now get dressed," he said again, turning back to her, taking her arm again to push her toward the bedroom.

Alex stepped forward, facing him. "Stop it. You can't do this."

A cold glance, running through Alex like a chill. "I can do anything I want. Anything."

"What? Have some goon beat her up? What are you?"

"What? A peasant. Ask her."

Alex looked at him, beginning to panic. The face set, determined. Just a matter of time before they searched Rykestrasse. The back stairs too, Erich cowering but trapped.

"This is all I am to you?" Irene said, angry, a different argument. "You'd do this? Send me to the Gestapo?"

"Gestapo," Markovsky said, sneering at the word. "Tell me where he is."

"Go to hell."

Markovsky raised his hand again, Alex reaching up to block it.

"Get away from her."

Markovsky grasped Alex's arm. "The hero," he said, then pushed him back, out of the way, and turned again to Irene.

Alex lunged at him, the force of it surprising Markovsky, who staggered back, bumping against the table. A baffled second, then a look of rage, leaping for Alex, knocking him back to the wall.

"Stop it!" Irene yelled, frightened, the room suddenly shaking with violence.

Markovsky pinned Alex against the wall, hand on his throat. "Idiot," he said, an end to it, having won the point.

Alex gasped, choking, but then brought both hands up, a desperate strength, shoving him away. Markovsky stumbled, not expecting this, off balance, his thick body reeling back, smashing his head against a shelf, the sound of dishes falling.

"My God," Irene said. "The china. Stop." The absurdity of it unheard, everything happening too fast.

"Idiot!" Markovsky said again, a roar this time, touching the back of his head, looking at his fingers, a smear of blood, reaching for Alex.

But Alex, hands already on Markovsky's chest, pushed again, the head snapping back, another crash.

"Stop!" Irene yelled, a quiver of hysteria now.

Not a fight anymore. No rules. The two bodies locked together, twisting, trying to throw each other over. One of the shelves, bumped again, collapsed. The clunk of something heavy hitting the floor. Markovsky pushed Alex's face back, stronger, trying to flip his body, then suddenly aware of Irene screaming "Stop!" and pounding on his back, her fists like flies, something to brush aside. The two bodies moved away from her, still locked together, both staggering, refusing to fall, and then Markovsky roared, a grunt of extra effort, and finally managed it, throwing Alex to the floor, then following him down, pinning him there, hand again on his throat to immobilize him, bring an end to it. Something else fell, the room noisy with thuds and the men panting, gulping air, Irene still yelling "Stop!" Markovsky grunted again, pressing his hand against Alex's throat, waiting for some sign, a raised hand, surrender.

"You'll kill him!" Irene screamed. "Stop! My God, you're choking him."

A growl from Markovsky, beyond speech now, tightening his hand to end it, all of his strength pressing into Alex, his eyes fixed on him, waiting for the sign, so that he didn't see Irene grabbing the candlestick off the floor, out of the jumble from the fallen shelf, see her raise it over him like a club.

"Stop! You'll kill him!" she said, bringing it down, not planning it, just some way to get his attention, surprised when she heard the crack, the bone splitting.

Markovsky reared back, stunned, blood welling out of the wound.

"Stop it!" she shouted, bringing the brass base down again, a splatting sound this time.

For a second Markovsky went rigid, his legs straddling Alex, his hand still on his throat, then he slumped, the hand loosening, and Alex pushed up, the body falling on its side.

"My God," Irene said, a whisper now. "My God." She looked at the candlestick, the first time she'd seen it.

Alex now changed positions, leaning over

Markovsky, putting fingers at the side of his throat, feeling for a pulse.

"My God. Is he — ?"

"No. He's alive."

"What do we do? What do we do?" Talking to the air.

Markovsky's face moved, a twitch, then an eye opening, a grunt. Alex looked down. Blood on his head, the eyes open now, but stunned, the same look as Lützowplatz. If he lived, they would die. The simple mathematics of it. No witnesses. Another gasping sound, coming back. Alex put his hands on Markovsky's throat and pushed. The eyes opened wider, a choking gurgle, his body moving, trying to gather strength. Alex pushed harder, feeling the body writhe beneath him, trying to move him away. A soldier, trained, would know what to do, how to smash into the windpipe, end it. Alex just held tight. A rasping sound now, struggling for breath.

"Alex," Irene said. "My God."

Don't think. Do it. If he lives, we die. Harder. The last line. An extra push, crossing it. And then a spasm, Markovsky twitching, a protest, the last effort. Hands tight, no air at all, keep pushing. Almost. And then he was there, the body suddenly slack, no sound at all. You could feel it, a split second, the rasp then the sudden quiet. He looked at his hands on the throat, no longer needed, and slowly moved them away, staring at Markovsky's face, blank, still. His own breath coming in shallow gulps, hands trembling. What it felt like. Murder.

He looked over at Irene, on her knees now near the china, the candlestick still in her hand. Blood on the base.

"It was my mother's," she said, in a daze. "Schaller. From her side." Something important to establish. She picked up one of the smashed plates. "It's the last of the china."

"Get dressed," Alex said. "Do you have an old towel?" And then, at her look, "For the blood."

"The blood," she said, an echo. She put her hand over her mouth, stifling a yelp, bewildered, like a wounded animal. "My God. My God. What do we do now?"

"I know," Alex said. "But we can't — think about it. Not now. We have to get rid of him. Clean up." Lists, tasks, the reassurance of the ordinary. "Frau Schmidt's away. So that's one thing."

"Alex," she said, shaking, still on her knees. "I can't. My God, look. What do we do?"

"Help me," he said steadily, offering his

hand up. "We have to get him out of here. Find someplace for Erich. You'll need a story —" More lists.

"It was this," she said, holding the candlestick. "Imagine. My mother's. Brass. To kill somebody with this."

"I killed him," he said, taking her by the shoulders.

"Both," she said. "Both of us. That's what they'll say anyway. Maybe he would have died just from the head."

"But he didn't." He waited a second. "Get dressed. I'll start here."

The cleanup didn't take long. Broken china in the dustbin, the shelf put back, candlestick washed, blood wiped.

"There's not so much," Irene said. "I thought there would be more."

"Not after his heart stopped," Alex said, matter of fact.

"Oh. No, not after that," Irene said, staring at Markovsky. "Well, now I've done this too." Her voice soft, distant.

"He's heavy. I'm going to need you to help. You all right?"

She nodded. "Where do we take him?"

"The river. It's not far. We just have to get him there."

"He'll float. You saw bodies floating there. For weeks."

"We'll weight him down. He has to disappear."

"Disappear?"

"To give us time."

Irene looked at him, not understanding, but nodded anyway.

"Okay, get his other side. We can use the banister, slide him down, but in the street we'll have to prop him up."

"Carry him? Sasha?"

"Like this. We're getting a drunk home."

The stairs were more difficult than he anticipated, Markovsky's feet dragging and getting stuck, so they finally had to carry him, Alex under his shoulders, the rescue position, Irene his legs. They were sweating when they reached the building door.

"All right, ready? Put his arm around your neck. We're carrying a drunk."

He opened the door.

"Oh God," she said, closing it quickly. "His car. It's a Karlshorst car. There'll be a driver. Someone waiting."

"All night? He does that?"

"Well, not when —" She thought for a second. "Can you manage? A few minutes."

"Here. Against the wall."

She fluffed her hair, then clutched the top of her coat. "Does it look as if I have clothes on under this? Can you tell?" He shook his head. "Good. I'm just out of bed."

He watched out of the crack of the open door as she went over to the car, leaning in to speak to the driver, pretending to feel the cold with only a nightgown on, then hurrying back.

"What did you say?"

"He's staying the night. He'll call for another car in the morning. Go get some sleep."

"Why didn't he come down himself?"

"Too much to drink. He passed out."

"Good. That'll work."

"What do you mean?"

"You've got a witness. That he was here, alive."

"And when he doesn't call?"

"Didn't he? He left before you were up."

"And they'll believe that?" she said, nervous.

"Let's hope so. Why would you lie? What motive would you have? He's no good to you dead. Anyway, he's not dead. Not until they find him. He's just — gone."

"Where would he go?"

"Anywhere but Moscow. He was worried about that all evening. Ivan will back you up. Ivan suggested it. He was afraid of going back. He was afraid it was a trap. For all we know, he was right."

She looked at him. "When did you learn to think like this?"

"Ready?" he said, not answering. "Shift most of the weight on me."

They started down Marienstrasse, dark without streetlights. At the corner, an S-Bahn train clattered overhead, on its way to Friedrichstrasse. Alex pointed north.

"Not the bridge?" Irene said.

"Too busy. Just this short block, then over."

But suddenly there were car lights heading down Luisenstrasse. They huddled in a doorway, Alex's back to the street. A couple taking advantage of the dark. If anyone noticed.

"Oh God, I don't think I can do this," Irene said.

"Yes, you can."

"But if we don't report it —"

"Then they don't have a body." He shifted his weight, pushing Markovsky farther in, as the lights passed. "And we have a little time."

They moved back into the street. Up ahead, the lights of the Charité, but everything around them dark, rubble and deserted building sites. When they reached the riverbank, the bomb-damaged Friedrich-Karl-Ufer, he sat Markovsky down on a pile of bricks covered with a tarp.

"Fill his pockets. So he'll sink."

Across the water, he could see the hulk of the Reichstag, like a jagged shadow in a nightmare. The Spree bent here, then again farther up, the arc of the Spreebogen, sluggishly winding its way toward Lehrter Station. An industrial stretch, bombed out, the empty Tiergarten on the other side, not likely to draw many visitors. As safe as anywhere, if they could get him to the bottom.

He handed her the bloody towel. "Tie this around some bricks," he said, loading Markovsky's pockets.

"And what if he comes up? What if they find him?"

"He should have been more careful at night. Big shot in the SMA? There must be a line a mile long waiting to knock his head in. Take the money out of his wallet, just in case. Maybe a robbery. Anyway, if he does float, let's hope the current takes him. You don't want him found here, so close. Moabit, anywhere downstream. Not here."

"But they'll know he was with me. The driver —"

"And it was still dark when he left — you were half asleep — and that's the last thing you know. Berlin's a dangerous place to walk around at night. Look what happened to him."

Involuntarily, she glanced down. "He wasn't so bad, you know."

"No, he just wanted to lock you up with an interrogator doing God knows what. Not so bad."

"He wasn't always like that."

Alex looked up, surprised, then nodded. "All right, fine, remember the good times. It works better that way. You're upset he's missing. He tiptoed out of the flat because he didn't want to wake you. He was thoughtful that way."

"Don't."

"No, I mean it. You're upset about him. They need to think that."

"*Shh.* There's someone."

They both stopped, listening for footsteps. A smoker's cough, then the sound of spitting.

"Quick," Alex said, moving Markovsky off the pile of bricks. "Cover him. Lie on him," he whispered.

"What?"

"I'll lie on you. He'll just see a couple, not what's underneath. Quick."

She dropped to the ground, lying faceup on Markovsky's body. Alex covered her, his open coat draped over them. They listened for a second, trying not to breathe. Irregular steps, unsteady, probably a drunk trying to find his way home, not a watchman or a guard. Closer, near the river, as if he were just out for a stroll. Irene's breath in his ear now, warm. The steps stopped.

"Move," Alex whispered. "Make him think —" Feeling her beneath him, the idea of it, public and reckless, beginning to excite him, the way they used to do it, the risk itself part of it.

Another cough, spitting again, then a noise of surprise, startled not to be alone. Alex imagined him looking at the moving coat, figuring it out.

"*Hure,*" the man mumbled. "*Quatsch.*" Disgusted, something offended in his voice, but moving on, not stopping to watch. In another minute, it was quiet again.

"In the street," Irene said.

"But he didn't see a body," Alex said, lifting himself off.

"And if he had come over? Then what?"

Alex looked at her, not answering. No witnesses.

"Get his feet," he said finally, lifting Markovsky from behind.

They half dragged him to the embankment edge. A drop, not high, just a small splash, all the drunk would hear. Feet over, positioning him so gravity could help slide the rest of him in. The body moved and then stopped, sleeve caught, the coat beginning to come off. Alex leaned over, frantic, pulling on it, away from the snag, some rusty rod sticking out of the blasted concrete. And then it was loose, the body falling away in a rush, hitting the water and sinking, the heavy coat stuffed with bricks dragging him under until there was just water, the wet shine of the surface. Gone.

"Come on," Alex said, holding her. "Before anyone else comes."

But there was no one out now, even Luisenstrasse deserted, not a single car heading for the bridge. Everyone asleep — where they were too, in their stories.

"Stay with me," she said at her door.

"I can't. I can't come here now. Not until it's safe again."

"I'm afraid."

He put his hand up to her hair. "Not you."

"But how will I see you?"

"I'll come to DEFA tomorrow. Fritsch offered me a tour, remember?" He smoothed her hair back. "That's all we can do now. Meet in public. You never could have done this alone. Get him to the river. So they won't suspect you unless they think —" He leaned forward and kissed her lightly. "It's just for now."

"They'll find out," she said, shivering.

"Not if we're careful. There are no witnesses."

But on the walk back, the city looming up around him, threatening, it occurred to him, a new wrinkle, that there had been a witness after all. Two people in the room. He imagined the small cell in Hohenschönhausen, one bright light. And she will tell us. That's the ending. If they suspected her. In her hands now.

In Rykestrasse there were no cars watching the street, no one in a doorway. He tapped gently three times before he used the key, but Erich hadn't heard, sound asleep. In the bedroom, the smell of medicine and night sweat, Erich's face had changed again, not Fritz anymore, but Erich as he had been, a boy, at peace. The living room was quiet too, the sleeping city outside. Only his heart seemed to be awake, beating fast, knowing he was running out of time.

■ ■ ■ ■

5
SPREEBOGEN

■ ■ ■ ■

He waited for a few minutes by Little Red Riding Hood, then moved on to Snow White, making a circle around the fountain basin. Just walk in the park, Dieter had said, and I'll come. But how would he know? There was morning traffic on Greifswalder Strasse, a roar of trucks loud enough to cover the sound of the airlift until they stopped for a red light and the droning came back, there even when you weren't aware of it, like a nervous tremor. He couldn't stay here forever looking at fairy tale figures. Maybe Dieter had meant him to walk through the park, toward the rubble mountain.

"Good morning," Dieter said, coming from behind.

Alex turned, almost jumping. "How did you know I was here?"

"I live across the street," he said, motioning with his head. "I keep a lookout. My cinema. You have a cigarette?"

He bent forward while Alex lit it for him.

"Something's wrong?"

"I need to hide someone. A safe place. For a while."

"One of us?"

"A German. POW. He escaped."

"And you want to help him? Take a risk like that? In your position? Didn't they teach you anything? Your training?"

Alex shook his head. "They just threw me off the dock and told me to swim. Can you help?"

"Who is he?"

"Somebody from the old days. He's sick. He needs to get to the West."

"Not an easy trip to make these days."

"He has something to offer. They had him working in the mines. In the Erzgebirge."

Dieter raised his eyebrows.

"So he has information. I'm sure we'd be interested. But first I have to hide him somewhere. He can't stay with me."

"With you? Are you crazy? You have an escaped prisoner in your flat? After we went through all this trouble — ?"

"If they catch him, they send him back. Worse. Can you help?"

"When?"

"Now," Alex said. "They know who he is.

His family. There's a link to me, so they'll ask."

"Wonderful," Dieter said, drawing on the cigarette. "All right, bring him to me."

"You? I didn't —"

"See the building across? With the missing plaster? Flat five. I'll be there waiting. What else? You seem —"

"When does Campbell get here? I need to see him."

"Why?"

"Something's come up."

"That you can't tell me."

Alex said nothing.

"So, now we're careful. Before, let's hide a fugitive under the bed, no problem at all, but now we're careful."

"It's important. I need to talk to him. Is he here?"

Dieter thought for a minute. "Go to the Adlon. Later. Four, five, maybe. See if any mail came for you."

"Then he is —"

"I don't know yet. Just ask. By then, maybe I'll have news. There's some hurry?"

Alex looked at him.

"All right," Dieter said, not pushing it. "What else? Have you seen Markovsky?"

"Last night. He was celebrating. They're sending him back to Moscow." Keep him alive, even to Dieter.

"What?" Dieter said, genuinely alarmed.

"I know. So much for our source."

"He's being recalled?"

"Promoted. Although there's some question about that. He seemed worried about it."

"Well, Moscow," Dieter said vaguely.

"The new guy's Saratov. Ever hear of him?"

Dieter nodded. "An old Stalinist. Close to Beria. And they're sending him here?" He tossed the cigarette, brooding. "Why, I wonder. The mines, there's some trouble there? Did Markovsky say?"

"No. He thinks he's doing a great job. They're making their quotas anyway. You think it means something, bringing Saratov in?"

"My friend, everything means something with them. It's a chess game, Moscow, one move here, another there. Except in this game the king is never put in check. Never." He looked up. "This is valuable, Herr Meier. A pity Willy isn't here — a feather in his cap. To know this before it happens."

"So should Markovsky be worried? He had a lot to drink."

"Well, that doesn't mean much with them. But it's interesting, yes. Worried about a promotion. We'll look some more at the tea leaves, see what they say. Your friend, she was with you?"

"That's why I was there. A drink at the Möwe. Well, drinks. He had a pal with him. Ivan."

"His flunky, yes. So what else did they talk about?"

"There was a story about Leuna. The heavy water plant there."

"Leuna?" Dieter said. "Just like that they mention Leuna? You must have a gift for this," he said, then grinned, an unexpected gesture, his whole face different. "We've been trying to find the exact location for months, and now — just like that."

"They had a lot to drink."

"Among friends," he said, nodding to Alex. "It's working. He trusts you."

"Not for much longer. He's leaving whenever Saratov gets here."

Dieter frowned, then looked up. "The evening went well? You might see him again? A dinner before he leaves?"

"I could ask Irene."

"A sad occasion for her," Dieter said, thinking. "She might prefer a dinner alone."

Alex shrugged. "She might be relieved. The POW's her brother."

Dieter stared at him. "And when were you

going to tell me this?"

"Does it matter?"

"Amateur. Such foolishness. You'll get us all —" He looked up. "Markovsky knows this?"

"No. At least, he didn't say and presumably he would have."

"Presumably," Dieter said, sarcastic.

"And he'll be gone. Not his problem."

"No. Ours."

"Look, Erich might have gone to her. Or me. So they'll check. But he doesn't know you."

"And that makes it safe," Dieter said, dismissive. "When did he escape?"

"Two, three days ago."

"Then you're already on borrowed time. You should have your head examined." He looked back at the statues, scanning the empty fountain. "All right, get him. I'll find a place."

Alex looked at him, a question.

"Somewhere safe, but not with me. No connection."

"Where?"

Dieter shook his head. "The fewer people know, the safer he'll be. No links to break. No chain."

"Part of the training?"

"No, I know how these things work. I was

for many years with the police."

"The Berlin police? During — ?"

"Yes, during the Third Reich." The hint of a smile in the corner of his mouth. "A conversation for another day. Better have him come alone."

"But —"

"A little trust, Herr Meier. Even in this business." He glanced down at his watch. "Is there anything else you're not telling me?"

"No," Alex said, his face suddenly warm. "Isn't that enough?"

"For one day, yes," Dieter said, another smile. "So. I'll expect your friend. Alone. And you? What's on the agenda today?"

"A meeting at DEFA."

"Such a life. Film stars. Say hello to Fräulein Knef for me," he said, turning to go.

"One last thing. Quick question. What does it mean if the Party calls your membership book in for review?"

"This has happened?"

"To an émigré. From America. I just wondered —"

"If it's only one, it could be anything. A travel request. Some personal problem. If it's several, many, then maybe a sign."

"Of what?"

"One of the great Russian spectacles. A purge. A great sport for Stalin, before the war. And now for us. We sit back and watch them pick each other off. They haven't tried it here yet, too busy stripping the factories. But an opportunity for us if they do. You've heard of only the one?"

"An opportunity how?"

"To recruit. A test of faith, even for the strongest believers. No sense to it. Why him? Why me? Think of the exiles, dreaming of their Socialist Germany. Here? No, in Mexico." He looked over at Alex. "America. So they come, still in their dream. And then they see what it's really like. A bloodletting. To cleanse the Party? Yes, to cleanse it of them, terrify them. And now where is your faith? An opportunity." He nodded. "Interesting times. Keep your ears open."

Fritsch offered to send a car, but Alex took the S-Bahn instead, a little time to think on the ride out. Charlottenburg, streets of charred, hollow buildings, as bad as anything in the East. Westkreuz. The big railway yards at Grunewald, a maze of switches and platforms, where the Jews had been collected to be shipped east, rounded up in trucks or simply told to report to the station. Had his parents brought suitcases? All

324

of it open, in broad daylight. Everybody saw. Everybody knew. Then the trees of the Grunewald itself, the lakes. Somewhere after that, no sign, they crossed back into the Soviet zone, the western sectors an island again.

He got off at Babelsberg, crossed over the tracks, and started the long walk to the studio. In Hollywood the soundstages were giant rounded adobes, baking in the desert sun. Here they were brick, tucked into the suburban woods, even the gates shaded by giant overhanging trees.

Fritsch was in a rush, darting around his office in a kind of blur, then stopping short and looking down, as if he were trying to remember something.

"I'm sorry, so rude, but I didn't know. I have to meet with Walter. Yesterday everything's wonderful and now suddenly a meeting. So. Irene can show you around, yes?" He looked over to her. "And we can meet for coffee later. You'll forgive me? Irene, why don't you start with Staudte's set. You want to see where the money goes? And he used to shoot in the rubble. Now —" He stopped, searching for something in his head, then looked at Alex. "He wants to call it *Rotation*. What do you think? You like the title?"

"Rotation. As in the planets?"

"What planets? No, like a printing press." He made a cranking motion with his hand. "For the *Völkischer Beobachter.* You see?" he said to Irene. "I told you it was confusing. What's the first thing you think of. He says planets. A film about a Nazi newspaper. So what good is that? Talk to Staudte, will you? He doesn't want to sabotage his own film with a title nobody —" He looked over his desk and picked up a piece of paper. "So let me get him some money. Then maybe he changes it. Herr Meier, you'll forgive me? I shouldn't be long. It's always quick with Walter. Yes. No. Never maybe."

"Who's Walter?" Alex said when he'd gone.

"Janka. The head. Matthias ignores the budget and then he's always surprised when — Come."

She led him out of the admin building, across the grounds to one of the soundstages.

"Did they come this morning?"

"Twice," she said, glancing around. "First Ivan and some driver from the pool. Where is he? Isn't he with you? I said. No. Ivan's still confused, of course, from all the drink. He left here hours ago, I said. I thought he was with you. Now more confused. Then, a

326

few hours later, another two. From Karlshorst. One I recognized — he worked with Sasha — so he knew me too. What time did he leave? Early. I was still half asleep. Not yet light. Well, maybe just getting light. Vague, the way we agreed. He didn't call for a car? I don't know, didn't he? Is something wrong? He's all right? Now concerned. And the friend tries to calm me down. It's probably nothing. And I say, but where is he? And they want to know, what did he say? When he was with me. Well, sad, of course, we were both sad. He's leaving. But we always knew this would happen one day. And then they want to know the time again — when did he get there, when did he leave."

"You didn't say anything about how he felt, about going back?"

"I didn't have to. Ivan already had. To make himself important, I think. How he told Sasha it wasn't a trick, but Sasha was worried. So they asked me did he seem all right to you, the same? And I said, well, there was something on his mind, yes, but I thought, he's thinking about leaving me. What else would it be? And of course they don't answer that. Anyway, now I'm very upset so they're not asking questions, just telling me everything's all right."

"Good. So they don't suspect?"

"Me? No. They suspect him. They're not sure of what. But when Ivan says he's probably sleeping it off somewhere they just look at him, like a fool. Oh, and they asked me, how did he say good-bye, what did he say? And I said he didn't say anything, he just kissed me here." She touched the back of her head. "He didn't want to wake me. He was so quiet when he left. So we're all right, do you think?"

"So far. But they'll come again. You have to be ready for that."

"Again?"

"You were the last person to see him. So where did he go? If he's hiding somewhere, the most likely person to be helping him is you. Unless he's afraid they'll tail you, so he's safer on his own. But they'll watch you. You have to be careful."

"For how long?"

"I don't know."

"So I don't see you?"

"Only like this."

She looked over at him. "You think it's so easy, once you start? That's how it is with you? Like a switch. On. Off."

He looked away, not answering.

They went in through a small stage door to a hangarlike space, busy with carpenters and gaffers shouting to each other as they positioned lights overhead. Against the wall were giant newspaper presses made of wood and painted plaster.

"So, the *Völkischer Beobachter,*" Irene said. "They worked from photographs. The dimensions are accurate."

"You can see through the paint," Alex said. A set patched together with rationed materials.

"But the camera can't. Look over there. The way it's painted, the lines. On film, the depth comes out — not canvas, loading docks. You can make the camera see what you want it to see." She glanced around the soundstage. "You know, when it was bombed here it was the only time I thought, that's it, that's the end. The set was just a silly room, for one of the mountain pictures, antlers and copper pots, stupid. And then it was bombed and I wanted to cry. A set like that. Well, that's all we were making then, Heidi pictures. And *Kolberg.* Months and months of *Kolberg.*

"Propaganda."

"Oh, propaganda. By then who was listening? Zarah Leander and her pilot? What's the harm? Think what was going on out there." She nodded to the door, the real world, then looked up at him. "I don't want to lose this. Now that Sasha's gone. I don't know if Matthias can protect —" She stopped, then put her hand on his arm. "They say Dymshits wanted you to come — a personal invitation. He'd do it for you, a favor, and I'd be safe." She hesitated, toying with it. "You'll be Sasha now."

He said nothing, taking this in.

"Isn't it funny. To be together again. After all these years. I never thought —"

"I've moved Erich, by the way. Somewhere safe."

"Where?"

He shook his head. "You can't see him. You'd lead them right to him."

She looked down. "So. This is what it's going to be like?"

"Not for long. Don't lose your nerve. Not now."

"My nerve," she said. "I survived Goebbels. Everything. Don't worry about me." Bravado with a quaver behind it, nervous.

"They have to think he's still alive. So we have to think it too. Act as if."

"Why?"

"Right now they've got a missing officer. Maybe a deserter. An embarrassment. If they have a body, they've got a homicide. A police case. And —" He stopped.

"And I'm the last one to see him alive."

Fritsch met them for coffee in the commissary, preoccupied, the meeting with Janka evidently not an easy one.

"You know, in the Ufa days there was a hierarchy here, a special table for the bosses, the directors, the technicians. Now it's democratic — sit wherever you like. And where do they sit? The directors' table. The technicians' table." He attempted a smile. "It's not so easy to change a society. Whatever Lenin might say. So, what did you think? The rebuilding, it's impressive, no?"

"Irene says you're back at full production."

"Almost. The Russians gave us a priority, for building materials. Otherwise —" He stopped, his mind drifting elsewhere.

"It's okay? The Staudte budget?" Irene said, reading him.

"The Staudte — ?" he said, confused for a second. "Oh, that's fine. Something else." He hesitated, glancing quickly away from Alex. "You haven't heard from Herschel, have you?"

Irene shook her head. "Why?"

"He didn't turn up. A shooting day, the set's already lit and no Herschel."

"He's sick, maybe."

"Walter sent someone to his flat. You know he's here, in Babelsberg, so it was easy to check. No one. And the landlady says she heard people in the night."

Irene looked up at him.

"At his door. She's one of those types, if you ask, I don't know anything, but she listens."

"Maybe some whore from the bars. He's done that before."

Fritsch ignored this. "You remember when they were looking for Nazis? Right after the war? Always at night."

"Nazis?"

Fritsch shrugged. "Whatever it is this time. A message maybe to DEFA. Walter's worried. Once it starts —"

"And maybe he's drunk somewhere," Irene said, her voice not believing it.

Fritsch looked at her. "A shooting day."

Alex watched them, back and forth, a tennis volley of unfinished sentences and code words, the way people talked now. He had forgotten where he was, a city where people could be snatched in Lützowplatz and disappear. He looked over at Irene. Face drawn, talking in glances to Fritsch. Don't worry about me. Now the inevitable suspect. How much time had her story really bought them? A man like Sasha couldn't just disappear. They'd never allow that. They'd have to hunt him down. Question the last person to see him. Over and over until she broke. The way they did things. Unless they could be convinced Sasha wasn't with her. He peeked at his watch. Was Campbell already here? When he looked up he felt Irene's eyes, trying to read his thoughts. Keep Sasha alive. Somewhere else.

"Maybe he left. For the West," Alex said, almost blurting it.

Fritsch sat back, a slight wince, as if the words themselves had made him uncomfortable.

"Herschel?" Irene said, dismissing this. "You remember how Tulpanov liked his work? He was a favorite of Tulpanov's."

"Yes," Fritsch said, still uneasy, "a favorite. Well, maybe some misunderstanding. The landlady." Eager now to move away from it. "So. What are you going to do for us? I know, I know, a book to write. But a film, it's time for you. I was thinking — you don't mind? — maybe something personal, from your own life? Would that interest you? Not the exile," he said quickly. "That's very difficult for film. But your parents, for instance. Your mother stayed with your father. Even to the camps."

"She had no choice."

"By then, no. But earlier. She wasn't Jewish and yet she stays to the end."

"She loved him," Alex said simply, glancing over at Irene. What did it mean to love someone that much? Something from another time.

"Yes, of course, a love story, but also a heroic one. He was a Socialist, yes? So imagine — take one step — a young Communist couple, who have to go underground when the Nazis —"

He began using his hand for emphasis and suddenly Alex was back in California, a producer pointing at him with a cigar, rewriting the world.

Irene, watching his reaction, interrupted. "Or maybe an adaptation. We have a list of possibilities. We could meet to go over that. Discuss things," she said, meeting his eyes.

"Good, good," Fritsch said before Alex could answer. "A meeting. You know the food here is off ration. So that's another thing. And now, you'll excuse me again?" He stood up, shaking hands, then stopped, remembering something. "Irene," he said, tentative, thinking out loud, "would you check with the gate? See if there's anyone else who didn't report today?"

Markus was waiting when he got back to Rykestrasse.

"You don't mind I let myself in? It's suspicious, waiting outside. People wonder."

"Yes," Alex said, thrown, not knowing what else to say. Had he already searched the flat? Poked through drawers?

"You've been ill?" Markus said, indicating the bedroom, a medicine vial left on the nightstand.

"I just felt a cold coming on. Better to catch things before they catch you. Would you like something to drink?" A quick scan of the room, the other medicines gone, no clothes left behind, just a rumpled bed.

"Where did you get it, may I ask? The medicine? Such a shortage just now."

Alex looked at him. Thrust, parry. "Where does anyone get it?"

Markus took his time with this, then sighed. "Yes. But could I suggest, given our association, that in the future the black market — we must respect the law in these matters. Otherwise —"

"What association?"

"Well, our cooperation, let's say. Our informal arrangement."

"Markus —"

Markus held up his hand. "Yes, I know. You prefer to leave the work to others. Protecting Socialism. But now such a unique opportunity to help. Think how grateful —"

"What opportunity?"

"You saw Irene at DEFA today?"

"Fritsch asked her to give me a tour."

"And did she tell you that her — what? friend? is missing."

"She said Ivan came looking for him this morning. And then some other people. Your people?"

"No. The Russians don't always share such information. Not at such an early stage. So think how valuable, if we could help them in this matter. Our new German organization. Not K-5 anymore. A certain level of respect —"

"Are you asking me if I know where he is? We had a drink at the Möwe. That's the last I saw of him. What makes anybody think he's missing?"

"He didn't sleep at Karlshorst."

"Is that unusual?" Alex said, looking away, pretending to be embarrassed.

"No. But he didn't return either."

"And?"

"And so he is missing. A man in his position, you see, it's a serious matter."

"He said he was going back to Moscow. Maybe he already —"

"No," Markus said, almost smiling. "That would be known. Your evening, it was pleasant?"

"I suppose. There was a lot to drink. He seemed —"

"What?"

"I don't know. Worried about something. Ivan got on his nerves, I think. But maybe that's the way he always is. I don't know him."

"He talked about returning to Moscow?"

"That's why the drink. To celebrate."

"So he was pleased?"

"Yes and no. Pleased about going home —" He hesitated, as if trying to get the description right. "But, well, antsy too. Ivan said something about the old Comintern days, how they tricked people home, and that set him off. Is any of this really useful? It was just the drink."

"Oh yes, very. It's as I thought. And all this time Irene — what did she say?"

"Not much. How she'll miss him. The usual. What you say when somebody's leaving."

"If he's leaving," Markus said.

"What do you mean?"

"Comintern days," he said, his mouth twitching. "Who talks about such things anymore? Ivan. Maybe a loyal Russian, but also a fool. You think Markovsky is afraid to go to Moscow? Everyone wants to go there. Afraid of his wife maybe, yes. Afraid to lose the easy life here. His — what does he call her? When they're together." Markus looked over at him. "She knows. A woman like that — you think she's so eager to see her man go? Stay with me. Don't go. I'll help you. Karlshorst, they don't understand this. They don't know her. So it's an advantage we have. An opportunity."

"An opportunity," Alex said dully.

"Stay close to her. Wait for her to give herself away. And when she does, you'll be there. Someone working with us. Let the Russians look wherever they want. We're the ones who find him. Right where she leads us."

"Us," Alex repeated. "You're asking me to — report on her?" he said, almost dizzy. "No."

"You're so fond of that family?"

"Her father saved my life. I'm not going to — what would I do? Follow her around? Like a detective?"

"You're an old friend. It's perfectly natural to see her. Talk to her. The more she talks, the sooner she slips. That's all. Something easy for you to do. Not so easy for the Russians. Or me. So, an opportunity." He paused. "And a great service. The kind of thing that would be noticed."

"Maybe even a promotion for you."

"I was thinking about you, your position here. A grateful Party — it's a very useful thing."

"But why would she do it? What good is he to her if he's hiding? What kind of meal ticket is that? If that's what you think he is."

"Who knows with her? Look at Kurt. So hysterical when he's killed. The love of her life. Until the next one."

"Was she? Hysterical?" Caught suddenly, trying to imagine it.

"Dramatics. Who knows what she's thinking? She has a sister in the West. Maybe —"

"He'd never do that. Go to the West. Would he?"

"Who knows what he does for that woman? All we know now is that he's gone. The Russians think, a political act, but they always think that. They don't know her, what she can do to a man."

"Markovsky? He can look out for himself."

"You think so? All right. Prove me wrong. Let me know what she says. If there's nothing, my apologies. But if she's helping him, we have something for the Russians. Both of us. You can't refuse this. To have this opportunity and not —" He stopped, letting the words hang in the air.

"Why would she tell me anything?" Alex said, running out of cards.

"She trusts you," Markus said. "You know, sometimes you work months, years for that and here it is, right in your lap. Well, I should go. Someone sees the car there so long — a visit between friends, that's one thing, but then why so long? Oh, and this, I brought this for you to sign." He put a folder on the table.

"What is it?"

"I took the liberty. Of writing it out. Your report on Aaron Stein."

"My what?"

"Just what you told me. You can read it for yourself. Nothing very important. Background."

"Then why file a report about it?"

"Sometimes we bring these things on ourselves. Resign from the Central Committee, of course it's necessary to look at the political file. It's only natural. Here, you can read it," he said, opening the folder and handing Alex the report. "No surprises. What we said. I wrote it up for you, but please feel free to change it or add something."

"GI," Alex said, looking at the boxes on the bottom. Ivan's joke. "Secret informer. That's what I am?"

"It means your work is not public, that's all. An internal matter."

"And this?" He pointed to another box.

"Method of recruitment. You volunteered cooperation — that's the best, of course. I made sure you had that designation."

"What are the other methods?"

Markus looked at him, not saying anything.

"Am I supposed to write these up for you?"

"No, I can write them. Just come and talk to me. As old friends do. Have coffee. You can read this before you sign, there's no hurry. Just bring it with you when you come to tell me how it is with her. Maybe another drink at the Möwe. Do you know what I think is possible?"

Alex looked up.

"She may ask you to help her. With Markovsky. It's hard to do this alone. And who else can she trust?" His face smooth, without irony.

Alex looked down again at the report. "What's *K*?"

"Your code name. So no one knows your identity."

Willy's voice. A protected source.

"What is it?"

Markus glanced to the side, flushing, oddly embarrassed. "Kurt," he said. "You don't mind? You remind me of him sometimes. So I thought —" He paused. "Maybe it brings us luck. In our friendship. Imagine, if we find Markovsky. What it would mean for us."

Surprisingly, there was mail waiting at the Adlon.

"Fräulein Berlau left these for you," Peter said.

An envelope with two tickets to *Mother Courage*. Compliments of Bert, the note read, but it was practical Ruth who'd probably remembered. January 11. Opening night, gold, worth cartons of cigarettes to someone.

"And this," Peter said, handing over a postcard.

Everything seemed to stop for a second. The Santa Monica Pier, his Peter's scrawl on the back. He looked at the postmark. The day he'd left. How many hands had it passed through since? Wondering if "see you soon" was code, not just what you said on cards. He read it twice: "Hope everything is ok, I went fishing but didn't catch anything, see you soon." An ordinary card but with his voice, flooding into Alex's head, then the sound of the gulls, the rides farther down the pier, the sun flashing on the water, his voice asking for ice cream, like some bright vision you saw the moment before you died, a moment of perfect life.

"Would it be possible, do you think, for me to have the stamps?" Tentative, formally polite.

Alex looked up.

"Stamps from America," Peter said, a complete explanation.

Alex nodded, an automatic response, still clutching the card. Could they steam them off, pry them away somehow? His thumb brushed across the glossy front, touching the sunny day, all he had.

But this Peter was waiting, eyes shiny with anticipation. Alex tore off the stamp corner and handed it across, then glanced down again at the card. The perfect day with a jagged edge.

"News from home?"

Alex turned to the voice at his side.

"Ernst Ferber, Herr Meier. We met at the Kulturbund."

"Yes, of course. RIAS. I've been thinking about — but you're here? In the East?"

Ferber smiled. "Oh, don't believe all the stories. Berlin is still Berlin. And people still have birthdays." He nodded toward the dining room. "But special occasions only. I try not to wear out my welcome. The police have better things to do than watch dangerous characters like me. And of course I bring friends with me." For the first time Alex noticed a cluster of men farther back in the lobby. "Safety in numbers, yes?" Ferber said, almost winking, his rimless glasses catching the light. "And you, are you brave enough to cross over? It's very interesting now. A city under siege. But the spirit is remarkable. Seventeen hundred calories a day. Do you know what that means? How many tablespoons? Electricity for two hours only. And yet —" He stopped. "It's a great story. And no one knows how it ends. You should see it while it's happening. Before it's history."

"I can hear it," Alex said, raising his eyes. "Do you really think it can work?"

"Frankly? I don't know. Dropping candy for children, it's one thing. Coal —" He opened his hands, a question mark gesture. "But come see for yourself."

"I'd like that," Alex said carefully. "You gave me your card. I've been meaning to —" A social call, in case he had to explain anything later. "You understand, a private visit. I won't do anything on the radio."

"No, no, nothing like that. Just coffee." He held up a finger. "Ersatz coffee, of course, not like here. No Adlon cabbage soup either. But conversation —"

"Yes, we'll have interesting things to talk about," Alex said, his voice flat but pointed, so that Ferber looked up, alert to shifts in tone. "How about tomorrow?"

"Tomorrow?" Ferber said, not expecting this, now all attention, an animal listening for snapping twigs. "Yes, of course. Excellent."

"Good. I'll call your secretary, fix a time? I should tell you, I don't have any West marks."

Ferber made a half bow. "My invitation, my pleasure. Anyway, you know it's not so much, ersatz. But the chance to talk —"

"I'll try to make it worth your while," Alex said, obvious code now.

Ferber looked at him, not sure where to take this.

"We can take a walk. See history in the making," Alex said.

Ferber waited for a minute, as if he were listening to this again. "Yes, a walk," he said finally. "That would be pleasant. Well, till tomorrow then." He glanced down, noticing the card. "Ah, it was ripped in the post? A clumsy censor perhaps."

"No, for the stamps," Alex said, nodding toward Peter. "A collector."

"It's from America?" Ferber said, curious.

"My son. He went fishing," Alex said, a

wry smile.

"May I see?" He turned the message over to the picture. "This is where they fish?" He shook his head. "What a place. He's coming here?"

"Soon, I hope. When things are better."

"In Berlin? You're an optimist, Herr Meier. Well, here's Franz," he said as a man approached them. "Tomorrow then. Kufsteiner Strasse. In Schöneberg."

Ferber left with his group but stopped at the door, looking back for a second, as if he were still not sure what had been said.

"Anything else for me?" Alex asked Peter.

"That's all the mail. It's still light out, if you want to go for a walk."

"A walk?"

"Have you been to the Reichstag? Many people find it interesting."

"Your uncle?"

"No. Someone else. The best view is from the Spreebogen side. You could go there now, before it gets dark." He nodded his head, a kind of dismissal. "Thank you for the stamps."

Outside, the misty afternoon was thickening. One of Berlin's winter fogs, the only thing the airlift pilots couldn't outmaneuver. He crossed Pariser Platz in the fading light and went through the sector control at the

Brandenburg Gate. They were checking cars, not as casual as that first morning, but he walked through unquestioned, then up past the back of the Reichstag.

The neck of land on the river bend was mostly open space now, littered with fallen beams and chunks of concrete, barely visible in the dense white air. He waited near the Reichstag wall, covered with Cyrillic graffiti, looking across the water to where Markovsky was lying with stones in his pockets. Unless he had somehow broken loose and floated away, his coat snagged on a piece of debris in Moabit or still drifting toward the lakes. Where he'd be found. How much time did they have? He looked around, hunching his shoulders against the damp. No one. But Peter was never wrong. There'd be a car any minute, headlights barreling across the Tiergarten.

Instead there was a workman, blue coverall and woolen cap, shuffling toward him out of the fog like a ghost.

"Been waiting long?" The voice as American as his haircut. Campbell himself.

"What's this?" Alex said, nodding to his clothes. "Something for Halloween?"

"Very funny."

"They'll spot the hair a mile away."

"In this?" Campbell said to the fog, but

pulled down the hat. "Christ, look at it. Nobody flies though this." He turned to Alex. "How are you? Dieter said it was an SOS."

"Where do you want to start? How about Willy? I left three people dead in the street."

"But no one saw you."

"There was a woman. If they ever match us up, I'll be facing a murder charge."

Campbell drew out a cigarette and lit it, a studied casualness. "But they haven't. Nobody knows."

"I know. I killed a man."

"You knew what this was."

"No. I didn't. You never said. Not that part."

"You're doing a great job. Stop worrying. Nobody knows."

"Somebody must. Whoever tipped them off that I'd be there."

Campbell looked at him for a minute, assessing. "That was Willy."

"Willy?"

"It wasn't supposed to go that way. They fucked up." He nodded. "It had to be him, the way it was set up. This is only for you. It's useful, looking for a mole. Keeps people on their toes. But it was Willy. We know."

"No witnesses, he said," Alex said, trying to piece this together.

"Against him. He couldn't risk that."

"But he was dying."

"Nobody believes that until it happens." He looked over. "It was him. But you were lucky, the way it happened. They still don't know about you."

"How can you be sure?"

"We have ears," Campbell said simply. "Look, I know, it's a test of fire, something like that, but you're sitting pretty. You're getting great stuff. We've been waiting for someone to confirm Leuna, not just rumors, and there you are. Saratov. That's coin of the realm. You're Dieter's favorite person of the week. And he doesn't have many."

"Really," Alex said, deadpan, but oddly pleased. "Now let's talk about how I got it."

"Your old friend? Well, that was lucky too."

"No it wasn't. You knew she'd be the target when you asked me to do this. Why didn't you tell me?"

"Would you have come?" He dropped the cigarette, grinding it out. "You never know how people are going to react to something like that."

"Spying on friends."

"It's easier when they're in place. When they see what's at stake."

"When it's too late."

"Don't think that. Look, your stuff is coming from Markovsky, not her. She's just the intro. She's a friend you haven't seen in — what? Fifteen years? It's not as if you're sleeping with her or —" He looked up. "You're not, are you? That'd be fast work. Even for a busy girl. It's never a good idea, though. Complicates things. And now she's a source. You don't want to get between her and the comrade."

"There is no more comrade. He's gone."

Campbell nodded. "They're burning up the wires, down at Karlshorst. Interesting, when people panic. They say things."

"Good. Then you don't need Irene anymore. Or me."

"What are you talking about? She's the key."

"To what?"

"Finding him first. You're right. She's finished as a source — unless she picks up a new friend. But he's not. He'd have a lot of interesting things to say. If we can find him."

Alex looked toward the river, invisible now in the fog.

"So you want to stay close. Closer." Markus's words, just as insinuating in English.

"I can't. I want out."

Campbell looked over. "That's not possible. Not now."

"You don't understand. That's why the SOS. Something's happened."

Campbell waited.

"You won't believe it."

"Try me."

"I've been recruited. To work for the Germans. They want me to do what you want me to do. For them. I have to get out. Now. Before it starts."

Campbell said nothing, turning this over.

"What Germans?" he said, as if he hadn't heard correctly.

"They have their own service now. The old K-5. I'm a *Geheimer Informator.*" He looked over. "A protected source. Both ways. It's a game of mirrors. I can't do this."

"Smoke and mirrors."

"I'm not good enough, not for this."

Campbell just stared, thinking, his hand over his chin, a smile beginning to crease his face. "You don't have to be good. Not when you're lucky. Don't you see what a chance this is?"

"To get killed. One slip and they know. One slip."

"But you won't." A full grin now. "You're the best idea I ever had. For chrissake, don't you get it? We've never had one."

"What?"

"A double. Their recruit. Now all you have

to do is tell them exactly what I tell you to tell them."

"And how long do you think I can carry that off? Playing both sides."

"You're only playing one. Don't worry, if things get sticky, we'll get you out."

"Get me out now. I mean it. I've done everything you wanted. But I didn't sign on for this. Get me out."

"I can't. Not yet. You're a unique source. And now this. You can see that, can't you? Just keep your shirt on. A set-up like this —"

"With me taking the risk."

Campbell looked at him. "Well, that was the arrangement, wasn't it?"

"No. Chitchat at the Kulturbund. That was the arrangement."

"So it got better. Much better. You've got a chance to really do something for your country now."

"Is that what I'm doing? Then when can I go back?"

Campbell turned away.

"We're in the British sector now. I'm already out. Why not just keep going? Just put me on a plane. I've killed a man for you. So when do I get my end?"

"Not yet."

"When? After they find out? I mean it.

Put me on a plane."

"Going where?" Campbell said, facing him.

Alex looked away, into the fog, everything now just wisps of vaporous cloud, no visible markers.

"Look," Campbell said, his most reasonable voice. "You've been doing a hell of a job. Now you have to hang on. See this through. If we're going to file an appeal, we need —"

"What appeal?" Alex said, dread rushing through him.

"For you." He hesitated. "There's some news you're not going to like."

Alex turned to him.

"The divorce papers came through. The final ones."

"And?"

"It's hard to control these things. She was lucky, she got a hardassed judge. Old school. Said when you left, you abandoned the kid. So you forfeit all rights. He awarded her full custody."

"We expected that," Alex said.

"And no visiting rights either. You didn't just leave — you went to the Communists. That makes you an unfit parent in his book. Your kid would need a court order to see you."

"She agreed to this? Marjorie?" His voice tight, a whisper.

"It wasn't up to her. Like I said, this judge —"

"But she didn't protest."

"She was advised not to."

"Advised by whom?"

"Her lawyer. Don't look at me. We had nothing to do with this. We're the good guys here. The judge thinks you're a traitor. So we tell him you're not, that you were working for us all along. We appeal."

Alex looked over at him, the smooth shave, the implausible worker's cap. "But you're not going to."

"Not yet. We need to have you here longer if we want to make this convincing. We're telling him he wasn't playing with a full deck. No one likes to hear that. He has to think you're a goddam patriot." He paused. "You need to put in some time."

"How much?" Alex said quietly, but he already knew. They were never going to send him back. They'd keep him here, where he could be useful. Until he wasn't.

When he turned to face Campbell, right next to him, a patch of fog seemed to make him disappear. There wasn't anybody else, not here, not at the other end. He was on his own.

"How much?" he said again. "What do I have to do?"

"What you've been doing."

"But that's not enough. To get me out. What would be?"

Campbell met his gaze. "Find Markovsky."

"Find Markovsky," Alex said, an echo, not turning his head to the river, the air like gauze. "What makes you think I can do that?"

Campbell shrugged. "I don't have anyone else with access. You know —"

"Her," Alex finished. "I use her."

Campbell shrugged again.

"And then you appeal."

"You have my word."

"Your word."

"He's a big fish. We could go to the judge with that." His voice smooth as his chin.

No one else, either end. On your own.

"I don't have a choice then."

"I don't see it that way. I think it's something you'd want to do. You've been here long enough to see what they're up to."

"And this will stop them."

"It's a move."

"And what if it doesn't work? What if she doesn't know?"

"I'll know you tried."

Alex took a step back, looking down, as if he were thinking it out. Yards away a body might be floating to the surface of the water. A phantom, like the judge. There wouldn't be any appeal, just its dangling promise. And knowing this, he felt the dread seep out of him, his body almost weightless now, suddenly free. No one else. No sides.

"I need you to help," he said finally.

"Anything," Campbell said, a sense of relief at the back of it. "What?"

"Put out the word — use your ears over there, however you do it. We have him. A man like Markovsky can't just stay in limbo somewhere, he'd have to defect. So he has, and you're the lucky guy."

"What good would that do?"

"It'll call the dogs off her. You think you're the only one who thinks she knows? They'll think it too and they don't like to take no for an answer. They'll try to beat it out of her and then she's no good to anybody. But do it quick. Today. Let them intercept something — make them think they're clever. Then back it up with a leak. Whatever you have to do. They've already talked to her and they'll talk to her again. But if they know where he is, then all they want to know is, did she help? That's a lot easier for her to deal with. And now they've got bigger things on their minds — what he's saying to you."

"Not bad," Campbell said, nodding. "Unless he turns up back in Karlshorst."

"He won't."

Campbell raised his head.

"Would you? That's a one-way trip." Alex looked at him. "No appeal. He'd have to defect. Sooner or later. So let's make it sooner. And get him out of Berlin — Wiesbaden, wherever the planes go — so they think he's out of reach. Otherwise they'll think they can use her to get to him." He glanced up. "We want her to ourselves."

Campbell stared at him for a minute, a cool appraisal. "Good. So we're back in business?"

"Look at the cards you're holding."

"Don't think like that. We're doing something here." He paused. "You have my word."

Alex ignored this. "There's more. I need an authorization to fly out of Berlin. Not for me. Someone else. I assume you can do this with a phone call?"

"I can call Howley, yes. Who?"

"An old friend. German POW. He's like Markovsky — he has to come over or they'll lock him up. Worse. So we need to get him out."

"We don't fly Germans back and forth."

"He's paying his way. Radio interview about the mine conditions in the Erzgebirge. They had him working there."

"The Erzgebirge? That's nothing new."

"Maybe not. But it's the best propaganda story we've got. The SED sending its own people to slave labor? Hard to top. And he can throw in an escape story if people start nodding off. RIAS will love it. And after we fly him out, he'll have a nice long talk with your people. Is that enough for the fare?"

"Where is he?"

"Hiding. Safe. I'll set it up with RIAS, get Ferber to do the interview. Then we get him out."

"You'll set it up? You don't want to expose yourself like that."

"Nobody'll know except Ferber. Isn't he one of ours?"

Campbell peered at him. "No. But he's done us a favor from time to time."

"Well, now we can do him one. But how do we work it? I'll get him to RIAS. But then we'll need to move. Fast. Before anyone can grab him. And we don't want him waiting around Tempelhof for a go."

Campbell thought for a minute. "I'll have Howley call the dispatcher. Clear him for any plane going out that night. What's the name?"

"Von Bernuth."

Campbell looked up.

"You want her cooperation, this is the way to do it. I save her brother, she owes me. Not to mention trusts. And you get a big story on the radio. And somebody who can tell you all about the mines. You'll be flavor of the month."

"After we find Markovsky," Campbell said evenly.

"Set this up, we at least have a shot. In fact," he said, pausing, as if it had just occurred to him, "clear two places. Same name. I might need that kind of leverage. People will do a lot if you promise to get them out of Berlin."

"She'd leave Markovsky behind?"

Alex took a breath, thinking fast. Sasha alive, not in the Spree.

"He has to go to the West eventually. He's a dead man here," he said. "She might give him to us if we guaranteed getting him out too." He paused. "Assuming she trusts us."

"Which brings everything back to you," Campbell said slowly.

Alex met his eyes. "Isn't that what you wanted?"

"What if the Soviets pick her up?"

"You forget. Markovsky's already with you. You're going to say so. They'll want me to find out what she knows. Just like you."

"I thought you said it was the Germans who recruited you."

"They work with Karlshorst, don't they? And now they'll have something to make themselves look good. I'll be considered a catch."

Campbell considered this for a moment, then grinned, a flash of teeth. "But we caught you first."

"Yeah."

"All right, we square here?"

"You'll set it up? How do I contact you?"

"You don't. Unless you've got a fire alarm. Use Dieter. He'll tell me when to make the call. I'm not really here," he said, beginning to step away into the fog, a ghost again. Then he turned. "By the way, who recruited you?"

"Who? Someone I knew from the old days."

"Yes?" Campbell said.

"Markus Engel," Alex said, feeling strangely disloyal. "Why?"

"We like to know who's out there fishing. Hard enough keeping track of the Soviets. Now we've got the Germans too."

"He was K-5. Promoted when they

formed the new service. I don't think he's a recruiter. He just happened to know me. From before."

"What was the approach?"

"Like you. He appealed to my better instincts."

Campbell looked at him for a second, not sure how to respond. "That's the way," he said finally, then drifted off.

Alex took a gulp of air, then another, calming himself, aware suddenly that his own breathing was the only sound he could hear. The planes had stopped, leaving an eerie silence. He held up his hand. Everything beyond was black, no moon or streetlamps, not even the pinprick of a flashlight. What drowning would feel like, swallowed up in the dark. He stood still for a minute, willing himself not to panic. They were going to leave him here, in place, to race between traps. Nobody could keep that up indefinitely. A matter of time and then caught. One side or the other.

He started to walk. Stay close to the wall, the only marker. If he moved even a few yards away, he'd be lost, going in circles. A pair of headlights swooped into the black. Where Wilhelmstrasse must be. He was about to duck, an automatic crouch, when he realized the car couldn't see him. The fog had made him invisible too. He could go anywhere and no one would know.

It must have been a piece of girder, something low to the ground, because nothing hit his shin as he tripped and pitched forward, suddenly flying. He put his hands out to break the fall, slamming onto the frozen ground, something sharp hitting the side of his forehead, a warm ooze of blood. He lay motionless for a second, angry at his clumsiness, then sank flat to the ground, the dread back, weighting him down. They'd keep him here. The cold spread across his face then moved down along the rest of him, a damp tomb cold. He'd never get out. He felt as if the marshy Brandenburg soil was reaching up to reclaim him, pull him under. He would die here after all, his exile just a reprieve from the inevitable. Did it matter who pulled the trigger? The Nazis. Markus. Campbell. The end would be the same. What his parents must have felt, climbing into the train, too dazed to resist. Their only comfort knowing they'd saved him.

And he'd come back. A bet against history. Now lying in the rubble. Waiting for what? To be a victim, like the others? No. He pushed himself up. He couldn't die here, not in Germany. One more Jew. He touched his forehead. Blood but not streaming, a Band-Aid cut. Think. Play your own side. Berlin had. On its knees for a cigarette. Now on seventeen hundred calories a day. He got up and began to pick his way carefully through the debris, then faster, more confident in the dark, suddenly feeling he could walk all the way back to Santa Monica Pier. He had one head start: he knew where Markovsky was. Make up the rest of the story. Isn't that what writers do? Smoke and mirrors.

If Campbell leaked Markovsky's defection tonight, Karlshorst would know by morning. They'd come to see Irene again, but what she'd already told them would fit. She just had to keep saying it, frame the story. Be surprised. Disappointed. Maybe even angry that he hadn't confided in her, just went off with a kiss to her head. But she had to prepare herself, know they'd be coming.

He turned up toward Marienstrasse, following the curb to the bridge. A street he could find in the dark. Maybe there'd even be a few window lights now that he was back in the Soviet sector, out of the blockade. Think it through. What could go wrong? Markovsky himself, bobbing to the surface. But there was nothing he could do about that now. The stones would hold or they wouldn't. As long as they bought him time. Campbell would know how to feed the story, add kindling. What did Markovsky tell us today? Reports leaking back to Karlshorst, everyone focused on them, not dredging the Spree. If they managed the story right, it could be more valuable than Markovsky himself. Assuming nothing went wrong, no weak link.

He stopped on the bridge, turning his back to a lone truck that was lumbering across. And if they found the body? You had to plan for the unexpected. Look at Lützowplatz. He heard Campbell's voice again, lodged somewhere in the back of his mind. It wasn't supposed to go that way. But how was it supposed to go? If they found Markovsky, there'd be hundreds of suspects. Berlin was a desperate city. A Russian alone at night. Anybody might have done it. But only one had seen him last. Nobody made it through a real interrogation. If it came to that. Three people in the room, one of them dead. They'd both be at risk, as long as she was here, easy to pick up, her protector gone.

He found the door with no trouble, then felt his way up the stairs. Underneath the door there was the thin flicker of candlelight. A soft three raps.

"Oh, you're hurt," she said, her eyes drawn immediately to the blood. She was clutching at her robe and holding a candle like some figure in a folktale wakened in the night. "What — ?"

"I tripped. It's nothing," he said, stepping inside, closing the door behind him. He lowered his voice. "Frau Schmidt. Is she still away?"

"What? Oh, Frau Schmidt. No, she's back." Fluttering, as if she were having trouble following. "But why — I thought you said we shouldn't see —"

"It's all right. Nobody followed."

"How do you know?" she said, her voice still distracted, clutching the robe tighter.

"Were you sleeping?" he said, finally noticing it.

She shook her head. "Why did you come? You said —"

"I know. I needed to see you. Do you have something for this?" He touched his forehead. "A bandage. A piece of cloth."

"Who's that?" A voice from the other end of the room, the German accented, Russian.

"A friend," Irene said faintly.

"Another friend," the man said, amused by this, stepping forward now into the candlelight, buttoning his uniform.

"No. A friend," Irene said, at a loss, looking over at Alex.

The room seemed to dissolve for a minute, as if he had brought the fog in with him, shrouding everything outside the reach of the candle, the flash of brass buttons, her eyes staring at him. Like that night in Kleine Jägerstrasse, a whole conversation in a look, everything understood in a second. The same bright sheen in her eyes, the tiny spark of defiance behind the dismay. When things came back into focus he almost expected to see the Christmas tree, Kurt lying among the presents. But there was only a Russian officer, buttoning his tunic, watching them both.

"I'll go," Alex said, not moving, his eyes still talking to her.

"No need," the Russian said calmly, picking up his hat. "I'm leaving."

They all stood still for another second, just looking, then the Russian started for the door.

"A friend," he said, smiling to himself. "I wonder, does Sasha know how popular you are?"

"Why don't you tell him?" A quick glare, then looking down, retreating. "It's not what you think."

"Ah," the Russian said, enjoying himself. "You should get an appointment book." He turned to Alex. "Or are you early?" He put on his hat, then stopped halfway through the door and looked at Alex. "You won't be sorry. Make sure she washes, though. Between friends."

The door closed with a click. Irene moved over to the table and put down the candle, then belted her robe.

"He works with Sasha," she said, low, almost mumbling.

"You don't have to explain anything to me."

"No?" She took a cigarette from a pack on the table and lit it with the candle. "I thought you weren't coming here anymore."

Alex raised his eyebrows, waiting.

"He came to ask me questions."

"That's some answer," Alex said, nodding at the robe.

She looked at him, then away. "Yes, isn't it? So now he knows. I'm a whore. Not somebody who would help Sasha. Somebody he'd stay here for. Because he loved her. Who loves a whore? So he thinks I'm innocent," she said, cocking her head toward where the Russian had been. "That's how they know if you're innocent now, if you're a whore."

"Irene —"

"Oh, look at your face. You don't have to — It's always in your face. You know, when I saw you at the door I thought, my God, he couldn't help himself, he had to come. Like before. Stay away? You?" She drew on the cigarette. "But that was when you were in love with me. Not now." She crushed the cigarette on a saucer. "So why did you come? We're supposed to be so careful."

"We need to talk."

"About this?" she said. "You already know. They think maybe I'm hiding Sasha. Now they don't think it anymore. So that's good anyway."

"They're going to think he defected."

"Sasha? He would never do that. Why would they think that?"

Alex hesitated for a second.

"What is it? Why do you say that?"

"Because it's the logic of it. It's how they think. What else could it be? Now that he's not holed up somewhere with you."

"In our love nest. You know the funny thing? I think he did love me. In his way."

Alex looked at her, disconcerted. "If you say so."

"You didn't know him. Anyway, he'd never defect."

"But they're going to think so and you're

368

going to help them."

She looked up at him.

"They're going to ask you again. And again. He didn't want to go back to Moscow. You thought it was because he didn't want to leave you. But now you know that wasn't true, because you haven't seen him. You've been thinking. He acted as if he was afraid to go back, that something bad was going to happen."

"And they'll believe that?"

"Bad things do happen. That's the world they live in." He paused. "Maybe it'll be your friend again. Asking. He'll believe you."

"Don't." She turned away. "You don't know what it's like."

Alex said nothing.

"So. That's what you wanted to tell me? Sasha was afraid of Moscow? That's why you came?" She looked over, her face softer. "Not to see me?"

"We need to talk about —"

"What?" she said, her voice intimate.

"Erich. I think you should go with him."

"To the West?" she said, surprised.

"He'll need somebody. I can get you both out."

"Oh, like a travel agent. Two tickets, please. Just like that. One way. You can't come back now if you do that."

"You'll be safe."

"From what?"

"Maybe the next one who questions you isn't your friend. Maybe it's someone who wants real answers."

"Why would they — ?"

"Bodies get found. Things happen. You're not safe here. You have to get out while you can."

"Leave Berlin? What would I do? My life is here."

"It won't be, if they find him. It wouldn't just be a few questions."

"I know what they do. You think I'd — ?"

"Everyone does. Whether they want to or not."

She looked at him. "You think I'd tell them about you. You want to send me away to protect yourself."

"To protect you."

"You think I would do that? Give them you?"

"You wouldn't be able to help it."

"And you? Would you tell them?"

He looked away, not saying anything.

"No, not you. A man of principles. Only a whore would do something like that."

"I didn't say —"

She came over to him, reaching up for his arms.

"Don't you know anything? I would never —"

"It doesn't matter. You're not safe here." He looked down. "It's not safe."

"The only one who knows is you."

He nodded. "I can't protect you here. Sasha's gone. You have to get out. Now. It's not safe."

"You keep saying that." She looked up. "There's something you're not telling me."

"You have to trust me."

"Trust me. When a man says that he's going to do something you don't want him to do. Trust me. And then he's gone."

"This is different."

"Yes? And are you coming too?"

"I can't. I'm not welcome there. You know that." He paused. "Not yet."

"Oh, not yet. So I sit and wait for you. And you don't come. And all we have is our secret."

"But you'll be safe. Erich will be safe. He'll have a life there."

"So it's for Erich, all this."

He looked at her. "It's for you."

"No. Once maybe. Not now. I saw it in your face before. Well, I don't blame you for that. I never get it right. All my men. When I was young, I thought everybody loved me. I just had to pick. And always wrong. Kurt, what did he love? The revolution, whatever that was. Sasha? One call from Moscow and he's off. Good-byes? He's so sorry? No. But you. I thought, well, we'll start over. But it's never like that, is it? And now you want to send me away. Because you're afraid I'll betray you." She shook her head. "I would never do that. Then what would I have left?"

He looked at her, feeling the heat in his face, ears buzzing. Never betray you. Tell her.

"Trust me," he said finally. "Just this once."

■ ■ ■ ■

6
ORANIENBURG

■ ■ ■ ■

RIAS already had ground rules in place for the interview.

"We've had trouble with the Russians — they just pick people up in the street after they're on the air — so we record now. Half an hour to set it up, see what he's comfortable with, what we're going to say. Then maybe an hour for the interview. We can edit later. By the time we air it, he's gone and the Russians don't even know he was here. Sound right to you?"

Alex nodded. The cadence of newsroom American with a German accent. Where had Ferber learned his English?

"Come by U-Bahn. Innsbrucker Platz. That what you did today?"

Alex nodded again.

"And no trouble, right? So do that. Then after I'll have a station car get you to Tempelhof. He's flying out right afterward, yes? Good. The important thing is that they have no idea until it's too late. I'll set up a recording studio. Any night. I'm always here nights. Last-minute, no leaks in between. Sound good?"

"Perfect."

"You tell him what we're looking for?"

"Personal story — what the work is like. Treating POWs like slaves. Everyone getting sick. Not the politics of it, just the human side. Don't worry, he wants to do this. He thinks it might help."

"The Russians won't like it."

"That's the idea."

"I mean, they'll have a marker out on him. As long as he's here anyway. Any idea when?"

"I'll call you. Need a code word? How about 'canary'?"

Ferber looked puzzled.

"The bird. They used to send them down into the mines. To see if there was gas."

Ferber smiled. "Erich will be fine."

Dieter must have been watching at the window because he was in the park before Alex had finished the first cigarette.

"How is he?"

"He sleeps mostly. To stay warm. There's no coal, so it's easier in bed. No more fever, but the medicine is gone. You'll need to

376

move him soon."

"He's well enough for the interview?"

"Mm. He talks about it. He wants to do it. Give the finger to Ulbricht, he says." Dieter smiled faintly. "He's a young man."

"We're almost there. Are we squared away at the airport?"

"Howley's been away. Back tomorrow. Just let me know when and Campbell will make the call. Don't worry, you have some time. They have better things to do in Karlshorst than look for POWs. Since the news."

"What news?"

"You haven't heard? I thought your friend might — It's Markovsky. We've got him. He's defected."

"What?"

"Your friend doesn't know?"

"I haven't seen her."

"See her, then. Interesting to hear what she knows."

"Where is he?"

"Wiesbaden. Very comfortable from what I hear. It's usually like that, isn't it?"

"But why? What made him do it?"

"They sent him a ticket, for Moscow, and he started wondering whether he should make the trip. Not that I blame him. People go back and —" Campbell's version, the one everybody must have now.

"Quite a catch."

"We'll see. But meanwhile Karlshorst — it's a sight to warm the heart. So don't worry about your young friend — he's got a little time." He looked over. "Except the medicine's gone. So you don't want to wait either."

He walked along Greifswalder Strasse, past the cemetery, then turned up the hill toward the water tower. The planes were back, humming across the sky the minute the fog had cleared last night. Unload, three minutes, take off to the West. With Erich on board. Irene, if she'd go. He saw her eyes in the candlelight, the Russian coming toward them. I'd never betray you. After she had.

Roberta Kleinbard was waiting by the courtyard door in Rykestrasse, hands nervous, fidgeting.

"Thank God. I thought maybe you'd gone away. All night — anyway, thank God. Please. I need your help. I need somebody to talk for me." Her voice quavering, matching the shaking hands.

"What's the matter? What's happened?"

"Herb. They've arrested him."

"For what?"

"I don't *know*. They just came and — took him. What is it, I kept asking and of course they'd answer in German and —"

"Okay, okay," he said, calming her.

"And they wouldn't let Herb talk — just took him. No explanation. So I went to the Kulturbund and nobody wants to touch it. I got somebody to make a call, at least find out what happened and you'd think I had the plague or something. He wasn't the only one, that's the thing. They're all scared there. The Party hasn't said anything. How can they not say anything? People just — taken like that. You've got to help me. Please. I don't know what to do. You've got a phone —"

"Come up," he said, opening the door.

"Oh God, finally. I didn't know what to do."

"Regular policemen?"

"I don't know. I guess."

"Uniforms?"

"No, clothes. Is that bad?"

"Let me try the police first."

"I'll never forget this. I swear. What do I say to Danny? Your father's a criminal? It has to be a mistake. I mean, Herb, he's been a Party member since — they can't just do that. It has to be a mistake."

It took a few minutes to be put through to the desk, a little longer to explain why he was calling, Roberta hovering, hands in her coat pockets, clenched.

"He's in Oranienburg," he said finally, hanging up.

"Oranienburg?" Her voice dropped, almost a whisper. "That's Sachsenhausen. A concentration camp. He's in a concentration camp?"

"Not like that — for political prisoners. If you want to see him you have to apply to the commandant. In person. That's all they'd say. Do you know someone in the Party you could — ?"

"My God, a concentration camp. Come with me. Please. I have to see him. I'll never ask another thing as long as I live. Oh my God," she said, breaking down now. "How could he be a political prisoner? What does that mean? He came to be with them, the Party. It's a mistake." She put a hand on his arm. "I have to know if he's all right. Please speak for me. You're an American — I can trust you. The others, at the Kulturbund, it's like I had the plague."

They took the S-Bahn north to the edges of Berlin, Alex feeling his chest tighten as they approached the last stop. In the street he looked at a passing truck, the way he'd come here before, packed in the back, standing. Then hit with clubs, climbing out. People watching. An ordinary suburb. But his prison was gone. He stood on the curb, unable to move, disoriented.

"What's wrong?"

"It was here. An old brewery. People could see in. They leased us out in work parties."

He asked an old man waiting for a bus.

"They closed that one in '34. Then they built the new camp. Over there." He jerked his head east. "The bus, you have to wait forever. You're young. It's not far, fifteen-, twenty-minute walk. Down there and then left at the corner."

On the walk they were quiet, Roberta finally silenced by fear. A place she'd never thought she'd see, something in a nightmare.

They turned down a street lined with trees, the walls of the camp on their left, barracks for the guards on the right. Where the SS used to devise new tortures, boot testing, the prisoners walking endlessly around a track until their feet were crippled. What did the guards say to each other at night, stories over schnapps?

"Oh God," Roberta said, faltering, grasping Alex's arm for support. "I can't."

Ahead of them, the camp gate with a wrought iron *"Arbeit macht frei,"* beyond it acres of barracks arranged in a semicircle, the open roll call field, electric wire fences and guards, men shuffling in the distance.

For one surreal moment, Alex felt as if they had entered a newsreel. All of it still here. Russian now. They had changed nothing, except the guards' uniforms. His throat closed. He'd never get out. Fritz was gone. His father's money. Nobody would buy him out this time.

A guard pointed them toward a large building in the outer courtyard. "Administration Offices," as if the camp beyond were a factory and the white-collar bosses had to be kept away from the soot.

The clerk, a thin stubble of hair over a broad Slavic face, had only rudimentary German.

"Kleinbard?" he said, a sneer in his voice that said "Jew," a sound as familiar to Alex as breathing. Nothing had changed. New uniforms.

The guard consulted a log. "Counterrevolutionary activities. Do you want to apply to visit?" He held out a flimsy paper form. "You can fill it out over there." He pointed to a table where a woman, white-faced, with the tight, forced calm before hysteria, was scribbling on a similar paper.

"Counterrevolutionary? What are you talking about?" Roberta said. "He's a good Communist."

The clerk handed her the form again, nodding to the writing table.

"I want to see the commandant. You can't do this. I'm an American citizen."

The clerk looked at her, his face a sullen blank. "It's not you in prison."

"Did Herb keep his passport?" Alex said.

Roberta shook her head. "He had to choose. He said, what difference did it make? The State Department was revoking it anyway. So he's German." She stopped midstream and turned to the clerk. "But where is he? My husband."

The clerk cocked his head toward the camp, his only answer, then pushed the form toward her again. "If you want to apply —"

"How long does it take?" Alex asked. "Usually."

The clerk shrugged.

"It's in German," Roberta said, looking at it. "German and Russian."

"I'll do it," Alex said.

The woman at the table looked up. "They lose them. This is my fourth." Her eyes cloudy, distant. "But they tell you if he's dead."

"Oh God," Roberta said. "He'll die here."

"No he won't," said Alex calmly. "Here, help me with this."

"What's the use?"

"Then it's on file. If you get somebody in the Party to intervene, he can say, we're moving up your application. Like any office. Otherwise you'll start over."

"They lose them," the woman at the table said.

On the way back they were quiet until they were out of the camp.

"Look at them all. Living right next door. All this time. Down the street. I said to Herb, how can you go to Germany? And he said, it's Socialist now, it's all different. But nothing's different. My God, a concentration camp. But why?"

"Something going on in the Party."

"But he's *in* the party. It's his whole life." She kept walking, brooding. "My father warned me. How can you do such a crazy thing? But he's not married to Herb, is he? So what do I do now? Take Danny and go home? And leave Herb? But what happens if I stay? What if they don't let him out? What kind of job could I get, with a husband in jail. The Party would never —" She stopped, as if not saying it would make it go away. "I can't go back and I can't stay."

"No," Alex said, just a sound. He looked around. Modest suburban houses, just a short walk from the barbed wire, the sky a heavy gray again, the color of lead.

On the S-Bahn they stared out the window, not talking. Finally Alex turned to her. "But you kept your American passport? It might be a good time to leave. For a while anyway. Until we know what this is. In case —"

"What?"

"In case they make trouble for you too. His wife. If anything happened, the boy would be on his own."

Her eyes grew moist. "But nobody's done anything. What did we do? He just wanted to be — part of it."

At Rykestrasse, she asked him in for tea.

"I can't really."

"Please. I'll go out of my mind alone. I'll be all right after Danny gets home. What do I say to him? My God, what do I say?"

She busied herself with the kettle and cups, the familiar ritual.

"They don't even say what you're charged with. Just 'Come with us.' I wouldn't have believed it if I hadn't seen it myself. Like Nazis. Well, in the movies anyway."

"What are these?" Alex said, trying to distract her, leafing through some architectural drawings on the table behind the couch.

"Schematics for the project. In Friedrichshain. You know it, that part of town?"

Alex nodded, thinking of the narrow gauge rail cars bringing rubble up to the park. "Stalinallee," he said idly.

"Well, he won the war."

Alex glanced over. A believer still, with a husband in prison.

"Thank you," he said, taking the tea. "Two buildings. They're both his?"

The pure geometry of the Bauhaus, white with lines of sleek horizontal windows, the inside presumably a model of efficient design, the old dream, postponed by the war.

"If they build them. There's a stretch across from Memeler Strasse, he fit them both on the plot, to make a continuous line on the street. Beautiful, don't you think?"

"But — ?" he said, hearing it in her voice.

"But they want these." She reached under the plans and pulled out a new set of renderings. "Wedding cakes, Herb called them. Oh God," she said, putting a hand to her mouth, "do you think it's that? He called them Stalin wedding cakes. In public. A dinner at the Kulturbund. With Henselmann, the other architects. He wasn't the only one. I mean, everybody thinks they're — well, look. Gorky Street. But that's what they like. You have to work with the client. In the end it's —"

"These are his drawings too?"

"No. He's supposed to study them. Learn from them. Herb. Who can design something like this. You don't think it's this, do you? Making fun of the plans? I mean, in the end he'll do it. You have to. Everybody was laughing, not just Herb." She looked down. "Maybe someone reported him. Out of spite." She raised her hands to her arms, crossing her chest, huddling in. "Oh God, what a place. I don't want to stay here. Not anymore. But we can't go back."

"He could go to the West. A German. They take in any German."

"The West? And work for all the old Nazis? Another Speer? No, thank you. This is the Germany he wants. You're here too. You understand how he feels. You don't go."

"I'm not in Sachsenhausen."

The boy came in just as they were finishing the tea.

"Danny, this is Mr. Meier. Also from the States."

Danny raised an eyebrow at this, intrigued. "From New York?" he said, politely shaking hands. About Peter's age, the same unformed features, hair falling into his eyes.

"California."

Danny said nothing to this, reluctant to

offer anything further, looking for his cue to leave.

"Mr. Meier's a writer." No response to this either. "Do you want something to eat?"

"Homework," he said, lifting his satchel and then, at Roberta's nod, "Very nice to meet you."

Alex watched him go, a shuffling walk, as if he were kicking fallen leaves.

"He's like that with strangers," Roberta said.

"Mine too," Alex said, his eyes still on the boy, suddenly wanting him to be Peter, an almost physical hunger. Just have him in the room. Not saying anything, maybe reading the funnies in the other chair while Alex flipped through the paper. Just there, in his presence. He turned to Roberta. "You have to think about him. What it's going to be like for him. I'm sorry. I didn't mean —"

Roberta sat up straight, about to chafe at this, then sank back. "I know. But I can't, not now. We have to get through this first. What do I say to him?"

What had Marjorie said? At least at first.

Roberta looked at him. "Please, I know I shouldn't ask, you've done so much already, but you're somebody there, at the Kultur-bund. I mean, they give parties for you. You could get to Dymshits. He won't talk to me but he'd talk to you. He's the one who *invited* Herb. You too, yes? He'd at least listen. You don't have to vouch for Herb — politically, I mean, if there's some kind of trouble. You're just concerned. There must be some mistake. Even some information —" She stopped. "I know I shouldn't ask. But it's not sticking your neck out or anything, is it? I mean, he hasn't done any-thing."

"Who?" Danny said, at the doorway again.

Alex looked at his face, grave and ap-prehensive, an adult's face, what Peter's looked like now too.

"All right," he said to Roberta. "I'll see what I can do."

The Kulturbund was quiet, no crowds hurrying past Goethe up the marble stairs, no one sitting in the old club lounge where Fritz had told his stories. Even Martin seemed to be alone in his small office.

"Where is everybody?" Alex said.

"The flu. You know, the winter," he said, evasive. "I'm glad to see you. Look at this." He pointed to a tape recorder on a small table, microphone next to it. "You can be on the radio here. For Dresden, anywhere. No need to go there. We just send the tape. We've been waiting so long for this. It's an expense, the trains. And you know the writers prefer —"

"I need a favor," Alex said, breaking in. "If you can."

"Of course."

"An appointment to see Dymshits."

"Major Dymshits? There's something wrong?"

"Not with me. Herb Kleinbard's been arrested. His wife is frantic. She's been trying to get through —"

"It's a difficult time," Martin said.

"What do you mean?"

"The major — so many requests. He can't involve himself. In Party business. The Kulturbund must operate —"

"What Party business? What's happening?"

"Periodically, you understand, the Party must examine itself. A matter of self-criticism, usually. It's easy for people to have failings. But if they go unchecked —" He paused. "As I say, a matter of self-criticism. In most cases."

Alex looked at him. "You mean they're arresting people. Not just Herb."

"We have heard of several, yes."

"Here? At the Kulturbund?"

"Yes, unfortunately. A difficult time. I was afraid when you asked that maybe you —"

"Then I wouldn't be here, would I?"

"As you say."

"But why would they arrest me? Why would you think that?"

"Forgive me, please. It's not that I doubt your loyalty. Your commitment. No. You know how I admire your —"

"But you thought they might have."

"The Party is examining comrades who have spent time in the West. Forgive me, I didn't intend —"

Alex waved this away. "Who else? Besides Herb?"

"Older comrades. Sometimes, you know, they have the old ideas. A conflict, maybe. So a correction is needed."

"Do you really believe this?"

Martin looked up at him, dismayed. "Herr Meier, please. How can you ask this? It's important for the Party to remain strong."

"By arresting Herb Kleinbard? What if it happened to you?"

He looked down. "I must perform a self-criticism, yes, but you must keep in mind —"

"You? You could write Lenin's speeches."

"Herr Meier, please."

"God, it's because of us, isn't it? The time you've spent —"

"No, no."

"I'm sorry," Alex said quietly. "If any of

this had to do with me. I never meant —"

"No, please," Martin said, upset now, façade beginning to crack. "It was an honor to be of assistance to you. Your name was never mentioned. We are so pleased to have you here." Recovering his poise, back on the job.

"You were happy to have Herb too. It must be a mistake. You know Herb."

"Herr Meier, I can't question Party decisions. How would that be, if everyone did that?"

Alex looked at him, the silence an answer.

"Who else? You said my name didn't come up. Whose did?"

Martin looked away, embarrassed, as if he'd already seen Alex's reaction.

"Comrade Stein has been arrested. And one of his editors. Not yours," he said quickly.

"Aaron? They arrested Aaron? What for?" Seeing the soft, watery eyes, the ones that had glimpsed the Socialist future.

"I don't know. They did not say. I'm expected to attend the trial, so I'll know then. Let's hope, nothing too serious."

"There's a trial? When?"

"Any day. We'll be told. Someone has come from Moscow. A new man in the state security division. Saratov."

"Saratov? So Markovsky was right after all," Alex said, unable to resist, keeping the story going. He looked up. "What do you mean, we'll be told? Are you testifying? Against Aaron?"

Martin said nothing, his face crumpling a little, as if he were in actual pain. Then he lifted his head. "I may be asked for an opinion. Of course, if I am asked —"

"You wouldn't."

"And you? What will you do if they ask you?"

Alex looked at him, time slowing in the empty room. Just a piece of paper in a file, signed. They wouldn't call him, risk exposing him as a GI. The anonymous report would be enough, a paper trigger.

"It must be a mistake about Aaron," he said weakly.

Martin looked up, miserable. "The Party doesn't make mistakes."

It was a short walk to Markus's office, in one of the buildings the SED had taken over near the palace. The new unit must have just moved in because there were no names listed yet in the lobby directory.

"The new K-5. It was K-5 before," he said to the desk clerk.

"Ah," the clerk said, suddenly conspiratorial, nodding to the elevator. "On three."

The doors, improbably enough, said Main Directorate for the Defense of the Economy and the Democratic Order, in fresh paint, not quite dry. A reception area with chairs, a typing pool, and a long corridor of offices. Markus's secretary, not expecting visitors, seemed flustered, and Markus himself was annoyed.

"You're not supposed to come here like this," he said, drawing him into his office.

"I thought that's the way you wanted to work it. A visit from an old friend."

"In a café. My flat. Not here. Who comes here? Unless they have to. Anyway, you're here. It's just as well. I was about to come see you. It's happening quickly now. You need to be briefed."

"About what?"

"Markovsky," Markus said, a cat with cream. "He's defected."

"What?"

"You're surprised?" He shook his head. "I'm not. A pleasure seeker. I always thought it was possible. So you can see, it moves quickly now. Such a lucky idea of mine. To have you in place."

"But she's here. He didn't take her. So what does she —"

"Yes, for how long? He'll send for her.

And when she goes to him, we have him."

"In the West."

Markus brushed this off with his hand. "We have him."

"So you're having her watched?"

"Naturally. But you know she'll be careful. She expects that." He looked over. "The best watcher is the one you don't suspect. You see now how important — this is your chance."

"My chance."

"To be of real value. But you don't want to draw attention to yourself. Not now. Coming here for a social visit. What did you want anyway? That you would come here?"

"They've arrested Aaron Stein."

"Yes."

"And others. Herb Kleinbard, for God's sake."

"I didn't know that you knew him."

"I met them at the Kulturbund. His wife's upset —"

"Well, yes. That's to be expected. I would be too, in her position. So you come to me? I have nothing to do with this."

"State Security? Who else would it be?"

Markus looked at him. "Our Soviet comrades. We don't interfere. It's not our role." He hesitated. "You don't want to get involved in matters like these."

"I'm not involved. That's the point. I don't want to be."

Markus frowned, not following.

"My little chat with Aaron? I don't want that used against him."

"That's not up to me."

"Yes, it is. Just pull it out of the file and throw it away."

"That's against the law."

"What law? Arresting innocent people? Aaron Stein, for chrissake."

"Be careful what you say. Innocent? You know this? Better than the Party does? It's trouble, thinking like this."

"Get rid of it. I won't be used against him."

Markus looked, then shook his head, smiling a little. "Writers. All dramatists. Brecht says this too. Not Aaron. It's impossible. Before anything is known of the circumstances." He walked over behind the desk, then leaned forward. "Now listen to me. As your friend. You don't want to compromise your position. There is nothing I can do about this, even as a favor to a valued collaborator. They already have Stein's file. Not a small one, by the way. They may ignore your report, they may not. They may ask you to appear at his hearing."

"I won't —"

"And if they do, I suggest that you speak willingly. Your concern must be the safety of the German Socialist state. That's why you came back. That's why you cooperate. There is nothing you can do for Comrade Stein."

Alex was quiet for a minute, letting this settle.

"He is charged with high treason and counterrevolutionary activities. These are very serious charges. You don't want to get in the way of Party discipline in a case like this."

"High treason? Aaron? And what's Kleinbard charged with? Laughing at Stalin's building plans?"

Markus stared, then came out from behind the chair. "Comrade Kleinbard is another matter." He put a hand to his chin, thinking. "There may be something I can do."

"I'd appreciate it."

Markus looked at him. "Why? Who are these people to you?"

"I just think it's the right thing to do, that's all. Germany needs people like him."

"And not people like us?" Markus said, his eyes amused. "Alex," he said, drawing the word out, an intimacy. "Everyone has his part to play. Now you." He walked to the door, hand on the knob. "Next time a café, yes? Like old friends. To come here

—" He let it drift, unfinished, then opened the door. "You understand about Irene? Stay close. The eyes she doesn't suspect. He'll send for her, you'll see. A sensualist. And then we have him."

The door opposite opened as they stepped into the corridor, a small confusion of people, two men leading out a short old woman. She looked up at Alex and stopped, her eyes puzzled, trying to place him. His heart stopped. The woman in Lützowplatz. But he'd had a hat then, half covering his face. No sign now that she'd actually recognized him, just some vague stirring. He turned his face away. Keep moving, don't draw attention. He started toward the reception area, expecting to hear the voice any second, a hoarse screech, finger outstretched, pointing.

"English overcoat," she said, low, half to herself.

Involuntarily he looked down. Why hadn't he got rid of it, flung it in the rubble somewhere or let it pass from hand to hand in the black market? But who threw away a winter coat in Berlin? Last year's, from Bullocks, now marking him like a fingerprint.

"English overcoat," she said again, still working it out.

"Yes, *Pani,* you've told us," one of the men

said, a little weary. *Pani.* Polish. Two men, one to translate. Things got lost that way, language to language, a police form of the telephone game. A longer process, cumbersome. "A few more pictures to look at, yes? And then you can go." Expecting nothing.

But Markus would know what she meant, ears up, alert. A woman he'd already interviewed, his only lead. He'd catch the smallest nuance. Alex felt Markus's eyes boring into his back. He'd know. After everything, Markovsky in the river, to be tripped up by a coat. Alex turned. Markus had stopped, staring straight ahead over his shoulder, his face white. The others stopped now too, the whole room suddenly still. Alex followed his gaze. Not the old woman, someone else, haggard, prison thin, standing by the secretary's desk, her head raised to meet Markus's eyes. A blank expression, and then a gasp, her face crinkling.

"Markus," she whispered, face moving now, some uncontrollable tic. "It's you?"

"Mother," he said, a whisper, still, not moving.

She nodded, eyes moist.

"Mutti," he said, another whisper, his body still rigid, the shock of seeing someone dead.

She started toward him, tentative, the rest of the room watching.

"Markus. This place," she said, a hand open to it. "What are you doing here?"

He said nothing, still stunned, afraid even, and when she reached him she held back too, extending her arms to him and then stopping short, as if he were some fragile object, easy to break.

"Markus." She raised a hand to his cheek, barely touching it, a blind woman forming a picture. "My God. You were just a child." Resting her hand against the side of his face. "A child." Her eyes, already moist, began to overflow. "What did they tell you?" she said, her hand now at his hair, Markus not even blinking. "Never mind. Tell me later."

"Mutti," he said, trying to make the ghost real or go away.

There was some movement to his side, the two policemen leading away the Polish woman. Alex watched them, hardly breathing, but Markus didn't notice, too dazed by the hand on his cheek.

"Markus. Am I so different? Let me hold you." She leaned into his chest, her arms around him, then turned her head, so that her gaze fell on Alex. A moment of confusion. "Alex? Alex Meier?"

"Frau Engel," Alex said, his head dipping.

"You went to America."

"Yes."

The sound of his voice, an outsider, seemed to snap some spell in Markus, and he began to move, disentangling himself, a kind of military correctness.

"It's a surprise, seeing you here. Where are you staying?" he said, polite, to a stranger.

"Where am I staying?" Frau Engel said, vague, then distressed, something she saw she ought to know but didn't. She turned, flailing, to a man standing near them.

"Comrade Engel will be at the guest house. Of the Central Secretariat," the man said.

"Oh, not with Markus?" she said, wistful.

"Perhaps later. When you know each other better. When he has had time to prepare for you. If you both wish."

"Know each other? Who could know him better?" Then she caught Markus's expression, someone watching a specimen, wary. "But perhaps later would be better, yes."

"Is she still — ?" Markus started to ask the man, then caught himself. "I mean —"

"A prisoner? No. Released," his mother said, opening her hand, an odd flourish. "I have the papers."

"I am merely escorting her to you," the man said. "To make sure she arrives safely.

Comrade Engel's sentence was commuted. In full."

"They gave me papers. So it must be. I don't know why. I was an enemy of the people. And then I wasn't. Like that. All these years an enemy." She reached up again to his cheek. "While you were growing up. Your whole life. They took away your whole life. And then one day I'm on a train. It's over."

"Comrade Engel —"

"Oh yes, excuse me. I didn't mean —" She pulled away from Markus, almost cowering. "Such talk. Pay no attention. I can't think —" Fluttering, wings broken.

"You were arrested for counterrevolutionary statements," Markus said simply, a policeman's voice. "This time away — to rehabilitate yourself — the Party must have felt —" He stopped, letting this trail off.

Frau Engel looked at him, her eyes getting wider, something she hadn't expected.

"Yes, that's right," she said quietly. "To rehabilitate myself."

Alex watched the elevator doors close on the Polish woman. She hadn't recognized him. A tweed coat. How many must there be in Berlin? Now Markus's secretary was coming over.

"I'm sorry, sir. It's Major Saratov. On the

phone. I told him you were —" She blushed, a kind of apology.

Markus glanced around the room, suddenly aware that everyone was still watching. "*Mutti,* I must work," he said, almost relieved. "I'll come see you later. We'll talk then."

"Yes. Later."

"Alex will go with you," he said, eyes brighter, pleased with himself, a way to ease Alex out too. "Get you settled. Isn't it nice, his being here again? Like old times."

Frau Engel stared at him, not responding, as if he were speaking another language.

"Alex, you'll make sure everything's all right?" Busy again, official.

"I have a car downstairs," the escort said.

"Good," Markus said, about to head to the waiting phone, then hesitated. A scene still public, not yet played out, people waiting for an embrace. He turned to his mother, at a loss, then put his hands on her arms. *"Mutti,"* he said. "You must be tired."

"Tired?"

"Get some rest. I'll come later." And then his voice softened, private, someone else talking. "Are you all right?"

She nodded.

Another second, the crack in the ice growing wider, then he dropped his hands and started for the phone.

Frau Engel insisted on taking the stairs.

"It's foolish, I know. But it reminds me, the lift. Closed up like that. You had to stand."

"In prison?"

She nodded. "The isolation box. It was a punishment."

"For what?"

She looked at him, surprised. "Nothing."

Two men in uniform overtook them on the landing, Frau Engel making herself flat against the wall to let them pass.

"What is this place? They're police?"

"State Security. German."

"He works here? He's one of them?" Her eyes large, apprehensive.

Alex said nothing.

"Markus," she said to herself.

On the street, she drew in some air, then shivered.

"I'm always cold now." In the winter light her face was ash gray, what Berlin had looked like that first morning, lifeless.

"Where did they send you? Can I ask?"

She shrugged. "A work camp. Near the nickel mines. Norilsk. Always cold. Well, so now that's over." She put her hand on his wrist. "What does he do for them? He's one of them?"

"I don't know."

"You don't know."

"He doesn't say. But he just got a promotion. He told me that," he said. "So he can help you."

"Help me?"

"Someone with influence. It's useful."

"I was afraid. When I saw him, his uniform," she said simply. "How is that? To be afraid of your own child? And did you see? He's afraid of me. Some disease you can catch." She touched her hand. "Contaminated."

"He was just surprised. In front of all the people. It's a — shock. So many years. It'll get better."

"But he's one of them. Not just a guard. One of them," she said, not looking at Alex, talking to herself. "How often I thought about this, what it would be like. Was he alive? What had they done with him? But I never thought this. That they would make him one of them." She stared at the ground for a minute, then looked over to the car, the escort holding the door. "Well, my carriage. Cinderella, that's what it felt like. I should have known. Are you all right, he asks. Can't he see?" She touched her skin. "Why do you think they released me? He doesn't see that. Only the old crime. What

crime?" She looked up. "I forgot to ask you
— your parents?"

He shook his head.

"No, of course not. Jews. And you came
back." Not a question, brooding. She looked
around "And so did I. And now what? He's
one of them. And everybody else is dead.
Kurt, my friend Irina, everybody. And what
was it all for? You know, it was me. I wanted
to go there, after Kurt was killed. Away from
the Nazis, what was going to happen here. I
was right about that. So I took him, Markus,
I was the one. On the train. I told him how
wonderful it was going to be."

Martin had arranged a lecture for Alex at
the university and a radio talk later in the
month, but now needed him as a last-
minute replacement for a broadcast with
Brecht. Anna Seghers was in bed with flu.
"You know how difficult it is to schedule
Brecht. A casual conversation only. Your life
in exile. Maybe even better this way. Comrade Seghers was never in America, only
Mexico, and everyone wants to know what
it's like in America."

"And Bert is going to tell them."

Martin looked at him, caught off guard.
"What do you mean? Oh, it's a joke? Please.
You know on the radio it's important to be

serious."

Brecht was serious enough for both of them: capitalism reduced everything, everybody, to the level of the marketplace, commodities for sale to the highest bidder, a system of inevitable debasement. "Life is not a transaction," he said, and Alex smiled to himself. One of those Brechtian lines it paid not to look behind. He imagined listeners nodding, like the congressmen, pretending to follow Brecht's testimony, befuddled but too cowed to try to pin him down. California, he said, had been the perfect example of this — hollow, a marketplace trading in souls. Didn't Alex agree?

Afterward they had a brandy at a local near the station, grimy, thick with smoke, Brecht's element. Away from the microphone he became the private Bert again, familiar.

"So now we're part of the cultural offensive," he said, underlining the words. "They always bring out the artists when they're up to something. Look, German culture, back again. Still, it's good for *Courage.* They want a cultural moment, and we open tomorrow. So the timing is there for us. Wait till you see Helene. We gave a closed performance last night for the workers from the Hennigsdorf steelworks. Not even the sound of a pin. Completely engaged. Steel-workers."

"What do you think they're up to?" Alex said.

Brecht drew on his stubby cigar. "You heard about Aaron?"

Alex nodded.

"It's a good time to be quiet. Write a book. The country, maybe. Then, when it's over, at least you have something."

"Unless you have a play to open."

"Well, me. I'm harmless."

"And Aaron?"

Brecht looked away. "The Russians. This mania they have for housecleaning. Where does it come from? And the acolytes are even worse. Ulbricht. One word and he's on his knees scrubbing."

"That's what they're doing, cleaning house?"

"Think how useful. A good broom can sweep so much away. Old nuisances. People in the way. Someone maybe too ambitious. *Pouf.* Gone. And the Party is pure again. So now it's the SED's turn. Maybe a test of loyalty for them, see how high they can jump when Stalin claps. And they will. Our new German masters. I knew them in the old days, when they were altar boys. Grote-wohl, Pieck, Honecker, well he really was a boy then. Now look."

"Altar boys."

Brecht nodded. "Now priests. You don't see it? It's not like before here — no more marketplace."

"Try in front of the Reichstag. Every morning."

Brecht dismissed this, waving his cigar. "It's a church now. And what do priests do? Defend the faith. Root out sin. Never allow doubt. Once that begins, everything crumbles. You know, really it's the same. I've been thinking about it. Maybe there's a play. I knew these men. All early converts, young. Some go to the seminary. In Moscow. Now they never doubt. If they did, what would happen to them? How would they keep their power? Then the religion itself falls. Someone raises a hand, asks a question. Aaron, maybe," he said, lifting an eyebrow. "He resigns. In protest. Protesting what? The religion? Maybe just the priests. But the questioning starts, who knows where it spreads? No religion can survive doubt. And, you know, they don't doubt. Not the Ulbrichts. What else do they have now? They live for the church. Who can be as pure as they are? Who can ever be so guiltless?" He smiled, then pointed a finger up. "Except the infallible one. It's all the same, isn't it? Rome, Moscow. So, now a little Inquisition. And then it's back to normal."

"But Aaron burns."

"Well, a metaphor —"

"Not for him."

"What do you expect me to do?"

"Help him."

Brecht looked at him through the smoke. "You know, it's very difficult to do that. Sometimes you have to work with things as they are. Look at the church, the real one. All those crimes, so many years, and yet there's the music. The art. We're not priests, we're artists. We accommodate, we survive."

"Ask the guy at the stake if the music was worth it."

Brecht shot him a glance. "It's better than before. Don't forget that. The Nazis were priests *and* capitalists. The worst of both. Gangsters. So it's better." He smiled. "Now just priests."

Alex sat back. "Accommodate. What happened to epic theater?"

Brecht turned his palms up. "I said sometimes. Never here," he said, tapping his temple. "You don't accommodate there." He looked at Alex. "And you? You're here too. So a radio talk. A small price, no?" He finished the brandy.

"You know he's being charged with treason. He won't just lose his Party card. It'll mean prison."

Brecht said nothing, staring at the empty glass.

"What if they ask you to testify against him?"

"They won't." He shifted in his chair, uncomfortable. "Ulbricht wouldn't allow it. He doesn't trust me. He thinks I'm making jokes half the time. As if he would recognize a joke. So I'm a risk. Better to keep me as I am, a feather in his cap."

"Whose opinion would matter. In public."

"What are you suggesting? A letter to the editor? In *Neues Deutschland*? It's begun. You remember the committee? In America? Once it started? There was nothing to do but get out of the way. Sidestep it, any way you could find. Then it goes on without you." He poured out another glass. "And there's the play to consider."

He caught the Prenzlauer Allee tram, hoping to work on the lecture, but had only been home for a few minutes when the phone rang.

"Alex? You'd still like a walk? What time is good for you?"

Dieter's voice, but gruff, pitched to anyone

411

listening in, barely recognizable.

"Anytime," Alex said quickly. "I could leave now if you like."

"Excellent. Till I see you then."

He turned left at the water tower, then down the hill past the cemetery to Greifswalder Strasse. Dieter never called. Something wrong with Erich maybe, his fever back. He waited by Snow White, expecting to have his usual cigarette, but Dieter was there almost at once.

"Erich's all right?"

"Fine. Something else came up."

"What?"

"A body. In the Spree. Near Bellevue."

"The British sector," Alex said automatically.

"Yes. In a Russian uniform. My old friend Gunther wasn't sure what to do. So he asked for advice. For once, some luck for us. Do you want to tell me what's going on?"

"They ID him?"

Dieter shook his head. "No. But I did. He'd been in the water, but even so. Except it couldn't be Markovsky, of course, because he's in Wiesbaden. So I didn't recognize him either."

"They call the Soviets?"

"No. I told Gunther to put him in a drawer under a Max Mustermann until I could look into it. He doesn't want to start trouble with the police here. Tell them you have a body, they start fighting over jurisdiction. Gunther thinks it's his murder case. Coming up near Bellevue. I told him I'd help. We're old colleagues."

"Murder case?"

"His head's bashed in. He didn't slip on a rock. Now do you want to tell me what's going on? He's in two places how?"

"He was never in Wiesbaden."

"Obviously. Not waterlogged like that. That was your idea?"

"Who's Max Mustermann?" Alex said, off the point, thinking.

"What? What you call John Doe. No one. This was you, the defection?" he said again.

Alex nodded.

"So?"

"When Markovsky went missing, they were all over Irene. Naturally. I thought this would give her a little space. Be the mistress he left behind. Not somebody hiding him."

"Was she hiding him?"

"No. No idea what happened to him." He looked at Dieter. "I believed her. But would the Russians?"

"And now they do?"

Alex shrugged. "They're not grilling her. They're too busy worrying about what he's telling us. Our defector. Anybody disappears, it's the first thing they suspect anyway. Another one to the West. So let them assume the worst — he knows their men in the field, all of it."

Dieter peered at him. "And when he did show up?"

"He'd have to defect. Once he already had. Not exactly a forgiving group. Would they believe him? Would you take the chance? Then we'd have him for real."

Dieter said nothing, still staring. "And this was you?" He looked away. "Campbell knew?"

"He had to. To set up the leak."

"But not me."

"It was safer."

"Mm. Except now he comes back as a corpse."

"No," Alex said, looking steadily at him. "He's still in Wiesbaden. Singing. As long as we want him to, as long as the Russians think we have him."

"And the body in the morgue?"

"Another Max — what? Mustermann. How many are there in Berlin now? Bury him and who's to know?"

Dieter shook his head. "It's murder. Gunther's a little lazy, maybe, but he's still a policeman."

"The Soviets aren't going to come look-ing. They don't even admit he went missing in the first place."

"He's a policeman. He has to report it. A floater in a Russian uniform?"

"Did you take it off?" Alex said suddenly. "I mean someone might recognize —"

Dieter smiled a little. "The major's stripes? We removed it, yes. It's in an evidence bag. Gunther doesn't know what he has yet. But eventually —"

"Eventually you'll tell him about the soldier the Soviets are looking for. Nobody special, just an Ivan who probably got rough with a whore, so her pimp — And he floats down to Gunther's sector. But if he sends the body back, he'll have the Russians on him. Another excuse to make trouble. They're not going to miss him. Nobody's going to miss him. Bury him. And we keep Wiesbaden going."

Dieter held his glance for a moment, then looked away. "You know, I'm a policeman too. A man's killed, you want to know why. Who."

"Markovsky? Half of Berlin would have loved to take a crack at him."

"But only one did. You're not interested to know?" He paused. "Or maybe you do."

"I don't care," Alex said easily. "They find

415

a wallet on him?"

"No."

"And he's alone at night? Anybody. Does it matter?"

"Gunther may not see it that way."

"Just for a while."

Dieter looked up.

"Let Wiesbaden play itself out."

"You won't be able to keep that up for long. The defector who isn't there? It's not a game, Herr Meier. Not that kind anyway."

Alex nodded. "Do what you can. We need to buy some time. If the Russians get Markovsky back now, they'll haul Irene in for more questioning. Let me get her out first. With Erich."

"She's going too?"

"I think she should."

Dieter raised his eyebrows. "That puts you in a delicate situation. You'll be losing your best source."

"She was finished anyway, the minute Markovsky got his marching orders. Saratov doesn't sound like her type. Unless they pass their women on."

"No," Dieter said, taking the cigarette Alex offered. "A pity."

"What? Saratov?"

"No, Markovsky getting called home. And then this. Not a very noble end. Fished out of the Spree."

"What's the saying? You get the death you deserve."

"Let's hope not," Dieter said, then looked back toward the street. "All right. I'll talk to Gunther. When are you moving Erich? He's a nice boy, by the way. We talked a little."

"Tomorrow night. Tell Campbell to make sure Howley calls with the clearance." He looked toward the sky. "And let's hope the weather holds."

"You have a car?"

"All arranged. From DEFA. Nobody'll miss it."

"You have to be careful. Especially now, with her. Why not do the boy first?"

"And wait for them to pick her up?"

"No, they don't want her in Hohenschönhausen, they want her walking around. But on a leash. Where they can see her. Which means they'll see you too. It's a risk, with her."

"Why do they — ?"

"Herr Meier. A man of action. Maybe you don't always think things through. Markovsky defects. So who joins him? The wife in Moscow or the girlfriend who can just walk across the street?"

"They why didn't she go with him in the first place?"

"Maybe he's testing the waters. Maybe she's not part of the bargain so he has to offer something. It's not easy to get out of Berlin. Or maybe —" He stopped, eyes on Alex. "Maybe he didn't defect at all. Maybe he was — picked up. You say it's the first thing they think? No, this. Kidnapped. A dangerous move in this game, by the way. They like to retaliate. Either way, what can they do? Watch and wait. She's the only lead they have. You don't think like a policeman. So it's risky with her."

"Maybe he never wanted her."

"Maybe. But who would you follow? She's a liability."

"Not if he's dead," Alex said, brooding.

"And how will you arrange that? Another leak?"

"I don't know. Something happens in Wiesbaden."

"Shot trying to escape?" Dieter said, his voice unexpectedly sarcastic.

"Maybe he can't stand the guilt. He commits suicide."

Dieter made a thin smile. "Not very encouraging to anyone who really might be considering such a move, no? Bad advertising." He took a last drag on the cigarette and flicked it into a patch of snow. "An interesting dilemma. How do you kill someone who's already dead?"

"Right now, we just have to make sure they don't know he's dead. That's you."

Dieter nodded. "And then you'll think of something. A little more carefully this time. If the Russians believe we killed him, it's a provocation. What they like — an excuse to be themselves."

"What about the truth? A street crime. He was careless and got —"

"Well, the truth, yes. But who believes that? Who knows what that is? You? Not me. May I offer you a piece of advice? You like to keep things to yourself. You think it's safer. Yes, maybe. But in this business at some point you have to trust somebody. You can't do it alone. Not everybody, just one."

"You?"

Dieter shrugged. "That's for you to decide."

"And how do you do that? Decide who to trust?"

"How? I don't know. You develop an instinct. You're still new to this." He sighed. "And I'm not so new. So why listen to me? You're still going to take the woman, aren't you?" Dieter looked at him for a minute. "So. Remember, they'll be watching her. And they're hard to lose. In a crowd maybe —"

Alex nodded. "How about a few hundred?"

Dieter looked up.

"At the theater."

■ ■ ■ ■

7
TEMPELHOF

■ ■ ■ ■

The play had an early curtain so cars started pulling up to the doors even before dusk. The Deutsches Theater was set back from the street, fronted by a small park and a semicircular driveway, designed for carriages, a more graceful time. Now the trees were stumps, burned black, and the coaches were jeeps and official cars with tiny flags on their radio antennas, but the building was lighted, almost blazing in the gathering dark, and there was the unmistakable hum of an event, voices rising, calling out to each other, car doors slamming, then sweeping back out to the street. Opening night, the ruins just background shadows, the neoclassical façade still intact, lit up by the bright lobby chandeliers.

"I didn't know there were so many cars in Berlin," Irene said. "My God."

They had walked from Marienstrasse, two streets away, and now had to weave through the line of waiting cars in the driveway.

All the Allies were here, many in uniform, so that the evening seemed a kind of international conference, the meetings they no longer had. Airplanes were still droning overhead, delivering coal, but they receded into the background too, like the ruins, while everyone faced the light. Alex thought of the photographs of the famous Weimar openings, white tie at the Zoo Palast, now bulky wool coats in the unheated salon, but the same eager sense of occasion, Berlin having its moment.

There were drinks for sale in the lobby, a crowded milling, no one prepared yet to go inside, the drama still here, heads turning to the doors as they opened, craning. The Kulturbund was out in force, wartime jersey dressed up with flashes of costume jewelry, sneaking glances at the Allied wives in better coats and permanent waves, everyone clinking glasses of *Sekt* as if the blockade were over, some bad memory.

"Remember, you're not going to be feeling well later," Alex said, handing Irene a glass.

"In our play," she said. "Look, is that General Clay?"

"I don't know. I've never met him."

"I think so. Or maybe they all look that way."

"Alex." Ruth Berlau, behind them. "You got the tickets? Well, of course you did, you're here. I'm so glad. You don't mind they're upstairs? The Americans all wanted the orchestra. So then the French had to — But of course you can see everything up there, the full stage." Fluttering now. "You can feel it, yes? Everyone so excited. All these years, and now — a million things to do. Everyone thinks it just happens by itself."

"How's Bert? Nervous?"

"Oh, you know him. Like a slug. He pretends — but he must feel it too. It's the homecoming. I said to him, you arrived in October but it's tonight that you come home. Be sure you make an entry in your journal. January 11, 1949. Years from now, people will look for that. How you felt when *Mother Courage* opened. I'm sorry," she said, finally turning to Irene.

"Irene Gerhardt," Alex said, introducing her. "An old Berlin friend. From before the war."

"The war," Ruth said vaguely, distracted. "Do you know what is so interesting? We were here at rehearsal. So in the Thirty Years' War. And I went for a walk in the

425

Tiergarten, and it was the same. The same landscape." She held out her hands, a scale weighing. "Outside, inside — the same. What a vision he had. And now everyone will feel the play is about them. A play about war. In Berlin. Who knows better about that?"

"Irene, how wonderful. You're here. I was hoping —" Elsbeth leaned forward to kiss her on the cheek. Still pale, the Dresden doll skin pasty, eyes retreating. "And Alex. You're here too. How is Er— ?" Stopping in time, a quick, awkward glance to see who might have heard, but Ruth had already drifted away.

"Better. He's better."

"Well, yes, Gustav helped him with the medicine. He's so generous, you know, and for family —"

"He's here?" Irene said.

"Getting drinks. But, my God, look at all these lights. We're down to two hours a day now. Electricity. It comes and you rush to do everything at once. The ironing. The sewing machine. Everything all at once, before it goes off again. And of course the refrigerator, it's hopeless. I said we would be better off if we had an icebox, like in the old hinterhofs. But then where do you get the ice? The worst part is you never know *when* the two hours come. Once it was one in the morning. So you iron when you want to be sleeping."

Alex glanced toward the bar, spotting Gustav's tall head, Elsbeth's litany of complaint indistinct, background noise. Maybe the way people talked during the Thirty Years' War too, consumed by domestic grievances. But someone who would try to keep Irene in sight, a possible monkey wrench in the plan.

"Where are you sitting?" he said suddenly, trying not to sound anxious.

"Where? With the Bowens," she said. She fished a ticket out of her purse. "Good seats, I think. You know, he's the British — Row D. So close. They said we should come. I don't like to, you know. I'm afraid to go to the East. But Gustav said, what could be safer? Travel with the British command. Who would dare to bother you? And I thought, well, that's right, isn't it? And it's Brecht." She looked at Irene. "Like the old days. How long has it been? You remember Papa?" Smiling now, dropping her voice. " '*Quatsch.* Plays about whores.' "

"No, he preferred the real thing."

Elsbeth giggled, suddenly a girl, then looked around. "Why don't you come see me?" she said, keeping her voice low, intimate. "You never come anymore."

"I will. I promise."

"And Erich?" Almost a whisper. "He's with you?"

"No. He went to the West," she said, looking at Alex.

"The West? How?"

"I don't know. Someone helped him, I guess. He sent a message. He's safe. Don't worry." Saying it to herself.

"Where?" Elsbeth said, pressing.

"I don't know. He said he would write. I'll let you know."

"We'll never see him again," Elsbeth said, looking down. "The Russians will squeeze and squeeze and then they'll come in and that will be that. That's how it's going to end. How else? They'll round us up. I'm sure Gustav is on a list."

"What list?" Gustav said, joining them. "Irene." Nodding to her, then to Alex. "How is your patient? It was TB?"

Elsbeth put a hand on his arm. "I'll tell you later."

"Ah, family secrets."

"He's fine," Irene said.

"And you? No Russian friend tonight?" he said, a suppressed sneer.

"He was called back to Moscow," Irene said evenly.

"For good?"

Irene shrugged.

"So you're alone now. No protector? I said this would happen, no? It's always the same."

"Alex protects me. So you don't have to worry."

Gustav hesitated, not sure how to take this.

"Oh, it's so nice to see you," Elsbeth said again, taking Irene's hand. "What are you doing after? Maybe we can —" Not noticing Irene's hand grow rigid, alarmed.

"What are you thinking?" Gustav said. "We told the Bowens —" He broke off and turned to Irene. "Our hosts. But another time."

"Yes, it's better really. I'm not feeling well tonight." In the play again.

"Yes, what's wrong?" Gustav said, a doctor's question.

"I don't know. My stomach. It's nothing, maybe something I ate. And the next day you're fine."

"Too many rations perhaps," Gustav said, the edge back in his voice. "You should come to our sector. Seventeen hundred calories a day. A stomach problem? No, hunger. Thanks to the Russians. Of course it's different for you. He probably gave you extra rations. *Payoks.*"

"Yes, that's right," Irene said, looking at him. "As much as I wanted. I never went hungry."

Gustav, held by her gaze, took a step back, a physical retreat. "Well, we should find the Bowens."

"They helped Gustav with the license," Elsbeth said, explaining them. "So he could practice again. They think the Americans are mad. To make it so hard, if you were a Party member. Everyone was, all the doctors."

"Some even believed in it," Irene said smoothly, avoiding Gustav's eye.

"Well, everything seemed different in those days," Elsbeth said. "It's funny, though, you know, to ride in a car with a British flag. Like the ones on the planes. That bombed us. Maybe even the ones that killed —"

"The British bombed at night," Gustav said, annoyed. "In the daytime it was the Americans."

"Yes, that's right," Elsbeth said. "It was the Americans. So at least we don't ride with them."

Gustav straightened himself to go, a heel-clicking motion. "I hope you feel better."

"Do you know the play?" Elsbeth said

suddenly. "I read it. She loses everything in the war. Her children. But she goes back to it. To make her living. So maybe she's part of it too. Do you think that's what he meant?"

Irene, not answering, leaned over and kissed her cheek. "With Brecht it's always more than one thing. I'll come see you soon."

Elsbeth nodded, letting Gustav pull her away into the crowd.

"Why did you tell her Erich was in the West?"

"Well, he will be, won't he? At least now Gustav won't be tempted to turn him in. If he's already gone."

"He wouldn't do that. He doesn't want to go near the police. Any police. You do that and before you know it, they start looking at you."

Irene lowered her head. "What if I never see her again?"

Alex said nothing.

"You know what it feels like with her?" Irene said quietly. "She's just waiting now. On a platform, maybe. Bags packed. Waiting."

"Irene —"

"There you are," Martin said. "Can I borrow him for a few pictures? *Neues Deutsch-*

land. Quite an evening, yes?"

"You'll be all right?" Alex said to Irene, waiting for her to nod. "She hasn't been feeling well," he said to Martin.

"I thought maybe you and Comrade Seghers," Martin said, not listening. "She's over here." Nodding toward the familiar white hair, pulled back in a bun. "Both friends of Brecht. And of course in your own right —"

"What news of Aaron? Any?"

Martin stopped, as if someone had clutched his shoulder. "No." His eyes darted anxiously, not here, not now.

"Does anyone know where he is? His wife?"

"I don't know. Herr Meier — Alex — please. Tonight —"

Alex looked around the room. Did anyone else feel it, the undertow? People slipping away under the bright lights. Not just late to work at DEFA. People everyone here knew. Now no longer talked about, like nervous tics kept under control, willed away.

"You say you'll come to see me, but you never do," Anna Seghers said, taking his hand.

"But I will. It's been a busy time."

"Oh, with this one?" she said, nodding to Martin. "Always arranging things."

"Stand together. Just there. That's right."

Flashbulbs.

"I wanted to ask you," Alex said, turning to her, another picture, casually chatting. "Have you heard anything about Aaron? Where he is? I'm worried —"

"No, nothing," she said, looking at him. "Someone said they're keeping him in Potsdam, but I think it's a rumor only."

"But why?"

"Alex," she said, touching his arm, a quieting, like a finger to the lips.

"Can't anyone do something?"

"But we don't know yet what is happening. Perhaps questions only. Maybe an indiscretion." Her voice low, one more smile for the camera. "We don't know the reasoning. The Party doesn't always explain. That doesn't mean they have no reason."

Alex looked at her, wondering if she could possibly believe this. The Party innocent until proven guilty, not Aaron. But her eyes gave away nothing, her voice even, not shaded with irony.

"It's not the Fascists," she said, then looked away, flustered.

"No," Alex said. "It's us."

Seghers looked up at this, about to respond, then caught herself, seeing Dymshits coming to join them. "Major," she said, her voice louder, a signal to Alex.

433

"My favorite writers. What a good picture, seeing you together like this." His glasses were shining in the lobby light, the slicked-back Thalberg hair gleaming. His body seemed to bounce, as if he were clapping his hands in delight. "Everyone is here. They say Emil Jannings might come. He hasn't been well, but for such an occasion —"

"A man who makes films for the Nazis?" Anna said, surprised. "He's invited?"

"Not invited. It's a question of getting tickets. Look around. They come from all over Berlin. So why not Jannings. It's not the old Germany anymore," he said to Anna, a gentle reproach. "Tonight it's the new Germany. And where is it? Here. In the East. They all come to us."

"It's a great credit to the Office of Cultural Affairs," Martin said, hovering.

"Well, that," Dymshits said, taking the compliment seriously. "No. Ask these two. It's about the artists, always the artists. Who else makes the culture? But we provide maybe the good climate, so it can flourish. That's our legacy, I hope. That we understood the importance of culture, that we made it grow here." A speech he must have made before, but the voice genuine, believing. "So we ask the artists to come home, and here you are. At such an evening." He looked around again, ready to be dazzled. "You know the play? To read, yes, but to actually see it? And now with Dessau doing the music — you've never heard the songs like this. I saw them rehearse — don't tell Brecht, he doesn't like it, people coming in."

"You're not people," Martin said politely.

Dymshits bowed. "Tonight, yes. Part of the audience only. So nice to see you all here. Zweig too, I think, somewhere." Vaguely looking around, everyone easy to lose in a crowd. "Ah, look who couldn't resist," Dymshits said, nodding to the door. "Even RIAS tonight."

"What?" Alex said, not expecting this.

"So, Ferber, no American jazz tonight? What will your audience think?"

"You can ask them yourself. They're all over here."

Dymshits lowered his head in a touché gesture. "As are you, I see. An evening of real culture for a change? You know these people?" he said, introducing them.

"We have met at the Kulturbund," Ferber said to Alex.

"Yes, at the reception. I thought you were at the radio station every night."

"Well, not tonight. Not now, anyway."

"You mean you'll be there later?" Alex

said, catching his eye, Ferber finally alert.

"Another night owl," Dymshits said pleasantly. "Maybe you're going to broadcast a review of the play?"

"I haven't decided yet."

"Oh, you mean you might like it. And have to say something good about our Berlin."

"Your Berlin. There are two now?" Ferber said, baiting him.

"If you listen to the Americans. But here you are," Dymshits said, not rising to it. "You see how easily people come and go? Despite what your radio says."

"As long as they don't leave the zone."

"Why would anyone want to leave?"

Ferber shrugged.

Alex watched them volley. Not the way he'd imagined, but maybe another piece of luck, something he could use. Ferber at the theater all evening. Ferber shot him a darting look, what? Alex glanced back.

"One more picture?" Martin said. "With the major this time?"

Anna and Alex grouped next to him, their backs to the door.

"I see all your usual theater critics have come out," Ferber said to Dymshits, another tease.

Dymshits turned to see a thickset man coming through the door. Receding hairline, head shaved on both sides, his face set in a scowl of suspicion. He looked, Alex thought, a little like J. Edgar Hoover, the same bulldog stance, the eyes sweeping the room, as if he were looking for snipers.

"Who's that?" Alex said, slightly mesmerized.

"Erich Mielke," Ferber said. "A great lover of the theater. Runs K-5 and the new K-5, whatever they're calling it now."

"Police, you mean."

"But not parking tickets. You better be careful. People have been known to disappear when Comrade Mielke's around. Now you see them, now you don't."

"Another American fantasy," Dymshits said. "Herr Ferber —"

"Suit yourself," Ferber said, holding up his hands. "Just don't go anywhere alone."

"Well, right now I want to use the men's room before we go in. Think that's safe enough?" Trying to keep his voice light, not an invitation, but Ferber heard it.

"In pairs," Ferber said, beginning to split off with him.

"American wit," Dymshits said. "But I wonder. How many of your security people go to the theater, take an interest in such things?"

Ferber grinned. "I'll give you that one.

But let's make a bet. Keep an eye on Mielke. See how long he stays awake."

"Of course he stays awake. Why would he come?"

"I'll give you that one too," Ferber said. "Herr Meier?"

But Alex had stopped, rooted. Behind Mielke, probably in attendance, Markus had just noticed him. Another complication, Markus not likely to ignore him, let him melt away. Obsessed with Irene, always eager to keep an eye out. He thought of Mielke's quick glance sweeping the room. Markus nodded, a polite secret smile between them. How do you become invisible when everyone is watching?

Ferber moved him toward the men's room.

"What's wrong? It's tonight? Why didn't you tell me?"

"I thought it was safer. You said you were there every night."

"Not this night."

"Never mind. Maybe it's better. We'll meet you there after the play. Nobody on your staff will be expecting it then. What's the setup down there?"

"Staff entrance in the back. With a parking lot. Just use my name at the gate. Studio one-ten. Ground floor. If I'm not there yet, anybody can set you up."

"No, be there."

"I came with people. I can't just —"

"They'll understand. You have to rush back. *Mother Courage* is news, no?"

"Let's hope so. How are you going to work this? You coming with him?"

Alex nodded. "The U-Bahn, like you said. But you'll have a car for us later, right?"

"Herr Meier, such a pleasure to see you." Markus, without Mielke in tow. "Herr Ferber."

Ferber gave him a perfunctory nod, then glanced toward the men's room. "Well, I'd better go before there's a line. Enjoy the play." Sliding off.

"What did he want?"

"What he always wants. For me to go on the radio. Don't worry, I said no. The last thing I'd want to do."

"That's right. You prefer the quiet life." Smiling to himself, some private joke.

"I see you're with the boss. Another promotion?"

Markus cocked his head. "It's good that I know you from before. Your true feelings. Someone else might misinterpret." He held his glance for a second, then moved on. "You're here with her?"

"Isn't that what you want?"

"I want you to be careful. A woman like that —"

"You don't have to worry about that. She's already making new friends."

"Yes?"

"Yes. You know how friendly the Russians can be."

"Alex —"

"And not a sign of Markovsky. I don't think she has any idea where he is. We're just chasing our tails with this."

"An American idiom?"

"Going in circles, getting nowhere. She's hurt, that's all."

"Hurt?"

"You spend time with somebody and he leaves without even saying good-bye? It makes her feel like —" He stopped.

"Yes," Markus said, amused. "She'd be convincing at that. Just keep your ears open."

"But does that sound like the kind of thing he would do?"

Markus looked up.

"I don't think so either. That's not the way it makes sense. He didn't say good-bye because he wasn't going anywhere. Something happened to him. You've checked with the police?"

"Of course we've checked," Markus said

quickly, annoyed. "Everything. It's not so easy to hide a body. Even in Berlin. Karlshorst doesn't think he's dead — they're still looking. So we keep looking too."

"What do they say, Karlshorst?" Alex said, curious, testing the ice.

"Well, Karlshorst," Markus said, unexpectedly sharp, an exposed nerve. "They don't always share things. It's for security reasons," he said, looking up, correcting himself. "In sensitive cases."

Alex nodded. The defection was still a Russian secret.

"Have you heard anything more about Aaron?"

Markus glanced up. "Don't ask about this. I was able to intervene in the case of your friend Kleinbard, but the other —"

"You mean you got him out?"

"A bureaucratic procedure only. A Party review."

"Thank you."

"Thank the Party."

Alex said nothing, letting this pass.

"And there she is," Markus said, talking half to himself, staring past Alex's shoulders. People were beginning to move in to their seats, the whole lobby in motion, Irene standing fixed in her own island near the doors, a rock in a stream. "As you say. New friends."

Alex stood still, a prickling at the back of his neck. The Russian who'd been in her room. Now smiling, making small talk. Irene's world. Something Alex thought he knew, had accepted, until it was in front of him and his blood jumped. What he really felt, the same wrench in his stomach, seeing Kurt's head in her lap.

"Everything is so easy for them," Markus was saying.

"Who?"

"That family. The von Bernuths. If you dropped something, someone was always there to pick it up. So why not do whatever you wanted? With so many servants. And we were the servants. We were glad to pick up, just to be part of that house. Remember at Christmas, the big tree? The parties. Even Kurt, a good Communist, but for her? A servant. Sometimes I think it was that house he loved, not her. That life. You fall down, always a soft carpet. I used to think, what is it like to be them? Everything so easy."

Alex looked at him, oddly touched. A boy with his face pressed against the glass.

"They don't feel that way now," he said.

"No?" Markus said, coming back. "Well, a

child's memory only. What does a child see?"

"It's gone. The money, everything."

"Yes, I know. You wrote about this. And then the war. But look how she stands. The shoulders. That's not money, something else."

"That's Fritz," Alex said. "Well, I'd better go rescue her."

Markus smiled. "Still the servant. But servants hear things, so it's good. Maybe you could bring her one day, to see my mother. Someone from the old days," he said, trying to sound casual.

Alex stopped. "I forgot to ask. How is she?"

"Not so well. Still at the Central Secretariat guest house. She prefers it there." He hesitated, weighing, then looked up. "Can I tell you something? You're the only one now from those days. The others —"

Alex waited, his silence a kind of assent.

"We're strangers to each other," Markus said finally. "I know," he said before Alex could answer. "She's my mother. But it's too many years maybe. Maybe that."

"Give it some time."

"She says things. I think, who is this woman? Does she know what it was like for me, to suffer for her crimes?"

"For you?" Alex said.

"Yes. All the children. After the parents were taken away. We were — orphans. Imagine what terrible things might have happened. Only the Party saved us."

Alex stood still, unable to speak, people brushing past on their way into the theater. He thought of her bony hand on the railing, too afraid to risk the elevator, a punishment box. He's one of them.

Finally, at a loss, he just nodded and said, "I'll bring Irene." But of course she'd be gone, another ghost after tonight.

He went over to her, still talking to the Russian. "We should go up."

"Yes," she said, relieved to get away.

"We meet again," the Russian said to Alex.

Alex acknowledged this with a look, taking Irene's elbow.

"But a minute," the Russian said, blocking them. "The general wanted to meet you." This to Irene.

"General?"

"Saratov. The one who replaces Markovsky. He had to use the toilet, but I know he wanted — ah, here. General, Frau Gerhardt."

"I have heard of you, of course," he said, a curt nod to Irene, but taking them both in.

Saratov was barrel-chested and dark, a short man with none of Markovsky's blond good looks — Georgian, perhaps, or Armenian, a permanent stubble on his face that suggested hair everywhere else, and an almost feral alertness in his eyes.

"I was told you were beautiful and I can see the reports were accurate."

A line meant to be charming but said without inflection, something memorized from a foreign language.

"Well, I think exaggerated," Irene said, "but thank you. When did you arrive in Berlin?" Making conversation.

Saratov ignored this, looking at Alex instead, waiting for the Russian to introduce him.

"Your friend," the Russian said to Irene, prodding her to do it, Alex unknown to him.

"Oh, Alex Meier. A friend since childhood. Here in Berlin. He's back from America to be with us again. A writer, very celebrated. You never think someone you knew as a child can be famous —"

"America," Saratov said, not interested in the rest. "You were there how long?"

"Fifteen years," Alex said, returning his stare. A hard-liner, close to Beria.

"A very long time."

"The Nazis took a long time to be defeated."

"But you didn't return immediately."

"No one did. It wasn't allowed. And then the Soviet Military Administration invited me to come home. So here I am."

Saratov grunted, frowning a little, as if Alex had been impertinent. He turned back to Irene.

"You were a friend of Major Markovsky."

"Yes, we knew each other."

"Then you'll be pleased that I bring good news of him."

"Yes?" Irene said, momentarily still, blinded. Only her hands moved, clutching her purse as if it were about to slide between her fingers.

"Yes, he is well. In Moscow."

Alex froze. Don't react. But Saratov's eyes were fixed on Irene, a beady relentless gaze. Her hands jerked again, tighter on the purse, and Alex thought of a hare in a trap, pulling at its leg.

"In Moscow," she said, buying time, even a second. Alex held his breath, the noise around them now just a hum. And then she found it, some miraculous reserve of will, and smiled. The von Bernuth shoulders. "Oh, I'm so glad. We were worried. People came asking questions — they said he was

446

missing. So you found him?"

"Not missing," Saratov said smoothly. "More misplaced. He became ill and he went to the infirmary, but not his assigned one. No one thought to look in the other. A foolish mistake. I'm sorry if anyone disturbed you —"

"No, no, I'm so happy to know it. So he's back in Moscow?" The hands still now, finding the part.

"Yes, with his wife." A jab, just to see the reaction.

Irene looked down. "Yes, of course. His wife."

"You knew he had a wife."

She raised her head, meeting his eyes. "Of course. He often spoke of her. She must be happy that he's back."

Saratov, not expecting this, said nothing.

The lights flickered, the call to go in.

"So," Irene said. "No more mystery. All is well in the end. Like a play."

"Yes, a good ending," Saratov said, his voice steady, almost insistent.

Alex looked over at him, uneasy. Close to Beria. They rewrote history, whole swatches of it, why not Markovsky? People erased from photographs, evidence fabricated, confessions taken down. The world was what you said it was. Markovsky was happy

447

in Moscow, Irene discarded — but wasn't that the way of things, the way it had to end? And now it had. But why?

"I hope you will be easy now in your mind," Saratov said, putting on his hat.

"Yes, thank you for telling me. You're not coming in?"

"No. Leon here is the one for the theater. I prefer facts."

Alex looked at him again. Was he toying with them? Watching the hare twisting in the trap.

"I came for the reception only. A courtesy to Major Dymshits. And my German, you know — I don't think it's up to this. A whole evening."

"It will come to you. Sasha — Major Markovsky — had only a little when he arrived."

"No doubt he had an excellent teacher." Dipping his head, but not smiling.

"And what good will it do him now?" Leon said. "In Moscow, I mean," he said, catching Saratov's glance.

"We'd better go up," Alex said.

"I'll say good night, then," Saratov said.

The lights flickered again.

"Don't worry," Leon said to Irene as Saratov left.

"Worry?"

"Sometimes his manner — but it's just his manner." He paused, a quick side glance to Alex. "Maybe we'll see each other again."

"And you," Irene said. "Is your wife in Moscow too?"

"In Perm," he said, a knowing faint smile. "Even further away."

Irene turned toward the stairs, not answering.

"Don't talk to her like that," Alex said.

"The family friend," Leon said, another smile.

Alex looked at him. Not here. Not tonight. "And what are you?" he said, then started for the stairs.

"My God," Irene said on the landing. "I'm shaking."

"No, you were perfect."

"He kept looking at me, just to see how — But what does it mean? Why would he say that? Sasha in Moscow."

"I'm not sure."

"To see what I know, I think. If I'm surprised. If I'm not surprised. And either way he suspects."

"Maybe. And maybe he wants you to think he doesn't suspect. They're walking away from it. So you don't have to worry anymore."

"And then put a rope around my neck."

He took her elbow. "They don't know he's dead."

"They must know something. Why would they make such a lie?"

"I don't know. I have to think."

"Oh, think. Look at me. Shaking. I really will be sick."

"We're almost there. Remember, go to the ladies' room before the curtain. Establish it."

"And he doesn't even come to the play. So maybe he's outside. Waiting to see who comes out. Who doesn't believe him about Moscow."

"*Shh.* Let's find our seats. Check the sight lines."

"The sight — ?"

"Who can see us."

They were in the first ring, three rows up, last seats on the aisle. Alex stood for a minute, trying to locate faces. The Russian, Leon, he spotted in the swarm of people below — a seat back in the orchestra, out of the way. But where was Markus, sharp-eyed Mielke? He turned his head slowly, scanning the mezzanine. Not up here. Beneath the overhang? Anna Seghers's white hair, Dymshits still working the aisle below, greeting people, Ferber next to a group of Americans. But what about the people he didn't know? Hundreds of eyes.

"Okay, go to the ladies' room now."

"I'm so nervous, it's for real."

He continued to stand, letting people get by him to their center seats, his eyes circling the theater. Markus and Mielke, there, in a box. Spotting him, nodding, but getting into chairs facing the stage — they'd have to swivel around to see him after the play started. Still looking for Markovsky, Karlshorst keeping things to themselves again, but neither of them aware there was a corpse in a drawer, fished out near Bellevue. Why say he was in Moscow? Maybe Irene was right — some trap, baiting them with surprise, just to see how they bit. Maybe Saratov, new to the job, wanted the whole thing off his desk, filed away. But the leak couldn't be filed away, still talking in Wiesbaden, Saratov's worst nightmare — a willing defector or a kidnapped one, did it matter? Someone who knew, who'd sat at the same desk. Unless — Alex stopped, looking straight out at the curtain, the noise rising up from the orchestra like heat. Unless they knew there was no defector, had never been. Unless they knew.

He stood for another minute, staring straight ahead, thinking, before he caught the movement, Elsbeth waving from below.

Front orchestra with the — what were their names? Now pantomiming "Where's Irene?" Alex signaling back, touching his stomach, then cocking his head toward the restrooms. Elsbeth nodded and excused herself, making her way up the crowded aisle. Not what he'd intended. Now she'd be concerned all evening, keeping them in sight. He looked again toward Markus's box. Leaning close to hear what Mielke had to say, but both facing forward. Dymshits taking his seat now. Where was Martin? Probably in the balcony. Ferber still with the Americans. Leon out of sight. He made another sweep of the first tier. No glasses looking away from the stage, no one facing backward. In the murmuring, expectant theater, no one seemed to be watching him.

Markovsky alive and well in Moscow. Some mischievous game, our phantom versus your phantom? We know. Not in Wiesbaden. But then where was he? Still somewhere in Berlin, waiting for Irene. Alex's eye stopped on two Russians, sitting in a box opposite, staring across. But they could be looking at anybody. If they knew who he was, what he was going to do, they wouldn't just watch, wait for an excuse. What would be the charge? Counterrevolutionary activities, like Aaron? Worse? In the end, did it matter? They took you to Sachsenhausen because they could. The charges came later.

"Herr Meier, what a nice surprise." Herb Kleinbard, taking the seat behind him, out free, just as Markus had said. "It gives me the chance to thank you. For your help. Roberta told me —" He turned to her, bringing her into the conversation.

"No, I made inquiries, that's all," Alex said, dismissing it, aware that Roberta seemed somehow embarrassed, awkward in his presence, as if she now regretted drawing him into their lives. "Everything is all right now, I hope?"

"Yes. A bureaucratic mistake. But of course, a worry if one doesn't know this," he said, a nod to Roberta, explaining her.

"Yes," she said simply, still in a kind of retreat. "Alex was very kind. A good neighbor." Glancing at him, then looking away, uncomfortable, eager to move on. What had she told Herb? How desperate she had been? How Alex had helped?

"And neighbors tonight, I think," Herb said. "You're sitting there?"

"Yes. And here's Irene. Roberta, you remember Frau Gerhardt?"

More awkwardness, Irene still a mystery to her, a woman with a car from Karlshorst.

453

"Feeling better?" Alex said. "She hasn't been well today. I think only Brecht could bring her out."

"A special occasion, yes," Herb said. Then, to Alex, "Thank you again. You're modest, but I know what it means. To help in such a situation. People don't want to get involved, they don't know it's a mistake, they're afraid. So I thank you."

Alex received this with a nod. "But it was Roberta, really. She wouldn't give up, and now here you are."

"We should sit," Roberta said. Not wanting to talk about it.

"Did they treat you — ? I mean, you're all right?"

"Yes. Such places, they're not pleasant. Well, we know that. Not country clubs. But you know, you put it out of your mind. An evening like this, to see this in Berlin, you forget the bad times."

Alex looked at him. "I was there. I never forgot."

Herb met his eyes. "No, that's right. You don't forget." No longer pretending, but still unsure what it meant, how he was going to live with it.

"Oh, they're starting," Roberta said, taking her seat as the theater went dark.

Irene leaned over to him as they sat down.

"Now what?" she whispered. "They're right behind us. People you know."

Alex said nothing, trying to make out the stage in the still black air, even the tinkle of voices disappearing, a void.

"What can we do?" she said even fainter.

"We go ahead. We have to. I'll tell you when. Watch the play."

Suddenly, a flash of light, the stage flooded with it, stark, exposed, nothing shaded or softened. The Recruiting Officer and the Sergeant talking, a sharp tang in the language, Brecht's German. An almost palpable pleasure went through the audience, street German, irreverent, theirs. *Off he's gone like a louse from a scratch. You know what the trouble with peace is? No organization.* And Ruth, as usual, was right: the stage was the Tiergarten, the street outside, the harsh bareness of it, another wasteland. The Thirty Years' War. No props or scenery needed. The eye filled it with rubble and scorched trees. A faint harmonica, the canteen wagon rolling onto the stage, Eilif and Swiss Cheese pulling like oxen, up on the seat Mother Courage with dumb Kattrin, Helene Weigel calling out a good day, the voice perfect, a whole character in a line, and then the first song and Dymshits was right too, Dessau's music gave Weigel her range, coarse and defiant, almost bawdy, the unselfconscious irony hinting at the horrors to come. Alex looked around. A magic in the theater, that moment of breathing together, seeing the extraordinary. And now happening here, with the rubble outside, Germany still alive, capable of art, a future.

Alex sat still, letting the language roll over him. Weigel fighting with Eilif now, drawing papers out of the helmet, omens of death. He shook his head. Pay attention to the audience, not the play. Over the railing, somewhere below, Elsbeth was watching a mother lose her children. Markus and Mielke, down right in a privileged box. How many in the audience were their informants, diligently filing reports? Maybe even on the play. Did any of them trust Brecht really, always slipping something by in a line?

He squinted, trying to see the faces, but the effect of the floodlit stage was to make the rest of the theater even darker. Unless you were in the first few rows, you were swallowed up in the shadows. These ring seats were even less visible. He could barely make out the audience, but they couldn't see him at all. Unless they were sitting right behind him.

Onstage Mother Courage had lost Eilif and now was opening the second scene selling a capon, a long screech of German that Weigel massaged like an aria, reaching for notes. No one was looking anywhere else. As good a time as intermission, when people get lost in the crowd.

"Now," he said faintly to Irene's ear.

She started, as absorbed in the play as the rest of the audience, then nodded and moved her hands to her stomach, waiting a bit, then bending over, a soft grunt, almost inaudible. Alex put his arm around her shoulders, helping her out of her seat and starting up the stairs to the exit.

"We have to go," he whispered to Roberta. "She's not feeling well. Take our seats, they're closer." And not empty if anyone looked, one body as good as another in the dark. "Her time of the month. She'll be all right tomorrow."

Roberta seemed to shrink from this, embarrassed again, and just nodded, turning her head back toward the stage.

At the curtain covering the exit door Alex turned, trying to make out the Russians across. Had they noticed? He waited for a second to see if anyone had followed, some furtive movement, but all he could hear was Weigel arguing with the cook.

They went down the hall, no ushers, Alex's arm still around her shoulder. The stairs would be trickier, visible to the concession sellers in the lobby. But everyone, it seemed, wanted to see the play, even standing in the back. They slid out the exit door, away from the waiting cars out front. A stagehand having a cigarette, shivering.

"Not feeling well," Alex said, still whispering.

The stagehand just looked at them, indifferent.

They headed toward Luisenstrasse, the way to Irene's flat, but then turned right at the corner instead, heading up to the Charité. If anyone was following, he'd have to turn too or risk losing them. They slowed, waiting a minute, but no one turned into the street. A car had come over the bridge and swept past without slowing. A man helping a woman get to the hospital, what you'd expect to see here.

"Where did he leave the key?"

"Under the fender," Irene said. "It's taped there."

"Hell of a risk. Anybody could —"

"It's DEFA's car, he doesn't care."

The car was in the faculty lot, just in from the street, the key still in place. Irene put her hand on the door, then looked up.

"What if something — ?"

Alex shook his head. "Ready?"

"If anything does, I'll —"

He looked up, waiting.

"I'll never forget you did this for him."

Alex opened his door. "We'd better stick to the main roads. At least they'll be cleared. It's easy to get lost if they're not —"

"Don't worry. I know Berlin. That's all I know, Berlin."

He headed north toward Invalidenpark, away from the theater and any cars that might recognize them, then swung east to connect with Torstrasse.

"You never told me where he is."

"Friedrichshain. By the park."

"So far."

"Not from me."

"No, from the radio. In Schöneberg, no?"

"We're not going to the radio. Not now, anyway."

"But I thought —"

"That's the choke point. The one place they don't want him to go. They don't want him to broadcast. So they'll be waiting to stop him there. If they know."

"But it's how he pays."

"He will. But not there."

There was more traffic than he expected, Soviet trucks sputtering diesel and a few prewar cars, so it took a while to reach Prenzlauer Allee. He turned up, then drove between the cemeteries and across Greif-swalder Strasse.

"I think we're all right," he said. "You see anything?"

"How would I know? They all look alike to me."

"You'd notice if it's the same one."

To be safe, he detoured in a short loop, then came down Am Friedrichshain from the east.

"Press number five," he said, idling the car at the green door.

But Erich was already there, waiting.

"Oh, so pale," Irene said, a mother hen's fluttering, as he got in the back. "You still have the fever?"

"It's better," Erich said. "Let's go."

"Duck a little," Alex said, "so no one sees your head."

"They're following you?"

"Not yet."

"I have a message for you. He said to tell you the refrigerator is still working."

Alex smiled.

"Who said?" Irene asked.

"No one." Alex looked at her. "No one."

She said nothing, turning to the side window. "But he helps Erich," she said finally. "How do you arrange these things?"

Not really a question. She raised her voice,

to the back. "You have your coat? It's cold."

"Yes, I'm warm enough. Don't worry."

"Enka's," she said vaguely. "I kept it. I didn't want to sell it. For those prices. He always had good things, Enka."

"It's lucky for me you kept it," Erich said.

"Yes," Irene said, "At least we have the coats on our backs. Imagine if father knew this. Leaving Berlin with nothing. Just the coats on our backs. And a purse," she said, raising it.

"How's your voice?" Alex said to Erich. "Still hoarse?"

"Not so much. I've been thinking what to say. What will he ask, do you think?"

"He won't. I will."

"You?" Irene said.

"Well, not on the air. I can't use my voice. They'd pick it up right away. I've written some questions out. You just answer, then say whatever you want."

"But we're not on the radio?"

"You will be. Make a tape recording, they can play it anytime. Don't worry, you'll sound as if you're there in the studio."

They were crossing the Spree now, into Spittelmarkt, and turning up to the center.

"We're going to the house?" Erich said, suddenly excited, head up.

"It's not there anymore, Erich," Irene said

461

gently, to a child. "It was bombed."

"But it's just up here. Let me see. I want to see it."

"There isn't time," Alex said.

"But it would be the last time. I can't come back."

Irene turned to Alex. "We have one minute? We can spare that? If he wants to see."

"Stay in the car. One minute."

He turned into Kleine Jägerstrasse, stopping the car by the mound of rubble where he'd had his morning cigarette. The street was deserted. In the moonlight you could see the jagged outline of the remaining walls, still, lifeless.

"Oh," Erich said. "Look. Only the door."

"I told you. It's gone," Irene said.

"So many years. And then gone. I thought it would always be like that, the way we lived here."

"So sentimental," Irene said. "It was an ugly house."

"Not to me. Not to Mama. She loved it. And to be like this — who was it, the British or the Amis?"

"I don't know. Does it matter? By that time it wasn't ours anyway. Papa sold it. To the Nazis. Well, who else was here to buy it? So it's not von Bernuth for a long time. You miss it? What do you miss? Your own child-hood, that's all. The house —" She waved, letting the house slip away.

"Still," Erich said.

"It wasn't the same after Mama died," Irene said, partly to herself now. "He let it go. Like everything else. I think he never liked it here anyway. He liked the farm. Where he could bully his Poles."

"He never bullied —"

"Ouf," Irene said. "More stories. Anyway, they have it now, the farm, so in the end —" She trailed off, then turned to Erich. "And we have our coats. So that's something. Maybe this time we won't be so careless."

"Who was careless?"

"Well, maybe not you, so young. Look at Papa, one card game and another piece of furniture's gone. Look at me." She stopped, gazing out the window at the house. "You know, when you put us in the book," she said to Alex. "The girl wasn't me."

"No, I —"

"You thought it was, maybe, but it wasn't. A story. Now I think you want to put me in another story. And I'm not her either."

Alex stared at her. "What do you — ?"

But she cut him off, turning to Erich again. "But you'll be safe, that's all that matters. So take a look and now it's gone, *poof.* Bricks. That time, too. Gone."

"Okay?" Alex said, putting the car in gear, anxious to start again.

"Never mind," Irene said, a stage cheerfulness. "We'll start over." She nodded to Erich. "Maybe for once a von Bernuth who amounts to something."

Erich smiled. "Do you remember what you used to say to me?"

"What I — ?"

"Remember who you are. You used to say that. Remember who you are."

"Well, in those days."

"Always proud of that, who we were. So you don't change."

Irene said nothing and turned back to face the street.

"Look, the French Church. The dome's gone," Erich said, still having his last look at the city. Alex thought of the day he'd left for good, Berlin draped in swastikas, everything intact. "What happened to St. Hedwig's? Is it all right?"

"No, bombed too," Irene said. "Where are we going?" This to Alex, who was looking in the rearview mirror. Nobody.

"The Kulturbund."

The club was quiet, the few people there already in the dining room. Up the stairs, past Goethe. Martin's office was dark, but unlocked, the tape recorder still on the side table. A portable mike had been attached to it, a makeshift studio, ready to send the word to Dresden and points east. Alex looked through the supply cabinet for a spool of tape and started threading it.

"Are we supposed to be here? What if someone — ?"

"He's at the theater. Let's just hope he doesn't count these," he said, tapping the spool. "Here, give me a voice check. Directly into the mike, don't turn your head. Your normal voice. Irene, close the door. Ready?"

Erich nodded, looking at the paper Alex had given him.

"Just introduce yourself, who you are, and take it from there. Use the questions if you need them. To keep things going. It's really what you want to say. What it was like for you there. Here we go," he said, switching on the recorder.

For a second, Erich said nothing, watching the spools turn, the machine a fascination in itself. Alex pointed to the mike.

"My name is Erich von Bernuth." Alex made a lowering motion with his hand. Erich nodded. "I'm from Berlin. All my life, until I joined the army in 1940. I was not a Nazi, but Germany was at war, so I thought it was the right thing to do. The army. My family had always been in the army." Alex raised his hand, steering him back. "Now I don't know, what was the right thing. I saw terrible — But I was a soldier, so you do what a soldier does." Now a circling motion with Alex's hand, move on. "But I want to tell you about what happened after. What is happening to other German soldiers. So many years later. I was captured, taken prisoner, at Stalingrad. We were sent to a camp, I don't know where, we were never told. Many died, of course, in the transport. The wounded." He stopped, waiting for Alex to nod. "The conditions in the camp were very hard. So more died. Typhus, other diseases. The work. But this was war, you don't expect — Maybe they thought we deserved this treatment, for everything they had lost in the war, their own men. Then the war ends. Those of us who had survived, we thought, now it's over, they'll send us home. Such conditions in wartime, it's one thing, but now — Of course you know they didn't. Your sons and husbands are still there. Slaves. Or they are back in Germany. Slaves here. I was one of these. I was sent to the Erzgebirge, to work in the uranium mines. Maybe some of you have heard of this. Have heard rumors. But now you hear the truth. I was a prisoner there and I escaped. This is what it was like, this is what I want to tell you."

Alex was nodding, clear sailing now. Erich had found his voice, unaffected, sure of itself, the quiet authority of a survivor. It would be a good radio voice, personal, artless. The barracks. The radioactive slime. The sick, sent back to work. The despair of knowing you would never be released, would be worked to death. The voice picked up speed, a steady rumble through the little office, unprompted now. Everything he had come to say.

By the door, Irene was watching, her face clouded over, near tears. What was she seeing? The boy he'd been? The prisoner dodging rat bites? A man at a microphone, no longer young. Maybe some daydream of what might happen next. Remember who you are.

And then he stopped — not abruptly, not fading away, just finished, an affidavit ready for signing. Alex glanced at the tape — almost near the end. Everything Ferber could want, questions spliced in, wrap-up added, the best kind of interview. More than airfare out. Propaganda that was true.

"That was perfect," he said to Erich, putting the reel into an envelope and replacing it with a fresh one on the machine.

Erich nodded, coughing, his body suddenly folding in on itself, as if the talk had exhausted him.

"Now let's get you out of here."

"Cargo," Erich said between coughs, a wry smile. "For the airlift."

They took Friedrichstrasse, safety in numbers, but there were only a few cars and nobody trailing behind. They were almost at Leipziger Strasse before they saw the roadblock farther along. Alex pulled over to the side, watching.

"They stopping everybody?"

"I can't tell," Irene said. "Maybe a random check. They do that sometimes."

"But why tonight? Let's try somewhere else."

He headed west and turned down Wilhelmstrasse, past Goering's Air Ministry, standing alone in the rubble, unscathed, a Berlin irony.

"They're here too," Alex said, idling again by the curb.

"Someone just crossed. Walking. They didn't stop him," Irene said. "Only the cars. Look, not all. They just waved that one on."

"We can't take the chance. Here, you drive and I'll walk him across."

"A woman driving? If they're after us,

they're looking for a couple, no? Not two men. Not you."

Alex looked at her.

"And then he's safe," she said, nodding to Erich, slumped in his seat. She opened her purse. "Here, give me the tape."

"What if — ?"

"And what if they find it on you?"

She took the envelope, not waiting for an answer, and opened the door.

Alex moved the car into the street. Two cars in front, the first being held up, guards looking at papers. The second pulled up, a quick check with the flashlight, another wave. Their turn.

"Papers?" a guard said, bored, shining his flashlight into the back.

Alex handed him his ID card.

"What's the matter with him?"

"Drunk. Let me see if I can find —" Beginning to fumble with Erich's coat.

"Never mind." He looked down at the ID card, making a show of reading it carefully, then handed it back. "Go." He motioned with his hand.

Irene was coming up on the sidewalk, slowing a little, trying to see if everything was all right. Alex watched her as she passed, purse clutched under her arm.

"Fräulein, out alone? All dressed up," the

guard said, the voice of a soldier in a bar. "Where to?"

Irene shrugged. "Meeting a friend. At the station," she said, cocking her head toward the Anhalter Bahnhof down the street.

"Be careful there. An American friend?"

"I don't know. I haven't met him yet."

The guard grinned. "How about a Russian friend?"

"For free?" Irene said, playing, then turned, beginning to move off.

"Worth it," he called to her back. She wriggled her hand, almost out of sight now.

The guard looked back, surprised to see Alex still there, and waved him through again. "Go, go. Next."

They passed Irene, not slowing until they were two streets away, dark to the checkpoint, then waited with the motor running, the roofless shell of the Anhalter off to their right.

"As good as Weigel," Alex said when she got in.

"It's what he thought," she said, then looked out the window as they started again. "What they think we all are."

They were heading straight for Hallesches Tor, no traffic, making up time.

"So, nothing," Irene said. "Nobody's following."

"See how Erich's doing. He's been half asleep. You need to get him to the hospital when you get there."

"An Ami hospital."

"That was the deal."

"The deal. Who made this deal?"

Alex looked at her. "Ferber."

"Oh, Ferber. At the play." She looked at her watch. "Swiss Cheese must be gone by now. Only Kattrin left. Do you think anyone sees we're gone?" Then, thinking, "And what happens, when they ask you? About me?"

"I took you home. After that —"

"Yes, after that. Then they watch you."

She said nothing for a minute, looking out as they crossed the canal and headed up the Mehringdamm.

"You say you're coming after, but you can't, can you?"

"We'll see."

"It's like going to America. You can't do it. You're a traitor there."

"Not that bad," he said, trying to be light. "Uncooperative witness, that's all." He paused. "Times change. It won't always be like this."

She looked up toward Viktoriapark. "But you had to leave. That's why she divorced you?"

471

"Lots of reasons."

"You didn't love her."

"Do you really want to talk about this? Now?"

"When else? I'm almost gone," she said. "Listen." Outside, the roar of planes, coming in low a few streets ahead.

"You didn't love her. Not like me."

He turned to her. "What's this about?"

"Nothing, I guess," she said, looking down. "I just wanted to hear it. Something pleasant to think about in my new life." She raised her head, facing the windshield. "And what will that be, I wonder. No Sashas anymore. All — what? Joes."

"It doesn't have to be like that."

She looked away. "But it will."

A kind of grunt from the back, Erich awake again. "They're so low. We must be close."

"We're here."

He pulled into the broad circular road that fronted Tempelhof, then the inner driveway that led to the building itself. Where taxis used to pull up, dropping passengers, now busy with jeeps and staff cars, the trucks out back on the runways, loading, leaving in fleets on the service roads. He had expected the airport to be bristling with guards, but there weren't any at the doors

472

— maybe all out on the field, where the goods were. The main building, with its square marble columns, was oddly empty, a passenger terminal without passengers, its soaring space echoing with the sounds of planes landing.

They hurried across the waiting hall to the departure gates. Through the windows he could see the floodlights on the field, shining on the runways. Planes pulled up in rows at the gates, assembly-line style, workers swarming over them like ants even before they stopped. German civilians, throwing sacks of coal down chutes from the planes, then lifting them onto trucks. A mobile canteen was making the rounds of the landing area, offering coffee and doughnuts to the pilots, quick snacks for the return trip. Mother Courage in a truck, Alex thought, selling her capon. Had anyone looked for them at intermission? Wind from the propellers was blowing dust across the field. Everybody busy. He had to ask two cargo workers before he was directed to a soldier with a clipboard.

"You the dispatcher?"

"The what?" Cupping his ear.

"With the manifests. What's going out."

"Going out?" he said, a wise guy smirk. "It's supposed to be coming in."

"You should have two passengers on there," Alex said, nodding to the clipboard.

The soldier glanced at Erich, then Irene, still in her theater clothes, giving her the once-over.

"Passengers," he repeated, as if trying to get the joke. "You think this is Pan Am?"

"Orders came from Howley. Direct."

"Not to me."

"Then get on the phone."

The soldier looked up, ready to argue, then stopped, thrown by Alex's voice.

"Now," Alex said.

The soldier waited another second, then crossed over to a phone.

"You better be right. Get my ass in a sling calling —"

"You don't and you've got trouble you can't even imagine."

"Who the fuck are you anyway?"

"They there?" Alex said. "Tell them Don Campbell. BOB. Two passengers. Howley already okayed it."

"*B-O — ?*"

"*B,* as in Bob."

"Very funny. What's — ?"

"Just say it. They'll know."

The soldier listened to the phone for a minute and hung up.

"Okay?" Alex said.

"Sorry. I didn't know who you were."

"What did they say?"

"Said give him whatever he wants."

"Okay, then one more thing. In case somebody else fucked up. Make sure somebody meets the plane and takes him to the hospital. Ours. Military. Get him taken care of, whatever the doc says. Anybody asks, use my name again. And if he has a problem with that, tell him I'll have General Clay call. But that won't be pleasant. She goes with him to the hospital to make sure everything's okay, then find her a billet. Decent. For a lady. You need a name for that," he said, nodding to the manifest, "it's von Bernuth. *V* as in VIP. Understood?"

"Listen, I didn't mean —"

"Just make the call. Now how about a plane?"

The soldier led them back to the gate.

"C-54 down there, as soon as it's unloaded. Nothing much going back, so they can even bunk down." He looked at Erich. "It gets cold that altitude. I'll get some packing quilts put in for them."

"Thank you."

"Sorry about — What is BOB anyway? Something secret?"

Alex just looked at him.

"Right. Okay. Let me go tell the pilot. As

soon as the krauts get the POM off, get them on board. Come on."

They went down the stairs to the field. A truck next to the plane was being stacked with boxes of dried potatoes, the handlers moving quickly, speeded up, like people in silent films. Everything around them, in fact, seemed to be in motion, trucks pulling away, propellers whirring, planes lifting off at the end of the field. Not on tarmac, Alex noticed. Hitler's showcase had never been paved, the runways just dirt though the grass, now covered with perforated steel plates, a temporary fix, like a pontoon bridge, to accommodate the traffic.

"My God. How low they are," Erich said, pointing to a plane coming in over an apartment block, from this angle almost grazing the roof with its landing wheels. He turned to Alex. "Where are we going? West, yes, but where?"

"Frankfurt. Wiesbaden, probably."

"Wiesbaden," Irene said, a wry smile to herself. "For the waters."

"Mm." A kind of grunt, preoccupied, working something out.

"What's wrong? You look —"

"Maybe nothing. Just thinking."

"Thinking," she said.

"It's all so efficient, isn't it?" he said, looking at the airfield.

"You about ready?" the dispatching soldier said. "The POM's almost off. Pilot says you're going to have some company. Layover crew being rotated back." He looked at Alex. "They'll make sure he gets to the hospital. Like you said."

"And you'll call. So the orders are there."

"And I'll call." He turned to one of the ground crew. "Karl, get a ladder." He nodded to Irene and smiled. "Better watch it in those shoes. Okay, that's the last of the spuds. You first," he said to Erich.

"How can I thank you?" Erich said to Alex.

"Just get well," Alex said, hand on his shoulder.

"But to do all this —"

"It was an old debt. Better get on."

He pointed to the ladder on the side of the fuselage. The rotating crew had arrived, throwing duffels up to the open hatch and climbing up after them.

"Wait," Irene said, suddenly grabbing Erich. "I'll say good-bye too. You'll be fine now. They'll take care of you."

"You're not coming?"

"Not yet." She brushed the hair off his forehead. "I want to listen to you on the radio."

"Let's move it," the soldier yelled.

"I'll come later. Write me where you are."

"Irene —" Alex said.

She hugged Erich and patted his shoulder. "Go, go," she said, pushing him a little. "Listen to the doctors." She looked up. "So tall. A man."

He hesitated, confused.

"Don't worry. I'll come soon. Alex will arrange it. Hurry."

She shooed him away then watched him climb the ladder and wave from the hatch.

"What are you doing?" Alex said.

"I've been thinking too. I'm going to stay." She turned to him. "With you."

"Don't forget why we're doing this."

"I know. To protect me. But this way, we protect each other."

"And when they find Markovsky?"

"Maybe they never do. And why should it be me? I'm the last one to do it. What am I now? Someone they can paw under the table. No one to say —"

"Irene."

"Don't you want me to stay?" She leaned forward, her mouth at his ear. "You didn't love her. Not like me," she said, her breath running through him. "It's what you wanted."

"You can't."

"And me. It's what I want. Do you know when I knew? After the checkpoint, on the road, when I saw the car pass. I thought, what if he doesn't stop? Just keeps going. What then? Go back to the guard, be what he thought? And Frankfurt, will that be any different? Passed from one to the next. And not so young anymore. So maybe not a Sasha. Just some —" She pulled her head back, looking at him. "You're my last chance. I saw it. So clear. Maybe that's why you came back. You didn't know it. But maybe that's why. Someone who still loves me. We can love each other."

"Until there's someone else."

"You want to wrap up the good-byes over there?" the soldier shouted.

"That's what you think?" she said. "That I want that life?" She looked up. "It's a kind of love anyway, isn't it? The kind we have." She leaned forward again, at his ear. "I'll make it be enough for you." The old voice, the way she used to sound, just the two of them. My last chance.

He pulled back, suddenly light-headed, weightless. What Campbell wanted. Markus. Stay close. "You have to go," he said.

"Oh, have to," she said, a von Bernuth toss of the head. "It's safe if we're together." She put her hand on his chest. "We'll be together." The only thing he'd ever wanted.

"Now or never," the soldier yelled.

They headed straight west on Dudenstrasse, passing over S-Bahn tracks and the Anhalter station yards. The bridge's walls were bomb damaged, patched with lumber rails, the street lined with ruined commercial buildings, another wasteland. For a while they were quiet, letting the air settle around them.

"We can still get you out," he said finally. "Another plane."

"To Frankfurt? And what's my life there?" She lit a cigarette. "Anyway, it's done."

"They'll still want to talk to you."

"Like before. I know. But then it's over. You're important to them. You have privileges. Not just *payoks*. A certain respect. They don't want to offend you."

"That's how it works?"

She glanced over at him. "Everywhere, I think."

"And Erich's interview?"

"I don't know. What do we say about that? RIAS taking advantage of a sick boy. I wish he had come to see me first, ask me what to do. But he didn't. And now he's gone."

Alex said nothing, then glanced at his watch. "The play should be over. Unless they're still taking curtain calls."

"You're still worried? What's wrong?"

"I don't know. Nothing."

"I thought you would be happy." She turned to him. "We can have a life."

"With all my privileges."

"Yes, why not? It's hard now. Without privileges." She drew on the cigarette. "It's not just that."

"I'm not Markovsky."

"No. You love me."

"I mean I can't protect you from them. I'm not Karlshorst."

"Well, but clever. You'll make a story for us."

He looked at her. Another story.

RIAS was a brand-new office building, horseshoe shaped and open at the back, its curved prow sticking into a small quiet square that seemed more intersection than *Platz*. One long side of the building bordered the park behind the Rathaus Schöneberg, pitch dark now, the only light coming from a few RIAS windows and the bulb over the entrance door. The one café in the square was closed. Alex drove past the back entrance gate and parked in the shadow of the shuttered café opposite the front door.

"What are we doing?" Irene said.

481

"Waiting. Ferber said to go to the back, so we'll use the front."

"You don't trust him?"

"But who's around him? Just in case. I don't want to leave the tape if he's not here. So we wait."

"How will you know it's him?"

"Who else comes to work this late? We'll see him pull in. The play must be over. Just a few minutes."

Headlights. A car approaching along the park side then stopping short of the turnoff for the back gate.

"Why is it parking there?" Irene said.

"I don't know. To watch maybe. They'd want to grab Erich before he gets in the building."

"But he's not here."

"They don't know that. Everybody's expecting the interview. As planned. Just wait. See if they get out of the car."

"Or if they're like us," Irene said, reaching for another cigarette.

"No, don't. They might see the match."

"You really think — ?"

"I don't know, but they're still in the car."

It was a long ten minutes before more headlights appeared, moving fast, then turned to the back gate, a few people getting out, heading toward the building as the driver parked the car.

"That must be Ferber. It's a station car. Let's give him a few minutes."

"The other car's still there."

"Waiting for Erich."

"You're so sure."

"No. Careful."

"*Ouf.* Then let me. I'll give him the tape and we're finished."

"No. Ferber's expecting me. You had nothing to do with this. You want to be able to say that. No idea what Erich was doing. Remember?"

"And if I knew? What then?"

"You'd need Sasha. And he isn't here anymore."

He reached up, fiddling with the overhead light.

"Now what?"

"It goes on when you open the door. They'd see. Okay, sit tight and keep an eye on them. If there's any trouble, start blowing the horn."

"You're serious. You think they — ?"

"They're still there, aren't they?"

He opened the door and crept out, still in the café's shadow, then crossed the square on the lower side, away from the park. When he reached the front steps and the overhead light, he climbed quickly, the envelope jammed under his arm.

A reception desk off the foyer, on the other side a waiting room with magazines.

"Yes, please?" the receptionist said, surprised to see someone at this hour.

"Herr Ferber. I have an appointment."

"Herr Ferber's at the theater."

"He just came in. Call him. Studio one-ten. Tell him his interview is here."

The receptionist picked up the phone, put out and hesitant, but Ferber responded immediately and came running down the hall.

"But where is — ?"

Alex handed him the tape. "He's here. Splice in questions or just run it with an intro. It's just what you want — everything we said."

"But where — ?"

"Safe. I couldn't take the chance." He touched the envelope. "It's the real thing. I guarantee it."

"Thank you," Ferber said, putting his hand on Alex's arm. "I'm not sure why you're doing this, but I thank you."

"They're Germans in the mines."

"You should come over to us," Ferber said, almost offhand.

Alex met his eyes for a second, then looked down the hall. "Is there another door? That way?" he said, nodding away from the park side.

"Mettestrasse, yes," he said, his voice careful, the way you talk to a drunk. "There's some trouble?"

"No. But it's bright out there. Why give anyone a look."

"I won't forget this."

"You have to. I was never here."

"Just a messenger."

"That's right. A boy."

They'd reached the side door.

"Listen tomorrow," Ferber said, holding up the tape. "You'll thank him? He's brave to do this."

"He's dying. That makes it easier."

"And you?"

Alex looked at him, not sure how to answer, and opened the door.

He walked back, away from the entrance light, circling around the car from behind.

"Oh, I didn't see you," Irene said, startled.

Alex closed the passenger door. "Everything quiet?"

"So suspicious. Someone just got in. A woman. They were waiting for her, not you."

"Good."

He started the car without the lights, turning right, away from the park, down to Wexstrasse.

"It went okay?" Irene said.

"He'll air it tomorrow."

"So that's that," she said, looking down. "And now he doesn't come back."

"No."

"So. And now?"

"Now we get you home. You weren't feeling well, remember? I forgot to ask Ferber. How the play was."

"How would it be? A triumph," she said, a radio critic's voice. "A landmark."

"See those lights?" he said suddenly, glancing in the rearview mirror. "Is it the same car?"

"Oh, not again. So they're going this way too. It's a busy street."

"Not that busy."

He stopped for a red light at Innsbrucker Platz, the other car still coming up from behind, then looked both ways quickly and stepped on the gas, shooting though the intersection. The car followed, running the light.

"See that."

At the next fork, he went right on Hauptstrasse.

"We're going back to Tempelhof?"

"That's what they'll think. They don't know we've already been."

"Yes, and maybe they just keep going to Potsdamer Platz," she said, skeptical.

"Let's see," he said, swerving onto a side street, dark, lined with tenements.

In a few seconds, lights appeared in the mirror.

"We have to get back to the main road," he said. "They'll trap us here."

He saw the car in Lützowplatz, screeching, cutting him off.

"What do they want?" Irene said nervously.

"Erich," Alex said, turning left, back to Hauptstrasse.

"Erich," she repeated, working this out.

"And whoever's helping him. Hold on. I'm going to speed up."

He shot into Hauptstrasse, making a sharp turn to avoid an oncoming truck, racing the motor.

Irene swiveled around, facing the back. "They're there."

Alex went faster.

"And if they catch up?"

"They'll try to cut us off. Christ, a light," he said, slowing for a red, too many trucks crossing to risk not stopping.

"They're coming," Irene said.

Lights brighter now, flashing in the mirror, pulling onto the left lane to overtake them.

Green light. Alex felt the car jerk as he hit

the gas pedal, a plane taking off. The other car now close behind. Then suddenly alongside, racing to get ahead, anticipating, beginning to move right, as if it were already in front and could make Alex stop by cutting him off. The cars almost touching. Alex moved farther right, away from the car, close to the curb now, then veered sharply left, into the other car's lane. A squeal as the car braked to avoid being hit, then the crunch of fenders, a jolt from behind. Alex kept speeding ahead, trucks coming from the opposite direction, boxing them in, a narrow raceway. Another bump from behind as the car tried to make them move over.

"What are they doing?" Irene said, alarmed. "They'll kill us."

"Hold on."

They were almost at the big intersection, traffic going in several directions, the streets like spokes. Alex held the left lane to continue on Hauptsrasse, then suddenly swerved farther left, then again, a U-turn effect, horns blaring, a truck's air brakes hissing, cutting off the chase car as Alex crossed back over Hauptstrasse and shot east toward Tempelhof. A tiny sound from Irene, too shaken to say anything, the car filled with the sound of their breathing, horns still blowing behind. An adrenaline calm, blood pulsing but his hands steady on the wheel. No need to be careful anymore, the speed carrying him with a life of its own, some rushing stream. The lights were back in the mirror, getting closer.

"Alex, stop," Irene said, her voice breaking, scared.

"We can't."

"You'll kill us. We'll die here."

"Here or Sachsenhausen. What do you pick? That's what it means."

"What, helping Erich?" she said, bewildered, a wail. "Oh God, look. Behind again. So fast."

An oncoming truck blinked its lights, a slow-down signal.

The car engine louder, making shuddering noises.

"They're still there. We can't get away," Irene said, almost sobbing with fear now.

"I know."

Alex had stayed in the left lane but now realized that if they gained on the right they could push him into the trucks. He banked right, the lesser of two evils, trying to straddle the lanes to block the other car. The Horch was beginning to throb from the strain, the car behind close enough again to smash into the bumper. They lurched forward, Alex hitting the steering wheel, Irene pitching farther, into the dashboard, her head knocking against the windshield. She clutched her chest, gulping air. Alex again moved right, near the overpass bridge wall now. The other car pulled sharp right, pushing them into it, a loud crunch as Alex hit the wall before he could yank the steering wheel left. The sound of scraping metal, Irene thrown against the door.

"All right?"

A grunt, no time for more, her eyes fixed on the other car.

"Alex!"

The car had gained again, about to repeat a push to the right, forcing them into the wall. Fenders near.

Alex slammed on the brakes, the stop throwing them both forward again, his chest on the wheel, Irene tossed into the dash, bracing herself with her hands then falling back, limp. The other car, caught in its own momentum, swept in front of them, across the lane, brushing against the wall as the driver tried to pull it out of a spin, jerking back left. The car swerved around, fishtailing back against the wall, now just a temporary wooden fence, the speed of its turn flinging it against the slats, splintering them. And then suddenly the back wheels were off the edge, the car stopped with its lights raised off the road.

Alex grabbed the gearshift, moving without thinking. Here or Sachsenhausen. No witnesses. He pressed on the gas, aiming for the front of the other car.

"What are you doing?" Irene shouted.

He heard the crunch as he rammed into the other car and hit his brake, then watched, a moment that stretched, like a held breath, as the car jerked back, the lights pointing upward now as it plunged down to the S-Bahn tracks. Distant screams. Irene gasped. Across the road, a truck was slowing. Move. It was then that he saw the other car had taken another chunk out of the damaged bridge, a jagged edge of pavement where Alex's front tire had caught and for a terrible moment he imagined the hole growing, bits of concrete falling away, wider and wider, until the side of the bridge was gone, swallowing the Horch, their own plunge down just seconds away.

He shoved the stick into reverse and gunned the engine but the sudden lurch had the effect of making them jerk forward, not back, he could feel it in his stomach, the right front tire slipping, heading into a fall. Then the rear tires gripped, pulling them back, even the right front, tugged up over the jagged edge, the car shooting backward until he braked again, then shifted and started away, the air around them suddenly flashing bright. More trucks stopped on the other side, one driver climbing down from his cab and running across the road, looking over the broken guardrail. The light must have been the gas tank exploding. How many in the car? Had anyone been conscious when it burst into flames, felt the sudden heat? More truck drivers on the road, shouts, yelling for Alex to stop. Don't stop.

"What are you doing? What are you doing?" Like a chant, hysterical.

Don't stop. No one behind, the traffic all airlift cargoes, heading away from Tempelhof.

"Oh my God, you killed them. Killed them." Covering her face with a hand.

"What's that?" Alex said, noticing the dark oozing. "Blood?"

"I don't know. My head —" She leaned back against the seat. "I hit my head." She turned. "How could you do that?"

"They were already over."

"No," she said vaguely. "Not over. Not yet. First Sasha, now — Oh, it's so hard to breathe." She clutched her stomach, a corset hold and sucked in air. "I feel —"

"What?"

"I don't know. Dizzy." She put a hand to her head. "There's blood. How is there blood?"

"You hit your —"

But she had slumped over, a thud as her head fell against the car window.

"Irene."

No sound, just the trucks and planes outside.

He took the first left out of the traffic, toward Viktoriapark, everything suddenly dark without the truck headlights.

"Irene." He tried to remember her smashing against the windshield. How hard? But he'd been looking behind, dodging. He said her name again, frantic now. More blood.

He pulled over to the curb. No one following. The blood was still welling on her head, a sign of life. He felt for a pulse on her neck, then tried to shake her awake, as if she were just napping. He took her hand, feeling her slipping away, like the smooth slide of the car going down. And she'd been right. It hadn't been over. Not yet. He'd pushed it. No witnesses. The car waiting at RIAS. Who'd known he'd be coming.

He took a breath, then another. No time to think about that now. Irene was unconscious, a head wound, not a hangover you slept off. Think. If Sasha were alive, he could call Karlshorst. But Sasha was lying in a drawer. Or in Wiesbaden. Or in Moscow. Why say that? To see her reaction. Or his. He looked over at her. Motionless. Think. Not Marienstrasse. A hospital.

He propped her against the door, head back, afraid to rearrange her limp body. A broken rib could puncture a lung. A hospital. He put the car in gear and headed toward Yorckstrasse to cross the Anhalter switching yards. The woman had come out of RIAS just after he went in. A leak, alerting the waiting car. Someone close to Ferber. Or sent by Ferber himself? Who went to birthday lunches at the Adlon, turned up at the Kulturbund, comfortable in the East. Who knew Erich was coming.

He glanced over at Irene, still quiet, breathing shallow. Faster. Pallasstrasse. Past the ruins of the Sportpalast, where Hitler had made his speeches. A thousand years. Where Elsbeth and Gustav must have raised their arms, shouting, glowing. Now home from the theater, with any luck still up.

All of Schlüterstrasse was dark, another electricity cut, but there was a flicker of candlelight coming from the front room. Alex stopped the car, put it in neutral and ran to the door, ringing the bell and knocking at the same time, everything urgent. A pinprick of light at the foyer door, Gustav peering out.

"Quick!" Alex said. "Open."

Gustav held the door ajar. "What do you want? Coming here at such an hour?"

"Irene's been hurt. Quick. Come with me."

"Irene?" Elsbeth's voice, coming from behind. Still dressed for the theater.

"Do you have admitting privileges at the Charité?" Alex said.

Gustav, not expecting this, gave an automatic nod. "But the Elisabeth is closer. Magdeburger Platz."

"That's where you volunteer?" Alex said to Elsbeth.

She stared at him, too startled to answer.

"They'd know you there, then. But you never go to the East."

"Why this — ? What do you want?" Gustav said.

"I want you to give her your name. A loan," Alex said to Elsbeth.

"My name?"

Alex looked at Gustav. "You admit her as Elsbeth Mutter. No one will question it. Your wife."

"What has she done?"

"Nothing. She fell in the dark. Charité

was the nearest hospital. So you brought her there."

"To admit her under a false name? Are you crazy? To think I would do such a thing?"

"You'll do it." He turned to Elsbeth. "She's in the car. Unconscious. We don't have time to argue. You used to borrow her clothes. Now she's borrowing your name. Just until we see what's wrong. And we can move her."

"Get out of here."

"Gustav, my sister —"

"First the brother. Now this. What has she done? No, don't tell me. I don't want to know. I never heard any of this. Leave us alone now, please. Go."

"She's hurt," Alex said. "She needs your help."

Gustav started to close the door. Alex put his hand up, pushing through, then shoved Gustav against the wall, hand on his chest.

"Now listen to me. Carefully. I have an old friend at Clay's headquarters whose idea of a good time is putting Nazis away. One call and I'll have him reopen your case. One call."

"They can't prove anything."

"Maybe not. But do you want to go through it all again? Defend yourself? And meanwhile your license gets suspended while they try to decide just how guilty you are. That usually takes a little time. Which we don't have. So decide."

Gustav glared at him. "Jew."

Alex went still for a second, then let it go. "Your wife just tripped in the dark. A nasty fall. Her head. You'll want her seen right away." He dropped his hand. "Get in the car."

"How can you talk to Gustav this way?" Elsbeth said.

"She's hurt," Alex said. "And that's all you can say? Be nice to Gustav?"

"He's a good man," Elsbeth said vaguely, not really following. "We're decent people." Shoulders back, the von Bernuth posture.

Alex looked at her, dismayed, then turned to Gustav. "Do you need anything? To admit her? Papers?"

"Just my signature."

"Then let's go."

Gustav checked Irene's pulse, her pupils, feeling lightly for broken bones.

"How long has she been unconscious?" he said, daubing the dried blood on her head with a handkerchief.

"Half an hour. Maybe more."

"Let's hurry, then."

In the car, Gustav was sullen.

"It's illegal, what you're doing."

"I'm keeping her safe. If anyone checks the hospitals, she's not there."

"And why would they check?"

Alex ignored this. "Remember, she tripped. In the street. No car. Nothing that needs to be reported."

"Except you. Like gangsters. What is it, something with the black market? I thought she didn't need that. Sleeping with Russians."

"When we get there, you're not just a doctor. You're her husband. Worried. Got it?"

They went to the emergency entrance and got Irene onto a gurney, wheeling her into the exam room, her eyes fluttering open, surprised, then closing again.

"She's awake," Alex said.

Gustav, on his own turf now, paid no attention, handling the admitting staff with efficiency, a doctor who knew what he was doing. Alex was asked to wait in the hallway.

"Just give me a second." He took Irene's hand, bending low to her ear. "Can you hear me? You're here as Elsbeth. Gustav will take care of you."

Her eyes opened, confused.

"If they check, there is no Irene. Do you understand? She's not here."

She took this in, then smiled faintly. "No,

in Wiesbaden."

"Somewhere. Anyway, not here. You're safe this way."

Another twitch, almost a smile. "Clever Alex."

"You must leave her now," a nurse was saying.

"Remember, you're Elsbeth, yes?"

She nodded, then clutched his hand. "Those people. They're dead?"

"You fell in the dark. In the street. That's all you remember. I'll be here. Just outside."

She grasped his hand again. "You were right. They were waiting for us."

"*Ssh.* No more. Remember, you're Elsbeth."

The wait in the hall seemed endless, a movie scene in a maternity ward, pacing, smoking, staring into space.

"No ribs broken," Gustav said, finally coming out with an X-ray folder. "Just a bad bruise. The concussion is something else. No major clotting. But a concussion is always serious. Let's see how she is in the morning."

"But she'll be all right?"

"I think so. But let's see how the night goes." He glanced at Alex. "Do you want to tell me how she did this?"

"Does it matter? I mean, for the diagnosis?" He caught Gustav's look. "In a car. We stopped too fast for a light. She hit her head."

"I see. And that's why it's important no one knows who she is."

"Can I see her now?"

"In the morning. We've moved her up- stairs. She's asleep." He began taking off his white jacket. "So good night."

"I'll give you a lift."

"In the getaway car? I don't think so. I'll call a taxi. I'm finished with this."

"But you'll be back in the morning. To see how —"

"Of course. I'm her doctor." He looked over at Alex. "And her husband."

"Thank you."

"Thank you," Gustav said. "For something like this. A criminal act."

"A small one. To keep her safe."

"And me?"

"Don't get caught. Then you'll both be safe."

Outside he checked the car for damage. There were dents on the bumpers and scratches on the side where he'd scraped the overpass wall, but nothing that would attract notice in a city of patched-together heaps. He moved the car back to the Charité faculty lot and picked up Irene's purse, fishing for her house key. Put her at Marien-strasse.

He made noise on the stairs, enough to reach Frau Schmidt's block warden ears, then knocked on the door while he slipped the key in so that it sounded as if Irene were opening it to him. Entertaining a visitor, the usual. Alex spoke to the empty room, a phantom Irene, hoping his voice would carry, and shut the door behind him, imagining Frau Schmidt below, nodding her head, pursing her lips. Or maybe already in bed, but aware of the sounds above in the flat, Irene moving about, making tea for some new friend. He left the curtains open so that the light would be visible, Irene at home.

In the bedroom there was the smell of her, powder and perfume, gifts from Sasha, and he stood for a minute breathing her in, staring at the bed. Where they'd made love. Where others had too. And now where she imagined some new life together, trusting him, living off his privileges. He gripped the bedpost, suddenly aware how impossible that would be now. He'd planned the evening to evade her watchdogs, but anyone following her would have stopped them earlier. Certainly at the airport, the escape hatch. But no one had. Instead they'd been waiting at RIAS, knowing he'd be coming with Erich. Which meant they knew about him. They'd been waiting for him. He felt a shiver of cold. They knew. How much? But just helping Erich would put him in Sachsenhausen. And the car burning on the S-Bahn tracks? Being Alex Meier couldn't protect him anymore, not the privileges, not the pictures in *Neues Deutschland,* the ode to Stalin. They knew. He had to get out.

He went back to the main room, breathing fast. Take some tea, think it through. Dieter's advice. He went over to the heirloom shelf and picked up the candlestick. Washed clean, no sight of blood, still their secret. Why say Markovsky was in Moscow? Toying with him, a cat with a mouse, knowing Sasha wasn't in Wiesbaden. Who knew about Erich's interview? Ferber? Who sent an assistant out to the waiting car? But that one was easy, just a matter of listening to RIAS tomorrow. If they broadcast the tape, then it wasn't Ferber. Someone else. They'd been waiting for him.

He sat down, still in his coat, cold again, thinking of that first night at the Adlon when he lay in a cold sweat feeling the dread creep over him. And now it had finally come. They knew. Think about the interview. He tried to work through the chronology, when, who knew, eliminating. Until there were two. Two. And Irene. Who didn't want to go West. Who wanted to make a life with him. He looked at the piano shelf, lined with framed photographs. Irene at DEFA, Irene in the old house, her hair now a period touch, Irene with a man who must be Gerhardt, in a flashy topcoat, Irene with Elsbeth and Erich, a golden summer, before anything had happened. Remember who you are. Who learned to do anything to survive. Who'd just had another Russian in her bed.

He stopped. He was mixing things up, confusing the issue. They knew. For how long? How much time did he have? Just leave now and walk through the Gate, into the park, his first morning again. And do what? Go to Föhrenweg, to people who didn't want him back, had never wanted him. Think of something. Make them want you. He was a mouse, wriggling in the cat's claws, waiting for the inevitable. He had to get out.

He switched off the light and crept quietly down the stairs, still in Irene's bed in Frau Schmidt's hearing. In the street he didn't bother to look around. If they were going to pick him up, they would. Or toy with him some more. Maybe wait to see if Erich was still with him. No one who'd followed his car from RIAS had survived. Irene had been home in Marienstrasse. So there was only Erich to account for, still stashed away somewhere.

He walked up to Nordbahnhof, then caught the late tram that ran along Danziger Strasse. You have to trust somebody, Dieter had said. He sat looking through the tram window at the dark city, juggling memories, what people had said. One more story. But even if his instinct was right, two now one, what he didn't know was who else knew.

He got off just before Prenzlauer Allee and walked down Rykestrasse. No waiting car parked in front, still in the cat's paw. On his door an envelope had been pinned with a tack. Inside he turned on the overhead light. An official envelope, in Russian and German. A summons to appear at the trial of Aaron Stein, a perverse gift of time. Maybe enough to work something out. They wouldn't come to get him until he'd helped them destroy someone else.

■ ■ ■ ■

8
BRANDENBURG GATE

■ ■ ■ ■

Erich was on the radio in the morning, crisp and clear, as if he were actually in the studio. Just as Ferber had promised. Alex imagined the interview playing at breakfast tables all over the East, the Erzgebirge slave camps no longer just rumors, Erich's fare paid.

He'd been up early, at the typewriter, drafting the letters he'd need later, ready to be retyped on official paper. Then his speech, weighing the words, getting the language right. The only writing he'd done since he'd come to Berlin. He looked at the small pile of manuscript on the desk, untouched, something from his former life. Leave the flat as if you'd just gone for a walk. But what writer would leave an unfinished book behind? He took out a large envelope and sealed the manuscript inside. A look around the room. Neat, but not abandoned, the bed still unmade. If anyone checked.

He walked past the water tower, its red bricks like embers in the pale winter sunshine, then down the hill to the park. Gretel, a sentimental pick, where he'd waited the first time. Wondering if he could do it, be two people.

"They get off?" Dieter said, joining him. "No trouble?"

"One of them did. She's still here."

Dieter waited.

"Answer me something."

Dieter opened his hand. Go ahead.

"What Gunther found. Did you tell anyone else?"

"No."

"I mean anyone."

Dieter shook his head. "Why?"

"You once told me I had to trust somebody. So now I am," he said, nodding at him.

"When did you decide, before the question or after?"

"Before. But you like to be right."

"And to what do I owe this honor?"

"Instinct. And a few other things."

Dieter grunted. "So?"

"I need your help. Someone tried to kill us last night. Down at RIAS. Hear anything yet on your grapevine? A car going over a bridge?"

"No. So they must be calling it an accident. But they know you're involved, with the broadcast?"

"Not the people in the car. Not now."

"But somebody." He thought for a second. "And me? Do they know about me?"

"I don't know. I'm going to find out."

"No, just go. If they know, it's no time for heroics. I heard the broadcast."

"They want me to condemn somebody first, so that buys us a little time. A little. I have to do this right."

"Do what?"

"What I came to do."

Dieter looked at him, puzzled.

"I'll explain later. First I need you to do something for me. You in?"

"It's your life you're playing with. You know that."

Alex nodded. "Go to the Charité. Irene's there. Under the name Elsbeth Mutter."

"Who?"

"Just a name. The point is, nobody knows it's her. Which means she's safe. Tell her to stay there."

"Another Wiesbaden? Or is she really sick?"

"She hit her head last night."

"On the bridge?" Dieter said, looking at him.

"Somewhere."

"And I'm the one you trust."

"Maybe she's better now. I don't know. But she has to stay there. Okay? Then call Campbell and tell him to meet me at BOB." He glanced at his watch. "Noon, a little later."

"You can't —"

"What's the difference. I'm no longer a protected source. Tell him to wait if I'm late."

"It's against all the rules. What's so important that — ?"

"I'm going to tell him where Markovsky is. In my own way. So don't ruin the surprise."

Dieter stared at him. "I don't understand what you're doing."

"Now you trust me. It works both ways. Just be ready when I call. One more thing. Do you have a gun I could borrow? Just in case."

"Just in case."

"You must keep one in the flat."

"No, I keep it here," Dieter said, patting his coat pocket. "Just in case."

"Can it be traced?"

"I was in the police. I know how to do

things." He took the gun out and handed it to Alex, one hand covering it, as if they were being photographed. "The safety's here. When you shoot, point outwards, not at yourself."

"I'm not expecting to shoot it."

"And that's why you asked for it."

Alex turned to go, then stopped, taking Dieter's hand. "Thank you. You'll see Irene? Now. So you'll be back when I call."

"I can follow orders. Frau Mutter." Dieter looked across the fountain. "Remember the first day? In the snow? You were offended, I think. I called you an amateur. And now look. Be careful," he said, touching Alex's arm. "Better an amateur than dead."

He caught the tram down to Alexanderplatz and walked past the palace. Scaffolding and scorched walls, what he'd seen that first night with Martin, everything circling back today, a completed loop. He stopped for a second on the bridge, turning around, wanting to remember it, the way Berlin looked now.

Around the corner from Markus's office a makeshift café had been set up in a bomb site, a few tables outside with people wrapped in coats, their faces turned up to the weak sun. Inside, under a sloped temporary ceiling, a coffeemaker was steaming, people holding cups and leaning across tables to talk, couples and — He froze, just for a second, then caught himself and kept going. A second, but long enough, Roberta looking out, meeting his glance, her eyes suddenly wide. She looked back to the table before Markus could notice. Coffee with Markus. How she'd paid for Herb. A small price, except you kept paying. Coffee every week, powdered milk and little betrayals, the neighbors, the Kulturbund, Herb's architect friends, all overheard now. Alex stumbled across the street. Markus's new GI. And another tomorrow and another, Markus and his coffee cups multiplying because there would never be enough. And after a while Roberta would forgive herself. They all would. It was just the way things were. Remember this, not Alexanderplatz. This was the future.

He'd been heading for Markus's office but Markus wouldn't be there, not until he'd heard Roberta out, so he kept going the few blocks to the Kulturbund. Martin was surprised to see him.

"I thought the trial was today," he said tentatively.

"Not until four. The Soviets never start anything early. Hungover, probably."

"Herr Meier," Martin said, but smiled a little.

"Are you going to testify?"

"No, no one from the Kulturbund," he said, clearly relieved. "Only people from Aufbau. The editor, his assistant."

Alex imagined them on the stand, facing the judges, not looking at Aaron.

"Good. For you, I mean. Not to have to do that."

"Of course, if asked, I would do my duty," Martin said, correct, a public answer.

Alex looked at him. His duty. Aaron in prison.

"Was there something you wanted?" Martin said, eager to move off it.

"I wondered if you'd do me a favor."

"Herr Meier, of course."

"I hope you won't think it's asking too much. I'd pay — I mean, I'd reimburse the Kulturbund for the tape. I know supplies are —"

"The tape?"

"Yes. You know I have a son in America. He has a birthday coming up, and it would be wonderful if I could record something to send him," he said, nodding to the machine. "So he could hear me wish him happy birthday. Hear my voice. Like a telephone call. I'd pay you —"

Martin held up his hand. "Herr Meier, please. I'd be so happy. A lovely gesture." He stopped, a sudden thought. "You know, of course, that a censor would have to play it. Any tape in the post."

Alex smiled. "I'm not going to say anything that a ten-year-old shouldn't hear. I think we'll be all right. It's fine, then? Would you show me how to use it?"

Martin busied himself threading the reels and setting the microphone levels, showing off a little, a teacher.

"When you're finished, just switch it off here. Well, I'll leave you. I'll be down the hall if you need me," he said, moving to the door, his bad leg making a shuffling sound.

Alex took one of the typed papers out of the big envelope and faced the microphone. The testimony Aaron would never hear, another gift to Ferber. His own airfare. He told the story everyone already knew: the exile returning to Berlin, the excitement of homecoming, the Socialist hopes. Then the disillusionment, the growing alarm at the Party's abuse of its own people, finally his refusal to condemn an innocent man. His decision to leave the East, burning every bridge now, every smiling *Neues Deutschland* picture turned upside down. Voting once more with his feet. He imagined

Brecht hearing the broadcast, dismissing it, a foolish self-immolation, maybe framing some sardonic twist to excuse the rest of them. But no turning back now.

He finished and put the tape in his pocket, feeling his heart racing, some clock ticking in his head. Almost there. When he left the office, waving thanks to Martin, he wondered if anything showed on his face. How did a man look with a gun in one pocket and a grenade in the other?

Markus was still out but his mother was at the office, perched on the edge of a chair in the waiting area, her eyes darting around the room, on guard.

"Alex," she said, her shoulders relaxing. "How nice."

"You're waiting for Markus?" he said, just to say something. Her face, if anything, looked thinner, skin stretched tight over the bones.

"He wanted to see me. The Commissar," she said, a wry edge to her voice. Alex looked up. A Berliner still.

"Won't they let you wait in his office?"

"I like it here. Where I can see. And you, you're well?"

"Yes, fine," he said, sitting down next to her. "How is it going with you?" He touched her hand.

"Well, how would it go with me? The coughing keeps me up at night."

"But you're comfortable? Your room — ?"

"They watch, I think." She looked down. "Well, maybe they don't, I don't know. But then it's the same, isn't it, if you think it?"

He said nothing, remembering Oranienburg, the months after, an eye at every window.

"Maybe Markus will find a bigger flat, so you can be together."

"Then he watches."

"Well, but to be together," Alex said, not sure how to respond to this. "It's a big adjustment. So many years."

"You know some of the German children, the young ones, were given away. To Russian families. So they're Russian now. Impossible to find. Even if you knew where. And the others? Dead, most of them. I never thought I would see him again. But all the time he's at the school. For the ones they wanted to send back." She stopped, going somewhere else. "Do you know what I remember? How your mother played the piano. The music in that house. Do you play?"

"No."

"Well, it's not like eyes or hair, is it? Something passed down. Maybe you'll come one day for coffee. We can talk."

"I'd like that."

She looked up, suddenly clutching his hand. "He thinks it was some kind of school. A classroom somewhere. Lessons. To correct myself. When I try to tell him, he doesn't hear. He thinks it was a school."

"No, he knows what it was. He knows."

"He knows and he doesn't know. Like everybody. All right, that's how he survives. But he doesn't just survive. He's one of them."

"Mutti," Markus said, coming in. "Alex." Looking at her hand, still clutching Alex's. "You're here?" he said to Alex, annoyed.

"Something came up."

"Yes, all right, come." Eager to get him out of the room, like sweeping dust under a carpet. *"Mutti,* I won't be long. They gave you some tea?"

"I'm fine." She let go of Alex's hand. "So you'll come see me?"

"Yes, soon. I promise." Another one broken.

"What's all that?" Markus said, pointing to the big envelope under Alex's arm as they walked down the hall.

"Papers. For a speech. On the radio."

"The radio. You heard about the brother this morning? And now it's our fault. 'How

517

could you let this happen?' The Russians don't tell us he escaped, they don't tell us he's here, and now it's our fault. Nothing changes with them." He stopped, hearing himself, and pulled back. "What did she say to you, *Mutti*?"

"Nothing. The old days. How is she doing?"

"I don't know. I think maybe a little —" He put a finger to his temple. "Fantastical ideas." He opened the door to his office. "I thought it was understood you don't come here."

"This couldn't wait."

"Yes? What?"

"I have something for you. But I want something too."

Markus looked up, surprised. "What?"

"I want to be excused from Aaron's trial."

"Again with this," Markus said, impatient. "There's nothing I can do."

"Yes there is. Say you need me and this will compromise my position. They've got plenty of others to hammer the nails in the coffin. Nobody's going to talk to me, if they think I'm part of this." He opened his hand to take in Markus's office.

"It's the Russians who hold this trial, not us. Do you think they consult me — anybody — who should be a witness? Saratov

518

doesn't ask for permission."

"No, but he'll do you a favor. He'll owe you."

"Owe me for what?"

"Markovsky. I know where he is. That's what I have."

Markus stood staring for a minute, not moving. "How?" he said.

"I slept with her. Irene. That's what you've wanted all along, isn't it? And you were right. Once we went to bed — well, you know what it's like."

Markus blinked, a tiny shift of his body, squeamish, and it suddenly occurred to Alex that he didn't know, that his contempt for Irene came out of some monastic ignorance. An unexpected piece of luck — something he wouldn't question.

"Where is he?" Markus said carefully, as if any sudden movement would scare Markovsky away.

"The Americans have him. Here. But they're going to move him. And that's our chance. I can deliver him to you."

"You?"

"Irene trusts me. So Markovsky does too. But I have to do this alone. If you come anywhere near him, they'll know and it's over." He opened his hand. "Gone."

Markus said nothing for a minute, standing still, only his excited eyes giving him away.

"You surprise me," he said. "To involve yourself in this." A question.

"It's what you wanted, isn't it?"

"I thought you would protect your friend."

"I am protecting her. You'd find him sooner or later and then you'd blame her. She had nothing to do with it." He held up his hand before Markus could speak. "I know, I know. But it was his choice. Now that you've got him, you can leave her out of it. They'll be too busy grilling him about the Americans to care about her. And congratulating you. Another promotion. At least. You wanted to work together. All right. This way we both come out ahead."

"Yes? What do you get?"

"A powerful friend in high places," Alex said, looking at him. "What could be more useful?"

Markus didn't answer for a second, looking for something in Alex's face. "Yes, what?" he said finally, his tone a kind of handshake. "I cannot guarantee that I can do anything about the trial. You must understand that."

"Get me postponed then. Saratov will be a lot more receptive tomorrow. One more thing? As far as Irene is concerned, I had nothing to do with this. It was all you."

"You want to — stay with her?"

"Markovsky's not coming back. She'll be alone." He looked over at Markus. "You take the credit."

"When does this happen?"

"They're moving him this afternoon. I'll call you when we leave. You don't want to have a car sitting around if you don't have to. Not in the Western sectors. They won't leave the West. You'll have to make the grab there."

"That's not a problem."

"I'll be in the car. So no fireworks. Just a quick snatch and you're gone. They won't be expecting this, so you won't need an army. Two should do it. Be quick and nobody will know. Except Markovsky."

Markus looked at him, the beginning of a smile. "You have a liking for this work."

"No. From now on we just have coffee, like you said. But this one fell into my lap. And you never know when you're going to need a favor."

Markus nodded. "Where are they taking him?"

"I don't know yet. I'll call. Then you'll be waiting for us." He paused. "We're not going to have another chance at this."

"We only need one," Markus said.

Alex took the U-Bahn, changing at Nollendorfplatz, a busy transfer station with several levels, an easy place to lose a tail. He let a train go by to see if anyone else stayed behind on the platform, then went downstairs. The train for Innsbrucker Platz was nearly empty, a weary late-morning crowd of rubble women and old men, their faces vacant. He thought of Markus, the eager eyes, so close now. What was the experiment? Two scorpions in a bottle, both safe if neither attacked. But one always did.

He got off a stop early, at the Rathaus Schöneberg, and walked across the park to RIAS. No one behind, on his own. He passed the spot where the car had been waiting and went in through the back gate. Ferber was in high spirits.

"We've had calls from all over to broadcast it again. People who missed it. Radio Berlin's ignoring it, which is always a good sign. They usually like to twist a story, confuse things. This one they won't even touch. *Ha.* Radioactive. Like the mines." He smiled, enjoying his own joke. "Tell your friend he did a great job. You know, I thought today everybody would be talking about *Mother Courage.* But no. The Erzgebirge. A great success."

"How'd you like another? Something to

follow it up." He took the tape from his coat pocket and handed it over.

"Another? From Erich?"

"No. From me."

Ferber looked at him, waiting.

"Why I'm leaving. For the West. The exile returns East, then says no. I won't testify against Aaron. You can splice in anything you like. But don't broadcast until tomorrow, okay? By then it'll be true."

"You're sure about this?" Ferber said gently. "It's an important step. You can never go back."

"I know."

"Then welcome," Ferber said, taking his hand. "You know they'll try to stop you. A name."

"Only if they find out before I leave. So don't tell them."

"No," Ferber said, smiling weakly. "It was Aaron? That made you decide to do this?"

"Not only. But it makes for a good finish," Alex said, indicating the tape. "What happens to a good man in a police state. What's going to happen to everybody."

"You know we were at school together? Boys. A Communist, early. A believer. Well, everyone was a little bit in those days. Unless you believed the Nazis. And now this."

"Are you going to cover the trial?"

"They won't allow anyone from the West. But I can tell you what it will be. Aaron's friends will be asked to attend. Anna and Stefan and — oh, anybody who might have a voice. And they'll sit there and hear lies about him and know they're lies and no one says anything. Only one voice now. Stalin's. They are there to bow in public. Aaron's punishment? They say it could be five years. In solitary. Five years. Maybe a madman after. My old friend. But the lesson's not for him. It's for them, the others. Now they know what is expected. And they'll applaud the verdict." He nodded. "You can hear it for yourself, on Radio Berlin." He held up the tape. "Thank you for this. One person who says no."

"The last time I did that I was deported," Alex said, brushing this off. "At least this time I'm walking out on my own."

"It's not a small thing," Ferber said, serious. "One step, but who takes it? Aaron can't, none of them. The idea is everything to them — they can't let it go. It was like that in Spain. I was there with Janka. In the brigades. Kids. And the Russians were heroes. Who else is helping? First advisers. Then they take over. And in the end they betray us — leave us to be picked off. The *Internationale*? Not in the Russian interest anymore. Everyone sees this. And no one will admit what's happening. Because then what would be left? So they pretend. That's what they're doing now, over there." He motioned with his head toward the East. "Still good Communists. But the Russians will betray them too. And then it's too late. Like the brigades. So," he said holding up the tape again, "not such a small thing. Where will you go?"

"I'm not sure yet. Let's see who listens to that," he said.

"Alex Meier leaves East Berlin? Everyone will want to hear this." He hesitated. "You know, you are always welcome here. RIAS. We need —"

Alex smiled. "I've said everything I have to say."

"I'm sure not, but — oh, excuse me." He waved to an assistant heading toward him. "One minute, please." He turned back to Alex. "It's a tragedy in the office. One of the girls last night left early, some boy I suppose, and then a terrible accident. They want me to help arrange the funeral. But don't worry," he said, fingering the tape. "I'll listen to this right away."

"What kind of accident?"

"Car. He was probably driving like a crazy man. That age."

"I'm sorry. How old was she?"

"Nineteen." He shook his head. "She just came over from the East last spring."

Alex changed trains again at Nollendorf-platz, this time going all the way to Friedrichstrasse, then walked to the Charité lot to get the car. The hospital door was busy, visiting hours. Dieter would have been and gone by now. So far so good. Dahlem was a long drive out. He thought about the girl from RIAS. How had they recruited her? Dreams of the future or a more practical bargain? Nineteen.

BOB turned out to be a large suburban villa on a quiet street off Kronprinzenallee, just up from Clay's headquarters. A high pitched roof, double stairs to a front stoop, ordinary, no different from the other houses on the street. Alex had somehow expected guards and wire fences. Instead, a simple wrought iron gate and a mail slot. Shades half drawn, nobody home.

Inside was another story, clicking typewriters and people carrying folders, a room with a big map of Berlin on the wall, ready for location marking pins. Campbell, waiting for him, seemed tense, not sure whether he should be angry or alarmed.

"All right, where's the fire? You realize that just by coming here —"

"They know. Someone tried to kill me last night."

"What does that mean, kill you?"

"What it usually means. They know. So the cover doesn't matter anymore. I can't go back anyway."

"Can't go — ?"

"No, so it's time for you to send a cable. Back home. Recommending the Agency go to the State Department and the court. I've drafted one here for you." He handed Campbell a paper from the big envelope. "And this we'll need to have typed up officially. Your orders to bring me in from the field, with an office here. I left the pay grade open because I'm not sure what it's supposed to be, so you fill that in. But we'd need a payroll listing to make it official, an Agency employee. What's the matter?"

"What the hell is all this?"

"It's what you promised. If I got the job done."

"We're not finished —"

"I am. I gave you everything you wanted. We had a propaganda coup this morning on the radio. Did you hear it?"

"I also heard you used my name to get him out."

"I had to think fast. Anyway, it worked. RIAS is over the moon. But somebody followed me and tried to kill me. So it's time to bring me in. It's all there. Read it. It goes out under your signature, so you should have a look before they code it. I assume you can send cables from here. You have a transmitter?"

"Tried to kill you how?"

"Run me off a bridge."

"Well, that could —"

"No. I know the difference. I've been learning on the job."

"What happened to them?"

"They went over instead."

"Then you're all right."

"Somebody sent them, Campbell. I can't go back. Read the cable. You want to get somebody to type up my orders?"

"What's the rush."

"Things have a way of not happening with you."

Campbell glared at him, then looked down, reading the cable.

"Quite a hero," he said.

"You can tone it down if you like. But why be modest? We're going to be petitioning the State Department. They'll want to know I put my life on the line for the Agency, don't you think?"

"What's this about a broadcast? The kid's in Frankfurt." He looked up. "On my say-so." Still annoyed.

"This one's mine. Another propaganda coup. Alex Meier leaves East Berlin for the West. Ferber thinks it'll make a big noise. None of the other exiles has gone back. Walked away. And I refused to testify at a show trial so we can float some balloons about the bad old days coming back, '37 all over again, with innocent Germans being put away this time."

"A man of principle," Campbell said sarcastically.

"The kind the State Department should take in. In fact, after this it'll look bad if they don't."

"What valuable information?" Campbell said, reading.

"Heavy water plant at Leuna. Saratov before he was announced. Add whatever details you like. I didn't know what you'd want classified. There's a second memo, for the files."

"This doesn't buy you anything."

"Invaluable assistance at great risk to himself? Two major propaganda victories, again at risk to himself? Your personal recommendation? Send it and see."

"I don't send cables like this."

"Then they'll really sit up and notice." He paused. "You said you would. That's why I did it. All of it."

Campbell looked at him. "All right. I'll go over it, send my own version later. Now, what do we do with you?"

"No, send it now. I want to see the confirmation copy."

"Don't get ahead of yourself. You're not station chief yet. This doesn't guarantee anything."

"There's something else. Not in the cable. We can follow up later. A one-two punch."

"What?"

"I know where Markovsky is. I'm going to give him to you."

Campbell looked up, startled.

"Where?"

"Send the cable."

"How do you — ? Oh, your friend. You got it out of her?"

"As you told me to. Send the cable."

Campbell looked down at the paper, now little more than an annoyance.

"Alan," he said, calling one of the clerks. "Have this encrypted. Mr. Meier here wants to see us transmit. He doesn't trust us."

"Just careful. It's important in this business, isn't that what you always say?" He gave the paper to the clerk. "And could you have somebody type this up on BOB letterhead?" He looked at Campbell. "You

530

decide on the pay grade yet?"

"Don't take chances." He scribbled something in the margin.

"And this," Alex said, handing another paper to the clerk.

"What's that?"

"My farewell to Berlin speech. A hard copy for the file."

The clerk waited for Campbell's nod.

"All right. Now where is he?"

"I'll take you to him. When we're finished here."

"You're being very cute all of the sudden."

"Have a smoke. It shouldn't take long." He looked around. "Some setup. Are there beds upstairs? Or do you put people in billets?"

"Depends. If they're at risk outside."

"So, here. With any luck I'll be out of your hair in a few days. The speech will make the news and that should move things along at State, don't you think?"

"You're so sure about this."

"When you give them Markovsky, you'll be able to write your own ticket. So you write two. One for me. That was the deal."

"Not quite."

"Well, things happen. And for once we got lucky."

"She just told you? Like that?"

"She doesn't know she told me. I figured it out."

"Figured it —"

"Don't worry. I know. Anyway, you can always send another cable if anything goes wrong."

Campbell, disgruntled, looked away and lit a cigarette.

"You might say 'Nice job' or something. I never thought we'd get him."

Campbell sat smoking, watching Alex, as if he were adding up columns of numbers.

"And where has he been all this time?" he said.

"Babelsberg. Out by DEFA. But she's moving him today."

"She's moving — ?"

"And we run interference."

"You're setting her up," Campbell said quietly.

"Would you have sent the cable otherwise?"

Campbell looked away.

"Sir? Sign here." Handing Campbell the authorization letter. The clerk turned to Alex. "Nice to have you with us. We all wondered who you were. The protected source."

"Not anymore."

"No, not anymore," Campbell said. "All

right. Now you're official. What else?"

"We wait for the cable, then we go." He made a show of checking his watch.

"Alan, get a car. Brady and Davis, I guess. That enough?" he said to Alex.

"She's only expecting me. Troops might scare her off. It's just the two of them. I think we can handle it. But your call."

Campbell thought for a second. "All right. Never mind, Alan."

"Anything I can do?" the clerk said, eyes excited.

"No. Just start a file on this one. He's worried about his pension." He turned to Alex. "And what's your next bright idea?"

"With Markovsky? He's all yours. I'd put him on a plane for Wiesbaden. Show him in public this time. Just for the hell of it."

"Is that what you'd do," Campbell said, stubbing out the cigarette.

When the cable confirmation came through, Campbell got up to go.

"I'll get my coat."

A minute, two. Time enough for Alex to make his calls. An empty office next to Alan's. Dieter, then Markus. Finished before Campbell got back.

Alex drove. "She knows the car," he said.

It was a long trip back into town, through

Wilmersdorf, then the more crowded West End.

"I don't think you're going to need that," Alex said finally, nodding toward Campbell's pocket. "They're not expecting —"

"You're new to this. You corner a man like Markovsky, you'd better be ready for anything."

Alex was quiet for a minute.

"New," he said. "It feels longer. What did you think? When Washington said they were sending me."

"Think? I thought you'd be a pain in the ass. First timer. In Berlin. You don't want to be a freshman here. It's dangerous."

"But maybe an opportunity for you. Somebody who doesn't know the ropes. Easier to play."

"To play."

"You told me Willy was a leak and I just swallowed it."

"Willy was a leak."

"After you said so. And he wasn't around to say anything. You know, I keep thinking about Lützowplatz. You said it wasn't supposed to go that way, but how was it supposed to go? I thought they were after me. But what would be the point of setting me up so soon? You hadn't even run me yet. But I'd make a great decoy if you wanted

Willy out of the way. He'd die protecting me. But the others weren't supposed to get killed. That's what went wrong. You thought I'd just stand there pissing my pants. No gun. You never thought I'd kill anybody."

"What are you talking about?"

"Willy said you had a Polish name. Hard to pronounce, so you changed it. You still have family there? Is that how they did it? Use that leverage? You were always interested in whether I had family in the East. You knew how that worked."

"How they did what?" Campbell said.

"Turn you. So was it family? It'd be easy to check, I guess, now that I know where to look. But maybe something else. Lots of ways to do it. Look at my friend Markus. Anything he can use. But I'd guess family. I don't see you as the believer type."

"Turn me. What the fuck — ?"

"It was you," Alex said simply. "Only two people knew I was taking Erich to RIAS. You and Dieter. But I changed things around. And when we got to the airport, what did I find? Howley's office hadn't called to clear us. All right, maybe a fuckup. Except everything there's like clockwork. No fuckups or the planes don't turn around. And Howley's office gives us the go-ahead like that." He snapped his fingers. "Like they would have if you had called. But you didn't. Why should you? You knew we were never going to get to the airport. We'd be dead. Or in a holding cell somewhere. Why waste the call?"

"You're out of your mind."

"Am I? Then there's the little comedy with Saratov. Our friend going to Moscow. Not your idea, I think. He just couldn't resist. Two can play at that game. But how did he know Markovsky wasn't in Wiesbaden? That we couldn't just pull him out of our hat and make the Moscow story go away? Only two people knew that. You and Dieter. So we're back where we started. It was you."

"And not Dieter."

"No. You."

"And why is that?"

"Because Dieter knows Markovsky's dead and you don't. You never would have gone on this little joyride if you didn't think he was alive."

"Dead?"

"But you didn't know that. So neither do the Russians. Or they'd have been all over it."

"Then what are we doing?"

"I want my life back. And you're going to get it for me. They won't say no to the Agency."

"Because I sent one cable? Wait'll you see the next one. What do you think you're worth now? To the Agency. You think anybody gives a rat's ass about you? Because you gave a speech? You're not useful anymore, that's all that matters."

"I thought you might feel that way. That's why the cable went first. And the speech is just what State will want to hear. So, now one more piece. A little insurance. To show the Agency how valuable I am."

"What? By telling stories about me? Who the fuck's going to believe you?"

"No one maybe." He turned to glance at him. "I don't care if you get away with it. I don't care about you at all. I just wanted you to know I know. Maybe Willy knew too, or suspected. Is that why? Tell me something. How long were you going to keep running me before I was just another Willy? Once Markovsky disappeared, I wasn't good for much. Gossip. Why were the Russians so interested in him, by the way? One of their own. Let me guess."

"More guessing."

"They wanted to get something on him. So Saratov could be the broom. Clean house. Man with a German mistress. This is the West to them. And he'd been here a long time. So a few personal details, for the files, just to make the case look real. Before Saratov came in to save everything. Start putting all those corrupting influences on trial. Jesus, Campbell, how did you feel doing this?"

Campbell was quiet for a minute. "You need to stop now. Before someone starts taking any of this seriously."

"It was you."

"Then you're taking a helluva chance."

"With you? Only a little one. I think you like other people to do it for you. And I have a gun too." He looked over. "When you corner a man, you'd better be ready for anything, right? And I wouldn't think twice. Not now. The last time I was in Lützowplatz I killed a man for you. That was hard. But that was a while ago. This time it would be easy."

"Corner a man. With what? Some wild story? You haven't cornered me."

"No. I'm going to let somebody else do that."

"What?"

"It's a pity your Russians don't share things with the Germans. Who you are, for instance. You should learn to trust them more. Otherwise, you start working at cross purposes."

"What are — ?"

"Here we are."

"Where?"

"Lützowplatz. You weren't here last time. You sent me instead. Into a trap. You wouldn't think it, though. All open like this. So I thought, why not Lützowplatz this time."

"For what?"

"To pick up Markovsky."

"Who's dead."

"Mm. How are you going to explain that?"

"Me?"

Alex started around the square, listening for a screech of tires, but they swept past the south side of the square in silence, then up the street where his house had been. Where was Markus?

"What are you doing?"

Now the north leg, toward the bridge, almost completing the square. Markus didn't know they were coming from Dahlem, from the south. Maybe he was waiting on the bridge, with a view of the whole square. Or maybe something had gone wrong. Another turn.

"What the hell are you doing?" Alarmed now. "Get out of here!"

Back to the bottom, about to turn and circle again. Where was he?

Campbell grabbed at the wheel, pulling

right, out of the turn, so that they were shooting south out of the square. "Drive."

Alex yanked back, breaking Campbell's awkward hold, stepping on the gas.

"Fuck," Campbell said and lunged now, fighting over the wheel, so that when he pulled it back the car skidded across the street, scraping into a standing wall. Alex stopped.

"Back up. Get out of here."

But now a car was swerving out of the canal embankment, where it had been waiting, racing toward them, a matter of seconds, the same screech, blocking the car, two men jumping out, guns drawn, yanking the car doors open. Markus looked in.

"Where is he?"

"He's got him," Alex said. "Careful. He pulled a gun on me. He's American intelligence."

"What the fuck — ?" Campbell said.

"Don't move. Hold your hands out," Markus said to Campbell. Then, to Alex, "What happened?"

"He tricked Irene. About moving Markovsky. But he didn't know I'd bring him here. To you. Just take him and question him. Whatever you have to do. He knows where Markovsky is. It's just a matter of getting him to tell you. Then you've got him."

"What are you — ?" Campbell said.

"Shut up. Get in the car," Markus said, waving the gun to his car.

"I wouldn't hold out," Alex said to Campbell. "It's never worth it."

"He's lying," Campbell said to Markus. Then to Alex, "You lied to me."

"You lied to me. That doesn't make us even."

"Alex, what — ?"

"Go ahead," Alex said to Campbell. "Tell him who you are."

"Bastard."

"He's Don Campbell," Alex said. "CIA in Berlin. He's got Markovsky. He can tell you where he is."

"That's right," Campbell said. "He's dead."

"Dead?" Markus said.

"Then what are you doing here?" Alex said. "And now you're wasting time. In the end we're going to find out anyway. Markus?"

Markus nodded to his partner, who stepped toward Campbell, waving him to Markus's car.

"Meier, for chrissake —"

"Just tell him what he wants to know."

Alex faced him. "I don't need any more cables. You've said everything you needed to say. You're not useful anymore."

Campbell's eyes opened wide.

"Cables?" Markus said.

"Better get him out of here," Alex said. "In case it's a trap. Someone else waiting."

"Trap," Campbell said, almost spitting it. "I'm working with you," he said to Markus. "Check with Saratov. He's lying to you."

"Working with me?" Markus said.

"Russian security." He caught Alex's eye, a second.

"With the Russians?" Alex said, sarcastic. "Don't you think they might have mentioned that? Or did you just join up now?" He turned to Markus. "We're wasting time."

Markus looked from one to the other, then nodded again to his partner, who grabbed Campbell's arm.

"You fuck," Campbell yelled at Alex, breaking from the partner's grip and pushing him away. He reached into his pocket, the gun out almost before the movement registered. Alex's eyes went to the barrel, pointed at him, as he fumbled for his own. No. A deafening sound to his left, the whole square filled with it, Markus shooting, Campbell's gun dropping out of his hand as he fell. Alex ran over. Eyes still open.

Markus had shot to wound, still hoping for questions later. Alex raised his gun. No more lines to cross.

"Alex — !" Markus shouted. The partner stumbled toward them and stopped, not sure what to do.

Campbell's eyes fluttered. "Don't," he said faintly, a whimper.

"You know what Willy taught me?" Alex said to Campbell. "Or was it you? No witnesses."

His finger on the trigger, unable to move, a stopped moment. Not who I am.

"Alex — !" Markus said again.

Alex fired, the explosion filling the air around them, Campbell's head jerking back, pieces splitting off, soft. Alex stood there shaking, his hand trembling. Not easier. Not who I am. But who I am now.

Markus was staring at him, his face moving, some storm passing over it, then still.

"The man in the English coat," he said. "It was you. She saw you."

Alex looked over. "Yes."

"Then you knew —" He nodded toward Campbell.

"Yes."

"You lied to me."

Alex nodded. "To both of you."

He turned to Markus's partner. "Help me

get him in the car. The trunk. See if there's something we can wrap his head in. We have to get him off the street."

Markus just stared.

"Well, you don't want him, do you? You don't want to go anywhere near him. Or Saratov —"

"What are you doing?"

"We were ambushed. It's a miracle I'm alive. He went down in the line of duty. Which will make his cable even better. Coming from a hero."

"Cable," Markus said, still in a fog.

"Never mind," Alex said, lifting Campbell's feet. "Point is, you'll need to think what to tell Saratov. If you stay."

"He was with the Russians?" Markus said, still working it out.

Alex nodded. "So let's explore our options. Thanks," he said to the partner, Campbell now stowed in the trunk. "Better wait in the car." The man looked to Markus, who nodded.

"Our options," he said to Alex. "You lied to me."

"Well, now I'm going to make it up to you. Let's see how this works. You just shot a Russian agent. And you recruited an American one. Which puts you in an awkward position. No, don't bother." He indicated

Markus's gun. "I'm on the radio tomorrow, on tape, turning my back on the East. A real embarrassment for the SMA. Your recruit. So you're still in an awkward position whether I'm dead or not. And Campbell here knew you recruited me — he asked for your name — so it's probably in a Russian file somewhere. Maybe you can talk your way out of it somehow. But Saratov doesn't look like the understanding type. So that's option one."

"And two?" Markus said quietly.

"You once offered me a job. Now I'm offering you one."

"A job."

"You wanted to work together."

"Work for you."

"Only for a little while. I'm going home. And you're going to help. My insurance."

"How?"

"I'm going to recruit you. A nice big fish. The Agency is going to be impressed. Maybe even grateful."

"A promotion for you."

"Better. A ticket. Home. You're a good catch, you know everything about the German security force. And even if you didn't, the embarrassment factor alone —"

"You want me to work for the Americans? Are you crazy?"

"Wake up."

Markus jerked his head back.

"You're not just in an awkward position. You're done here."

"Go to the West?" He stopped. "Leave? You don't understand what we're trying to build here."

"You're building a prison. You just can't see it. You're one of the guards right now, so it looks all right to you. See how it looks tomorrow. If you're dumb enough to hang around that long. Markus, I'm offering you a chance."

"To be a traitor."

"A chance for you and your mother."

"*Mutti?* You want her to go to the West too? She would never —"

"It would be nice to think there was another way to do this."

"Do what?"

"Make you see. Have you been out to Sachsenhausen? That's where she's been. Worse. It would be easier if you could see that, how things really are. But it's probably too late. The hook's in. So we have to take a different approach. You know how it works. Some leverage. Some pressure. Snap." He made a closing sound with his fingers. "And you've got him. Like you had me."

"So you're blackmailing me."

"And how does it feel? Ask Roberta. Ask any of them. Your GIs." He cocked his head. "You're finished there."

Markus said nothing, staring, his mouth slightly open.

"I'm offering you a lifesaver. Grab it. Get your mother and go to twenty-one Föhrenweg in Dahlem. Now. Before anybody starts asking questions about him." He looked toward the trunk. "Before your friend there starts telling people what an exciting day he had. You really think you can talk your way out of this one? Nobody's that good. The Russians never blame themselves. They'll blame you."

Markus looked up, a point that finally seemed to hit its mark.

"Who are you?" he said, his voice distant. "I never thought, when you came —"

"Neither did I."

"I thought we were friends."

"Did you?" he said, suddenly dismayed, seeing Kurt's little brother. "Then trust me now. It's your best option. The only one."

"You don't do this for me. For you. To make yourself important. And then what about me? What's my future?"

Alex looked at him.

"I don't know. But at least you'll have one."

■ ■ ■ ■

Dieter met him at the hospital lot.

"Where's Campbell?"

"In there." He pointed to the trunk.

Dieter looked up. "You?"

"Why would you think that."

"I started going over things. After you left. Who else knew you were taking Erich to RIAS?"

"Only you. And Campbell."

Dieter took this in, then nodded. "What are you going to do with him?"

"Take him back to BOB. I couldn't just leave him in the street. After the ambush. You don't desert somebody when he saves your life. Takes a bullet for you."

"Ah."

"He died for the Agency. Who's to say otherwise? The Russians? They get quiet, times like this."

Dieter looked at him, a smile at the corner of his mouth. "Amateur," he said. "It's lucky I was there. So you have a witness."

Alex looked at him, a conversation in a glance. "Yes, lucky."

"And did you find out? Whether he told them about me?"

"No. Sorry."

"Well, but the odds are yes. And who risks his life for odds. You're going out to Dahlem?"

"You want a lift? Markus may be arriving later."

Dieter raised his eyebrows.

"I'll tell you in the car. But I have one more thing," he said, glancing toward the hospital. "I won't be long."

"I'll wait for you on the other side. By the Gate. You don't want to risk a border check with a body in the trunk."

"But you risk it."

Dieter shrugged. "And what do you want to do about Markovsky?"

"Can you get Gunther to bury him as Max Mustermann? The Russians love a mystery. Let's give them one."

"He won't like that."

"Nobody will ever know. Except you and me."

Dieter looked at him. "And whoever killed him."

"That's right. And whoever killed him."

"Another mystery," Dieter said. "You ought to stay in this work. You have the nerves for it."

"What, and work with you?"

"They're all amateurs out in Dahlem. New to it. The Russians aren't amateurs.

For this one thing, they have a genius." He paused. "You could be useful. I'd help you. You're in this now."

"I'm not in anything."

"No?" Dieter said, glancing at the trunk. "Once you start, you know, it's hard to turn your back. No one else understands how it is, what we have to do, unless they're part of it too. It's important work. You could be valuable."

"Is this what BOB said to you?"

Dieter smiled. "No, I was easier. They got me for a letter. To wash my sins away. 'A Nazi of convenience,' that's the phrase they used."

"Were you?"

Dieter shrugged. "Everyone on the force. Now an Ami of convenience. You do what you have to do. Terrible things sometimes," he said, looking toward the trunk again, then back at Alex. "You try to keep a piece of yourself. Something they can't get. And then it's over and you think, my God, I did that. I was part of it. So in the end what did you keep? And now," he said, extending his hand to take in the car, the city beyond. "A new side. More things we don't talk about. You think you don't pay, but — you carry it with you." He looked over. "If you go on with this work, keep something for yourself.

Not just a piece. Otherwise they'll take it all. And then you're not good for anything else."

Alex felt cold on the back of his neck.

"Well, my friend, better hurry," Dieter said. "You still have a body to explain."

Irene was sitting up, wearing a pink bed jacket, frilly, with girlish silk ribbons. She giggled at his expression.

"Elsbeth's," she said. "She dresses like a doll. So, finally. That strange man before. 'Don't leave the hospital.' Why? 'Wait for Alex.' So now we can go?"

"Are you all right?"

"This?" she said, touching a white head bandage. "It's better, I think. Gustav says I should rest a few days, but I could do that in Marienstrasse, no?"

"You could also go to Elsbeth. Then Erich. I can still get you a plane out."

"Oh, again with that."

"It would be better for you."

"What's wrong? Your face. They found him, Sasha?"

"No. They're not going to. I'm taking care of it. You'll never have to worry about that. It's safe. It would just be better in the West, that's all. Easier."

"What do you mean, you're taking care of it?"

"I don't have time to explain. It never happened. You don't know anything. You never did. Okay?"

"And Elsbeth's name?"

"Just a precaution. If they checked the hospitals. After the accident. And your name popped up —"

"The accident."

"That's what they're calling it. You don't know anything about that either."

He waited for a moment.

"I'm going to be on the radio tomorrow."

"Like Erich?"

"Yes. Just like Erich. So I have to leave. I've come to say good-bye."

"Good-bye?" she said faintly, almost dazed. "You're leaving? Where? Frankfurt?"

"No, I'm going back."

"Back where? You can't go back."

"I can now. I made an arrangement."

"Clever Alex," she said. "Always —" She looked up. "You mean you're leaving me."

"I have a child. I don't want him to grow up without me. That's all that matters now."

"That's all? Not us?"

He sat on the bed, putting a hand up to her face. "Us. There is no *us*. It was just an idea you had."

"I don't believe you. It's not the child. It's something else."

"No, it's him. It's what I came to Berlin for — to go back."

"What does that mean? You're not making sense."

"I know. Never mind. I have to go. I can't stay in Berlin."

"But why?" she said, her voice rising, a kind of wail. "You never said —"

"The people who were following us last night were following me. Not you. You're safe, but I'm not. I have to go."

"But what about me? What will I do?"

"Go to Elsbeth."

"Oh, Elsbeth. This stupid jacket," she said, taking it off. "You're leaving me and I'm in this ridiculous jacket. In bed. No," she said, getting out. "I can stand. Tell me standing up. This is what you came to say? You're leaving me? I thought you loved me."

"I do," he said softly. "But I can see you better now. All of you. Erich. Elsbeth. You. Before I just saw what I wanted to see."

"Oh," she said, flailing, clutching the bed jacket. "See me better. What does Erich have to do with anything? Elsbeth. I don't understand —"

"Can I ask you a question?"

"What question?" she said, distracted, a

kind of pout.

"When you told them things, did you tell them about me?"

"What?"

"It's important to me. To know. I don't blame you. I just want to know."

"What are you talking about?"

"You should have gone with Erich. And I should have known then. You weren't scared enough. You should have been. I was. But you weren't afraid to stay. I thought it was the usual von Bernuth foolishness. Nothing can touch us. But it wasn't just that. You still felt protected. Even with Sasha gone. Did it start with him? Or before? Of course, he wouldn't just sleep with you. He'd ask you things. Nothing special. DEFA, probably. Did you report on DEFA? Tell them what people were saying? Fritsch? Which doesn't matter much, until somebody doesn't turn up for work."

"Stop this," she said, shoulders back now, standing still.

"And then I came. Somebody from the West. They'd want to know everything. What I did, what I said. And you were in such a good position to help. Maybe that's what Leon was doing the night I came to the flat. Just getting a report. Be nice to think that's all it was since we'd just — But probably one thing led to another. You'd want to keep the DEFA job safe. With Sasha gone. And once you start something like this, they never go away. There's always somebody."

"That's why you're leaving? Because you think this?"

"I know how it is. When I saw Roberta, I thought yes, just like that. A coffee, checking in. That's how it's done. But not with Markus. Maybe that's why he's so angry with you — I'll have to ask him. He couldn't get to you, you were already in another league, with the Russians. No wonder Markovsky was so upset when he found out about Erich. Lying to him. You expect better from a source. Especially one you're sleeping with. Feels like she's cheating on you. An insult."

"Stop it."

"And after? I kept thinking they were going to haul you in for some serious questioning, but no. They never seemed to suspect you. Why would they? You were still co-operating, still one of them. In a small way, maybe, but they'd look after you. A kind of protection racket. How else to get along?"

"Alex, please."

"I don't care why you did it. All the usual, what else? Maybe they forced you. They don't give you much choice. I know how it works."

"Oh, you know," she said, eyes flashing. "You think you know."

"But if you stay here, they'll never leave you alone. That's why I thought the West —" He looked up. "Did you? Did you tell them anything about me? It's important to me to know."

"Why?" she said, turning her back to him, walking, then back, pacing in a cage. "So you can hate me?"

He took her by the arms. "Did you? Please. Tell me."

"Nothing. Unimportant things," she said, wrenching away from him. "That's all. Unimportant things. They don't care. Anything. They just like to collect —"

"I know. They asked me about Aaron. Unimportant things."

"You think I wanted to make trouble for you?"

"No."

"No. It was just, what does he say? Does he like it here? Unimportant things. So, yes, he likes it here. What's the harm in that? All good things, what they like. They respect you. You have a position here."

"Not after tomorrow," he said.

"What's tomorrow? Oh, the radio. What

do you say?"

"Things they won't like. I can never come back."

"So it's like before. In America. The great gesture. And where do you go this time?"

"I don't know. Wherever I can see Peter."

"But not me. It doesn't mean anything to you, how we are?" She reached for him, drawing him closer. "You can't just walk away. You can't. I'm not like her. The one in America."

"No."

"This nonsense I tell them. It's so important?"

He stroked her hair. "No. I just wanted to know. It makes things easier, that's all."

"What things? I can stop all that. We could —" She pulled back. "You're not even listening. It doesn't matter what I say —" Her voice quivering, then suddenly calm. "How can you leave? You always wanted this."

"Yes, I always did."

She stood taller, gathering up her pride like a skirt. "Well, then. And later, how will you feel?"

He looked at her, the same defiant eyes, Kurt's head in her lap, feeling time dissolve. He slipped out of her arms and walked to the door, then turned.

"What?"

"I just wanted to look." A snapshot moment, what he'd felt on the bridge.

"Alex, for God's sake —"

"You used to think everybody was in love with you."

She shrugged. "So maybe they were," she said, her face soft. "In those days."

"Maybe. I was. I wonder —"

"What?"

"How different everything might have been. If you'd been in love with me."

He walked down Luisenstrasse and over the bridge. In the dusk, moving headlights were lighting up the Brandenburg Gate, the world divided by a few steps. Nobody was stopping traffic. A crude wooden sign. You are leaving the Soviet sector. He passed under the arches expecting to hear a police whistle, pounding feet. But in another minute, East Berlin was just a patch of dark behind him. Out of it. Through the Gate. Where everything would be different. Where he would be himself again. Dieter was leaning against the trunk of the car, smoking, waiting, indifferent to what was inside. What he would become. Maybe what he already was. You're in this now. You do what you have to do. Then you carry it with you. But he was here, on the other side. He stopped for a second, taking a deep breath, somehow expecting the air itself to be different. But the air was the same.

ABOUT THE AUTHOR

Joseph Kanon is the Edgar Award–winning author of *Istanbul Passage*, *Los Alamos*, *The Prodigal Spy*, *Alibi*, *Stardust*, and *The Good German*, which was made into a major motion picture starring George Clooney and Cate Blanchett. Before becoming a full-time writer, he was a book publishing executive. He lives in New York City.